The Heart of Blackbeard

Patricia Cooper Baker

Top Shelf Tales Book Two

The cover design and some internal art are creations of the author with licensed images from Shutterstock.com.
Printed in the United States of America
Cooper's Peak, Publisher
Cooperspeak.com
ISNB: 978-1-7359250-3-5

Tribute and Thanks

My story rests on the diligent work of dozens of Blackbeard biographers, but I must offer special thanks to three recent researchers.

Baylus C. Brooks showcases the records pointing toward the origins of Edward Thache.

Kevin P. Duffus brings Blackbeard to life through his magnificent prose, personal insight, and illuminating photography.

David D. Moore makes everything possible through attention to facts and primary sources.

Thanks also to my team of friends and family, who listened to a million complaints and kept me on the rails as this work developed. And many thanks to my supporters who cared enough to volunteer to be early readers.

Special thanks to my writer buddy, **Dr. Bob**, and to Dylan Grimes and Gabriel Baker, who stood for the images of Drake and Ody Saunters.

In memory of my beloved brother, advisor, and fan**, Rusty Cooper**.

Sixteen Bones on a Dead Man's Chest

There are dozens of histories about Blackbeard's life. But from shortly before Edward Thache came to Bath until his death, there are only sixteen trusted events upon which to build his story—Blackbeard's sixteen bones.

Hardly any historian can approach the subject without clothing these bones in veils of inference and speculation—familiar tools for fiction writers.

Some historians think the evidence of Blackbeard's marriage to a young girl in Bath is insufficient. But the records tell us that the wedding happened. The story of why this pair chose each other and how they navigated the sixteen critical events of their short marriage speaks to the desire, needs, and circumstances that bring any couple together and how love endures even when the ending is bittersweet.

I was lucky to have a team of time travelers to tell me what happened around Pamlico Sound, but you may refer to notes at the end of the book to hear what history has to say.

Enjoy your visit with Blackbeard and his family.

Patricia Cooper Baker

Table of Contents

Top Shelf Tales Book 2
THE HEART OF
BLACKBEARD
PATRICIA COOPER BAKER

Act One: Home Port

Wedding (or Wager) Cup

1 Wedding Crashers

Aurora Saunters

Oh, no. A crowded room? Thank goodness my arrival was a mere ripple in the fuss.

What went wrong this time?

My target, a prayer book, lay on the floor under the hand of an unconscious woman. But she was too old to be Elizabeth Glover, and I wasn't sure she was breathing.

Quick! Where is this?

If I didn't return home soon, Ody and Drake would arrive at the wrong destination, and wherever this was, it was not safe—not for us, anyway. The situation called for a do-over, but I couldn't get home without my walking stick. *Where was it?*

"Make way, make way," a feeble male voice called. He leaned on a cane, and his wife supported the other arm. But when he reached the lady on the floor, he freed a hand to pick up the prayer book and passed it to a convenient bystander—*me*. Then with his wife's assistance, he knelt by the woman.

My foot wedged against a wooden object until half a dozen arms pushed me aside, and the gentleman's wife took my arm to steady me, whispering, "The Governor will soon be here."

Could she mean Governor William Glover? Elizabeth Glover was his daughter. Maybe things weren't as bad as I thought.

The wigged wife gripped more tightly as she bent to whisper to the kneeling man, "Tobias, send for a doctor. We mustn't upset the bride."

"Quite right, my dear." Then he spoke slightly louder, "Will someone fetch a doctor?" His request traveled through the room, each iteration somewhat louder than the one before, "Mr. Knight requires a doctor."

Finally, the loudest voice, deep and musical, with ringing notes that reminded me of a steel drum, replied, "I'll fetch him for 'e, Mr. Knight."

Tobias … and *Knight*. *Tobias Knight.* I knew the name, but how?

I turned toward the musical voice but only caught the tip of the man's coattail as he dashed through the door. Then, through a forest of limbs, I spied a girl in pink at the top of a mahogany staircase. She peeked around the skirt of the young lady who held her hand. But when the girl saw trouble in the hall, she pulled loose, ran down the stairs, and headed straight for me.

No, *not me*—it was the book she wanted.

"That's mine," she said, then she snatched the book and placed it on the fallen woman's palm. "I lent it to comfort you, Widow Bellieu. And see, you needed it."

The young lady took the girl's hand. "Come with me, Lizzy. She needs a doctor, not your book."

"Not yet, Penelope," the girl begged, but Penelope gripped Lizzy's fingers and pulled her away.

Tobias Knight tugged the skirt of the woman holding my arm. "Bring water, my dear. Please hurry."

In her haste, Mrs. Knight shoved my arm aside, and once free, I bent to search for my cane. But dozens of feet shifted around the woman lying on the parquet tiles. My staff clattered from boot to boot as it moved toward a corner, where a young hand grabbed it.

Then, the musical voice called from the yard. "The doctor's in the old Towne, Sir."

Mr. Knight turned to a man in a plumed hat who knelt on the other side of the fallen woman. "What say ye, Captain Thache?"

"We'll make do," the plumed man said. "But the party can't start till this lady rouses."

"No, it cannot," Knight replied. "Is the Widow Bellieu able to sit?"

Captain Thache lifted the Widow so that her dangling head rested against his brass-trimmed satin sleeve. "Can anyone here help us?" he asked as he looked around the room.

I scanned the crowd, and through the frame of someone's crooked elbow against someone else's waistcoat, I found a sight even more upsetting than the ailing woman—Drake with mouth agape and Ody holding my stick. Unfortunately, I had lingered too long, and now my grandsons were here.

My hand fumbled for the charms that would take me to the boys, but I searched in the wrong pocket and pulled out a mothball instead.

With a finger to my lips to warn the boys against speaking, I jerked my head toward the door. While they wormed through to the exit, I knotted the mothball into my handkerchief and approached the Captain.

"This may help 'e, Sir," I whispered. "'Tis an aromatic I keep for faintin' spells."

His eyes widened as he sniffed it. "*Phew.* This pong'll do it," he said as he placed the pungent knot under the lady's nose.

Wide-eyed and sputtering, she roused.

"'Ello, Mother," Captain Thache said. "You've rejoined the living just in time for your daughter's wedding." His charming grin held a touch of mischief as he added, "You wouldn't want to miss that, now, would 'e?"

Pale, wrinkled lips gasped for air, but the woman clutched her chest as she whispered, "No, Sir. No, indeed."

"Very well, then."

Thache returned my handkerchief and helped Mrs. Bellieu to her seat. Once the woman could sit straight without help, the captain addressed the crowd. His red coat commanded enough attention, but he must have been nearly seven feet tall with the long feather in his hat.

"All is well, ladies and gents," the Captain said. "Gov'nor, are we ready to proceed?"

Tobias Knight waggled a finger to direct a man in robes and a powdered wig to the front of the crowd. Then, after the man tugged his golden neck stole into place, he said, "I see no reason to wait."

Thache turned to the crowd. "Then take yer seats, everyone. Governor Eden says we may begin."

My head spun as I summed up what I had seen. Then I fought through the incoming crowd, down brick steps, and across the yard to Ody and Drake, waiting patiently under a shady oak. I took my stick from Ody, and after short embraces, I held tight to Drake's shoulders as the boys peppered me with questions.

"Where *are* we?"

"*When* are we?"

"Was *that* Elizabeth Glover?"

And Drake added, "And whose ship is *that*?"

"How would I know?" Words stuck in my throat as I scanned the hull of the ship in the creek. It was far longer than the house behind me, with a mast taller than any tree in the plantation yard. The weathered hull held a freshly painted sign touting the name, *Adventure.*

Oh my! *Thache* was *Teach.* It made sense.

"Oma?" Ody called me back to reality. "Where are we?"

I gulped before squeaking out a broken reply. "This is Bath—the first town in North Carolina. As for when, well, it is summer, and by the sun, it's past noon but not much after."

"Do you know more than that?" Drake, my younger grandson, asked.

After a long, cleansing breath, I replied, "I do. It's 1718, and this gathering is in the home of Tobias Knight, Secretary to this colony under Governor Charles Eden."

"Well, at least you got the *governor* part right, even if it's the wrong one," Ody said. "Why are all these people here?"

I shook my head, dreading to say the words. "It appears we are wedding crashers. Today Captain Edward Thache will marry a local girl. I believe her name is Mary."

"Who is Edward *Tayche*?" Drake asked, exaggerating the unfamiliar name.

I sighed. "You may have heard the name pronounced Edward Teach. But if you say *Tayche* with teeth clenched, as a Bristol man would, you can hear *Teach* instead. In most records, the name is T-h-a-c-h-e, but people hear it as *Teach*."

"You're kidding me, right?" Drake asked with a grin.

"No," I said, "In this century, people often write what they hear. But, unfortunately, not many are good at spelling."

"That's not what I meant," Drake said. Then he pulled away and ran toward the stairs.

Ody called after him. "Where are you going?"

Drake laughed from the foot of the brick steps, and thankfully, everyone was inside as he shouted, "I'm not going to miss Blackbeard's wedding. Come on, cousin. There might be cake." He turned back to Ody with a gleeful grin as he added, "Or rum!" Then he hurried through the door.

"Get him out of there," I whispered.

Ody dashed into the hall and returned with a tight hold on Drake's elbow.

"Oh, wow," Drake shouted. "I met Blackbeard! My friends will never believe it."

"*What?*" I replied, nearly shouting.

"Can't you remember even one rule?" Ody asked. "It's the most important one."

"Oh right," Drake replied, every bit of excitement gone. "The first rule of time travel: I can't tell *anyone* about this … *ever*." He shook his head as he kicked at the ground. "What a waste."

"Should we go home?" Ody asked.

I huddled with my grandsons. "It will take time for us to find another trial run. And if we fail now, we will have wasted our chances for this summer."

"Oh, don't twist your hair in a knot," Drake said. "I'll behave. Let's get this lesson behind us so I can play baseball."

2 Water Streets

Ody Saunters

Since I was seventeen and the more experienced commuter, Oma named me captain of this mission. Time travel was new to my cousin, Drake. He had a lot to learn, and he was lucky I was there to teach him.

"I hate to disappoint you, Drake, but we won't find baseball in Bath." He grumbled while I scanned the yard, the great creek, and the boats tied at the landing. "How about a boat ride, instead?"

"That sounds fun," Drake said. Then, he turned to Oma, asking, "Can we get away with that?"

Oma nudged him in the shin with her walking stick. "We can *if* everyone follows the rules. We don't want to make anyone suspicious that we're visitors from … err … out of town," she said, cocking an eyebrow.

I snickered, "Yeah, let's avoid that."

A wide creek flowed past the house, and I looked for anything interesting along its banks. "Wonder where we can find a ride; Bath Towne is upstream from here."

"Maybe I can help you." The voice was deep and familiar. I'd heard it in the hall, but now the black man it belonged to leaned against a nearby tree. He was muscular, nearly thirty years old, but not as tall as Drake. He had a friendly smile, and as he stepped toward us, he carried himself like a man accustomed to fitting in to this situation and probably any other.

"I'm Caesar, one of Cap'n Thache's men," he said. "Today, he asked me to ferry townsfolk to the point if they need it. Can I take you somewhere along the creek?"

He stood by a small craft that should hold us if the water behaved. So, Oma asked, "Is there a tea house near the docks? One with decent food?"

"There are two ord'nries. I can unload 'e there if 'e wish it."

"Thank you very much, Caesar," she replied.

We helped Oma settle on a plank bench in the middle of the boat while Drake and I sat behind a tall, thin oarsman. Long voyages under the sun had tanned the sailor's leathery skin, but his vest was weather-beaten to a dull, indescribable color. The two greasy braids dangling over his ears were mousy brown without a touch of gray. I guessed him to be in his late twenties.

"This here's Coleman Adler, but we call him The Crow," Caesar said, slapping the oarsman on the shoulder. After Adler forced a gold-toothed grin, his crewmate ordered, "To the dock, Crowman." Then Caesar stepped over Oma's bench to man the rudder.

Drake and I laughed at otters playing as we pulled away from Tobias Knight's plantation. But Oma had warned us against speaking. Luckily, Caesar chatted enough to fill the silence.

"This here's Knight's Landing, and over yonder lies Plum Point," he said, pointing across the creek to land jutting into the stream. "I work on both sides of this creek. Plum Point is the Cap'n's place now. 'E'll be moving there with his new lady, Mistress Marybeth Thache. 'Twas her mother, Widow Bellieu, who fell sick in the hall."

"'Tis a fine house," I said.

"Aye, 'twas the Bellieu house, but it suits the Cap'n. Part of the weddin' agreement was he pay the widow rent for her land. 'E topped some of the pines and turned the old bell tower into a crow's nest so 'e can see down to the sound. He makes a habit of watching ships come and go."

When Adler stopped snickering, Oma wished the new couple every happiness.

"I wish it, too, Ma'am," Caesar said. "The Cap'n has had his share of trouble with the ladies, and even though Miz Marybeth carries herself well, she is barely more than a girl. They're both gamblin' on this marriage and 'twould be the best if it makes them happy, too." Then, he went silent as he guided us toward swifter water in the center of the creek.

"If you have a spare oar, my grandsons can help," Oma said.

"Thank 'e, but short though I may be, I'm stout as an oak stump, and The Crow carries more seawater than blood in his veins."

Once the boat was on course, Caesar pointed to the left bank, where a large frame house sat high on the knoll, sheltered by massive oak trees and a windbreak of pine saplings. "'Tis Thistleworth, Gov'nor Eden's farm till lately, but before Eden, it belonged to another governor named Cary."

"That's the land over the tunnels, ain't it, Ceez?" Adler asked.

"Mebbe," our rudder man replied.

"Did you say, Charles Eden?" Oma asked. "Is he the one who performed the marriage?"

"I heard he would do it," the black man replied. "So, I reckon he did."

"What are the tunnels for?" Drake asked.

Caesar shrugged. "I can't say if there are any tunnels. It's just what folks say." Then he grinned, "Besides, if I did know and told it, I might be sharin' a secret, and the Cap'n can't abide loose lips."

When we pulled to a floating dock extending from a sandy point, Caesar nodded toward the row of buildings running roughly parallel to the creek.

"Is that Bath Town?" Drake asked.

"'Tis most of it. This is Water Street. That's the town fort ahead of us," Then he pointed along the row of buildings. "There's the grist mill about halfway up, and the shipyard is over yonder," he said, pointing toward the north end of the street. "And The Marsh Moon Tavern, just this side of the mill, is the best ord'nry for gentlefolk. Tell the innkeeper Caesar sent ye. 'E'll treat you right if 'e thinks the Cap'n pointed 'e there."

Oma fiddled in her pouch for a few coins, but Caesar stopped her. "'Tis the job the Cap'n give me today, Missus. 'E'd slap me silly if I took yer gold."

"You've been very kind, Caesar, and I thank you for ferrying my family and me," Oma said.

I hopped out of the boat first and offered a hand to Drake, and then we helped Oma and her walking stick off the floating pier and onto the boardwalk. Once up a gentle rise, we stepped onto Water Street, a walkway of packed earth and oyster shells.

Oma stretched her legs and fluffed out her cloak. "So, now that we're on dry ground and in Bath proper, 'tis time to do what we planned. I promised you a visit to remember, and North Carolina's oldest town is quite a landmark."

Drake scanned Water Street to the south, and I looked north. The town was small and dusty, and besides a few citizens strolling, the only thing that moved was a tired horse walking around the grinding stones.

Drake whispered, "This isn't going to take long; I'm not sure we will find this trip as memorable as Grandma thinks."

I shrugged. "Don't fret. Oma promised we'd be home by nightfall, and when we get there, you can check off your first commute. That alone is worth the journey."

Drake shook his head. "What a waste of a time trip," he muttered as we watched the jollyboat sail down the creek.

I punched Drake's arm. "Get over yourself, Cuz. Who else has done what we're doing?"

"I wish I knew," he replied.

Oma tucked her walking stick under her arm as she straightened her mob cap. "It's your first time out, Drake, and we'd be wise to keep a low profile, so follow Ody's example and watch what you say when anyone might be in earshot."

"OK, OK," Drake said, rolling his eyes toward Oma before glaring at me.

As mission captain, I reckoned I should take over the tour. After all, I wasn't ignorant about Bath. It was the site of many North Carolina firsts: the first town, port, library, church, and the earliest de facto state capital, but in 1718, most of that hadn't happened yet. Still, the most exciting thing I had ever heard about Bath was happening here and *now*—Blackbeard was in town.

Drake agreed. "We're going the wrong way," he said, pointing after the jollyboat.

Oma gave him the side eye and motioned to remind him to be low-key, so he whispered, "But the pirates are down *there*." He kept his eyes on the boat's wake as I dragged him forward for the tour.

"I thought you missed baseball," Oma whispered, with the touch of an elbow to his side.

He turned to her, and with two quick lifts of his eyebrows over a playful smile, he whispered, "Blackbeard trumps baseball."

Oma tugged at his sleeve. "Let's move on. We don't want to draw too many questions. The shipyard is further up the way."

Herons stood guard at the far end of the harbor as the marshy ground gave way to a sandy knoll where chains rattled, saws zipped through massive cedar logs, and hammers sang against iron in the shipyard. We watched dock hands heaving wood spars onto the stacks of masting timbers; barrels thudded as hands stacked kegs of turpentine and tar.

Drake sighed his boredom, so we turned back toward town, stopping to watch a few boats come and go from the various points jutting into the creek along Water Street. There were a few small sloops, vessels with oars, poles, or sails, and several larger periaugers, but nothing as grand as the sloop at Tobias Knight's landing.

"Those are big for canoes, aren't they?" Drake asked. "And is it still a canoe if it has a sail? How far can those periaugers travel?"

Oma was the history expert, so she replied, "They're shallow draft vessels, and with sails and oars, they can go about anywhere around here, creeks and the big sound, too. But they're small enough to be carried anywhere aboard a larger ship. Then when the ship reaches the next port of call, the tenders are launched to ferry cargo to and from the landings. But since there aren't many roads here, these probably bring crops from the plantations."

"I wonder where that one is going," I said, pointing to a periauger named *Black Sam Bellamy*, anchored at the end of a floating dock.

Then, just as the crew finished scrubbing the boat clean, a parade of Bath's citizens—sailors, tradesmen, mothers, and children—marched down a boardwalk toward the landing. They came in small family groups, and each cluster bore a basket of figs, wild grapes, or small cakes to the *Bellamy*. A bosun took each gift and placed it on one of the seats.

Oma stopped one of the fruit-bearers when she reached the walkway. "Is this part of today's wedding?" she asked.

"That and more," the young woman replied. "'Tis to honor Capt'n Thache and our Mary."

"Is that a common custom?" Oma asked.

"Not that I ever saw, but we're hopeful that Capt'n Thache and his men will break the chain of misery in Bath."

"What misery is that?" I asked.

She looked me in the eye, nodding as she summed me up. "You're new here, but since the Tuscarora uprising nearly seven years ago, we Bath folk lost our men from war and fever, then we lost women and children through the drought and poor harvests that followed. As a result, we hardly grow enough to survive, and most ships take their goods to bigger ports."

Oma smiled, saying, "And yet you offer such a bounty to the newlyweds. 'Tis very generous of you."

"These baskets carry prayers for the new couple and Bath, too," the woman said. "We hope Captain Thache and his ship, along with the blood and muscle of his crew, will bring better days for Old Town."

The woman beside her added, "Don't forget Marybeth, Maude. That girl was the key to keeping Captain Thache here, and I reckon she did that for Bath as much as for love."

"She did it to live, Edith. There ain't a soul in Bath that's not lookin' for more to hope for than dying young."

Oma's smile turned to puzzlement. "But you have the Governor and other men of influence here," she said. "Isn't that strength enough?"

"Gold lining the pockets of the rich brings them all the luck they need. But we count on Captain Thache to bring life to us common folk." Then with a nod, Maude walked on till we lost sight of her among the clapboard houses lining the street.

I turned to Oma. "Will he bring good to Bath?"

"I'm not sure he'll have the time," she replied as we walked on. Then she lowered her voice to a whisper, adding, "He's near the end of his days." It made sense that she whispered, as spreading information about the future was one of her no-no rules of time travel.

Watching the dock hands spar as they worked was fun, and British colors in the harbor made history come alive. Still, when Oma said *no* to boarding one of the vessels, Drake's brief spurt of enthusiasm fizzled, and soon, we all agreed there wasn't much left that we strangers could do in Bath.

"I bet the wedding party is more fun than this," Drake said. "We should've stayed at the hall."

I scanned the landings up and down Water Street. "Well, the jollyboat's not here now, and we can't swim down this creek." I turned to Oma, asking, "Should we go home?" Surprisingly, Drake was the first to say no.

"Not so soon. Not yet," he said. "Not with Blackbeard in town. Maybe we'll get another chance to see him."

"I'm not sure you'd like that," Oma replied. "I hear he can be quite fearsome."

"Then what's left for us to do?" Drake asked.

Oma shrugged, "We could always eat."

3 Under the Marsh Moon

Ody Saunters

Oma pointed across the street to a painting of a table loaded with vegetables, mutton, and wine under the watch of a melon-colored moon rising over the water.

"Drake hasn't tried any eighteenth-century food, and I have coins to pay for a meal," she said. "Let's see what the ordinary has for dinner."

"The *ordinary*? That's a tavern, isn't it? There'll be pirates in there for sure," Drake said, grinning again. Then, without a worry, he pushed through the black-paneled door, and Oma rushed after him.

Oh, well, it was too late to hope the tavern wouldn't be a bawdy place. So, I scrambled after Oma before the black doors slammed shut.

Luckily, the Marsh Moon was not unfit. After all, this was Bath. Oma said the population was well under one hundred, and most of them were sailors, dockhands, and now pirates, but it was also the home of plantations for governors, a few with royal titles. So, Marsh Moon served a blend of classes, with the roughest of seamen seated near the back, and for the genteel, there were tabletops of heavy polished pine near the bottle-glass windows. Oma picked a table at the far end of the window array. From there, we could make out silhouettes of those passing, but from outside the dim tavern, no one would see us clearly, much less peg us as strangers in time.

A busty barmaid dodged fingers that snatched at her skirt tail as she ignored shouts from the back: O*'er here, Sally,* and *Where ya been, lass?*

Drake hid his chuckle. "Look at Sal go."

Sally nimbly threaded her way to our table. Oma said most patrons were too deep in their cups to slow her down.

When the barmaid reached us, she straightened her apron and pointed to a sign by the door. "The fare's marked on the board, and the prices are there, too. What'll ye have today?"

The menu was a mystery to me, but Oma ordered Scots Venison for us and a dish I'd never heard of for herself.

"Very good," Sal said. "And I'll bring you the fish and roast squash from the fire." She looked around the table, probably noting Drake's fresh face and my half-stubbled beard. "Will it be cider for all?"

After Oma relayed our order and passed our coins to the cook, Sal returned to us with a question. "Did ye folks happen to see any of the weddin' today? I hear tell the bride had a dress fit to crow about."

We looked at our grandmother as she took a moment to pick her phrases.

"We were there by mistake for a few minutes," she replied. "But I saw nothing of the bride."

"'Tis a shame. I hear 'tis a glorious frock. Some say Cap'n Thache hisself took it off a French ship trying to make it to Charleston," and from behind her hand, she added, "I hope there weren't no *mamozel* still inside it." Her eyes widened as she hid a giggle behind her palm. Then she wiped the humor from her face and said, "But, I'd still like to see it on our Marybeth."

"Is the bride your kin?" Oma asked.

"No, but till this week, she was a server here, and her Ma was a coo ...." The young woman stopped mid-sentence and dropped her mouth as she recognized three silhouettes passing the green glass and heading for the door. "Lordy!" she said. "'Tis the Cap'n."

Drake and I straightened as Sal hurried back to her work. My cousin held his breath with eyes fixed on the creaking door as two women entered the room, pausing as their eyes adjusted to the changing light.

I remembered Mrs. Bellieu from the hall. She was on her feet again, but the lady was still pale, and her downturned lips twitched as if she were praying.

"That's his wife," Drake whispered, nodding toward the younger woman. "She and Thache were standing by the Governor when you yanked me out of the hall."

I turned toward my cousin. "I was getting you back to safety."

Drake scowled as he replied, "Nothing happened."

But then, the bride looked my way, and the room faded as I fell captive in the net of long brunette curls pouring over pearly shoulders.

"I believe that gown is blue damask over satin," Oma whispered. "It must be French."

I had no idea what fabric she wore, but I had never seen a girl with beauty compared to hers. Marybeth's sapphire eyes sparkled in the lantern light, exactly matching the skirt of her overdress. And beneath that, a sheet of glimmering white slid against her like fresh snow over rounded hills.

I sat, entranced, till Drake's snort and a kick to my shin weakened the girl's spell on me. But then the door widened, and it was Drake's turn to drop his chin.

A sea breeze wafted through the room on the coattails of a tall shadow. Scents of leather, salt, and fresh-pine timbers washed away the odors of beer and fish. Blackbeard, tall and mighty as a ship's mast, had arrived. His entry made the tavern a new place, just as his presence in the Pamlico Sound changed the world of Bath.

"Watch yourself," Oma whispered. "Edward Thache is not a man to bear slights easily." But luckily, Sal's amazement at her friend's transformation drew attention to the new bride.

"Oh, Lordy, Mary," she cried, a free hand to her face. "Is that you? You've turned to a dream." She dipped a little curtsy as Thache directed his bride and her mother to a table between us and the door.

The new groom helped seat the pair, but before he took his chair, he noticed our table in the corner and stepped toward us. I was half afraid he meant to put me in my place for gawking at his wife, so I tried not to stare at either of them as he walked our way. Luckily, Grandmother was his target, not me.

I had paid little mind to the famous beard during my glimpse of Thache in Knight's Hall, but now it was very close to Oma's face. Though thick and curly, his beard was much shorter than I expected, perhaps trimmed for his courtship and wedding day. I had seen a sketch of him where the beard nearly covered his face, but he had shaved some of the hair away, revealing high bare cheekbones and clear, smiling eyes.

His plumed broad-brimmed cap covered a black mane, now combed away from his forehead and tied at the nape of his neck with a blue ribbon. Ruffled lace cuffs rested against his palms, and his red satin jacket fell open over a tooled leather waistcoat covering a white linen shirt.

"Madam," he said as he tipped his hat to Oma. "I be Cap'n Edward Thache, and 'tis my pleasure to see ye again. After the wedding, I sought 'e in the hall, but 'e must have left us quickly."

Oma's eyes pleaded for us to keep silent, even though she had no choice but to speak.

"I beg pardon for intruding on the festivities, Sir. I'm the widow of Ephraim Saunters, and these are my grandsons, Odysseus and Drake. We are strangers to Bath, and unfortunately, we arrived at the wrong house. Our best wishes to you and your new family."

"But 'twas a blessing you were there to help care for our dear Mother Bellieu."

"I was grateful for the opportunity to help. Will your party follow you here, Sir? We will gladly give up our tables if you need."

"No, no. Our celebration lies elsewhere, but my wife's mother, Henrietta Bellieu, needs a quieter evening. Since she is known here, we hope to secure a room for her for the night. 'Tis bold of me to ask, but I wonder if you would be willing to do us another favor. Will you keep her company and see to her health should she fall ill again?"

What would Oma say to that? We should go home, but did she dare disappoint Blackbeard?

While she searched for words, Drake reached for her hand, whispering, "We can stay one night, Grandmother. Don't you agree, Odysseus?"

My eyes widened at the prospect of staying, not to mention Drake using my full name, but my grin grew as I caught the gist of his game and played along.

"I don't think Uncle would mind our staying a little longer, and if we can help, we should do so, don't you think?"

With a tiny twitch of her head, Oma replied, "But ... but we made no plans for that."

Thache had the answer. "I'll arrange for all," he said. "And 'twill be my pleasure to pay for your lodging and board for a night if you agree." Oma was silent for a moment, so Thache sweetened his offer. "By noon tomorrow, I can offer transport to wherever you need to be."

I stifled a chuckle; how did he plan to get us to another century?

Drake's face glowed; he was all in, and I was wavering.

Oma tapped her walking stick, reminding me we had an out—a backup plan. That sealed it for me. No one asked, but I would have voted to stay. Oma must have agreed.

"Very well, Sir. If it suits you, we will be happy to be company to your good mother for a night. We thank you for your hospitality," she said.

"'Tis our great pleasure, Madam," he replied.

Henrietta Bellieu huddled with her daughter, their hands clasping as Thache arranged our lodging.

"Don't fret, Mother," Marybeth said. "Edward treats me as a gentleman should, and how else can we survive without Father?"

Mrs. Bellieu wiped her tears and stuffed the wet handkerchief into a palm. "You've paid for our security, daughter, and now we can work our farm instead of this kitchen. But the price is too great; you know little of the ways of men like him," she said.

"I have friends who are wives—some with children already. I know more than you think, Mother—enough to get me through this night." Marybeth traded her fresh handkerchief for her mother's soppy one. "We will return tomorrow; you'll see all is well."

Henrietta snuffed back her tears as Thache returned to the table.

"'Tis done," he said. "Two rooms with two beds paid for, including board through the morning." He helped Mother Bellieu stand and then bent to speak to his wife. "Marybeth, we should be going." Mrs. Bellieu held tight to her daughter's fingers for as long as she could, but when she finally let go, the Captain escorted Mrs. Bellieu to our table.

The gray-templed woman watched as her daughter passed the door and headed toward the landing on the arm of her new husband. Then Henrietta Bellieu burst into tears and sobbed a puddle around her daughter's handkerchief.

Wavy green glass marred my view, but I had seen the soft, smooth fingers that brushed Blackbeard's sleeve and noticed how Marybeth's dimples deepened as she smiled into his face. The stroll looked like a dance as she pranced to match his gait until they reached the landing. Then they boarded the gift-laden periauger, where scruffy sailors snapped to attention as Edward Thache escorted his bride and settled her into the *Bellamy*.

And as we watched them pull away and the sails slowly unfurl, I was surprised to find that Drake and I had finally agreed on something. We both wanted to stay in Bath. My cousin wanted to know more about Blackbeard, and I wanted at least another moment in the glow of the radiant Marybeth. True, she was a married woman now, but Oma had said it: the groom's days were near an end.

4 Sun, Shadow, and Time

Aurora Saunters

The boys dug into their venison, and the tasty meal lifted our spirits. But there was not so much as a smile from Henrietta Bellieu, not even when Ody chuckled at Drake gagging on his first taste of frog leg pie.

"Did your boys never go a-frog-gigging?" Henrietta asked.

"The boys are from colder climes where frogs are not as plentiful, so this is a new delicacy for them."

When we finished, Sal asked if she could show us to our room.

"Not yet, please," Mrs. Bellieu muttered. "I need air."

"You remember our rules for travel, don't you, boys?" I asked. They nodded, and after Ody promised to watch his cousin, the boys dashed to the shipyard.

I followed Henrietta as she gravitated to the dock where Marybeth boarded Thache's *Bellamy*. She stared toward Pamlico sound, clutching her daughter's soggy handkerchief, repeatedly muttering until I understood the words, *What have I done?*

"Have you done something wrong?" I asked.

Henrietta studied the toes of new leather shoes as she said, "I bargained with the Devil, and the price I paid was a life I had no claim to."

I prodded her for what she meant. But she scanned the street and the landings on the shoreline and then replied, "Such deeds are only fit for the shadows."

"Then, walk with me," I replied. "Let's find my boys and keep them from mischief. The sunshine and sea breezes will do us both good."

We strolled on Water Street as if we were in different places. I walked in Bath's sunshine, and Widow Bellieu carried the shadows of grief with her. Our conversation was sparse as we walked, but we agreed on what we should call each other; we settled on Aurora and Hetty.

We finally reached the shipyard, where we found Ody and Drake fascinated by craftsmen working on a new sailing vessel.

"Look at this," Drake called. And the excitement of one teenage boy tumbled over the other as they explained how a giant cedar becomes a periauger.

"They have one ready to test at the landing ahead. May we go?" Drake asked.

"They invited us," Ody added.

It was good to see the light in Drake's eyes again. I couldn't say no, so I looked to see that their pendants were in place and nodded my permission.

"But that's an untested boat. Do you not fear for the boys' lives?" Hetty asked.

"The world is full of rough seas," I replied. "The main point of our journey here is to teach my grandsons how to survive more than life's usual dangers."

Hetty's smile twitched as she watched them, full of questions and observations for the crew. Each cousin corrected the other as they tried their hands at the oars.

"They're a noisy pair, aren't they?" I asked.

Her smile faded as she replied, "At least they aren't thrust into being adults before their time." Then her eyes followed the course of Old Towne Creek, but she soon turned from the view, saying, "I should sit down."

We found a bench on the boardwalk along the row of townhouses and shops, where we watched the gulls dive while the sun lowered. When the boys returned, we enjoyed clam chowder and corncakes at Marsh Moon. After that, we found our rooms and settled in for the night.

Henrietta Bellieu said little as we prepared to sleep, but when she was in her part of the trundle bed and I in mine, she told me how Captain Thache had wooed her daughter.

"After my Bert died, we had no hands to run the farm. With war and the fever, the town was already short of men, and we had no crops to barter, so Mary and I took work here."

"Did Thache's arrival put an end to that?" I asked.

"Aye. The town was happy to have more manpower for the yard, and 'twas a bonus that the sailors had silver to spend. On top of that, they swore they had given up on their pirating ways and meant to live as proper men do."

"That must have been a great boon to the town," I said.

"Aye, 'twas so. We were glad of the crewmen until they decided to find women. Several had their eyes on my Marybeth, and she had a harder time keeping hands off her in the tavern. But Thache shooed the rest of them away. He had his pick of women in town but wanted my girl."

"Did she want him?" I asked.

"Not at first. Mary had a sweetheart. 'Twas I who told Thache about Wallace McNeil, and at first, that put him off her, as I hoped it would. Bath was full of widows and young women, too, and a few hoped for the Captain's attention. But when Sal convinced him Mary was yet unspoiled, he turned to her again."

"Did she welcome him this time?"

"She needed him. We both did. We'd seen war and liked having a man with followers at his command who would protect our home. And after being poor, Mary liked the finery he brought her. You can't blame a girl for that."

"Of course not," I said.

"But she loved Wallace and had promised to marry him."

"What happened to change her mind?"

"He went away." Then Hetty would say no more about Wallace and turned to the wall, quietly sobbing until she fell asleep.

So, now Marybeth Bellieu was married to Edward Thache. He may not have been her first choice, but perhaps he was the best.

But what would happen to her and her mother after his last battle in November? Would the girl live to see that? Would Thache give her to his crew as some old books suggested? Guilt already wracked poor Henrietta. What would she do if her daughter lost her life due to Blackbeard?

I hadn't come prepared to meet pirates, and my memory of Thache's legend was spotty, but I had facts and a few more Spanish coins at home. So, with my grandsons and Henrietta sound asleep, I slipped clothes over my nightshirt, and with shoes, cloak, and walking stick, I stepped into the shadows outside the tavern. Then, after a quick review of why this was the right thing to do, I grabbed the walking stick and found myself back in my study at Cooper's Ridge.

Everything was as we left it. Elizabeth Glover's prayer book was on the floor where the last commuter dropped it, and Drake's baseball mitt was still on the sofa.

I sighed, thinking of how Drake balked at doing the commute. He wanted a summer of diving, climbing, and smacking a baseball around a diamond with his friends, and in our century, those were the battlefields where boys became men. It was Drake's time to enter manhood. But even though baseball was more fun than hanging with Grandma, it wouldn't teach Drake what he needed to know about the dangers *he* might face—dangers the other boys would never encounter.

The bell jar holding my pendant collection was on the desk where Ody had left it. Each of the boys had a pendant of my hair that would bring them to me, and I had one for each of them in case they needed a rescue.

That was part of my job on this mission. I was an advisor, rescuer, and scout. But I had been a miserable scout this time, directing the boys to the wrong place and time.

The mantel clock struck one. It was still the middle of the day—precisely when I left expecting to meet Elizabeth Glover. Odd. Until now, there had always been a time gap between leaving and returning via my walking stick. It was a gap I had to measure to keep up with two timelines.

There was so much about the time-travel mystery that we didn't understand—had my commuting powers evolved again? If so, I should hurry back to the boys. If the time differences on this commute were not as I expected, I might fail as a rescuer. And as for advisor, I'd better get on with what I came for—information about Blackbeard and Bath.

I had no time to memorize facts and dared not take an entire book back to 1718. A glance at the indices showed no mention of Wallace McNeil or Bellieu. The only name associated with his wife was Mary Ormand, and that record was unproven.

Luckily, I found a source with bullet points on Blackbeard's life, including dates of critical events. After printing that page, I tucked it into a secret pocket in my eighteenth-century garb. Then, I gathered all my Spanish coins and dropped them into my skirt pocket.

At last, I had collected all I dared carry, so I clutched the pendant that would take me to Ody, but where would I find him? And when? If the commuting powers had changed, the timing might not be as it had been with Ody in Old Salem. Now I couldn't trust that the forty minutes I spent visiting home would be forty minutes for Ody in Bath. Either way, my grandsons would be surprised I had made an unannounced time jump.

There was no choice. I had to find the boys, so I pressed tightly on the ring of Ody's hair, hoping he'd still be safe in bed when I arrived and that Drake would be there, too.

5 Pirate Songs

Drake Saunters: Time-travel Trainee

Ody sure took his time going up those narrow tavern stairs, and the air grew more stifling with every step. My cousin stumbled as I gave him a little push. "Hurry, find windows that open."

He scowled over his shoulder but grabbed the rail and picked up the pace. After all, our stomping up steps and banging doors didn't matter. The Marsh Moon was an inn, and sometimes the guests were noisy sea captains and their crew. We soon found our room and tumbled onto a set of trundle beds.

"Good grief, it's hot in here. We won't get much sleep," I said.

Ody punched my shoulder. "Don't state the obvious, Drake. Oma hates that."

"Well, can *you* sleep in this sauna?" From my perch on the lower shelf of the trundle, I kicked off my shoes and peeled the stockings down from the knee band on my knickers. "Jeepers, I miss air conditioning."

"Yeah," Ody said. "Let's see what we can do about that." He pushed open the heavy curtains and opened the window. "There, that should be better."

The breeze helped, but it wasn't enough. "Any idea where we can find ice?" I asked.

Ody kicked off his shoes and stretched out on the higher of the two beds in our trundle. "The North Pole? I don't know. You can check beside the vending machine, I guess."

I threw my pillow at him, and a puff of feathers clouded the air.

He threw it back. "Just lie still. The night air is bound to cool."

"Maybe, but not anytime soon." I moved to the window, fanning my long nightshirt to stir the breeze. "Too bad they don't have a pool."

"There's a big creek out there," Ody replied.

"Are you telling me to go jump in the lake?"

"Well, all that fanning will make you hotter," Ody said.

"Oh, yeah?" I fanned even faster out of spite, but he was right; I was making it worse. "Let's go sit outside awhile," I said.

"Oma won't like that."

"Who's going to tell her?" I replied, stuffing my shirt back into the knickers. "Come on. I remember a bench by the street."

Ody shrugged and looked for his shoes and stockings. "Just remember the rules," he said.

"Fine, but I'm not putting those socks back on. It's hot enough without them."

"Oma wouldn't like that either. Folks will spot us as odd without stockings."

"There's nothing there but starlight and not much of that. So, no one can see us, and who could we run into anyway? Do you reckon they have a town crier?"

Ody slipped his shoes over bare feet as he said, "They had a nightwatchman in Old Salem, but that was decades ahead of now and in a bigger town. So no, I don't think there will be a town crier. Just remember Oma's rules."

I waited till Ody put his shoes on, and after that, we stuck to the shadows till we reached the landing and chose a bench at the point's edge.

"You're right; this is better," Ody said, stretching his feet to waves lapping onto the point.

"Told you. But I don't get why we're doing this. Why would anyone want to go back in time? Everything's backward here—especially air conditioning."

"You know why. My trip to Salem was an accident; I might have been stuck there. Your being here proves you have the gift, too,"

"*Gift?* I'd say it's more like a family *curse* that can kill you if you step wrong."

"That's why Oma wants you to learn under safer conditions than I had."

"Ha!" I said. "How's that working out? You had Moravians. Now we have pirates."

Water splashed, and ropes groaned as boats pulled against their tethers. Then the rattle of a kingfisher broke the silence, and moonlight turned the ripples on the water's surface into frothy orange soda.

Then, the night became brighter as the moon lifted into the sky. Ody sat up, fidgeting on the bench as he looked around. I felt it, too. We were exposed and unsafe.

"Listen," he whispered.

To our right, a boardwalk creaked as someone went to a boat on a nearby landing, and softer steps trudged southward toward the Towne Point.

I nodded to Ody, and we hurried to the shadows of the Water Street buildings, an easy escape from trouble.

The moon provided sufficient light for the sailor to our north. We watched his boat sail down Old Town Creek toward some unknown dock. As he passed the fort, the boatsman south of us pushed slowly into the current, following the first man. Then we were alone again.

Despite the night birds, croaking frogs, and rocking boats, we detected the sound of tapping mallets followed by the brushing zip of tools used to shape wood.

"Do shipyards operate at night?" I whispered.

"Doesn't seem likely," Ody replied.

"Maybe it's a secret project," I said with a grin. "Let's go see."

We crept along Water Street, tiptoeing toward the sounds and low lantern light at the harbor's north end.

"There. I see someone," Ody whispered as he pointed to the shadow of an arm at work.

We snuck closer. Someone was smoothing boards. Suddenly the sounds stopped, and the lantern light faded. I held my breath until footsteps shuffled quickly over the sandy ground. Once the steps hit Water Street's packed-earth walkway, they became softer as they moved away.

"Well, so much for solving that mystery," I said, shrugging.

"Come on," he said. "It's safer at the fort." So, I followed Ody to the south end of Water Street, where we found a bench on the far side of the palisade. From there, we watched ripples made silver by the risen moon.

"What do you reckon those two sailors were up to?" I asked.

"Going home would be my guess," Ody said.

"Or smuggling."

Then a new voice chimed in.

"I know where those men are going."

We turned to find the stranger.

"I know, and I don't care much for the thought of it," he said. But his somber tone became a chuckled as he spotted our shins shining in the moonlight.

"You lads ain't from here, are you?" he asked. Then, when we quickly tucked our legs under the bench, he added, "Don't fret. I'm not from here either—not exactly." Then he motioned for Ody to scoot over to make room for him between us.

"So, what were they up to?" I asked. "Those sailors, I mean."

I reckoned the man wasn't much older than Ody. He bent forward, resting his arms on his knees, a blue and white striped headscarf in his hands. And when the moonlight struck his scalp, he looked like he'd shaved his head with a scaling knife. Maybe he was new to shaving, too. Even with a safety razor, Ody did nearly as bad a job on his face.

"Do you see those lights there?" he asked, pointing to the left bank, far downstream. "That's Plum Point. And that's where they're going."

"Isn't that Edward Thache's plantation?" Ody asked. "Our ferryman pointed it out to us today."

The young man spat into the creek. "It ain't his. He's Blackbeard, the pirate, and there ain't nothing here that's his. Plum Point belongs to the family of Bertram Bellieu."

Ody tapped a finger to his lips, reminding me to be silent, but the stranger had more to say. "Thache paid the tavern keeper for rum today, and his men are on the way to enjoy it. The rich folk had their fancy party, and now it's time for the pirates to play."

"But … but what about his bride?" Ody asked. "Will she be safe?"

The man laid his head into his fingers, holding the scarf over his eyes as his shoulders shook.

I wasn't sure what to do, so I looked for Ody's lead. My cousin bit his lip to keep silent, gripping the bench edge until he couldn't hold back. His throat was tight as he asked, "They won't hurt her, will they?"

The man sat up, twisting the headscarf around a fist. "Not tonight. She will come to no harm tonight nor any other night if I have my say. She's a lady, she is, and fit for better than the like of pirates."

"She's a girl worth some trouble, I'd agree with that," Ody said, "And I'd be willing to help you, but my cousin and I can't stay here for long."

"'Tis fine. I will be here for Marybeth, providin' I can avoid Blackbeard and his men."

Then broken bits of faint voices mingled with the night sounds.

"Do I hear singing?" I asked.

When we trained our ears to ignore the sounds of waves and docks, we heard the low strains of dozens of male voices wafting over the breeze. Even though they sang in unison, we couldn't make out the words, but the tune ebbed and waned like waves, and the rhythm pounded, reminding me of old movies where a drummer kept time for the oarsmen. Then, as the chorus picked up the tempo, the song became shouts and cheers.

The stranger's jaw stiffened, and his white knuckles curled into fists.

"Do you know the words?" I asked.

"Aye," he replied, "I reckon they are singing for the newlyweds, but those words ain't fit for a lady's ears."

"But you said she would be safe," Ody repeated.

"Aye. Safe but uneasy, I reckon."

When the song ended, the sounds of the night swallowed the remaining incoherent wisps of male voices. After a time, the stranger relaxed his fists, but his jaw stayed set as he nodded. Then, even though his voice was quiet, it pierced the night like a sword as he whispered across the waves, "I'll watch out for you."

Ody slapped him on the right shoulder. "I'm glad she has you," he said.

It was a tricky question, but I had to ask it. I lay my hand on the man's forearm, saying, "I mean no offense, but … does she want to be watched?"

He turned toward me, jaw set, eyes steely, "She *will* want it, and I'll watch out for her till I'm convinced otherwise."

I nodded, clapping his free shoulder, and the man jerked as Ody and I fist-bumped behind his head. We were on the same team when it came to Marybeth.

"We will do our best," I said.

Ody agreed, saying, "Aye, we will."

"Call me Carver," the young man said. "That name is safe for me here, but it won't be if the pirates find me out. Since you lads are strangers, maybe I can help you, too. If you need to reach me, ask Captain Harding at the shipyard—no one else. He'll find me."

Ody opened his mouth to tell him our names, but he paused, no doubt deciding whether to say who we were, so I filled in the pause.

"We might be in danger here, too. So, call us Wolfie and the Dragon," I said, pointing toward my chest.

Carver turned to me, asking, "Because you can fly, or do you breathe fire?"

Ody scoffed. "He's a drake, not a dragon. Call him duckie."

I pushed Ody's shoulder, and he shoved me in return. Carver snickered at us, but he stood to shake our hands. Then we joined him at the water's edge, and Carver's smile faded as we stared silently toward Plum Point. I reckon we were all wondering about the welfare of Marybeth Thache.

Then for no reason, Ody stumbled, and Carver's quick grab saved him from falling into the water.

"Oh! Oh, my!" The voice was female. We turned to see Grandma steadying herself as she leaned against the bench.

"Grandma? We thought you were sleeping. What are you doing here?" I asked.

"I'll ask you the same question. I thought I'd find you boys in your room," she replied.

"I don't mean to be rude, Ma'am, but how did you get here without making a sound?" Carver asked. He bent down to pick up a coin. Then, after he studied both sides, he asked, "Is this yours? I don't think I ever saw one of these unless cut into bits."

"Thank you, young man," Grandma said as she accepted her coin. "I'm so sorry to have startled you, but I've been worried about my grandsons and was hurrying to find them. What happened to your head?"

"'Tis no worry. I should be on my way." Carver tied his headscarf, slipped into the shadows behind the fort, and kept running. We held our tongues till he was too far to hear us speaking.

"Where have you been?" Ody asked. "Where did you get that coin?"

"Nevermind. Let's go to the inn. I'll explain."

We led Grandma to our room, and she checked the hallway before closing the door behind her.

"Did you go home, Grandma?" I asked. "Did you leave us here alone in the past?"

"I hoped you be safe sleeping here," she said. "Besides, if you weren't here, I'd have no way to return to Bath." Then she looked at Ody. "What happened?"

"Drake was hot, so we decided to sit by the creek. That's all."

"That's all?" she asked, and from the suspicious slant of her brows, I don't think she believed my cousin.

I shrugged, saying, "We watched a few boats come and go. Nothing else."

"Did you speak to anyone?" she asked.

"Just the guy you met. He took a break from his work at the shipyard to watch the boats. But, I tell you, nothing happened," Ody replied.

"Well, we heard pirates singing," I said, smiling.

"And where were these pirates?" she asked.

"Further down the creek," Ody said. "It was nothing, Oma. Seriously. But why did you go home?"

"Yes, why did you leave us here?" I asked.

Grandma opened her cloak and fanned her neck as she sat in the only straight chair in the room. "Mrs. Bellieu worries about her daughter—what Blackbeard may do to her. So, I went home to get more Spanish money and look up facts about Blackbeard's last months."

"You aren't going to alter history, are you, Oma?" Ody asked. "You've warned us about that."

Grandma grimaced as she replied. "I can't change the history about Blackbeard's wife because there's barely any record of her. We know he married, and not long after that, he was dead, but we don't know what became of his bride. Some books suggest he didn't treat her well, but that isn't fact, only rumor. So, if all history has is hearsay, we can't cause damage that would reach our century."

"What about the grandfather paradox?" Ody asked. "What if someone careless … just as an example, let's say Drake … what if Drake kills an ancestor of ours? Would we all disappear from history?"

"Wha …?" I asked. "I'm not going to kill anyone. Who do you think I am?"

"Calm down," Grandma said. "Drake obviously didn't kill an ancestor because we are here."

"But that's a famous time paradox, Oma," Ody said. "Aren't you worried we will change history?"

"Not as worried as I used to be," she replied. "I'm still untangling time knots, but a theoretical expert, Vincent Peregrino, suggests that if we are here, we are part of history, and what we do in this century was either always done or didn't matter."

Ody's look was as puzzled as mine.

Grandma shrugged. "I'm still working it out, but he had some theories that made sense. But to be safe, let's not do anything drastic."

I rolled my eyes at Grandma. "Ok, I'll make a note: *no murdering folks*. Check."

"Ease up on the sarcasm," Ody said, shoving me. Then he turned to Grandma. "Then why did you need notes on Blackbeard?" he asked.

"Blackbeard's history is written. Things won't turn out well for him, and maybe that history harms Marybeth and Mrs. Bellieu if they get caught in his wake. But if I know when things happen, a word well-placed might keep the women safe."

"We aren't going to be here that long, are we?" Ody asked.

"Well … no. Probably not. I just wanted to be armed with facts. And I discovered something that might be important."

"To Blackbeard?" I asked.

"More to time travel in general. It seems our gift has evolved. For example, when I used my walking stick to return home, I arrived precisely when I left. That's new. It hasn't worked that way before," she said.

"Does that mean, if you return home and we transport to you, it will be as if we never left? Our parents won't miss us?"

"I'm not 100% sure, but I think that's right," Grandma said.

"That simplifies things," Ody said. "We can stay here as long as we like. No one will know."

"No one at home," I replied. "But our being here might still upset the past."

"I hope that upset doesn't cause a shipwreck," Ody said.

"Or a murder," I added. "Especially ours."

"I'm glad to hear that we can stay if we need to, Oma," Ody said. "Blackbeard's wife might be in trouble. If we stay longer, maybe we can spare her some grief."

"Sounds good to me," I replied.

"Ok, boys. Let's not rush into things. Henrietta Bellieu should return home tomorrow, and that may be the last we'll hear of Thache."

"But at least we'll see him tomorrow, too," I said.

"Yes, let's see what tomorrow brings, and then we can decide what to do," Oma said. She draped her hood over her head and wrapped the gray cloak around her. As she reached the door, she looked back over her shoulders. "Please. For all our sakes, don't go anywhere else."

We promised we wouldn't, but I crossed my fingers just in case. After all, Ody and I might need to help Carver.

6 The Fever

Aurora Saunters

Eager for sleep, I hurried to the rough pillow of my trundle bed, but the odor filtering into the hallway was not the smell of sweet dreams.

Hetty Bellieu was retching into the chamber pot she had pulled from under her bed. When she paused between vomiting spasms, she rested against the mattress, weak, but since she wasn't at death's door, I grabbed the empty water pitcher and rushed back to Ody.

"Mrs. Bellieu is ill. Find a maid. We need towels, water, and a spare sheet if you can find one. Hurry, please."

Ody ran for help, and Drake swapped my empty pitcher for his and ran to find more water while I hurried back to Henrietta's side. She sat on the floor with one hand on the chamber pot, her head flat on the bed, mouth open, gasping. I wet a towel in our wash basin and cleaned her face and neck. Then after a rinse and wring, I used the wet towel to cool her feverish brow and wrists.

"Was it the clams, dear?" I asked.

She rolled her head slowly from side to side, indicating *no*.

Then I whispered, "Is it the same thing that caused you trouble at the wedding?"

Her breathing was heavy, but this time she whispered, "I … I don't know." Then after a pause, she groaned, saying, "I … ache … everywhere."

Ody pushed the door open and set a bundle of towels on a chair by the bed. "How is she?" he asked.

Henrietta was too weak to answer, but Sal replied, "We've seen this before. We hoped it was gone, but I believe she has the fever."

Mrs. Bellieu tried to raise her neck, and when she could not, she lay her head flat on the bed again, whimpering.

"What fever?" Ody asked.

"Yellow fever," Sal replied. "We've seen customers take ill from it more than once. 'Tis what killed her man."

Henrietta turned her body to one side and cried into her arm. "I can't go yet. My poor Marybeth."

"Is there a doctor close by?" I asked.

"No, Mum," she replied. "We might find Doctor Maule in the morning, but we have no one in town right now."

"Bring me the coolest water you can find, a bit of soap, clean sheets, the best bread you have, and a pot of weak tea with a little bowl of honey."

Sal wrung her hands, "The fever won't spread, will it, Ma'am? This ain't another plague, is it?"

"Have you seen other cases recently?"

"No, Ma'am. Not for ages now."

"That's a good sign."

"Oma, what else can I bring for you?" Ody asked.

"Drake went for water. Find him and bring as much as you can." Then I turned to Sal.

"Yes, mum?" she asked.

"Bring clear red wine if you have it and the strongest whiskey you can find."

"I'll do it and find cups for 'e, too."

"Cups for the tea and wine, but the whiskey's not for drinking. 'Tis for rubbing. And if you need help, ask one of my grandsons."

"Yes, Ma'am." And she was off like a scared bunny.

Within minutes Sal and the boys had delivered everything. Henrietta had stopped vomiting, but she was still burning with fever and faded in and out of consciousness, moaning in pain when she roused. Sal set the tea, wine, and whiskey on the bedside table, within easy reach. Then she emptied the chamber pot and freshened the basins and water pitchers while Ody and Drake changed the sheets on Mrs. Bellieu's bed.

"Do you need anything else, Grandma?" Drake asked.

"Shall we take turns staying to help you?" Ody offered.

"No, boys, but please do exactly as I say. Pour fresh water into your basin and wash any part of you that isn't covered. Use the soap. I'm not positive this is yellow fever, but you can't catch it from Mrs. Bellieu if it is. Keep covered against mosquitos, just in case."

"Are you sure, Oma?" Ody asked.

"Yes, I have what I need here. You boys should sleep. Eat your breakfast when it's time, and if Marybeth Thache arrives before you've seen me, ask her to come to the room." They nodded and left me with Sal.

"Sal, please spread the used sheets on the floor, and I'll bundle all the dirty things in there."

"Yes, Ma'am," she replied. "Do you have a clean nightshirt for Mis'ress Bellieu?"

I checked the little sack the Captain had brought for Henrietta. "I do, Sal. Thank you. If you will, please, help me change her." Sal helped me put Henrietta in clean clothes and on clean sheets, and the stack of dirty things grew in the corner of the room.

"Wash your hands before you leave, too, Sal. Use the soap."

"What about the clothes I'm wearing, Mum? Should they be boiled too?"

"It's unnecessary unless you find vomit or blood on them, but it can't hurt to be safe. You've been a godsend. Mrs. Bellieu will rest easier now that she's clean."

"'Tis no worry, Mum," She grinned as she added, "I reckon Cap'n Thache will pay for all this, too, and he's good to chip in a bit extra when pleased. I reckon his wedding night will have him in a good mood."

I don't know if Henrietta was lucid enough to understand Sal's last words, but she groaned. I opened the whisky and rubbed some on my patient's neck, face, hands, and feet before exposing them to the night breeze. That should reduce the fever. I also had a small pill hidden away; it would bring down her heat without causing bleeding. A sip of whiskey with honey might help if she continued to be in pain. The tea, honey, and bread would strengthen her should she rouse.

The wine? Well, that was mostly for me.

7 Pressed Into Service

Aurora Saunters

Once Henrietta's fever cooled, she drifted to sleep. I dozed off shortly after the early birds began their calls. But then, Henrietta's weak gasps woke me.

"Miz Saunters … Au … Aurora … the fever … did it break?" she asked in a whisper.

I hurried to her side to find she was barely warmer than I was. "You've done well, Mrs. Bellieu. How do you feel?"

She tried to turn onto her side, and while she could shift her body, the pain wrenched her face as she tried turning her neck, and her head fell back to the pillow.

"Lie still, dear." I put a cool, wet cloth on her head. Then after a check for skin color and clarity of vision, I said, "You're going to be fine."

She nodded, then rested her head on the pillow. And with eyes shut and lips barely moving, she muttered, "I'm too weak to fight."

"You won't have to fight; you're recovering well."

"From the fever, maybe, but … my daughter …."

"She has a husband now. He will watch over her."

The widow shook her head slowly. "But he's the reason she needs protecting."

Mrs. Bellieu had reason to worry, but history had an unknown plan for her and Marybeth, and I had to get the boys safely home. Still, I had to ask, "Why are you so fearful?"

"'Tis the men he sent here. Caesar seems nice enough, but the other man, Coleman, tells me things about Thache. He said the Captain had several wives before Mary but left each behind soon after they wed. And if they put up a fuss, his anger could bring him to blows."

"That sounds like tall tales to me. Men sometimes tell stories about the women they caught and the fish that got away. Try some tea; it will give you strength."

She roused a bit after a couple of sweet sips. "I hope that's all 'tis," she said, "But there's something else. Before Thache came to town, my Mary kept company with a stone mason out of Beaufort, and I told the Captain about him."

"Yes, last night, you said you meant to discourage Edward."

"Aye, but it didn't work. The young man, Wallace McNeil, disappeared without a trace. His brother came asking about him. No one in Beaufort knew what had happened to him, and no one in Bath was talking. He just vanished."

"Do you think the Captain scared him away?" I asked.

"I fear Thache put an end to him, and if he did, I've cast bad bread on the waters around Plum Point, and only bad can come of that. God willing, the Captain will put an end to me and not my daughter. But if he loses interest in her …."

Hetty's sobs took over again, but finally, she sat up, propped on one elbow. "Aurora … please stay at my home till I'm stronger. I need your help."

When Henrietta kept her tea down, I offered her a bit of bread with honey. After that, she felt well enough to sit in a chair. But when Marybeth called from the hall, Hetty returned to her sick bed and complained more loudly of her aches and fever.

Mary hurried to her mother's side. "What happened, Mother? Sally says you have yellow fever. Is that so?"

Henrietta resumed her low tones. "I can't say what the fever is, but, aye, it might be the same that took your father. I was lucky to have a healing angel to care for me. Aurora Saunters stopped the retchin' and soothed my fever."

"And how do you feel now, Mother?" the girl asked.

"Still weak. The fever was worse at night, and I ache when I move. I fear I won't be much help around the house for a while." Then Hetty smiled weakly, saying, "But don't worry about me. How was your night, my darling? How are you now that you're a married woman?"

Marybeth's face brightened. "It was beautiful, Mama. Ned was so gentle with me, so thoughtful. His men anchored the tender at Knight's landing, and we rowed home for the night. Some of his crew camped outside and sang for us while his cook prepared a dinner of turtle soup and fresh king mackerel for his officers and us."

Mrs. Bellieu choked a little at the mention of food, then said, "Go on, my dear."

Marybeth beamed as she continued. "Israel Hands, Edward's first mate, toasted us with Edward's prize silver cup, my wedding gift from Edward."

"That must be a treasure," I said.

She smiled, "'Tis, indeed. Then this morning, we counted stars from the lookout. Then at dawn's light, we boarded his sloop and sailed into the big river, so I could feel the sea wind in my hair and hear the slap of the sails as we watched the sunrise over the sound. I never knew such happiness, Mama. He's as strong as a storm, and under his command, his crew can outwit the waves. We need never be afraid again with Edward Thache to protect us."

When the smile faded from Henrietta's pale face, Marybeth tried to cheer her.

"Mama, we've come for you now as we promised. The sloop is still downstream, but we brought the periauger to bring us home."

"I fear I'll be abed for days to come," Henrietta said. "How will you manage?"

"I'm more concerned about how we can care for you." Then she turned to me, asking, "Widow Saunters, tell me what to do. Or better, bide with us; stay and tend to my mother. Please."

Henrietta looked at me with wide, sad eyes. "Yes, please, if you can. Come stay with us."

As they pleaded, the door swung open, and Blackbeard swept into the room like a hurricane in September. But after finding Mrs. Bellieu on her sickbed and his wife near tears, he tempered his boisterous entry and became a sheltering oak, hovering over Marybeth.

"Sal told me about your illness, Mother," he said. "Again, I must thank Widow Saunters. There is a doctor on board with my crew, and he may have remedies, too. But you look well on the way to recovery."

"Thank you for your encouragement, Captain," Hetty said. "If this is the same fever that took my husband, it could return for days before it takes me. Or it could go away; no one can say. Either way, I can't promise to be much help to Marybeth, and she can't run the farm alone. What will she do if she must sail to Bath?"

"You're not to fear, Mother Bellieu," Thache said. "I'll fetch my doctor and leave two men to help while I'm away. You've met Caesar. He is as strong as a bull. I've known him all his life and trust him to guard you."

Henrietta nodded.

"And Coleman Adler hurt himself when my great ship ran aground. While his leg mends, he can fish for you and find anything else you need. Just ask The Crow, and he will bring it to you."

"But two men can't handle an ailing woman, and I'm too much for Marybeth alone," Henrietta said.

"No, the men can't be of use while you're abed, so I'll ask another favor of this kind lady." Edward Thache turned to me. "Widow Saunters, is there any way you can stay on Plum Point? We have plenty of room for you and your grandsons. Please stay until my physician comes; then stay as our guests as long as you like."

"But 'tis your honeymoon, Captain," Oma said.

"Nonsense, Mis'ress Saunters. Sadly, we won't have much of a honeymoon right now. The Governor and Tobias Knight let me keep the *Adventure*, but the ship is for Bath's benefit as much as mine. The whole town is low on supplies, and I reckon they want my crew out trading to remedy that. I fear I'll be away more than my new wife will like, and I'd be grateful for someone to keep her company."

"Captain Thache ...." He didn't let me finish.

"Mis'ress Saunters, I do not know what business you and your boys had in Bath, but I suspect you didn't finish it. I'll give you a jollyboat and rowers to ferry you to town for your needs, but please stay in my home and take care of Mother Bellieu until she has recovered. Then we'll see what comes next."

By this time, Ody and Drake had heard of Blackbeard's return and were listening at the open door.

"We agree, Grandmother. We'd be happy to stay and help out, too."

I shook my head to clear the dread of looming danger. And even though that didn't work, I gave in anyway. "I suppose another day can't hurt," I said. "But, Captain, please bring your doctor around within that time."

"He's on *Adventure*, but we'll get ye settled, and I'll have 'im on Plum Point by morning."

"One more night, then," I replied.

Captain Thache laughed as he clapped the boys on their shoulders. "I figured you pair might be pleased to stay."

Drake and Ody grinned till I thought their smiles would rip through their ears.

I shook my head, but even while I considered the worst case, there was a glimmer of relief. At least we could return to the exact moment we left our home. So, we wouldn't be putting a wrinkle in two different timelines.

8 Sailing with the Devil

Drake Saunters

The *Black Sam Bellamy* required more muscle than the jollyboat, so two more oarsmen joined Caesar and The Crow as we sailed to Plum Point.

Once we boarded and Captain Thache was satisfied with the balance, he cast the rope from the dock and shoved us off before climbing between Ody and me.

"So, which of you boys is which, and how old are ye?" he asked.

"I'm Ody, Sir," my cousin replied. "I'm seventeen."

"Ah yes, Odysseus," Edward said. "And you must be Drake. About fifteen, I reckon?"

"Aye. Francis Drake Saunters," I replied, breathless, to believe I sailed with the real Blackbeard.

"Francis Drake, you say."

"Aye, Sir, did you know him?"

When the Captain stopped laughing, he said, "No, no, he lived a century before me, so we didn't meet. But, in a way, he's the father of all the English freebooters."

"How so, Sir?" I asked.

"Well, he started like many did, as a privateer for Queen Elizabeth. He gave Spanish ships a fit to protect the English traders. So, the English gave him the title *Sir* Francis Drake, but the Spanish called him a pirate. They named him *El Draque*, the dragon."

I punched my cousin's arm. "See, Ody. I told you I was a dragon."

"And they called you Blackbeard, Sir?" Ody asked.

Edward chuckled. "They did. I have Black hair, like Black Sam Bellamy," he said, fluffing his beard. "But that wasn't the only name they called me. To them, I was also *El Gran Diablo*, The Big Devil."

"But what's the difference between a privateer and a pirate, Sir?" Ody asked.

"It depends on which country you serve. Governments don't hang their privateers, but they hang pirates. But it doesn't matter who holds the rope if they mean to hang you with it."

When I went silent, contemplating the rope, Edward shifted the topic from hanging.

"Sir Francis was more than a privateer, though; he was the first Englishman to sail around the world. He fought the Spanish Armada, and when he and his men went for the Spanish treasure ships, they found so much silver they couldn't carry it. So, they buried the silver but brought the gold back to England."

"I heard he was the richest pirate ever," Ody said.

"Well, I cannot say who was the richest ever, but I know one that topped Drake. This boat carries 'is name, *Black Sam Bellamy*. And that pirate was a mate of mine, probably the finest man I ever knew."

"How did you know him?" I asked.

"'Twas the story of Drake's success that started sailors searching the Spanish wrecks with Benjamin Hornigold's fleet. I captained a ship with Ben, and Sam was his mate; I never met a sea rogue I thought more of than Sam."

"Why is that?"

"Sam figured men who went a-piratin' were often forced into it. Some of his men had been slaves; others had been pressed into sailing on English warships and got little pay—some got no payment at all. Sam called that dishonorable. He figured fighting men had as much reason to wage war out of their own courage as governments did while hiding behind laws. Those ideas are what made Sam part with Hornigold."

"How did that happen?" I asked.

"Hornigold would not attack English ships, but Sam saw no difference between England and any other government. Finally, enough men voted Sam as captain, so by signed agreement, he got Ben's ship, and his crew took off without us. Folks started calling him Robin Hood, and his men called themselves Robin Hood's men."

"If you thought so much of his ideas, why didn't you leave with him?" Ody asked.

"I stood behind his ideas, but I had been in the Royal Navy, and, like Hornigold, I wouldn't fight against England."

"But Sam got rich?" I asked.

"He did. His crew took The *Whydah*, and that prize topped even Francis Drake."

"But were you a rich man after returning from the treasure ships?" Ody asked.

"Not as rich as Francis Drake, but I won more money than the Royal Navy paid me, and my family needed it. So I chose to put my fight in providing for them instead."

"You fought for gold, Sir?" Ody asked.

Edward sighed, "Country, family, or gold, any or all of them from time to time." Then he grinned, "And 'tis true I enjoy a good fight when necessary, but I reckon the love of adventure was always a part of it."

"Are you in Bath for adventure, Sir?" I asked.

He tossed his head left and right before replying, "Maybe so. New challenges are a kind of adventure, but no, that is not the main thing. Times are changing, and while there's not much as grand as the sea, 'tis the land that pulls you back." Then he turned to me, winking, "I yearned for a home port."

Then he touched my shoulder, saying, "Don't forget what Francis Drake proved, lads. Sea roving works best when at least one government offers a friendly harbor."

It wasn't long till our boat was mid-stream in Old Towne Creek. Edward clapped us on the back. "'Tis a downhill run now, boys. If we stay on our mark, the current will do most of the work till we dock at Plum Point, and thar it is," he said, pointing the way.

9 The Bride's Tower

Marybeth Thache

The Captain swept me into his arms as soon as all passengers stood on dry ground. And even though Mother's face was none too happy seeing the Captain hold me close in broad daylight, I didn't pull away from his embrace. She finally turned to lean on the Saunters lads as they helped her to the boardwalk.

"I'll miss ye tonight, my l'il Beth, but I promised Tobias Knight we'd discuss business. He's not well enough for the creek today, so we must meet at his house this time. You have my word; I'll row home in the morning as soon as the waves allow."

"Business?" Mother asked. "Does that mean you'll be sailing away soon, Captain?"

Edward had warned me he'd need to tend to business, and on several occasions, he mentioned trading missions for Bath, but the thought of a pending departure jolted me.

"Surely not all that soon, Mother," I said. "We only married yesterday. Mr. Knight and our neighbors in Bath must give us longer than that before my husband is pulled to sea again."

Edward held me tighter as reassurance, but he spoke to Mother, addressing her concern.

"I'll go no farther than across the creek tonight, Mother Bellieu, but I reckon Tobias has a venture in mind that will set us on the waves before too long."

Mother looked away as Edward and I enjoyed an embrace. Then he pulled me close to his chest and stood with his arm around me while giving his next set of commands.

"Caesar, see to the grounds, and Coleman, you check the provisions." Then he turned his warm smile to me, and with a wink, he said, "Mis'ress Thache, I trust you'll see to the comfort of our guests."

Then, we cleared the dock while Ned and the rest of the crew headed to Knight's landing to tend to his business, which included fetching his physician for Mother.

Mother seemed in better spirits once we turned toward the house with Edward rowing in the opposite direction. She leaned on the shoulders of Aurora's grandsons as they helped her over the plank walkway, past our dockside tunnel, and to our front steps.

The Crow set out to gather fish for our dinner, while Caesar's job was to tidy the land where the crew camped the night before. It was yards from the house, where our Plum Point gut emptied to Old Towne Creek. Edward had ordered the cleanup as he thought it might distress Mother to see signs of what he called *men at their worst*, drinking and partying on our farm.

I longed for Edward to be at my side, but as the lady of the house, I had duties. So, I opened the door wide to give Mother and the boys space to enter, and then they helped her to her room left of the parlor.

"Make yourselves at home, boys. I'll show you around as soon as your grandmother and I settle Mother in bed."

The boys whispered and rattled box lids as they explored the parlor. They commented on our lantern clock and Edward's work coat on the peg by the door.

Then the younger boy gasped as he found the room I shared with Edward. "Is that Blackbeard's sea chest?" he asked.

So, they preferred *that* as a name for Edward. I wondered if they had heard the vicious legends I believed before meeting him. The boys turned from my bedroom door as I asked, "Are you finding everything in order? Do you have any questions for me?"

The older boy removed his hat as he replied. "We were wondering about your clock," he said, pointing to where it hung on the wall. "How did it come to have only one hand?"

Mis'ress. Saunters joined us. "Oh, that does look rare," she said. "I'm not sure I ever saw one like it."

I smiled as I replied, "My father brought this lantern clock from his boyhood home in France, but I never thought it unusual. My father couldn't abide a house without a timepiece."

Then I turned back to the boys. "I heard you mention Captain Thache's sea chest. Follow me. I'll show you to your rooms and something else you may like."

One flight of stairs led to a narrow landing where I paused to point toward the rooms where our guests would sleep. "Mis'ress. Saunters will prefer the room to the left, and hopefully, you boys will be comfortable sharing the room to the right."

They peeked in before following me to the back of the landing and up a second flight of stairs to an attic room Edward used to store his belongings.

"Wow, look at all this gear," Drake said, eyes wide.

"There's more," I said, and she pointed to a set of thick blocks bolted to a corner wall. "We call this the tower ladder. The hatch above leads to a belfry my father built to warn neighbors of danger."

I squinted against the afternoon sun glittering on the water as I watched Edward's ship bobbing across the way.

"Is this a crow's nest?" Ody asked. "Caesar mentioned it when he took us up the creek yesterday."

"No, not a crow's nest," I replied, "My husband calls it my *Bride's Tower.* The old bell is still here, but Edward fitted it with a telescope and lantern so that when he sails, I can watch for his return." I peered through a brass telescope Edward had mounted to the railing, and when I found his ship, I smiled and stepped aside to give Ody a turn at the lens.

The *Bellamy* rocked beside *Adventure,* and even without the glass, I saw my husband's dark sleeve against the sails as he waved. I blew kisses to his silhouette as crewmen tied the boat to the landing.

"This is quite a view," Ody said.

"Yes, wait till there's a full moon. Then, you can see the sun setting and the moon rising on either side of the creek," I replied. "'Tis a shame your cousin is missing it."

Ody looked around. "What happened to Drake? He was right behind me." Then he shouted, "Drake, come here."

Boots knocked against the blocks, and soon Drake emerged from the attic hatch. "Sorry, I was fascinated by the room below. It's just how I imagined a captain's cabin."

"Oh," I said. "Edward likes to keep his treasures nearby. Maybe you saw the drawing of his mother."

"I don't know. I was afraid to touch anything, but it was full of maps, chests, and sailing tools I didn't recognize. I'd like to know more about how they work." Then he scanned the view, "Wow, this is fantastic. Is that the Captain's ship?" he asked.

"Yes," Ody replied, "But he may be in Tobias Knight's house by now. You missed him."

"What's the other ladder for?" Drake pointed to a rope ladder outside the railing, I had seen similar ladders hanging from the sides of ships, but this one dangled to the roof below.

"Oh, yes. Edward plans to use this tower as a lookout to watch who enters the creek and keep an eye on the grounds. This ladder drops to the roof ridge, and another is fastened to the eaves and leads to the yard. So, he can climb up or down without disturbing the household."

"Is that Coleman?" Ody asked, pointing to a fisherman far up Bellieu's Gut.

"Yes, I believe it is. I hope The Crow gets a good catch for supper."

"Do Thache's men stay in the house? Will they share our meals?" Drake asked.

"Until last night, they sometimes slept on Ocracoke Island, where the Captain anchors his ship. Edward fitted sleeping quarters on these grounds for Caesar and Crow. We have yet to determine how we will do meals, but no one goes hungry on Plum Point. Not unless we all do."

"Where is Caesar? Can we see him from here?" Drake asked.

"From the sounds of their singing last night, the crew camped on Plum Point Gut, our stream to the north boundary. Caesar was to clean up after the men. Can you see him?" I asked.

We peered through the pines to the north until Drake said, "There, I see him moving through the trees. I think I'll help him if that suits you. I'll take the shortcut," he said, then he straddled the railing and slid down the path to the ground.

"Is that Coleman?" Ody asked, pointing to the mouth of Bellieu's Gut. "No, I don't think that fellow is tall enough."

I found the man he meant leaning on the railing of my father's summer house by the edge of the creek. "You're right. That's not The Crow."

Then I gasped. W*as it a ghost?*

"Is something wrong, Mrs. Thache?" Ody asked.

"'Tis nothing—only the flash of a memory," I replied. "I wonder if one of the Captain's men has come with a message. If so, he'll be at the door soon. I can no longer see him on the point."

"There's no sign of a tender boat, but I'll find out," Ody said, and he dropped to the ground to see who may be prowling on our property.

Aurora soon found me in the tower, and I pointed through the trees to help her find Drake working with Caesar.

"Did all that carousing bother you last night?" she asked. "The boys said they heard singing from the docks in Bath."

"No, it was no bother. I heard little of it. Once the officers toasted us with Edward's prize cup and left the house, my husband closed the windows and finally asked his men to keep it to a mouse's roar. He wanted nothing to upset me or spoil our first evening together,"

"He seems to be a very thoughtful husband, my dear."

"He is," I said. Then I chuckled. "You must think me silly to believe I know all my husband's secrets in such a short time, but our first day together has been lovely."

"I hope they all are, my dear. Enjoy every minute you can."

Ody returned within an hour without news of the stranger we saw at the summer house. But he had found Caesar and The Crow and reported they were roasting some good-sized white fish over the fire by their shed. The boys ensured we had fresh water and sufficient fuel for our fires while Aurora made valerian tea for her patient.

The widow Saunters helped me gather corn and peas from the garden during Mother's nap. And by the time the corn roasted and the peas were tender, Caesar and Drake returned to trade crispy fish for a healthy supply of corncakes and vegetables. Then Caesar carried supper to his shed-mate.

After supper, Aurora entertained us with the story of Sir Walter Raleigh, another of Queen Elizabeth's privateers who met an unhappier ending than Francis Drake. King James I, who came after Elizabeth, beheaded Raleigh in the Tower of London.

Drake must have heard that story before, as he begged to go to bed before his grandmother finished the tale. But I lasted till the end, hoping to remember it to impress Edward when he returned.

Even though I had only had a husband for one night, I had trouble falling asleep. And after my eyes closed, the sounds of our house guests woke me in the night. Did I hear the boys moving in their room above mine? And did Aurora walk past the stairway to settle them?

Happily, our guests soon quieted, but I still tossed and turned, wondering how much of our marriage Edward would spend at sea at the request of Tobias Knight and Governor Eden.

I tried to push such thoughts away. Time would tell how our life together worked. But worries about the future drifted to when I wrestled with my decision to marry Edward.

After Wallace left me without a word, Edward wanted a quick answer to his proposal. I preferred to wait, but Mother convinced me Wallace wasn't coming back, and I shouldn't let the opportunity slip away.

It wasn't just Mother, though. We both needed this marriage. There was never an anxious night at Plum Point when my father was alive, but there was hardly a night without worry after he died. We both hoped I'd choose a husband who would provide for us at least well enough so that Mother wouldn't need to work at the Marsh Moon and we could run our farm.

I agreed to the wedding, and Edward made me happy; I had not hoped for more. But even so, a few troubling questions surfaced in the shadowy moments between wakefulness and sleep.

What security would Edward bring to Plum Point? How would he fit into life here, especially with Mother? Would Edward be as faithful as my father, or was I hoping to resurrect the impossible?

Years of marriage would hold the answers, but even after only one day, I missed my husband—the warm, strong, loving man he was and the guardian, provider, and faithful companion I believed he would be. So, I touched his pillow and fell asleep, hoping for the sun to rise quickly and for Edward to return.

10 The Healers

Aurora Saunters

Waking up in a different century was unsettling, but a tin of British tea on the Bellieu mantel improved my outlook. I shifted the kettle over the fire to boil the water while I looked in on Hetty.

She had no fever, so I figured I had time to savor a sip while I enjoyed the sweeping view from the Bride's Tower. So, with a cup in one hand, I climbed the block ladder, hoping to watch the sunrise over Old Towne Creek.

I was surprised to find Drake there. My grandson was sleeping with a hand sandwiched between his face and the sturdy railing.

"Wake up, Drake," I whispered. "You fell asleep and could fall farther than that if you're not careful." His head jerked from the rail despite my best efforts not to startle him.

He gasped as he saw me. "Grandma … oh … Sorry, Grandma, I didn't hear you. But I wasn't sleeping," he said, despite the red knuckle marks on his cheek.

"How long have you been here?" I asked.

"I … I don't know. I couldn't sleep, so I came here—eventually."

"Is something wrong?"

"No … no, not really. I just wanted to watch the sky."

"Me too. Finding something that looks like home is a comfort when the world turns over, as it has for us. Look, the sun is rising." I finished my tea and set the cup on the railing as we watched nature's light show.

We couldn't see the ocean nor much of Pamlico Sound from our perch over Plum Point. But we watched the dark blue water of the river turn rosy in the rising sun, and eventually, rays washed up from the mouth of Old Towne Creek, slowly filling the vein of black water with a blood-red glow.

"It's beautiful, isn't it?" I asked.

"Yeah. Sure."

"I see the edge has worn off your pirate enthusiasm. Are you sure you're OK? You didn't catch Hetty's fever, did you?" I pressed my hand against his head.

He pushed my hand away. "I'm fine." Then after a beat, he spoke more softly. "I *think* I'm fine."

"You look all right to me," I said. "Perhaps a little tired."

"Grandma, explain something to me so I'm sure I have it right."

I looked around for errant listeners, then whispered, "About commuting?"

He nodded. "Will you tell me the three ways again?"

"I thought you mastered that in our training, but I'm happy to review it for you. Do you want the simple version or more details?"

"Simple will do, thanks."

"Very well, we know of three ways to commute. The first only works for me so far. My walking stick takes me home. No matter where or when I am, it brings me to my home in my century. We haven't learned how this works, but the stick and the mantel in my study grew around my father's grave, so the best guess is that the wood and my father are connected somehow."

"And do you think the stick might work for Ody or me one day?"

"It's possible. We don't know enough to guess when the powers or the objects that make us travel, the commutators, may change. But we have evidence that they evolve."

Drake nodded, "OK, now tell me about method two."

"The second method works for all three of us with the gift. We can travel to each other with something made of our genetic material."

"Our hair charms, right?"

"Yes. I pinch your charm to go to you; you pinch the charm with my hair to come to me."

"OK," he said. "Now, the third way."

"We've only found a few examples of the third way, and each one was unexpected. So, we never know what might work, making commuting unpredictable, an ever-present danger."

"Like when the bugle took Ody to Old Salem, right?"

"Exactly. Here's our best guess. When our ancestors experienced extreme emotions, they sometimes created a commutator without knowing it or meaning to do it. The object connects to its moment of creation. For example, Clayton Robins empowered the bugle when his dying friend passed it to him."

Drake nodded. "Elizabeth Glover is an ancestor, and her prayer book commuted us. But what was the emotion?"

"I can't say, but a wedding and a sick lady can create strong feelings. Elizabeth was there. But I didn't expect her to be a child."

"And if we used that prayer book again, would we return to that moment? The wedding?"

"I think so."

"Thanks, Grandma. I've got it now."

"Don't worry about it too much, Drake. Just be careful while we're here, and we'll review everything that happens when we're safely home."

I leaned forward to pat his shoulder and noticed a silver frame by his boot. "What's that?" I asked.

The corners of his eyes turned down as he picked it up and looked at the image inside.

"Where did you get that?" I asked. "What is it?"

With a sigh, he turned the image toward me. "It's Blackbeard's mother," he said. "It was in his room below. She looks like you. Do you see it?"

As the sky brightened, I could see the image more clearly. The subject was a mature woman in a white, flowing shawl. Hair combs decorated with silver shells secured her white top knot. Her eyes and cheekbones were similar in shape to mine, and her nose and lips were about the same proportion, but I didn't recognize my face in the frame.

"There's a rough resemblance," I said. "Why do you think this portrait looks like me?"

He studied the face again. Then he muttered, "I just do."

"Does the picture make you sad?" I asked, leaning forward. "Why?"

"I believe she died," he said.

I grabbed his shoulder. "But *I'm* beside you and still kicking," I said, tapping his shin. "Did you have a bad dream?"

"No. I don't think so. But I better put this back. Thache might not like that I moved it."

I grabbed my cup and followed Drake down the ladder to Edward's attic retreat, where he returned the image to a vacant spot on the desk. He rearranged a few items, probably restoring them to their original positions. Then he walked to the desk and used my handkerchief to polish a few shiny objects before repositioning them.

I hugged my Grandson and smiled as I studied his eyes. "You've been snooping, haven't you? That wasn't a good idea, but it's probably not harmful. Have you left all as you found it?"

"I think so."

I tightened my arm around his shoulder. "Then let's go find breakfast. You'll feel better with food in your belly. The Captain will probably be back before midday. Let's see what we can do to help around here."

We collected Ody on our way downstairs, and with the help of my boys, Marybeth and I brought breakfast to the table. And then I held Henrietta's arm, escorting her to the dining kitchen. She seemed much better, Drake was cheerier, and Marybeth was thrilled at the prospect of her husband's return. But even though it was a happy morning, I looked forward to passing Henrietta's care to a proper doctor and returning home with my grandsons.

After breakfast, I helped Marybeth with the household chores. And later, Ody and Drake tended to tasks in the backyard while I chatted with Henrietta on the porch. Then, once dinner was stewing, Mrs. Thache went to the Bride's Tower to watch for her husband.

Marybeth sounded a large brass bell when she spotted a small boat with four men rowing across the creek.

"Edward's home," she shouted, and the new bride ran to the landing to greet her husband. Edward Thache gathered his wife into his arms, and then the newlyweds escorted their guest to the house, where Edward introduced us to Dr. Asjen Nuevo, his ship's physician.

"'Tis a pleasure to see you again, Mrs.Thache," he said. Then he turned to me and, after a short bow, "Enchanting to meet you, Widow Saunters."

"And these are my grandsons, Ody and Drake," I said, nudging the boys forward.

"What fine fellows. And look at those new black boots. I should learn your secret for keeping them black," Neuvo said, shaking his head at his own footwear.

"My grandmother insists on it, Sir," Drake replied.

Then he patted the boys on the shoulder as Marybeth led our party inside to dine.

After our meal, Marybeth asked me to attend to her mother during the examination, and I took the opportunity to study our visitor.

It's hard to guess the age of a man who has spent time on the sea, but Dr. Nuevo was at least sixty or seventy. He dressed more like a town tradesman than a sailor, with his knickers, coat, and tricorner hat instead of a seaman's loose-fitting breeches and wool cap.

As befitted a physician, his grooming was as immaculate as his attire. He was clean-shaven, as was the fashion, and he wore his long salt and pepper hair tied with a grosgrain ribbon at the nape of his neck.

The only part of him that was less than perfect was his footwear. Scuffs and scratches marked years of wear, but the boots were clean, despite lacking a good polish by the standards of my century.

After checking Henrietta, the doctor said, “Your kind nurse has taken good care of you, Mis’ress. Bellieu. There is hardly anything else you need from me.”

Henrietta nodded, and with a hint of a smile, she said, “I haven’t asked the Widow Saunters how she learned so much about healing, but ’tis clear my friend took care of patients before me.”

I chuckled. “Oh, not so many, dear. But we all learn from caring for others, and everyone pitches in when sickness passes through a town.”

Hetty studied me knowingly as she replied, “Aye, that may be, but my mother and the mothers before her came from Bristol, and they spoke in whispers about those who heal. The old ones say healers are oft born knowing about plants and potions as if they came into this world already trained. And some of them can see into the future.”

“Oh, my. Well, I hope I don’t turn out to be a disappointment to you, Hetty. I could never live up to such a promise.” Then I turned to Dr. Nuevo.

“How about you, Sir? Have you been a ship’s doctor for long?”

Nuevo chuckled, “Longer than I like to admit, but only recently with Captain Thache.”

He offered no more about how he acquired his healing skills, but when Henrietta rose to the edge of the bed, he encouraged her efforts.

“Since the widow Bellieu is so well, perhaps she would like to visit with the others in the parlor. No doubt ’twould cheer Mrs. Thache to see her moving about,” he said.

Henrietta smiled and offered her arm to Dr. Nuevo, who escorted her to her favorite chair in the sitting room.

“Are you feeling better, Good Mother?” the Captain asked. “How do you like my ship’s doctor?”

“He’s very skilled. Even Aurora gave him a stamp of approval.”

“And I, her,” Neuvo said, chuckling. “There was little left for me to do, but at least I have a tin of fever powder to leave with you.” Then the doctor raised a finger as he turned to Edward. “Captain, you and I should find more medicine soon.”

“We shall take care of that on our next voyage,” Edward promised.

Just then, Ody and Drake returned from carrying dinner to the crews’ hut, and Ody chimed in on our conversation. “Oh, yes, please tell us how you came to sail with the Captain. Did you meet him in your travels?”

“Well, yes and no,” he replied as he lit a pipe. “I learned medicine while tending to soldiers in my regiment. Then, between wars, I kept a surgery to see patients in the various towns where I lived. I first met Captain Thache when I cared for his mother years ago.”

Edward interrupted. "And I met the good doctor for a second time when all manner of ailments plagued my crew. I was near Charleston, looking for medicines and a practitioner, among other things."

Nuevo added to the story. "And since I was acquainted with the Captain, I didn't fear treating his crew, as some local physicians did. And by the time he left the harbor, I had accepted his offer to sail with them."

"That he did," Thache said, slapping Nuevo on his shoulder. "And my men and I are better off for it."

The doctor paid little attention to the boys, but Ody studied the man's face as if he were solving a puzzle. Then I noticed Drake; his face was pasty white, and his breath shallow. I rushed to his side. "Drake, are you well?' Did you eat anything strange?"

"No, Ma'am," he muttered. "I'm fine."

Did he say, *Ma'am*? He was definitely not himself.

"Perhaps the boy needs a bit of rest," Marybeth said. "He couldn't have slept much; I believe I heard him wandering at night."

"Then my wife is right; he should rest," Thache said, "and the doctor should return to my crew. Who knows how many scrapes and broken bones they have by now."

We walked to the porch to wave farewell to the doctor. He and Edward chatted as they walked to the jollyboat, and before Nuevo boarded, he tapped the fingertips of one hand as if ticking off a list. Then after Edward smiled while clapping his friend on the shoulder, the two oarsmen took Nuevo to join the crew on the *Adventure*, and the newlyweds climbed the boardwalk back to the house.

Ody spun to face me. "Oma, will you walk with me to the summer house? I want to look around there again."

Drake didn't say a word, but he stumbled along with us to the point where a weathered frame pavilion rested on a stone base, complete with a few steps to access the shelter.

When we settled on the benches, Ody could wait no longer. "Oma, do you recognize Dr. Nuevo?" he asked.

"He seems familiar, but I can't place meeting him."

"I thought the same thing, but the more he talked, the more familiar he became. Oma, I think he's Augustus Neumann."

I was stunned to silence for a moment, but what Ody said was impossible. "Ody, we met Neumann in 1783. He must have been upwards of 70 years old. That puts his birth year around 1713. So, he'd be five years old now; that man couldn't be Neumann."

"When I shook the doctor's hand, he had the same steely fingers of the man who cared for me in Salem. His eyes are the same despite his face being a bit younger. But it wasn't his looks or touch; his voice gave him away. And the story of taking care of soldiers—Neumann told that to me in Salem."

"It can't be him, Ody. By 1783, I guess Asjen Nuevo will be … well … dead. If he's in his sixties now, he'll be over 100 years old by then."

"Then it must be a relative. They are too much alike."

"Neumann said he was searching for family members to solve a mystery. So maybe we've found one for him. Too bad we'll never be able to tell him," I said.

Drake had remained silent and pale during the walk and the conversation that followed. Now he cleared his throat, and his voice squeaked as he said. "Grandmother, I need to tell you something."

We both turned to Drake, who was rarely quiet and never subdued. But now, he kept his eyes on his toes and swallowed at least three times before speaking.

"Is this a confession, boy? Out with it," I said.

He pursed his lips, and his chin quivered as he turned saucer eyes toward Ody and then me.

"You two are not the only ones who have met Dr. Nuevo. I've seen him, too."

I reached a hand to his knee. "Before today? How is that possible? You weren't with us in Salem. You couldn't have met him when we did."

"I … I saw him last night. I don't think he saw me, though."

"You must have dreamed of someone similar, Drake. Perhaps from all the talk of a doctor coming to Plum Point."

He shook his head. "You must believe me, Grandma. I saw him." Then after a long pause, "I … I broke a rule."

He stiffened his chin, and I thought his lip might bleed from him biting it. Then, summoning his courage, he confessed.

"I commuted without you, Grandma. I didn't mean to, and I was only there for minutes. It scared me, and I came back to you. But I traveled, and I landed wherever Asjen Nuevo was. I'm sure of it. I saw him."

Ody shook my shoulder. "Oma, should we go home right now before we get into more trouble?"

I took deep breaths as I pondered our predicament.

"What do we do, Grandma?" Drake asked.

I cleared my head. Then, I swallowed hard before speaking.

"Augustus Neumann was the first person we ever met who had something to do with our time travels. He said we might meet another person, but it was to be in Europe, not here. So maybe we found someone else with a clue."

Ody spoke, "And maybe if we learn what he knows, we can keep the time travel without the danger."

"Is that possible?" Drake asked.

"It's possible, but far from sure," I replied. "Let's sleep on it; then we can decide. But we have a rare opportunity here, and I'm not sure we should pass it by."

"Marybeth might need us," Ody said.

I nodded. "And we need to know how this happened to us, and Asjen Nuevo might have the key." Then I turned to Drake. "But not tonight. No one goes anywhere tonight. However, I do have a question for you."

Drake sheepishly looked into my eyes. "What is it?"

I struggled to frame the question just right. "Could you tell if time had passed between when you left this house and when you returned here?"

Drake searched his memory for clues. Then finally said, "Yes, I think so. I left while the clock was striking midnight, and it might have been a half hour after I returned when it chimed once. But time had passed; I'm sure of it."

Ody added it up. "Was your time there about half an hour?"

Drake nodded, "Maybe less."

"What do you think, Oma?" Ody asked.

"Time passed here and there, too, and the time gaps may be the same. If that's correct, it's good data to have."

Beneath furrowed brows, the boys nodded in agreement. Drake's unexpected commute gave us another worry, but it also gave us a clue we couldn't ignore. This rare opportunity could impact my grandchildren's lives, maybe for the worst.

But what if it were for the best?

11 A Fair Heart

Drake Saunters

I breathed easier after telling Grandma about the commuting incident. She knew the time travel ropes better than anyone, and now that the worry was on her shoulders, I could get on with … well, whatever I was supposed to do here. Ody was still sleeping, so I tiptoed down the stairs for a trip to the outhouse, but before I got back to the porch, a deep voice called my name.

"Drake, is that you?" Caesar scratched his head beside an unhappy nanny goat. "I can't get the hang of this," he said. "I reckon the Cap'n won't be best pleased wid' me; this old girl won't give up her milk."

I knelt to watch him at work. "Hmm. Let me try."

"Did you milk goats where you come from?"

"No, but I did it once or twice; let's see if I can remember." Grandma had dragged me to some pioneer farm reenactments. And after a few failed attempts, I got the pinch right, and we cheered as milky success spilled into the bucket.

"I see what you're doing. Let me try," Caesar said. I turned the stool over to him, and once Caesar got his rhythm going, he relaxed enough to chat as he worked. "Did you grow up on a farm?" he asked.

"No. I just visited a few. How about you?"

Caesar kept milking as he replied. "I was born on the plantation owned by old Cap'n Thache, but we had no goats."

"I saw a picture of the Captain's mother. Did you ever meet her?" I asked.

"I did. Mis'ress Elizabeth was as good as they come. She had a chore raising young Ned, though. He was a brawny boy, built like his Papa, but his Mama cared that her boy's heart worked as good as his back and that his brains took charge of that temper of his'n."

I chuckled. "How did she do with that?"

Caesar grinned back, “She won more times than she lost, I reckon. She valued the prize of Edward’s soul above all else.”

“She told you that?”

“No, I didn’t see much of her once she took to her bed. Edward told me, and her spirit lived on in him over the years. She had her share of victories even after she passed.”

“So, how did you come to be on the plantation?”

“My Mama and Papa were part of the farm when I was born, so I belonged to it, too.”

“Were you a slave?” I asked as he carried the pail to the porch.

“’Tis how it was.”

“Then how did you get here?” We took seats on the porch step, and Caesar told his story.

“I reckon I’d still be on that farm if not for Ned,” he said. “When I got old enough to work the plantation, the foreman didn’t appreciate what I could do. Being built close to the ground, I couldn’t reach as far as the other workers. Then, of course, being a young’un made it worse, but he thought I was slacking.”

“What happened?”

“I always tried to do my best, but when I was a lad, that didn’t always work out, and he’d scold me for disobeying. He threatened the whip, too.”

“Did he ever use that whip on you?”

“He came close once. A gentleman complained about my treatment of his horse, and McGruder, the stable master, felt ’twas his duty to punish me. But young Ned saw what happened and stopped the stableman from striking me.”

“That must have made him angry.”

“He was none too pleased, and worse, The Old Captain Thache disapproved of Ned’s steppin’ in the middle, and they had harsh words about it. ’Twas so hot that I thought the old Captain might whip the young master instead of me, but somehow, they struck a deal. After that, the Captain made Ned my overseer, and I’ve been with him ever since.”

“Did you become his servant then?”

“’Twas like the old man give me to Ned as a punishment. He claimed his son would suffer enough by havin’ a man in his charge who won’t obey.”

“Does he own you now?” I asked.

“Not no more. But I was his after that day. He gave me work I could do, and I earned my keep. That was part of his deal with the old man. Young Ned was my foreman, and I had to do my share.”

“Were you with him in the Navy then?”

“Ned and I left the plantation when he went to sea. He was on a merchant ship before he signed onto the Windsor. But there was no place for me on a Navy ship, so Ned left me to care for his family. And then, once he was free of the Navy and started up with Benjamin Hornigold, he signed me on his ship as a free man. Men signing on with Cap'n Thache's ship are free unless they choose serving over following our ship's rules. As Stede Bonnet used to say, 'All men are either sea rogues or slaves.' I was a sea rogue. 'Tis our way."

"If you're on his crew, why are you milking goats?"

"My job now is on land under an agreement between Tobias Knight and the Cap'n. But even here, I'm part of the Cap'n's company, so I'm bound to follow his orders and rules. But, as part of the crew, I get my fair cut of the take on any venture, just as we wrote down. We know the prize we get when we do our job and the punishment if we cross his line."

"And what if you don't want to do what he says?"

"Well, that ain't happened yet with Cap'n Thache, but any man that feels that way can leave once he's on dry land, or, if most of the crew are discontented, they can choose a new Captain."

"Why would he let you do that?" I asked.

"Because ship rules are fairer than what happens to a man like me unless he has proper papers. And if a man thinks he can fare better on land, Captain Thache won't stand in his way. He's a man who honors the rules."

That seemed a contradiction to me. "How can men who steal on the sea be rule-keepers? How can pirates be fair?" I asked.

"I've seen plenty in this world that ain't fair, but more than one pirate has tried to be—Black Sam Bellamy, for one. The Captain told you about him."

"So, is pirate life a fair one?" I asked.

"You're full of questions, lad," he said. "The captain of a freebootin' ship is like a king; men do well if they sign on with a fair-minded captain. But freedom on land is tricky, especially for a man like me. On the land, a man's future might depend on more than one person in charge, and sometimes the leaders bicker amongst themselves over his destiny. 'Tis why I'll stick to Captain Thache. He's my best chance. I've known him since I was born, and I know what's in his heart—what his Mama put there. That's what proves he's fair."

That gave me an idea—one cut out for me alone. If I wanted to see deeper into the heart of Edward Thache and prove to Ody that the Captain was worth following, I should see how it started.

But breakfast was not the right time for that, and as it turned out, Captain Thache had plans for us the next day, too.

12 Captain's Men

Drake Saunters

Ody slept through the smell of sausages, but I hurried to the kitchen where Captain Thache stood behind his bride, arms around her as she stirred grits over the fire. Grandma put a platter of sliced boiled eggs and fresh tomatoes beside a bowl of ripe plums, and Mrs. Bellieu set out trenchers and mugs.

"Don't worry, Drake. I've been spyin' for 'e," the Captain said. "Bangers, goat cheese, and corncakes are coming up, too. 'Tis my duty to see that my men are well fed."

Marybeth kissed her husband on the cheek, saying, "And don't forget the salt fish, my love." She stroked his beard, smiling. "'Tis your favorite."

She happily allowed the Captain to grab one more hug as she fetched a ladle for the grits. But then, seeing me with idle hands, she asked, "Drake, would you mind scattering a bit of feed for the hens? It's in the sack by the door."

Thache cocked his neck back. "Feed? In the summer? Have you spoiled the hens till they're too lazy to scratch?"

Her face glowed as she caught the twinkle in his eye and replied, "I spoil all under my roof. 'Tis the job of a good wife, Captain Thache, and our way here at Plum Point."

"So 'tis," he replied. "You carry on as the Princess of Plum Point, and I'll stick to being Master of the Waves."

She waggled her head as if straightening her crown, and Thache gave her a little spank as she turned toward her chores.

"And are you next, young man?" The Captain asked. "Do you need a little push to get your feet moving?"

"No, Sir, Captain," I replied, and he chuckled as I hurried to tend to the hens before returning to breakfast.

"There we are," Marybeth said, plopping a platter of corncakes beside a small pot of molasses. "I hope that's enough for two young men and one hungry captain."

"'Tis a bounty to me, my love," Thache said.

Grandma chuckled. "It must suit my boys, too. Look at them digging in."

"Good enough that they are," Marybeth replied. "We have work for stout men around here."

"Full bellies make happier workers," Widow Bellieu added. She nodded at her daughter. "At least that's what your Papa always said."

Edward swallowed his first bite of saltfish before speaking again; then, he pointed at me. "Is all well, boys? Do you have more questions?"

I washed down my corncake with a swig of cider before replying. "I have one. Caesar told me about ship rules and how the crew could pick a captain."

"Like they picked Sam Bellamy when he won Hornigold's ship," Ody said.

"Right. Does that happen often?" I asked.

"Well, military ships and those owned by trading companies don't elect Captains. But 'tis common practice on freebootin' ships like mine, where the crew works for a cut of the haul."

"Do you mean on pirate ships?" Ody asked.

Marybeth looked up in shock, and Thache threw my cousin a dark look.

"That word *pirate* might bring a man to the noose, lad, and Governor Eden pardoned me of that label. Then Tobias Knight called his Board of Admirals to study me, and they declared me a respectable tradesman. 'Tis only legal trading that I do now. I reckon he let me keep my ship for just such business. 'Twas a sea prize we took in the old days, but we give her a clean start by renaming her *Adventure*."

"Did the crew have to vote again to keep you as Captain? Could they vote for a new man to captain *Adventure*?" Ody asked.

"They could. But we're in transition these days and must see how the wind blows. So far, we're under our old rules, and I'm still Captain."

"So, do you know any voted out of being captain?" I asked.

"Well, here's an example. Not long after we added David Herriot's ship to our fleet, Stede Bonnet caught up with my crew in Turneffe. Have ye heard of him?"

"Not that I recall," Ody replied.

"Rightly so. Bonnet ain't that much to remember. He had a ship and crew, but his crew wasn't satisfied with him and voted him out as captain. They did not have a choice they agreed on, so they begged me to choose a new Captain. So, I put a man, Richards, on Bonnet's ship, and my first mate, Israel Hands, captained Herriot's sloop."

"What happened to Bonnet?" Ody asked.

"Well, he was a gentleman, more port wine than port 'o call, and not cut out for command by my reckoning, so I convinced him to stay on my ship as a guest. So, everyone was satisfied," Thache said. "Now, why all these questions?" he asked. "Are you lads ready to sign aboard?"

"They are not," Grandma replied. "They have more schooling to finish."

Thache grinned. "Another time then, boys. But my wife is acquainted with Hands; she can tell you more. Mrs. Thache, give these young gents your take on it. What do you think of Israel Hands?"

Marybeth turned her eyes to the table, and one hand knotted the napkin it held. "I only met Master Hands during our wedding party. He was polite but a little frightening." Then she met her husband's eyes. "And you were with me at every step. So, I couldn't get a sense of how he might treat me without you there."

The Widow Bellieu's eyes widened, and Edward's face went dark, his neck tendons bulging.

"He'll treat you respectfully, or he'll pay this piper. And the same is true of any other in my crew," Thache said.

Marybeth smiled at her sliced eggs, and when she timidly reached to pat the Captain's fingers, he squeezed her hand.

Then Thache pushed back his chair and turned his attention to Ody and me. "Boys, if you mean to help in this backwater place, I reckon you should know more about sailing. Your best way of getting anywhere is on the water, and ye should be ready for it should my wife need ye. So, what say we give it a try?"

"Today?" I asked.

"The sooner, the better," he replied. "You never know when you may need to take to the water."

"Then lessons sound good," Ody replied.

Thache beamed. "Let's see what ye can do with the jollyboat."

After that, we left the kitchen work to the women and followed the Captain to the landing. As Ody and I boarded the boat, Thache said, "The sooner we get you water-worthy, the better. I haven't told my wife, but I may have to sail sooner than expected. So, I need to get you started."

Then he chuckled and pointed to the creek. "Looky there," he said, "'Tis Israel Hands, in the flesh." Thache raised his hand in salute as a long sloop sailed toward the dock in Bath.

It was easy to pick out Hands from the rest of the crew. For one thing, he was the only one with an eyepatch. The others were all busy with the rigging or the rudder, and in the summer heat, they wore cut-off sleeves and breeches that flowed loose around their calves. But Hands wore a faded green linen coat, buckled knickers, and stockings with holes. Even with his head scarf, it was clear his hair was sparse on top, but thin gray stands hung from his temples to his shoulders, and the rest of his hair, bound with twine, trailed down his back, more the muddy color of a copperhead snake. He nodded in response to Thache's salute, but the crew paid us no mind. Their full attention was on their temporary captain—Hands.

"What do you make of him, boys?" Thache asked.

"That long braid is scary; it looks like a snake coming down his back," I said.

The Captain nodded. "'Tis one reason they call him the basilisk."

"The name fits," Ody said. "Is there another reason?"

Thache chuckled. "Well, a basilisk is the king of snakes, and I hear they can stop a man's heart by looking him in the eye. So maybe his eyepatch has something to do with it. The men tell me there's a fright behind that flap."

"He's headed into town, Captain," I said. "I thought the *Adventure* was off to Ocracoke."

"Change of plans, me boy," he replied. "We picked up a new order from the Governor, we need to lay in supplies, and the men want to spend a few coins here before we set sail. 'Tis the main reason I want ye as fit for sailin' as can be done in one day."

"What can we learn in one lesson?" I asked.

"Not enough to be sure of survival, but enough to give it a fair chance," Thache said.

"Where do we begin?" Ody asked.

"Lesson 1: Don't die. Do ye see the mouth of the creek down there?" he asked, pointing downstream. When we nodded, he continued, "Don't go there. Not unless you'll die if you don't. Down there, where this creek feeds into the big river, fresh bait like you will likely die anyway."

"Where should we go then?" Ody asked.

"Upstream to Bath Towne for supplies if you need, or if the Indians attack, get to the fort. It's in the town, too. Today we'll see if we can train ye enough for that."

We nodded and took positions the Captain chose for us in the boat.

"Lesson 2: Go where you mean to and keep the boat oar-side up. Let's aim for that."

We spent most of the day practicing entering the stream, getting around obstacles, and reading the water to tell where it was shallow or running too quickly. Then, he taught us how to hold the boat in the stream.

"Good job, men," he said. "Now I will show you what all that work is good for. Lesson 3: Let's see if ye can cross a creek."

"Do you mean crossing this creek?" I asked. "Where?"

"Right there." He pointed toward Knight's landing. "Ye might have business with Tobias Knight, so learn how to get from one side of this creek to the other without being washed to the river and learn it both ways 'cause east to west ain't the same as the other way round."

"Won't we have Coleman and Caesar with us?" Ody asked.

"Ye might and ye might not, depending on circumstances, and if they are not handy, you better be able to do it alone."

"Aye, Sir," I replied.

We spent most of the afternoon rowing back and forth, nearly half a mile each way, until our arms ached. Then, finally, after more passes than I care to remember, Thache had seen enough.

"Good job, lads." The Captain tapped the brim of his hat and winked, saying, "You've mastered the current on this creek, and I won't fear for my wife to ride across wid ye. Your next lesson will be the wind."

"I hope that lesson doesn't come tomorrow," Ody said, rubbing his arms.

"Ah, the wind must wait for another day, but I'll give ye a lesson that doesn't require wind nor water." He pulled us both toward him till his beard tickled our faces. Then he whispered, "Remember this for certain. If ye ever sign on to a proper ship, listen to every order the captain gives ye and be quick about followin' it."

I nodded, eager to hear what he would say next, but Ody's eyes narrowed. He was one to make his own choices and was skeptical of anyone who'd take that from him. But Thache grabbed his neck and pulled him in closer.

"Are ye listenin', boy?" he asked. When Ody nodded, the Captain continued.

"Ridin' the waves is tricky, and the captain won't have time to explain every order. He's the brains of the ship, and you're the arms and legs. So trust he's right without questions. No arguing. Bringing you safely to shore is his job more than any other. If you can't trust him that much, you're on the wrong ship, and you better bail at the first port you come to."

"Aye, aye, Captain," I said, saluting.

Ody grinned at me, saying, "I'm glad you agree because when it's just the two of us, I'll be the captain you obey."

The Captain gave us his big Blackbeard belly laugh and slapped us both on the back, saying, "Ye'll make fine sailors yet."

Once he tied our boat to the landing, he ran up the boardwalk to his wife, and we sat on the dock, soaking our feet and rubbing our arms.

"So, what do you think of the Captain?" Ody asked.

I shrugged. "What do *you* think?"

Ody's grin faded as he studied his toes in the waves. "I'm not sure I can trust any man who wants to make decisions for me, not when it means life or death. And he doesn't know everything about us, either."

I nodded. "I trust Thache. Deep down, he's a good man."

"And how do you know that more than I do?" Ody asked.

I lifted my chin, grinning. "I've known him longer than you have."

"Wha …?" Ody leaned back, looking at me over his nose. Then, figuring I was making a joke, he shoved my shoulder. "You're spouting nonsense, you silly duck."

I wasn't ready to tell him the truth, so I let my cousin enjoy his joke as we teased each other about being Blackbeard's men.

13 Change of Plans

Ody Saunters

After supper, the Captain took his pipe to one of the porch rockers. Drake and I chose perches on either side of the top step, leaving the other chairs for the ladies. There, leaning against the porch posts, we could keep one eye on the water and one on Captain Blackbeard.

In the lowering sun, the sky and clouds changed from blue and silver to teal and gold, and as they cast their colors on the water and sails, they lent a storybook look to the boats returning to Bath. But one ship sailed in the opposite direction.

It was thrilling to see *Adventure* dancing downstream on her way back to Knight's Landing. Even as the sky dimmed, crewmen tested the sails and studied the clouds from the deck of the sloop, and when a sailor spotted Blackbeard enjoying the evening on his porch, he elbowed the man next to him, and they waved greetings to the Captain and his bride.

"And here I thought I'd be the wife of a low country planter," Marybeth said. "Instead, I find myself part of a sea captain's court."

Thache emptied his pipe and refilled it from his pouch. "You know, my dear, the Governor had other plans for me all along. But I can't fault him; he's just putting me to work at what I do best. I've always been more for salt than silt. Knight probably won't come in person due to his health, but his man will bring the Governor's wishes, and Tobias Knight's signature will be on that page, too. We will find out what they have in mind."

The Widow Bellieu looked up from her mending with the disgust of someone who finally found the rabbit eating the cabbages.

"So, will you be off with your crew now?" she asked. "And what will become of my daughter? Do you mean to leave her to the wolves?"

Thache laid his pipe on the round table beside him and stiffened his back.

"Mistress Henrietta," he said without a hint of humor, "Your daughter is more my treasure than yours, now. But you can trust that while she and I both live, I'll never let anyone harm her. That's the deal we struck on our wedding day, and I'm a man of my word."

Marybeth turned to Hetty and whispered, "Mother, you do Captain Thache a disservice. He has been generous and thoughtful to us both. You should be grateful. After all, this is his plantation now. He paid you good silver for rent, and we couldn't farm it without his help."

"S'pose so," Henrietta replied, "'Tis true we're short-handed. Beg pardon, Captain Thache." But there was no smile as she gathered her mending and left for her room.

Oma leaned toward Marybeth. "Don't worry, my dear. I'll check on her when she fiddles through her frets."

The Captain leaned back into his chair. "You need not worry either, kind Lady," he said. "Hands' crew is bringing a supply of cornmeal and rice, and my men will be here to help with any difficulty."

"How long will you be gone?" Drake asked.

"I don't have a list of all the Governor needs for the town just yet," Thache replied. "But 'twill probably be a short run up the shoreline, and we'll be back before you know it."

"Are you going to Charleston?" I asked.

Thache chuckled, "I reckon I made a splash in Charleston last time I was there. I'll find friendlier ports on this voyage."

"I'll miss you, Edward," his wife said.

"You'll travel in my heart, my love."

"Will Caesar and The Crow stay with us?" she asked.

"Aye, and there may be another runner to fetch things from here to town. I'm not sure of that yet," Thache replied.

Drake turned to the Captain. "Caesar told me some about himself this morning, but what is Adler's story?"

Thache nodded. "Aye, The Crow. Coleman Adler came to us first as part of Bonnet's crew, but in the shuffle of assigning Hands to be their new captain, The Crow, Bonnet's barrel man, shifted to *Queen Anne's Revenge,* as we had more need of him than the sloops did. 'Tis a shame he was wounded, but he'll soon be fit to sail again."

"What happened?" I asked.

"'Twas just over a month ago when I first came to these parts. You may not have learned this yet, but the seabed here is famous for shifting something terrible. We failed at sailing through Topsail Inlet. My frigate, *Queen Anne's Revenge*, was too big for the channel, and she grounded in a sand bar."

"A ship bigger than *Adventure?*" Drake asked.

"Aye, much bigger and with 40 cannons ready to fire."

"That must have been a sight," Drake said. "So, what happened to The Crow?"

"We call The Crow our barrel man because he's the one most likely to climb up to the crow's nest and get a bird's eye view of land and sea. So up he went to check out the damage to the high rigging, and the ship listed even more. Israel Hands was in another sloop in our fleet, and I called him to throw a kedge anchor to wench *Queen Anne* off the bar. But despite the best efforts of Crow and the crew, the *Queen* shifted, Adler fell to the deck, and we lost both ships. 'Twas only by quick-done work that we saved our cargo and most of our powder and got all the men to shore."

"How many men did you have that day?" I asked.

"About 300, I reckon."

"And you saved them all, even with two wrecked ships?" Drake asked.

"All accounted for," he replied.

I shook my head. "So far, I haven't seen 300 men anywhere in Bath. Is that the size of *Adventure*'s crew?"

He chuckled, "No, without *Queen Anne*, we couldn't carry a crew that large. So, some men sailed north on Stede Bonnet's ship. Others took the King's Pardon and then drifted to employ themselves at other ports. Some of the braver black men chose to find the Maroons in Dismal Swamp. We were on dry land, and our biggest ship was underwater, so they had a right to choose."

"How many do you need to man the *Adventure*?" Drake asked.

"We can always use a good hand. Are ye still looking to sign up, boy?" he asked, chuckling.

Grandma pursed her lips as she shook her head. "Drake's fifteen with years of education ahead of him. He won't be signing onboard a ship anytime soon. 'Tis mostly his natural curiosity, I believe," she replied.

"Well, a sloop ain't as fearsome as the *Queen*, but 'tis quick, agile, and load-worthy, and best of all, she's fit for shallow creeks and deep water, too. Moreover, the shifting sands around here ain't likely to trap her. We carried a crew of over 120 on her before, but we can get by with a few dozen. So, we're fit for trading, I'd say."

"Was Dr. Nuevo with you when you lost *Queen Anne*? Did he attend to Coleman's wounds?" Grandma asked.

"Aye, he did. His hands were full with all the men he had to patch up. His skill probably saved The Crow's leg, but it will take time before he can scamper up a mast on a rolling sea. He ain't exactly happy about being land-locked, but he's healing fast, and his time will come to sail again." Thache replied.

"And he's well taken care of, isn't he?" Drake asked.

"Aye, he is. He'll get his share of the treasure we salvaged and earn a bonus for his injuries. 'Tis in our agreement."

Drake pointed to the middle of Old Towne Creek. "What's that light?" he asked.

"Ah. Knight's messenger," Thache said. "They've lit a lantern to show the way."

I peered toward the faint light in the water. "Looks to be four in the boat. Who's coming?"

"Two rowers with Israel Hands, and I reckon the fourth is Tobias Knight's man, Edmund Chamberlain." Thache turned to his wife, "Could ye fetch me a bottle and three glasses, my dear?"

"Of course," she replied. "I'll bring your drink and leave you men to your charts." Then she turned to Grandma, adding, "Have a pleasant evening, Aurora."

Grandma leaned on her walking stick to stand. "Boys, I believe we need to say good night, too. The Captain has business."

"Aye, you'll need to be up early to see us shove off. We'll be making way at dawn," Thache said, emptying his pipe.

I followed Drake up the steps to our room, and he was asleep as soon as his head hit the pillow, but I could not rest as easily. I saw something from the porch that bothered me, and I wanted proof that what I saw was no trouble. So, I crept down to the parlor, walked out the back door, and then to the peony bushes at the corner of the house. From there, I could watch the men on the landing.

Maybe it was mischief or nothing, but I saw the same puzzle again. There was nothing unusual about Chamberlain and Israel Hands chatting as they approached. The mystery was the two men left behind at the dock. I had seen the portside crewman pass a sack tied with a flat leather strap to the man on the right, and that man brought the bundle ashore. The peony bushes hid me from the porch, but I spied the man moving north till he reached Plum Point gut and followed it upstream toward the crew hut.

Glasses clinked against a bottle as Marybeth brought spirits to the porch. As the visitors climbed the stone steps, Thache scraped his chairside table across the porch boards and pushed it to the middle of the group. I hid deeper in the bushes, and as Chamberlain hung his bright lantern on the rafter hook, I rechecked the dock. The roving crewman had returned but didn't take his oarsman seat. Instead, he scanned the grove around the landing, and then I lost sight of him in the shadows of the oak and cypress trees.

Finally, the whiskey cork popped, and drams spattered into three glasses. Then Marybeth wished a pleasant evening to the guests and left the men to their discussion.

I could not see the men, but the deeper they got into their cups, the louder their voices became, making it easy to hear their conversation. Thank goodness for the lessons Oma shared about listening to language. Blackbeard's deep voice and Bristol accent were easy to recognize. Chamberlain's accent was similar, but his voice was higher pitched with more of a nasal tone. Israel Hands' voice was gruff from age, and his accent was born in southwest England—Cornwall or Devon.

It may have been my imagination, or perhaps it was how voices carried through the night air as the temperature cooled, but as I listened from the peonies, Thache's voice carried the hint of a threat when he spoke.

"What's the Governor after, Edmund?" Thache asked.

"The Governor says we need rum more than anything," he replied, "but here's the rest of the list."

"Rum and gunpowder," the Captain said with a snort. "Why is there never enough rum?" Then, after a moment, he added, "Molasses and sugar, too—they're easiest to find in the Indies, but I don't reckon we'll go there on this trip."

"Where should we go for wheat?" Hands asked. "Do they have flour to spare in the northern colonies?"

"We might have luck with dry goods and the medicines my crew needs from the northern ports. 'Tis unlikely, but if their season was good, we might find a surplus of flour on this side of the Atlantic," Blackbeard said.

"Let me see that list," Hands said. Then after a moment, he asked, "What about the river ports in Virginia, Edward? And where will we find spectacles?"

"Knight gets his eyeglasses from Philadelphia," Chamberlain replied.

"Well, Philadelphia, maybe," Thache said, "but I reckon we'd better stay clear of the Royal Navy out of Virginia."

Hands nodded, saying, "True enough … unless we can get to a ship willing to offload before it gets to port."

"And providing we find these things, what do we trade for them?" Thache asked.

"We loaded the *Adventure* with all the turpentine, pitch, shingles, and salt pork we could spare. According to Mr. Knight, that and skins are about all we can pull out of North Carolina," Chamberlain replied.

"And what if we can't find these goods?" Thache asked. "Or, say that we find dry goods from England in Baltimore, but Baltimore wants to keep them?"

"Knight says you no doubt have a cache of silver," Chamberlain said. "Silver's in short supply, so maybe you can find a profitable trade for coin."

"And what's our cut on this venture?" Thache asked.

I shifted a few branches and risked a peek through the leaves. But the men were engrossed in their negotiation and didn't notice me as they studied the list.

"Here's what the Governor set as the fair value of the cargo we loaded, and you can keep track of whatever silver you spend. We'll divvy the profits with some for the town and some for the traders." Chamberlain replied.

Thache leaned back till his face was only two bright eyes peeking over his black beard. "I reckon there's a cut for the Governor and his man, too?" he said. "How does that figure in?"

Chamberlain shoved the glasses aside, making room on the table for the eight silver bits snipped from a piece of eight coin. I heard them scrape as Knight's man divided them: four, then two, and another two. "The Governor thinks a half share of the profits for the town, a quarter for the crew, plus another quarter to split for the Governor and me," Chamberlain said. So, if we can agree, we're fit to make way at dawn.

Thache scratched his beard. "I can see how the town might need half. After all, 'tis mostly their goods we're trading, but they don't deserve more than the men that go to find the trades. Besides that, I reckon you and the Governor will also get a share from the town."

"I agree with the Captain," Hands said. "'Tis our necks at risk, and we do more than sail the ship. We know where to find bargains and how to get them. And we know which ships sail to which ports and what they might carry to these shores. So Thache and me being on board can multiply your profit by a good margin."

"What do you find fair?" Chamberlain asked.

After a pause, the Captain leaned forward and rearranged the bits into two sets of four. Then he replied, "How about we deliver a half share to Knight? Then he and the Governor can decide how to divvy that with the town and each other. Then the other half goes to the ship, and we'll split it according to our rules."

"Will the Governor agree to that?" Hands asked.

"I can't say for sure; he isn't in town. He's busy with a new property by Queen Anne's Creek," Chamberlain replied.

"So, are we sailing in the morning or not?" Hands asked.

"Half share to a half share is my offer. I reckon I have as many men on my ship as you have in your town, and 'tis our ship and lives at risk," Blackbeard said.

"Knight gave me the authority to agree for him, and I think Eden will be satisfied," Chamberlain replied. "The town needs goods, your ship is the best chance, and it sounds fair enough. Shall we shake on it?"

"It works for me," Hands replied, but Thache hesitated.

"Gentlemen, this is my first time making a deal with the Law; we should put it to paper."

"Then write it up, and 'tis a bargain," Hands said.

Chamberlain grimaced as he nodded. "Write it and hide it somewhere safe."

Thache found paper and ink, and then by lantern light, they signed the deal, with Chamberlain's signature specifying it was on behalf of Tobias Knight. Finally, they poured the dregs of the bottle, and the three men toasted their bargain while the ink dried.

Afterward, Thache slipped the agreement into the bottle and promised to leave it in the hands of his wife on Plum Point. "In case things run afoul, my wife will need to know what happened, and she'll be no trouble to find here," he said.

As they shook hands, I slipped around the house and into my room before Edward Thache left the porch.

I was tired, but another puzzle kept me from falling asleep as I reviewed the whispered conversation from the dark porch. Drake might believe Thache walked on water, but I wondered if Blackbeard was becoming an agent of the crown. Or could it be that the King's men were becoming pirates?

Was there any difference?

14 Uneasy Feelings

Marybeth Thache

Edward knew every port and mud puddle on the Eastern seaboard, and he must know sailors and traders along those shores, but I had never been out of Bath County. To me, his voyage was a mysterious journey, and the uncertainty kept me awake that night.

My husband was a master of the sea, but this time he was following the orders of Governor Eden and Tobias Knight. They were well-respected men who presented themselves nobly, but could the temptations that drew men to piracy also corrupt those of higher social stations? Had Edward taken the King's pardon to fall prey to another master? Or another set of thieves?

No. It couldn't be that. My husband was kind and strong-willed. No one could sway him.

But then he brought a bottle to our chamber. At first, I thought it was empty, but as it landed on the bed beside me, a paper scroll wobbled inside it.

"What's this?" I asked.

"'Tis the agreement I made with Tobias Knight on behalf of the Governor. I want you to put it somewhere safe when I leave tomorrow."

"What should I do with it then?" I asked.

"Hopefully, you'll never need it," he replied, "but dealing with men who hide behind smiling faces and under powdered wigs is a new game for me. If anything goes wrong, I want you to have proof of our partnership that spells out the expectations of this voyage. If it is profitable, you need to benefit from my share, and if it fails, you need protection from anyone who might try to take things from you, including this plantation."

"Do you think such a thing could happen?" I asked.

"I don't know Eden as well as Knight, and I'm unsure what to expect. But I promised to protect you, and I will."

"Stay with me, Edward. None of this is a worry if you're here. That will be protection enough."

"I can't do that, my love. I'm neither a planter nor a shipbuilder. But I know the sea, and the sea is where I can provide for you and the town too. 'Twould be a pleasure to taste white bread, wouldn't it? And a town with tea, ribbons, and gunpowder is better than one without."

"Take me with you. Then I'll be safe."

His laugh was more than a chuckle. "Oh, my darlin', you have no idea what 'tis like among a ship full of sailin' men."

"They wouldn't dare harm me with you there, would they?"

"Well, to begin with, sailors are a superstitious lot, and a woman on board a ship is the worst kind of luck to them. So, if we come upon a storm, they might throw you overboard to calm the waves."

"You're making that up."

"No, no. 'Tis as bad as killing an albatross."

"An albatross?"

"Aye. 'Tis lucky if one follows your ship, but not if ye kill it. They carry the spirits of dead sailors, and we wouldn't want to kill one twice."

"They'd kill a woman but not an albatross. Your men certainly don't believe that."

He cocked his head, shrugging, "I fear they do."

"How can I bring you good fortune and help you return home? What charm is there for that? Should I wish you an albatross?"

"That could be a tricky one. Dolphins are lucky. Oh! I have a better idea. Do you have a star on ye?"

"Well … no."

"Then give me one of your hair ribbons."

I plucked a blue ribbon from my braid, and Edward pulled me to the writing table.

"Here. Draw a star on the end of your ribbon."

I did my best. The ink bled a little, and the shape was ragged around the edges, but it was a star. "How's that?"

Edward smiled as he examined the ribbon. "It's perfect. Now, tell me it's the North Star."

"Edward, I present you with the North Star," I said as I passed him the ribbon.

With a smile, he tied it around a lock of hair in his beard. "There. 'Tis done. The North Star will bring me home to you with the greatest haste."

"Oh, good," I said, reflecting his smile.

Edward led me back to bed, saying, "Now, come. Call me Neddie, and let me hold you. Dawn will be here too soon."

***

I woke before Edward, but the dawn had not yet come. The sky was turning from black to inky blue. Over the pines, Polaris shone brightly above Bath, and I prayed to the wind, seas, and God above to bring my husband safely home.

Soon after I returned to the kitchen to put the kettle over the fire, I heard footsteps above me. "Edward, is that you?" I called.

"Sorry, my love, just gathering a few things I need."

Our calling to each other woke the house, and soon the boys joined us at the table. Mrs. Saunters chatted with Mother as Aurora helped her dress. Edward looked even taller in his sailing boots and hat. And the brass buttons on his long, red coat made him every inch the sea captain. His beard had grown a bit since he trimmed it for our wedding, but he had braided it into tight rows with a colorful ribbon at the end of each one. My blue ribbon sat on his longest braid that hung toward the left side of his chest.

"You're a fine-looking man, Edward Thache," I said as I straightened his lapels.

He chuckled. "Few can say that with a straight face," he said, smiling. His arms were warm around me, but he turned as Ody interrupted our embrace.

"Sir, I have something to report," Ody said. "Last night, when I left the porch, I saw one of the sailors who brought Hands to your dock carrying a sack toward the north creek, then he came back without it."

"Was he causing trouble?" Thache asked.

"I can't say, Sir, but I wanted to report it. He isn't the first stranger I've seen on the point. I saw a man by the summer house on our first night here. Could someone be up to no good?" Ody asked

"Doubtful," Thache replied. "He was probably taking gear to mates on land. No one from my ship will bother me, nor mine. But just in case, you lads rally Caesar and The Crow to breakfast here. I'll give the Plum Point crew my final orders."

When we finished a quick breakfast, everyone gathered around to hear what Edward had to say. The captain donned his hat, buttoned his coat, and slipped his sword into the scabbard on his belt.

"Caesar, Crow, we'll miss ye on this trip, but your orders are to watch my land and take care of my household as I would," he said. "Let them want for nothing and keep a sharp eye out for trouble no matter from sky, land, or sea. That goes for you, too, Ody and Drake. You're part of my crew here."

It wasn't much of a chorus; the words were staggered, but all four spoke agreement, "Aye, aye, Captain."

"I'll count on ye then," Thache said, tipping fingers to his hat. "God willing, I'll be back here soon."

"We will be here if we can, Captain, but either way, I'm sure of your safe return," Aurora said.

Mother gave her a strange look. "Are ye making prophecies now?" she asked. Then she turned to me, saying, "I told 'e she was a seer."

While the women argued over Aurora's ability to tell the future, I walked to our dock with Caesar, Coleman, and Edward. And as Edward took his place in the jollyboat, he whispered, "'Tis far enough, my Lady." He jiggled the blue ribbon in his beard, and I smiled at his little North Star. Then I told him to say hello to the dolphins. All in the boat were chuckling as they started across the creek.

I hurried to the house and climbed the Bride's Tower to watch them depart. Drake was in the Captain's den, but I nearly missed him as he bent over, looking behind a table.

"Did you drop something?" I asked.

"Yes, Ma'am. I dropped a shell I had in my pocket."

"Hurry up to the tower if you want to see the Captain leaving," I said.

Ody was already at the spyglass.

"Do you see any strangers on the grounds, Ody?" I asked.

"None at the moment, Ma'am," he replied.

Drake soon joined us, and we watched the sails unfurl as the *Adventure* headed into the rising sun.

"I wish them a good voyage," Drake said.

When we lost sight of sails in the river, we left the lookout to face whatever the day brought. But Drake stopped me in Edward's den.

"Did you find what you were looking for, Drake?" I asked.

"Yes, Ma'am. I did." Then he pointed toward Edward's drawing of his Mother. "Was that star always there?" he asked, pointing to a gold pendant draped over a corner of the frame.

"I don't spend much time here, but I believe it was always there. Look, Mother Thache wears the pendant in her painting, too."

"So, she does," Drake replied.

"I didn't know this till last night, but that star has special meaning. It is the North Star, and it shows sailors the way home. Perhaps Old Mrs. Thache wore it for her husband."

"Yes, Ma'am. That makes sense."

The boys went to their farm chores, and I went to the porch, where I joined Aurora and Mother.

"Did you see the ship sail?" I asked.

"Yes," Aurora replied. "It was quite a sight."

"Hmph," Mother said. "Maybe this place can feel like home again now. Or it would if we could get rid of those pirate pups."

Aurora swallowed a giggle, and Mother apologized for being so ungracious.

I took a porch chair and looked to the sky and water for direction, but I had no idea how to read the clouds or gauge the wind. I tried to think of Edward and our last evening together. But those happy thoughts were intruded upon by images of strange men on my farm and Edward in the company of former pirates, completing shady dealings with the rich men of Bath.

And what would happen to my husband on this voyage? Would the ship and crew lure him back to piracy? He'd meet friends and visit ports I knew nothing of. Would he stay faithful? Would he return the same man?

I had wrestled with these questions before, but how long would Edward be gone this time?

There were many reasons to be wary, but no matter how many times I tossed the questions around, I wouldn't have the answers till the sea brought my husband home again.

Act Two: Against Stiff Winds

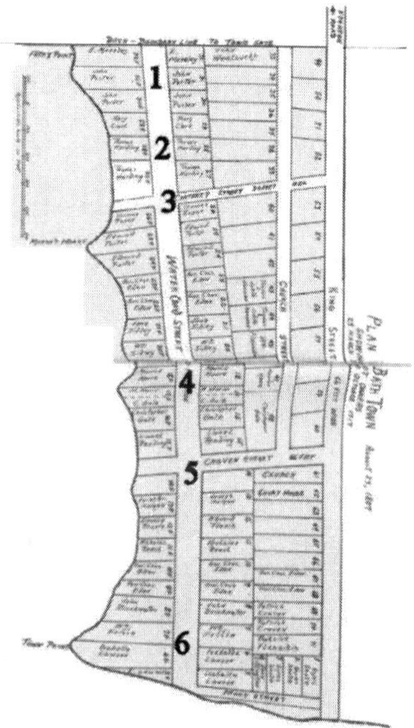

Town of Bath as presented in ***The Heart of Blackbeard.***
This map is based on a map redrawn around 1807 with owners of lots around 1717.
The left side (west) is Bath Creek
Rough positions of locations mentioned in this book.

1. Shipyard
2. Home of Captain Harding
3. The Hornpipe Inn (fictional)
4. Grist Mill
5. Marsh Moon Inn (fictional
6. Town Point and Lawson's Fort *[Reed, pp. 48-49]*

15 The Intruder's Secret

Ody Saunters

From the tower on Plum Point, Drake and I watched *Adventure* sail until we could no longer see the tip of her mast.

"What will Bath be like now?" I wondered.

"It's different, isn't it?" Drake asked as he pointed to the jollyboat returning to our landing without Blackbeard.

"Yes, we're a crew without a captain."

My cousin dug his elbow into my side. "I thought *you* were the captain." Then before I could catch him, he dropped down the hatch and ran through the house, shouting, "We aren't crewmen now; we're farm hands. You can be captain of that."

I followed Drake to the front porch to join the rest of the household. But since throttling my cousin wasn't in anyone else's plan, we pitched in to do our part of running the plantation. The Widow Bellieu felt well enough to air her bedding, so she and Oma went inside to bundle sheets and quilts. But Marybeth, eager for any messages from Captain Thache, joined Drake and me on the porch to wait for the jollyboat to dock.

Caesar soon joined us, but Coleman ran toward the crew hut. He soon returned to the landing with his tow sack and headed the jollyboat for Bath.

"Where's Crow going?" Marybeth asked.

Caesar shrugged. "Said he had business in Bath."

"What business was that?" she asked.

Caesar shook his head. "He didn't say, Ma'am. I hoped he'd help me check the pens and corrals, but there he goes, up the creek."

"I'll help you with the pens, Caesar," Drake said. And they headed to the backyard to care for the livestock.

"That leaves me, Ma'am," I said. "What work do you have for me?"

"Please call me Marybeth. It can't offend my husband if he isn't here, and 'twill make me more comfortable. Besides, I'll rely on you to be my lieutenant now that you're the oldest man on Plum Point who hasn't been a pirate."

"Yes, Ma'am," I replied. I was disappointed to be downgraded from captain but thrilled that she trusted me. "What shall I look for?" I asked.

"Oh, anything around the perimeter that needs repair or is out of place. If you find something dangerous, let's fix it."

I reached to grab my hat, but Marybeth stopped me before I could leave.

"Oh, there's one more thing." She raised a finger, signaling me to wait as she hurried to her quarters and returned carrying a flat glass bottle. When she held it at arm's length, I noticed a paper scroll corked inside it.

"My husband told me to hide this. Will you find a safe place for it? He said it could be important if he has trouble on his voyage."

"Yes, Ma'am," I replied, tucking the flask into my vest pocket. "I'll check the perimeter from the tower first."

She agreed with the plan, so I returned to the Bride's Tower, where I found something suspicious on my first search—a man creeping among the brush lining Bellieu Gut. When he paused between the berry bushes and oak seedlings, I thought he might be looking for an open window to invade the farm. But the stranger kept on his path downstream till he reached the little summer house on the point.

With the stiff breeze blowing, he couldn't hear me calling, so I slid down the rope ladder and raced to the shelter, yelling at every step. "Wait! Who are you? What business do you have at Plum Point?"

I was out of breath when I reached the pavilion, and the man was nowhere to be seen. So, I scoured the banks around the mouth of the gut and then searched the banks of Old Towne Creek, looking for clues—a shoeprint or clumps of broken seagrass, but there was nothing.

When I gave up on the creekbanks and turned back toward the summer house, I finally found something amiss. There was a hole in the stone underpinning of the little pavilion, and one cantaloupe-sized stone had broken from its mortar and lay on the ground.

Only bits of mortar lay in the hole where the stone had been, but upstream along Bellieu Gut, I found footprints among broken reeds. My quarry was on the move.

With only sticks and stones nearby, I chose a strong oak branch as my weapon. It fit my hand well, and although it was lighter than a baseball bat, it might still pack a wallop should I have a reason to use it.

The trail stopped at a ditch lined with similar greenish rocks that channeled runoff to Bellieu Gut. But up the slope, this rocky gully led to a sassafras hedge by the house. Three-fingered leaves waved as if recently disturbed, so I pushed the branches aside to find an open wooden door in the underpinning.

When I stooped to peek into the rocky tunnel behind it, I found a man in a plain muslin shirt and blue-striped headscarf crouched like a toad in the hole. But he was no stranger; I had met him on my first night in Bath.

"Carver," I shouted. "State your business or be on your way. This land belongs to Captain Edward Thache and his family."

"Blackbeard owns nothing here," he replied.

"Neither do you. Be on your way."

He crawled out of the tunnel and stumbled down the ditch, eyeing me at every step. Then, when he gathered his balance, he sat on one side of the gulley and pointed for me to sit opposite him. On our first meeting, he struck me as having honest concern for Mrs. Thache, so I rested the oak branch across my knee, ready to hear what he had to say.

"You're wrong. Marybeth Bellieu belongs to me."

Clearly, his concern was born of some affection for Marybeth, but how could he imagine she belonged to him? "Marybeth Thache is a married woman now. If she was yours once, she isn't anymore."

"Then she must tell me so," he said.

This fellow obviously wasn't at the wedding, and from what he told us that first night, he needed to keep hidden. But he knew she was married; he said as much when we heard the pirates singing. Perhaps he needed a reminder.

"I reckon Marybeth said as much to everybody in Bath the day she stood before the Governor and vowed to be his wife," I said.

"She was misled. Some folks at the wedding knew it was wrong and didn't speak up. She doesn't know the whole story."

"Don't you think it's too late to speak up now?" I asked, shrugging. "I've seen them together, and it's in her eyes. She's happily married."

"And I say, she was lied to, and if she knew the truth, she'd want out of that vow and be right to break it."

"Well, she seems satisfied to me. What kind of story could change her mind about that?" I asked.

"It ain't you that I need to convince, but I won't stop till I tell Marybeth the truth."

"What are you doing here? Were you sneaking into the house? How did you open that tunnel anyway?" Then another thought startled me. "Did you plan to kidnap Marybeth?"

"Of course not," he replied. But then he looked me in the eye. "I might better ask *you* what you're doing. You don't belong here."

"Captain Thache asked us to keep watch over his family while he's away, and part of that is looking out for trespassers—like you."

He reached into his head scarf and pulled out a rusty iron key.

"Where did you get that?" I asked, eyes wide.

"I hid it for Bert Bellieu," he said.

"Why? How?" I stammered. "Isn't Bert Bellieu long dead?"

"He is," Carver nodded. "But my Papa was a stone mason, and I was his apprentice. He did most of the brickwork on this place, and 'twas I who put these ballast stones in place. My Papa and I built the cellar and all the rock work you see along this creek."

"Are you saying that tunnel leads to the cellar? I thought the dockside tunnel did that."

"Aye, it does. But Bellieu wanted an escape route for his family should the Tuscarora attack. So, the dockside tunnel goes to the cellar, and the hole where you found me comes out here. Only me and my Papa knew about it because Bellieu had us build it for him, and he asked us to make a hiding place for the spare key, too."

"Anyone along this creek might find that tunnel," I said.

"Why would anyone bother with what looks like a potato hole, and where would they find a key?"

"Did you mean to invade the house?" I asked.

"No. I meant to hide from you when you chased me, but you trailed me too quickly."

"Then give me the key, and I'll give it to the Widow Bellieu."

He shook his head. "That night on the Towne Point, you promised to help me, and now's the time to do it. Arrange a way for me to talk to Marybeth, and I'll give you the key."

"Is this the only one?" I asked.

"There were two. Bert kept one with him and hid the spare."

"All right. Here's what I will do; I'll talk to Marybeth, and then she can choose if she wants to see you. Do you see the roof tower?" I asked.

"I know it."

"I'll tell Marybeth about meeting you, and if she wants to talk, I'll tell her to be in the tower tonight. So, if you see her there, you can climb that ladder behind the fig trees to meet her."

He grimaced, but he gave in. "Make it tomorrow night. I can't get away again today."

"Well, there's more to the bargain. If Marybeth doesn't show up on the tower, she doesn't want to see you, and you must promise to leave her alone and never come here again."

He hung his head between his knees. "I'll promise to leave her alone," he said.

"Then give me the key, and we have a deal," I replied.

"Well, since you're here to guard Marybeth, I'll do it."

After passing me the key, he added, "If she doesn't come to the tower, I'll leave her alone. But mind you; I'll never stop watching out for her."

"Suit yourself," I replied. "Now, clear out of here till Mrs. Thache decides."

Carver dusted his breeches and went toward Old Towne Creek, sneaking from bush to bush. I climbed the ladder behind the rain barrel to watch him till he boarded the boat hidden near the south gut. Once he rowed away from Plum Point, I dropped to the yard again.

The fig trees that wrapped around the corner of the house hid me from Oma and Henrietta, who were busy hanging quilts and blankets over the clothesline. So, I followed the oyster shells along the house's foundation till I came to the sassafras stand that hid Carver's oak door.

This time I entered the hole where stones lined the walls and the tunnel floor. The space would hold a few crouching adults if they huddled. The back wall, comprised of small, mortared stones, sloped upward till it reached a flat crawlspace under the floor joists. A short stack of loose rocks at the edge of the ramp made the opening look too small to pass through, but moving them aside gave clear access to the crawlspace.

When I locked the door behind me and began to climb through the passage, the Captain's bottle rattled against the stones. Fearing it would break, I hid it under loose rocks in a back corner of the tunnel and left it there as I explored.

Even lying prone in the crawlspace, I had only a few inches of clearance from the floor joists, and from the right, light seeped through the mortarless underpinning, giving a dim view of a few spider webs and snake skins abandoned there. But I shifted left, where I could drop over a seven-foot brick cellar wall to the earthen floor below.

I clambered down and found enough casks and crates to allow anyone to climb to the crawlspace. But who would bother to visit a drain? The underpinning wall allowed no entry or exit unless an intruder wanted the house to fall on his head.

Outside the Bellieu family, only Wallace and I knew about the second cellar exit. And since I had the key now, the potato hole tunnel made a perfect place to hide the Captain's bottle, so I left it there.

After securing all access to the hiding space, I climbed the cellar steps that ended in a storage area under the stairs in the main house. The bottle was safe. But what should I do with the key? I should ask Marybeth.

She wasn't in the house nor working with Hetty and Oma in the yard, but they pointed me toward the garden where she gathered vegetables for dinner.

"Just in time, Ody," she said. "Do you feel like getting your hands dirty? I could use some help here."

"I fear they're dirty already," I replied.

She dropped her basket and stood eyeing the grime ground into my vest and knickers and the dirt smudging my sleeves and face.

"What have you been up to?" she asked.

The garden was too close to Oma and Hetty. "Follow me," I said, pointing past the vegetable patch to the apple orchard.

She was puzzled and reluctant to leave the gardening but followed me to the apple trees.

"What has happened?" she asked, impatient for an explanation.

"Mrs. Thache, I found a man in the yard today, and he wants to speak with you. You don't have to do it, but he begged me to ask if you'd meet him."

"Who is it?"

"Do you know a fellow named Carver?"

She shook her head. "I never heard of a Carver family,"

"He wants to talk to you. He says he has a claim on you, despite your marriage to the Captain."

"That's impossible. What do you mean?" Then her brows knit toward her nose, and she paused before stepping closer. "What does he look like?"

"He's a young man, a year or two older than I am, and he's almost as tall. He doesn't have much hair, but he wears a blue-striped headscarf. He says he did brickwork with his Papa."

She stepped back, mouth agape. "Who put you up to this?"

"Just the young man, Ma'am. I don't know much more. He wanted to explain it to you himself. Do you know him?"

"Wallace," she whispered. "But it can't be him. He left me. Why would he come back now?"

"I can't say, Ma'am."

"What did you tell him?"

"I told him if you agreed to meet him, you'd be on the tower tomorrow night, and if you don't show up there, he's to leave you alone."

"Did you say tomorrow night?" she asked.

"Aye, Ma'am. He said he couldn't come tonight."

She brushed her skirt as she shook her head. "I'll think about it."

I stepped closer to whisper. "I told Wallace you were married and happy. If you don't want to bother with him, I'll make sure he hears it."

"I have a day to decide, you say?" she asked.

"Yes, Ma'am."

"I have questions, and he might have answers—or at least, excuses. Let me sleep on it, please."

She started for the garden but turned around after a few stumbling steps. “Please. Don’t speak of this to anyone. We’ll talk more tomorrow.”

16 Ghosts

Marybeth Thache

Even after collecting pulling peas and digging onions, I was still stunned by Ody's news. Thank goodness preparing dinner was more a routine than an art; otherwise, the stew would have been a disaster. The science of chopping carrots was the last thing on my mind; Edward was the first.

Was he in danger? What shallow shoals and rocky coastlines must he cross to find the goods for Bath? Another hazard worried me, too, but I resisted being jealous of the unknown female friends he may meet.

After all, an old love of *mine* had surfaced, and questions about him mingled with my worries about Edward. *Why did Wallace leave me, and where had he been? And what could he want now?* Wallace's return brought up issues so upsetting that I tried to lock them in forgotten corners where I hoped they would fade into the darkness, but instead, they kept pushing back at me.

Did he think we could pick up where we left off?

Could I turn away from him if he did?

The swarm of stinging questions hovered like wasps, and try as I might, I couldn't wave them away. Not completely. So, I stirred the dinner stew. At least something useful could come of that.

When Caesar came for the crew's dinner, he told us The Crow was missing. No one had seen him since he rowed to Bath. His mysterious absence took a minute of mealtime conversation, but talk soon shifted to the animals and fences on Plum Point. I paid little attention to what was said or what I ate. From the corner of my eye, I noticed Ody watching me, probably puzzled by my distraction.

After dinner, Caesar and Drake left for chores, and while we ladies cleared the table, The Crow returned wearing a fancy blue coat with brass buttons. Such a coat was nothing like Coleman's typical garb, and the change begged an explanation.

"That's a mighty fine jacket you're wearing," I said. "Have you been shopping?"

"No, Ma'am, the Cap'n give it to me before he left, and part of my pay, too. Look here."

The Crow opened his sack and felt around the bottom before pulling out a tin of tea.

"Hope it's the kind you like, Ma'am," he said. "And I have more to offer."

Who would have imagined The Crow dressed for company and bearing gifts? What was the story behind this change?

"Is that your new fishing jacket, Crow?" Ody asked when he returned from slopping the hog.

The Crow huffed, replying, "A man can look his best for a day in town if he's a mind. This look served me well; even Edmund Chamberlain felt at ease speaking to me today. He sent a message from Tobias Knight for Widow Bellieu."

I raised my eyebrows as he passed a note to Mother. "What does it say?"

"She chuckled a little. Knight wonders if we would accompany his stepdaughter to the scripture readin' Sunday. Fancy that."

"Will you go?" Aurora asked.

"I'll think on it, but I'd be uneasy leaving our farm with no one besides Thache's men. We'll see."

The rest of the day passed, and since Mother's blackberry cobbler wasn't quite ready at supper time, she asked Drake to fetch Caesar and The Crow to join us on the porch for dessert. We enjoyed the pie, made even better with a dollop of rich cream, as we watched the ships enter Old Towne Creek, but something was missing.

"Edward should be here," I said. "Even though he hasn't been in Bath long, he knew every ship and crewman passing here. I miss his stories."

Caesar wiped blackberries from his mouth and said, "I've known him since a boy, Ma'am, and I reckon I know all 'is stories. I can tell a few if you like."

I didn't have to reply as Ody and Drake clambered to hear of Edward as a boy. 'Twas a blessing to have Caesar entertain as I fought the wasps that battled inside me.

So, The Crow, now back to his sailor's garb, chose a willow stick to whittle, and Ody followed suit as Caesar turned every question the boys had into a story.

My thoughts drifted, so I only remembered bits and pieces. But I noted a few points I'd want to learn more about. And whether I focused on the stories or not, the rhythm and music of Caesar's voice soothed me.

He started by telling of how an earthquake struck Jamaica when he was a boy, ruining the plantation where he lived. And even though he said that was before Edward's family came to manage the farm, I fretted over what storms Edward may face on his current voyage.

And after I calmed those fears, Caesar told of what a wild pirate haven Jamaica had once been, and that suggested all the freebooter ports and bawdy women Edward may visit. But then I remembered the little star he jiggled before he left, promising to find his way home.

The last part of the story may have been the worst. Caesar told how twice Edward claimed to have seen the ghost of Sir Henry Morgan. Morgan was once the Lt. Governor of Jamaica, but before that, he was a famous privateer and friend to the pirates. Morgan's ghost gave Edward the same caution twice—a warning that young Edward should not follow in Morgan's shoes.

That omen was frightening, but Edward was under the King's Pardon and was no longer part of the pirate life. So, I fussed at myself for fretting over nothing more than dreams and fanciful stories.

I wasn't a good audience for Caesar, but the boys were transfixed. So, I left the group and went to the Bride's Tower to find comfort in the light of the North Star.

The star twinkled as if promising to bring Edward home soon, but as fears about my husband calmed, the other source of worry came to the forefront.

Wallace.

Why had he disappeared, and why had he come back? Regardless of his excuses, it was too late to change things, but I needed answers to those questions.

Had another ghost resurrected just like Sir Henry Morgan? Was this one still flesh and blood?

I'd find out tomorrow.

Maybe.

17 Sticky Business

Marybeth Thache

I began my day in the Bride's Tower. There, the refreshing morning breezes relieved some of my wasp questions, but my new status was prickly, too. My husband was gone, and I was the mistress of Plum Point, but I wasn't prepared to make decisions about the farm.

With Edward away, I had become the caretaker of food, water, shelter, and access to the sea, everything that meant survival to those on Plum Point. Now I knew how my mother felt when Papa died, and the weight of our farm fell on her shoulders. I felt the burden, but I had no clue how to manage it, but I knew housework, and that was a start.

Even sweeping the floor was part of guarding my father's life's work. And by the time I reached the porch, my sweeping wrought fury on any speck of debris threatening our threshold. Bits of dried leaves and grit swirled like tiny dust clouds, forcing Mother and Aurora to swing the laundry hamper over their heads for protection.

Mother called to me from beneath the wicker, "Hold on to your broom for a moment." And when I paused, she peeked out, pointing to the fig tree beside the steps.

"Good heavens, Marybeth. These figs have ripened overnight; we can't let these go to waste. Fetch me the fig basket."

Oh, that felt better—Mother in charge—Mother giving the orders. She had taken only remote interest in farm matters lately, but the ripe figs had renewed her spark.

Mother's fire began to die when Father passed, and the years of a failing farm sapped her even more. Her hope brightened when she thought I might marry Wallace McNeil, but her grim face returned when he left Bath—and me—behind.

Then Edward came calling, and even though Mother said the choice was mine, it was clear that she saw his courtship as a path forward. Once I said yes, she smiled more often. But her hope for our marriage turned to doubt somewhere along the way, and she became sullen again.

But today, she glowed. Something as insignificant as a fig made her smile.

Aurora handed Mother the tray as she asked, "Will you make preserves?"

"If we have enough sugar," she replied as she inspected the fruit.

I smiled. "We do, and you can thank Edward for it. He brought a sealed hogshead to Plum Point the day you approved our marriage."

"Yes. I remember," Mother said. "And I remember what we paid for that, too."

"Mother, if you're speaking about me, I can assure you I'm not a price paid. On the contrary, Edward is a blessing, and I'm happy with him."

She nodded, then muttered softly. "But you're not *all* that was paid."

I couldn't solve her riddle, but Ody appeared, and the conversation shifted.

Aurora's face glowed as the boy joined us on the porch. "Perhaps he can fetch the sugar for us."

"Ody, let me show you the cellar," I said. "What do you think, Mother? Two or three cones?"

"High-quality cones are small, so bring two for sure." Then as she turned the figs in the tray, she added, "Bring three, just in case."

I was surprised that Ody knew the way. He walked directly to the cellar door, passed the lantern, and helped me down the steps.

"Have you been here before?" I asked. "Did Edward take you to the cellar?"

"Edward? No," he replied. "But I was here, and there's something I should show you."

"Well, let's get the sugar for Mother first." After delivering the cones to the outside kitchen, I stopped Ody at the back door. "What did you want to show me?"

When Ody was sure we were alone, he pulled a large iron key from his vest pocket. "Do you recognize this?"

I looked it over from every angle, but I had never seen it before as far as I could remember. "It's like our cellar key, but the ironwork is different. Did you find this near the sugar cask?"

Mother's harsh voice interrupted his answer.

"Where did you get that?" she asked. "That belonged to Bert." When I turned to face her, she grabbed the key from my hand.

"What does it fit?" I asked. "I don't recall Father having a locked chest that would take a key this large."

She turned toward Ody. "Did Thache give you this?"

"No, Ma'am," he replied.

I took the key, holding it upright near her face. "What does this fit, Mother?"

"'Tis a cellar key."

"But Edward has charge of the one that fits the dockside door. Was there a spare?"

"No. Not a spare key. But there is a spare door."

"Why didn't I know about that?"

"'Twas for emergencies, and lucky for us, we never needed it. Your father kept this key till he died, and I … I buried it with him."

I turned back to Ody. "So, did you find this key?" I asked.

"No. It was given to me."

Mother pushed close to Ody's chest, demanding answers. "Did one of the pirates dig into Bert's grave? Does Coleman know the secret?"

Ody took a step back, shaking his head. "I heard nothing like that, Ma'am."

Luckily Aurora found us and broke the tension, saying, "Pardon me, but I'm not sure what I should do with these figs?" Then, noticing our tense faces, she asked, "Has Ody done something wrong?"

"No, Oma. I promise I have not," the boy replied.

"No one alive knows where that key was hidden," Henrietta said. "Tell the truth, boy."

"I can only tell Mrs. Thache," he replied.

Mother nodded as if she had solved a riddle. "Then Thache has something to do with this, doesn't he?"

"If he does, I don't know how, Ma'am."

Aurora Saunters took my mother's arm. "It seems my grandson has a secret for your daughter. First, let's tend the figs; afterward, Marybeth may share it."

Mother was reluctant to let the matter lie, but this stranger, Aurora Saunters, had sway over her, so she followed her new friend to the kitchen.

"What's this about, Ody? Who gave you that key? Where does it fit?" I asked.

"'Twas Wallace McNeil who gave it to me, so I'd ask you to meet him."

My eyes filled with tears as I asked, "Did he dare take it from my father's grave?"

"No. Wallace knew where Bert hid the spare key."

"Show me what this unlocks."

Ody led me to the crawlspace and explained the rocky tunnel and escape hatch behind it.

"I hid your bottle in a cluster of rocks down the ramp," he said. "The key fits a door beyond that. It's hidden behind sassafras bushes along the house wall."

"How did I never see that door?" I asked, but I remembered the rocky drain when he led us outside to see the tunnel from the yard. "Papa. He's the reason. He told me this ditch was dangerous and to stay away from it." I offered the key to Ody, but he wouldn't take it.

"You should keep it, Marybeth. You're the mistress here now."

I studied the key again. "I'll give it to Mama. She's been the mistress longer than I have."

"Carver says your Papa wanted a place to hide his family and escape trouble," Ody replied. "He hid behind that door when I was chasing him. He'll be in the yard tonight, and if he sees you, he'll climb up to the roof."

I gripped the key, lost in memories of a young boy toting rocks for his father.

"Will you meet him?" Ody asked.

"I don't know."

"If you want to speak to him, I'll stand guard," the boy promised. "I vowed to the Captain that I'd keep you safe."

"I'll think about it."

"Then, I'll leave you to that, Ma'am, and I'll finish scouting the perimeter." He tipped his hat and headed toward the east fences.

I stumbled to the summer house, and as I sat, gripping the key, I let my thoughts of Wallace McNeil roll with the waves in Old Towne Creek. Those were the days when I was safe under my parents' roof—when I could be a child who dreamed of a life with a thoughtful, handsome boy who would someday make me feel as safe as my father. Most of those memories were as sweet as the sticky figs cooking in our kitchen. But they could not explain why Wallace McNeil had deserted me.

18 Wallace's Story

Marybeth Thache

The decision to meet Wallace flipped and flopped like a trout on the shore, but finally, one truth settled it—he had the answers I wanted. So that night, after everyone had gone to bed, I climbed to the Bride's Tower.

Not long after, Ody peeked through the hatch.

"I'll be here. If there's trouble, shout, and I'll be ready."

When Ody dropped into Edward's den, I leaned on the railing, staring toward the Pamlico River. But images of sails in the night sky intermingled with memories of a fourteen-year-old boy who slipped away from his masonry work to share his sugared orange peel. Then, when he was fifteen, he touched my hand when he brought me flowers or seashells. After that, he gave me my first kiss, and when he was away, I longed for him. So, I answered *yes* when he asked to marry me. But then, he vanished into thin air.

And now there was Edward—somewhere on a dark sea, but also invisible, and part of me wondered if he had left forever, too.

Thuds.

I turned to sounds from the roof near the rope ladder.

Ody shuffled about in the room below but stayed in Edward's den. I went toward the sounds, watching as a striped headscarf rose to the roof.

When Wallace looked up, my tears spilled over the brim.

"Where have you been?" I asked.

He nodded and kept climbing till he could cross the rail and stand before me.

His fists clenched as if to grab for me, and part of me wanted that, but things between us had changed forever. I was devoted to my husband, but Wallace McNeil had answers.

"I never left you, Marybeth," he said. "No matter what you think, I never left you. I was taken from you."

"What happened?"

"Thache took a mind to have ye," he said.

"I won't believe Edward hurt you. He's as gentle as a lamb."

"He did not hurt me," Wallace replied. "But word got back to me that he wanted you and that I'd better watch myself."

"So, did you run away?"

"I did not," he replied, standing straight before me. "But I was taken, and I reckon Captain Thache was behind it."

"What happened?"

"The Drucker family called me to lay bricks over a grave at the burial grounds. So, I was there when they dug the grave and spoke the words. Then, after his family buried him, my job was to cover him with bricks to keep the ground around him."

I nodded. "You did the same for my father."

"Aye," he replied. "But when the bricks were in place, two salts told me what a good job I did, and they brought me to the sailors' tavern for a drink." He looked at me sheepishly, adding, "It might have been three."

"Three men?"

"No. Three drinks."

"Hm," I said, nodding. "What then?"

"I can't remember what was next. When I came to, I was on a beach around a fire, and the two men who took me to the tavern were there with three or four more sailors deciding what to do with me. One said they should have thrown me in the sea, but another said they should cut off my hand and send it to you."

"Who were these men?" I asked.

"I can't say, but I reckon they were part of Thache's crew. His men are the only sailors I know who would behave that way."

"How did you get away?"

"I didn't," he replied. "They pulled out their knives and argued over what part of me I might spare. One wanted my ear, and another thought a finger would do for a prize. But a third man said he'd scalp me, and no woman alive would want me after that."

I stood at that part of the story and turned away from Wallace. *Who would do such a thing?*

"I'm sorry, Marybeth. I'm sorry. Turn here to look if you can. I'll show you what they did."

I expected the worst as I turned to find him kneeling with his headscarf in his hands. Scarred scalping victims were part of the nightmare tales from the Tuscarora War, but this wasn't scalping. Instead, his tormentors had shaved his hair to the skin, and it had grown back stubby and white as snow, nothing like the honey-colored curls I remembered. Beneath the fuzz, I saw the red and blue scars, a skull roughly carved into his scalp.

I gasped, and Wallace covered his head again as my tears streamed.

"They left me bleeding on that beach," he said. "I washed the wound with seawater and spent the night wiping blood and stirring the fire embers they left. The next morning, I saw I was on an island with no water or food besides what I could pull from the sea."

"How did you live?" I asked.

"I figured I couldn't be far from home, so I was determined to find a way to get to my family. I collected driftwood and vines and was working on a raft when someone came to the island. It was as if he had been looking for me, and he took me to his boat, bandaged my head, and gave me a jug of water and a piece of hard tack."

"Who was it?" I asked.

"He was familiar, but I couldn't place the face. He was older than the Captain but a man of the sea. He took me to land and told me never to go home and to never speak to you again if I wanted to live."

"So, it wasn't Edward, then,"

"No, it wasn't," he replied. "But the message was loud and clear. It was because Edward wanted you, and I was to leave you alone."

"So, why are you telling me this now?"

"Because, even if I can't speak to you, I mean to watch out for you. And I had my chance once Captain Thache was off to sea."

Memories of the sweet romance we once shared mingled with those of Edward's courtship. I had once loved Wallace, and perhaps I still did, but my bond with my husband was deeper. We hadn't just agreed to marry, we had crossed that threshold, and love had taken on a new meaning.

"Wallace …."

"I know," he said. "You're married."

"That's right. And I'll be faithful to my husband."

He nodded, and when he spoke again, there were tears in his voice.

"You will stand by him; that's who you are. And he has every reason in the world to love you for that."

Then he lifted his chin, resolute. "If he's a man who deserves you, then I'll let it be. But I'll watch until I believe he's good enough for you."

"Did you go home?" I asked. "Your family came looking for you."

"I must keep them safe, too, My parents won't speak of it, but they know I'm alive and can't go home yet."

"Then where are you?"

"Close enough to know if you need me," he replied. He touched my hand briefly before hurrying down the ladder. Then I watched him cross past our landing toward Plum Point Gut, where I lost him in the trees.

But someone else was in the yard; a thin man with a lantern walked from our dockside tunnel. A full sack hung by a leather strap over his shoulder. In the dim light, I recognized the blue coat and bony profile of The Crow.

A voice from behind me whispered, "Is all well?" It was Ody Saunters who had climbed up from Edward's den.

"Look at this," I said, pointing to the intruder.

Ody watched as The Crow crossed our land. When Coleman reached the last place I had seen Wallace, he looked around, confused, and then looked back toward the lantern on the Bride's Tower.

With the sack resting on one hip, he lowered his lantern to see us in the tower light. He stared at Ody and me, and when he was sure we saw him, too, he nodded coldly, then held his lantern toward us, pointing an accusing finger. Then he disappeared into the trees along the gut.

We entered the cellar from inside the house and found nothing amiss. Then I passed the potato hole key to Ody, and after he climbed to the crawlspace ledge, he reported the hiding place locked and the glass bottle safe.

But when he returned the key to me, he said, "Either leave this key in the drain tunnel or give it to your Mother. She'll know where to hide it."

So, I went to Mother's room and passed the key to her.

"Are you ready to tell me who had this key?" she asked.

"'Twas Wallace McNeil," I replied. "I just spoke with him. He's come back to watch over us, even though I've married."

"He's alive? You're sure it's him?" she asked.

"As sure as I stand here, Mother. Papa had him hide a spare key."

She grabbed me, sobbing, but she smiled beneath the tears. "Then I didn't kill Wallace," she said. "Perhaps I haven't brought ruin to this house after all."

"Is that what you thought, Mother?" I asked, eyes wide. "How? Why didn't you tell me?"

She tightened her hold on me for a moment. Then she pushed me away as she wiped tears with her apron.

"Go to bed, girl," she said. "We have work to do tomorrow." Then she pushed me out the door, and soft laughter mixed with the water splashing in her wash bowl.

Was she well, or had the news of Wallace been her last straw? I peeked back through the door. "Mother?" I asked.

She was a tiny woman who needed a step stool to draw water from our well, but now she stood straight as an arrow, holding her head high. She had resurrected as the confident mother who knows better than her child. Her eyes were as clear as rain as she spoke.

"I told you, girl. Go on now. Go to bed."

I listened as she crawled under her quilt. And as soon as her head hit the pillow, she snored soundly.

Sweet dreams eluded me, but it was a comfort that Mother had found hers and was ready to stand with me as we guarded Plum Point.

19 Monsters in Bath

Ody Saunters

Why did The Crow point his finger at Marybeth and me? And why was he coming from the tunnel with that sack?

The cellar held no clues, and no one had tampered with the door to the potato hole. Marybeth was more troubled about the sack than The Crow, but she asked me to keep an eye on his comings and goings as I could.

Over the following days, Coleman found excuses to run errands in Bath or to fish from the jollyboat. But, not even Caesar, who knew The Crow best, saw anything unusual in his behavior. So, we pushed worries about The Crow to the side and continued the business of farming on Plum Point.

The following Saturday, Edmund Chamberlain, assistant to Tobias Knight, came to find out if any in our household planned to ride with Knight's stepdaughter to Bath for the Sunday scripture reading. His instructions were to wait for a reply, so I left him on the front porch while I found the ladies shelling peas in the back.

"He calls it a scripture reading. Is it a church service?" I asked.

"We've never had a real church in Bath," Marybeth answered. "There's plenty of talk about a building, and there's a prayer meeting now and then, but no church."

Henrietta lifted her head from the pea sack long enough to raise an eyebrow. "No," she said with a snort, "the closest we came was when the lawyer, Christopher Gale, held weekly readings at his office."

Marybeth sighed as she dropped the peas in her lap. "Governor Eden is trying, Mother. But with all the troubles in Bath, he's had no luck so far."

Hetty looked up from her pea sack. "Well, if he doesn't get a meeting house for us, something else will fill the void, and Quakers ain't the worst of what could happen when men don't pay attention to what's inside them."

I nodded, "You have a point there, Hetty. Cary's Rebellion wasn't that long ago."

"Indeed not," the widow Bellieu replied. Marybeth remembers the day two governors were in an armed fight across this creek from us—three governors if you count Lt. Governor Daniel. He owned Knight's plantation then, and Cary lived at Thistleworth. But it was Cary and Hyde quarreling over who should be the rightful governor.

They'd been battling north of here, but on one fine May day, Hyde marched on Thistleworth with seventy armed men to capture Cary, who ran to Daniel's farm. Daniel's five cannons and forty armed men persuaded Hyde to withdraw.

"The cannons, muskets, and shouting less than half a mile from our home frightened me. I couldn't sleep for weeks," Marybeth said.

"What brought that on?" I asked.

"Some silliness about whether or not a Quaker man could serve in office without swearing an oath. It shows you what men can become when they let the evil inside them take hold. In this case, 'twas lust for power that turned otherwise good men into villains disrupting life up and down the sound."

When Marybeth finished her opinion on Cary's Rebellion, she dropped peas into the bowl and turned to her daughter, saying, "Never mind the politics, daughter; you should attend the service. Regardless of which side is readin', I reckon hearing the scriptures nurtures good and binds evil. It might lift your spirits, and maybe Aurora will accompany you."

"Mr. Knight was of great service in arranging our wedding. And since he isn't well, we should help him with Lizzy. Come with us, Mother."

"I can't leave those pirates here with no one to watch what they are doing; I'll stay here."

When Drake learned that those staying at Plum Point would shell more peas, he decided to go to the reading instead. But since Marybeth had asked me to keep an eye on The Crow, I figured I'd better stay at the farm.

So, I returned to Chamberlain to report there would be three passengers from Plum Point.

***

Shelling peas seemed a dull duty for a summer day, but Oma pulled me aside, asking me to keep the peace between Henrietta and the crewmates while she was in Bath.

"The Widow Bellieu sees these men as outsiders," Grandma whispered. "She feels she should be in charge of her farm, especially with the Captain gone. But the sailors might not like taking orders from her. So, keep the fires low. Don't let sparks fan to flames."

It surprised me that Oma thought the Widow Bellieu had an angry side. But if she did, perhaps peas would not be as boring as I first thought—and maybe Hetty had more stories to tell about the Cary Rebellion.

After we waved the party off our landing, the Widow Bellieu put us to work.

"I've set all we need on the back porch," she said. "Those peas won't dry themselves in the shell."

Caesar opened the door for Hetty to pass through first, but The Crow had other ideas. He jumped off the side of the porch. But before he disappeared around the corner, Caesar stopped him.

"Where are you going?"

"Shellin' peas ain't part of my work here," he said. "I'll be fishin'."

"Well, the work at hand is peas," Henrietta said, hands on her hips.

"Come on, Coleman," I said as I stepped beside the Widow Bellieu. "The Captain made you the provisioner; part of that's taking care of the food."

"Fish is food," he replied, turning toward the sideyard.

Caesar planted himself in The Crow's path, saying, "Thache's orders are for us to mind the farm and care for the ladies here. The Cap'n won't be pleased if you leave the widow alone and don't help with her safety. You wouldn't want to put him in a black mood as soon as he comes to port, would ye?"

Coleman had thunder in his eyes as he turned back. "What would 'e care if I shell peas or not? How would 'e know? Are ye plannin' to tell on me, Caesar?"

The Widow Bellieu had no patience for the uncooperative, so her eyes shot daggers as she stood to her full height.

I backed her up, saying, "If the widow doesn't tell the Captain, I will."

"So there," Henrietta said, "Two against one."

The Crow grumbled, but he followed us to the porch and grabbed a handful of peas from the sack.

As we got into the rhythm of shelling, spilling good peas into a bowl, and saving the rest for fodder, I asked, "Does the Captain often have black moods? Is that why they call him Blackbeard?"

Caesar answered first. "They never called him Blackbeard on the plantation, and even then, his anger roused when he had a righteous reason for it, so it ain't just his temper."

"Isn't it because of his black beard?" Hetty asked.

"'Tis only part of it," The Crow replied.

"Well, that's true, Crowman," Caesar said, flicking one of the Crow's ear braids. "If we named crew after their hair, we'd call you *mousetails*."

Crow grimaced, "And you'd be *baldy*."

Caesar ignored him and continued, "The name stuck after the Cap'n refitted *Queen Anne's Revenge*. More ships joined us, and the *Queen* was the flagship of a fleet. Seeing a mighty warship with forty guns leading the fleet and hundreds of men scattered over the decks was enough to make our targets yield the battle. They gave us no fight when we boarded."

Coleman picked up the story. "True enough, but there's more to it than that. The Cap'n was part of the terror. He's a towering man, and he made himself more fearful by letting his hair and beard grow and flow around his head. And when we approached a ship as if to broadside, he brandished his blade and flashed the six pistols strapped to his body. And he growled with that black look of his'n. He even lit fuses in his hair to make smoke swirl around his head."

"Well, that's when he got the nickname Blackbeard, all right," Caesar said, "But lighting fuses in his beard is nonsense. How could he fight without setting himself on fire?"

"I didn't see it myself," Crow admitted, "I was on Bonnet's ship in those days, but 'tis how Thache's crew told it."

"A fearful reputation is a mighty weapon," Caesar said. "The Cap'n told me half of winnin' a battle is puttin' fear in those you'd defeat, so they'll back down from the fight. He said he learned that from stories about Henry Morgan."

"So, in a way, Blackbeard looked scary to keep from hurting people. Is that right?" I asked.

"Aye. You could say it that way," Caesar replied. "He took ship after ship without spilling a drop of blood, and if he wanted to keep one of the ships he took, he put the captured crew on another and sent them on their way without harm."

The Crow snorted. "My take is that fear made stealing easier but 'twas more than a show for the crews of his targets. Thache's crewmen told of an unknown man walking below deck at night, like a giant gray ghost in the mist. They say it was the devil himself, looking for the Captain so they could plot evil together."

Henrietta shrugged, adding, "Now, there's a fairy tale if I ever heard one. That sounds more like the Captain putting on a fear show for his crew. I'd wager it took a little fear to keep his men in line."

Caesar added, "Or maybe it was the crew trying to put a little fear into you, Crow."

Adler took a menacing step toward Henrietta. "If that be the case, your daughter might toe the line, too, Widow. I've seen her in the tower talking to other men. The Captain loves her enough for now, but if he catches wind of her cheating on him, he might bend to his dark nature, and your precious Marybeth wouldn't like that, not even a little."

That was enough for me. I pushed between Henrietta and The Crow. "Marybeth is as true as a woman ever was. She loves the Captain with all her heart."

"And I reckon you'd say that, seeing as how I've noticed ye spending a bit of time alone with her, too," Crow said.

The Crow had powerful arms from climbing in the rigging, but I couldn't let his insult stand. So, I set down the peas and held my fists at the ready. "Don't spread rumors to stir up trouble. Marybeth is as good as gold."

Henrietta pulled me back to my chair and handed me my bowl, but then she turned to The Crow.

"Do you think I'm afraid of sailors?" she asked. "Do you think I fear ghosts in the dark or big men with frightful hair?"

"Well, if ye don't, ye should," The Crow said.

"My daughter and I have seen real monsters," the Widow replied. "And those frights weren't from faraway fairy tales. They were here on this river and so recent that my daughter could draw pictures of them for you."

We dropped our peas to listen, and images of a raging Blackbeard faded as Henrietta replaced them with worse terrors.

"The Cary Rebellion settled down, but yellow fever came the next summer, and drought followed that. Then, in September, when Marybeth was still a child, John Lawson, one of Bath's founders, was murdered by the Tuscarora. Her father and I tried to shield her from the horrible death of a friend, but the word spread. First, they slit Lawson's throat with his razor, stuck big pine splinters into his skin, and lit him alive to slowly bleed and burn."

"Why would they do that?" I asked.

"As I said, monsters spawn when evil festers in the hearts of men. The Tuscarora had had their fill of the settlers enslaving their people, cheating their traders, and taking their land. Even John Lawson said the natives were better to us than we were to them. They always fed us when we passed their lands, but we let them walk by our doors hungry. Too many of the European settlers were callous, unkind, and unwilling to understand the Tuscarora. So, the resentment built, and soon the natives, filled with hatred, sought vengeance. But regardless of the reason, both sides suffered once the last straw broke and war began."

As Henrietta retold the story, she closed her eyes against the terrors she remembered.

"By the end of September in 1711, The Tuscarora had had enough insults, and some of their leaders decided this land would be better without the English. On 23 September, about a week after they killed John, a horde of 500 Tuscarora and their allies struck in force throughout Bath County, armed with arrows, blades, and guns. Their full war paint showed one eye in a circle of white, the other blackened."

"Like painted eye patches?" I asked.

Hetty nodded. "They rampaged through farms, burning houses, massacring families, trampling crops, and butchering cattle. Then, they hit plantations along the Neuse and the south side of the Pamlico. And since they planned to drive us away, once they had murdered the farmers and their families, they set up a fear show of their own, leaving bodies in grotesque poses to make others run instead of standing their ground. Did Blackbeard ever display such terror as that?"

"Well, no, Ma'am," Caesar replied. "But as I said, Captain Thache tried to avoid killing."

Crow's smirk disappeared after the widow's story. "After such a raid, how can Bath still stand?" he asked.

"Have you looked around? Would you call this standing?" Hetty asked. "We escaped most of the early carnage but feared the terror coming to our doors, so Bert watched the creeks. The first sign of trouble wasn't the natives; 'twas those fleeing from them. Bert sounded the bell and passed his gun to me. Then I grabbed Marybeth, and we fought through the brambles to reach the ford on East Creek. We finally reached the makeshift fort, a refit of John Lawson's first house. My husband, with no protection but his axe, followed with as much food as he could carry. But we didn't feel much safer inside those palisaded walls."

"Did the Tuscarora reach the fort?" Caesar asked.

"No. The invaders hit more plantations on the edges than the main town, but we feared they'd be in our streets and creeks any minute. The men were still raisin' the palisade when the victims came—over 300 women and children screaming from the horrors they witnessed and shouting that the invaders were following.

"Every day more came, half-crazed with grief and fear, clawing over each other in their hurry to get behind the wall. Once inside, they spouted horrors we could barely stand to hear as they prayed for the men, sick, and elderly they left behind so the women and children could survive. There was little medicine and not much food, and we had no way to gather any. So, these remnants of families who had lived happily on their farms just days before now huddled in corners begging for their ration of cracked corn or beans."

"How long did you stay there?" I asked.

"We had little news from outside Bath Town, so we followed the soldiers' lead. When they came and went, the people did the same. And soon,

Bert wanted to return to our farm. Then, either he or I stayed watch on the roof, and he showed me a hiding place to run to with Marybeth in case the natives invaded."

"But you never used it?" I asked.

"No, but we came close. When we spotted a scouting party wearing eyepatch warpaint, Bert told me to run, but I couldn't leave him alone. He fired at the invaders while I reloaded, and Marybeth sat on the tower floor, pulling the bell rope. Then the invaders vanished into the woods."

"Was that the worst of it?" The Crow asked.

"No. Things went from bad to worse."

"How could it be worse?" Caesar asked.

"The Indian attacks settled for a while, but yellow fever came next. It took my husband, leaving my young daughter with no father to protect her. So, I latched Marybeth in the chicken coop while I buried Bert beside the garden. Then, we returned to the fort.

"All the time, the Tuscarora continued fighting until we finally signed a treaty three years ago. But the war and fever left us with shattered families and few men to rebuild our homes and tend our fields."

She turned to face The Crow.

"As I said, monsters breed inside men when they give way to the evil inside them. Those few years ago, monstrous invaders shattered all we gave our blood and bones to build while women and children went insane with fear and grief. Some of them that lived became monsters, too, barely more than angry, hopeless, hate-ridden shells. But my girl and I looked the monsters in the eye, survived illness, and endured men who brought terrors of another kind, coming to blows over who believed what.

"Who cares who can sit in which government seat when you can't make peace over who fishes which stream or sleeps in which field? Ghosts of those monsters and the beast-like victims they spawned walk this ground, but we don't fear them. We were among those who helped each other and defeated the tormentors. Despite one assault after another, survival was our victory."

She set her peas down and faced The Crow. "Do you think we're afraid of a few dozen pirates? We are not afraid of you; we need you. And if you are worth the bother, we welcome you. We're still building back what we lost. And, pirates or not, you might help us if you grow your goodness and not your evil."

"And if we don't behave?" The Crow asked.

Henrietta stood up, poured her peas into a drying tray, slapped the large sack of unshelled in the middle of us, and dusted her hands on her apron. She stared The Crow in the eye, saying, "If ye are no help, then we have no need of 'e in our town."

Then, she went to the yard and grabbed Bert Bellieu's axe from the chopping block. She held the axe across her chest as she turned to face us. With eyes narrowed and lips as tight as a trap, she said, "Shell the peas." Then she began to split logs.

Should I say something? Could I comfort her? "Widow Bellieu …," I began.

"Not … *whack* … another … *whack* … sound," she replied. And tiny as she was, she ripped pine to tinder between each word.

***

When we finished shelling peas, Hetty served dinner, and we were free to choose what we did in the afternoon. Coleman brought her three large trout for supper, Caesar took special care of the goats, and I went to the Bride's Tower to scout the farm. I viewed Bert Bellieu's brass bell differently as I imagined Tuscarora warriors coming through the pines.

When Oma returned that Sunday, she waved at me from the landing and joined me in the tower. I quizzed her on what she knew about the Tuscarora War and why the natives acted with such violence. She nodded and took a few moments to word her reply.

"It was the same as other conflicts we had with the natives," she said. "Foreigners washed over the ancestral lands of those before us, and the European invaders didn't respect their wise men, warriors, or way of life.

"It's usually not just one thing, but one thing after another. The Tuscarora were proud and dignified people who felt no one responded to their complaints of insult and unfair trading. No one can tolerate such abuse forever."

"I guess we learned what happens in such cases," I replied.

"The treatment was wrong, and the response was wrong, too. But sadly, we humans seem to be slow learners." When I nodded, she added, "So, you found a moral lesson today, even though you didn't attend church."

"I learned a *few* lessons," I replied.

But learning wasn't over for the day. Those who spent the day in Bath brought revelations, too.

20 Secrets of Bath

Aurora Saunters

"We're waiting for you, Elizabeth," Edmund Chamberlain called. Then he smiled at us over his shoulder. "Mr. Knight and his wife send their regrets, but Lizzy will be delighted with a new audience for her chatter." Then with a wink, he added, "And I'll be glad of more hands to help keep her still."

Drake whispered, "Is this *the* Elizabeth Glover—the one we expected when we commuted?"

I pressed a finger to my lips as I nodded. We were new to Bath, so no one expected us to know Lizzy, and they'd never guess she might be our ancestor.

The little girl's dress and the ribbon around her straw hat were the color of summer lettuce, and her neckerchief was an oversized silk scarf printed with green leaves that matched her outfit. She hopped into the boat beside Edmund Chamberlain, craning her neck to read the words on the paper he studied. But when Mr. Chamberlain put the page away, Lizzy twisted around to face the three passengers who shared her boat.

"I remember you," she said, pointing to me. "You took my prayer book." She held up the same book that had transported Drake and me to Bath.

"I'm so sorry," I replied. "I wasn't sure who it belonged to."

She scrunched her lips into a knot. "All is well now. I have it for Sunday, and Papa Knight wrote my name in it." Lizzy flashed the name inscribed on the inside cover before turning to her escort.

"Do you know if Penelope will sit with us today?" she asked.

"Not that I'm aware of," he replied. "But Miss Penelope may sit with her Papa Eden if they decide to come."

"I'm glad she isn't here. She won't let me move from my seat."

"You should sit still anyway, Lizzy. Now, and in the meeting, too. Your mama said so," Chamberlain replied. "She'll be unhappy if Mrs. Thache has a bad report on your behavior."

Elizabeth twirled around again, examining Marybeth's yellow print dress and lace shawl. "Your blue wedding dress was beautiful, but this gown is pretty, too."

Marybeth smiled politely. "Why, thank you, Miss Lizzy."

"I thought the Captain might marry Penelope. She's very wealthy, you know. But he married you instead."

Chamberlain tore his eyes from the page as he pulled the girl's arm. "Turn forward, Lizzy. Mind your manners." But the girl had the last word as she twisted back toward us.

"'Tis just as well; Penelope has a new beau now. And she lent me her scarf to match my hat." Then she beamed a sunny smile before settling forward again.

Marybeth's smile faded as she turned to me with eyes wide.

Drake shrugged. "She's just a kid," he whispered, rolling his eyes.

Mr. Chamberlain changed the subject. "Before the war, the scripture readings were held at Christopher Gale's house by the grist mill, but these days we meet in our makeshift fort refitted from a house that once belonged to John Lawson. There it is on Towne Point," he added, pointing to a palisaded structure on the nearby landing.

The fence, made of tall, masting timbers from the shipyard, was much newer than the house it surrounded. The home had two stories and an attic, and like the house at Plum Point, there was a bell tower on the roof.

Marybeth's jaw tightened. "They rang the bell here as Papa did at our house," she said, frowning. "From either bell, eight rings warned the town that trouble was coming, and we were to rush here for shelter."

The young bride sat silent for a moment, twisting the end of her shawl. Then her frown deepened, and with shallow breath, she said, "I should not have come today; the fort dredges up frightening memories."

Chamberlain turned to her with soft eyes. "I understand, Mrs. Thache, and if you like, the men will take you and Lizzy home, but I must stay; Mr. Knight has assigned me other duties."

I patted Marybeth's hand to comfort her, but as Lawson's Fort at Bath did not survive till my century, I was curious to see it, so I added, "If you don't mind, I'd at least like to see inside the fort. And if you prefer, Drake can sit with you by the water, and then Lizzy and I can join you for tea. Either way, we won't interrupt Mr. Chamberlain's business."

"I hope I can visit the shipyard," Drake said. "Maybe I can show Captain Harding what I've learned about rowing."

Marybeth set her jaw stiff and nodded. "Yes, we don't want to trouble Mr. Chamberlain after he was kind enough to bring us here, and Mrs. Knight must feel it's important to have Lizzy at the service. Come, I'll go with you. I should at least try."

"Gale's Wharf, please, Mr. Onslow," Chamberlain commanded, and we rowed past the Towne Point landing.

Onslow and crew pulled the boat to shore not far from the center of Water Street. And when we disembarked, a boardwalk connecting the landing to the street saved our shoes from the sand.

When we reached the Grist Mill, Edmund referred to his paper, and by the time he looked up, his young charge had run to the Mill fence. "Leave the horse to his day of rest, Lizzy," he called. And when she returned to our group, he wagged a finger at her. "Behave now, as your Papa said. Your Mama will hear if you do not." Then after wishing us a good day, Chamberlain turned northward while we walked south to the fort.

Lizzy constantly chattered, dancing circles around us as we walked till she noticed Marybeth's puckered brow.

"There's nothing to be afraid of, Marybeth. I've been here dozens of times," she said. "I hope my friend, Isabella, is here. If she is, may I sit with her?"

Aurora raised an eyebrow as she turned to the girl. "Perhaps you will both sit with us. I think your mother would like that best."

"Very well," she replied, "but I won't be noisy; I promise to be good."

But she was still full of news for Marybeth.

"Mother said Mr. Schute will read about Noah's ark today, and I like that story. My dear Papa gave me a toy ark, and if I'm good, Papa Knight promised to buy me a pair of pelicans for it. It can't have every animal in the world without pelicans."

"Why would pelicans need an ark?" Drake asked, grinning. "Can't they just fly over the water?"

"Pay no mind to my grandson, Lizzy," Aurora said. "He's just playing smarty breeches today."

The bouncing girl paused long enough to find an answer. "Well, Mister-Drake-Smarty-Breeches, perhaps you aren't so very clever. Birds get tired, too, you know. They can't fly for forty days and nights straight."

Drake's smile broadened as he snapped his fingers. "You've got me there, girly. I guess your ark needs pelicans, after all."

Lizzy giggled, and a smile broke through Marybeth's grim face. "I believe I can stay, Aurora," Mary said. "It might be comforting to hear a story of God watching over a ship."

The little girl skipped forward and turned around to skip backward, facing Marybeth. "Do you want a ship story because your husband is at sea?"

"That's right. Captain Thache is away, and I miss him," Marybeth said, then added, "Come here. Stand still a moment so I can fix that scarf for you."

After all her skipping and twirling, Lizzy had yanked the scarf free, so Marybeth pulled her close long enough to straighten the cloth and fold the square into a triangle. She paused to study the letters *ML* embroidered along the hem before repositioning the neckerchief and setting Lizzy free.

The girl giggled and led us to a small group waiting among the earthen banks and ditches in front of the tall, wooden barricade. There, she took the hand of a slightly older girl, and the two of them scouted for pretty pebbles at the water's edge.

"That's Isabella Lawson," Marybeth said as we sat on a bench by the fort gate. "This building was the first house her father built."

"Was that the same John Lawson that Mr. Chamberlain mentioned?" Drake asked.

"Aye," she replied. "I barely remember Mr. Lawson, but his wife, Hannah, helped feed those of us in the fort. Mother said the Widow Lawson mourned for her husband by caring for other widows and their children."

Drake could hardly sit still longer than Lizzy. So, he walked around the fenced yard, peeking through the planks to examine every inch of the fort.

"Are those gun ports?" he asked, pointing to holes cut through the logs of the top story.

Marybeth twisted her handkerchief. "Yes. The garrison slept in the attic, rotating watch in the tower and standing guard at the ports. It eased our fear to have them watching over us, but no one could stop the hunger pangs or the grief we shared." She turned to me and whispered, "I wish Edward were here."

A scraping noise stopped the conversation.

"What's that?" Lizzy asked, turning as our lector, Mr. Schute, pushed aside the great wooden beam bolting the gate. He welcomed us inside the walls and pointed to the log house's open door.

Lizzy tugged Mr. Schute's arm. "Is there food in the house? My friend is hungry," she said.

Marybeth blushed as she pulled the girl to her seat.

"Shall I fetch Mother?" Isabella asked.

"No, Dear," Marybeth replied. "Lizzy misunderstood. I said I was hungry when we had to shelter here some years ago, but I remember the thoughtful attention of your mother." Isabella smiled and ran to Hannah Lawson, who beckoned from the door.

"Ah, yes," Mr. Shute said. "Hunger was common in those days, and even now, we suffer from it."

Four rows of six chairs waited for us inside the fort, and since there were only twelve attendees, it was no trouble for us to find a row together. Mr. Schute ignored the low attendance as he greeted each cluster of gatherers.

When he came to our row, he patted Lizzy's hat, saying, "I know Miss Elizabeth Glover well, but who is your company today, Lizzy?"

The girl grinned, happy to play hostess, as she introduced us. "Mr. Schute, you may know Mis'ress Marybeth Thache, wife of Captain Thache, and our friends are Widow Aurora Saunters and her grandson, Drake." Then she curtsied.

Schute bowed in greeting and turned to Marybeth. "Those gathered here hope that your husband and his friends may help with the hunger pangs we still feel in Bath." Then he turned to me to explain, "After the drought, war, and sickness, our fields are more barren than usual, and European ships pass us for bigger ports in Charleston and beyond. So, we look forward to Captain Thache's ship bringing supplies and food to this port, and his friends are welcome workers as we rebuild."

A man nearby sniffed before adding. "Thache *may* help *if* he and his men do not rob us blind first."

Mr. Schute turned to the new arrival, saying, "Mis'ress Marybeth Thache, allow me to introduce Mr. Edward Moseley. As the Treasurer of our province, he is the guardian of taxes, income, and theft too, it seems."

With a hint of a smug smile, Moseley asked, "Are you here to pray for the Captain, Mrs. Thache? I hear he may need a little guidance from Heaven."

Marybeth stiffened but found a ready reply. "I pray for my husband at every opportunity, Sir. But just as he now sails in service of Bath Town, my friends and I are doing a neighborly favor for Tobias Knight. And 'tis our pleasure to be here with Lizzy."

Moseley's smile faded, and he moved to sit alone in the back row where he could watch everyone else.

When Mr. Schute passed us again on his way to the podium, Marybeth grabbed his sleeve. "Please pray for the Captain to return home safely," she begged.

With a kind smile, Schute patted her hand before moving to the Bible stand in front of the room.

Marybeth had flinched at Moseley's insult, but Schute's kind words encouraged her, and she listened intently to Noah's story.

After a chorus of "Praise God to Whom all Blessings Flow" and prayers, we stood to leave. Mr. Schute mingled among those gathered, but Moseley observed and listened more than he conversed. Most of those who greeted us had questions about the Captain, his men, and we strangers to

Bath. But once we had satisfied their curiosity, we left the fort and walked toward the Marsh Moon Tavern for tea.

The smell of pit-cooked pork reached us, drawing us to the Tavern yard, where the scents of ducks roasting on spits and sweets baking in brick ovens filled the air. Drake looked longingly toward the shipyard at the north end of the street, but the aroma was too tempting. He decided to stay long enough for tea.

We took our familiar table by the windows, and while we waited, Edmund Chamberlain walked past the mill in a civil but smileless chat with Mr. Moseley. Their conversation ended when a stocky, red-haired man joined the group. Chamberlain tipped his hat before continuing his brisk walk toward the shipyard while Moseley and his companion watched as if curious about Chamberlain's destination. They must have lost sight of him because they soon entered the Marsh Moon, choosing a table in the back.

Then Sal arrived to take our order, and I thought no more of Moseley.

"So nice to see you again," she said, beaming at our young companion. "And Miss Elizabeth Glover, 'tis a pleasure to see you here today." Then she turned back to her friend. "But where is your mother, Marybeth? The fever doesn't still have her, does it?"

"Nice to see you, too, Sally," Marybeth replied. "Mother is quite well, thank you. She'll come with us next time."

"It smells wonderful here," Drake said. "Mr. Schute said Bath was still hungry, but I can't see how anyone could go hungry here."

"We do our best," Sal replied. "The folks here know that we feed locals more often than strangers, so some men trade us fish and game for a well-cooked meal, and the folks at the grist mill put us at the top of their customer list. The local farmers scrape the bottoms of barrels to put meals on the table, and we collect a little of this and that to make recipes from what we have."

"Do you have tea?" I asked.

"None from England, Ma'am, but we have gingerroot, lemon balm, and a few types of mint. And today, we have gingersnaps and peach tarts, too."

Lizzy's eyes widened, and she licked her lips in anticipation. "Did you say peaches?"

"One of the planters had a booming crop this year, and he traded two bushels for cornmeal and silver from Cap'n Thache's men."

Soon, Sal brought a tray of treats and a pot of gingerroot tea brightened with a bit of orange peel. I sipped my tea as Drake and Lizzy dug spoons into their tarts, and Marybeth chose two gingersnaps.

Then, as Sal set a honey pot on the table, she turned to Marybeth. "So, how is life as the wife of Captain Thache?" she asked.

Marybeth beamed. "'Tis happier than I ever imagined, although 'tis less pleasant when he must be away."

"I see you have another lovely frock. Is that a gift from the Captain, as well?"

Marybeth blushed. "'Tis one of the gifts he gave me when I promised to marry him."

Sal nodded. "Several girls in town are quite interested in the men the Captain brought to Bath. Sadly, the sailors don't always show the best manners, and they get much rowdier at the Hornpipe Tavern than in the Marsh Moon. But despite that, we may have more weddings coming soon. One of the girls has a new dress, too."

Lizzy looked up from her tart. "Does it have a hat to match, like mine?" she asked.

Sal grinned, saying, "As I heard, she only got the dress yesterday, and I haven't seen it yet, but if it has a hat, it couldn't be as lovely as yours."

"Who is her beau?" Marybeth asked. "I wonder if I've met him."

Lizzy tugged at my sleeve. "May I have a gingersnap, too?"

I passed a snap to the girl, then repeated the question, "Yes, Sal, who is the beau?"

"I don't know him yet," Sal replied. "But I'm sure I will know soon. By then, perhaps, I'll be promised, too."

Marybeth perked her ears at the news. "Oh, will you now? And who might you be fond of, Sal?" she asked, smiling broadly.

Now it was Sally's turn to blush. "I can't say just yet, but I might have my eye on a captain, too. We will see how that goes when the ship returns."

A bell tinkled as a new customer entered, and Sally rushed to attend to a raw-boned, weathered man with a touch of gray at his temples. He carried a large stone under each arm. Sally smiled as she examined each one and sat them on her counter. Then, with a nod, she left him, and Mr. Malone, the tavern owner, soon joined the new customer.

"Could that be her beau?" Marybeth asked. "He has the air of the sea about him."

Drake shook his head. "No, I met that fellow on our first day here. That's Thomas Harding of the shipyard. He took me on a boat that day."

"Is he a sailor?" I asked.

"More than that," Drake replied. "He's a captain, and he builds ships."

While Harding spoke to the tavern man, Sally returned to our table.

Lizzy impatiently tugged Sally's sleeve, asking, "What are those stones?"

Sally patted the girl's shoulder. "Captain Harding brings those to us lately. We trade them for food that he takes back to his home."

"What do you do with them?" Lizzy asked.

Marybeth wondered, too. “How can stones be worth food?”

“Just a moment. I’ll show you,” Sal replied.

When Thomas Harding left with two food parcels for his family, Sal fetched one of the stones from the counter and brought it to our table.

“Here it is,” she said. “You might think this is an ordinary ballast stone, but ’tis more. Guess what it is.”

Drake turned the stone, and we saw someone had carved around the surface to show an animal with wings, a beak, and tail feathers. “Is it a dove?” I asked. “Or a crow?”

“Captain Harding brings us all sorts of figures. We’ve seen doves, cardinals, and owls. Sometimes the rocks show faces or angels. We can sell these or trade them for ingredients we need here.”

“But if food is so scarce, who would want to trade it for a rock?” I asked.

Sally nodded. “’Tis a question I had too, but Mr. Malone reminded me that hunger is not the only pain we feel in Bath. We grieve over our lost loved ones, too.”

“’Tis true,” Marybeth replied. “During the war, some women cried more over bodies left to the wolves than for their hungry children. And even those buried had nothing but a sand pile covered by a few loose stones to mark their graves. We were lucky to get bricks over my Papa.”

“Now, they buy these stones to honor the dead,” Sal replied. “They choose a figure that reminds them of the ones lost and use these to mark the graves. Sometimes they want something fancier and choose a piece of driftwood carved into a cross or engraved with a name.”

“Does Mr. Harding carve these?” Drake asked.

“I don’t believe so,” Sal replied. “He has only brought them to us lately. I think one of his new boatwrights makes them. I don’t know who he is, but that’s his maker’s mark.”

Sal turned the stone to show the bottom. There was a mark that looked like two tall letters X standing side by side, touching at the points.

“Does someone use that mark for his name?” I asked.

“Not that I’ve ever seen,” she replied.

Lizzy studied the stone. “Does he make pelicans?”

Sally patted the girl as she bent to pick up the stone. “I can’t say I ever saw a stone pelican,” she replied.

“Let’s go see Captain Harding,” Lizzy said, pushing back her chair and tugging at my sleeve.

Drake was eager to visit the shipyard, too. So, I paid Sally for our tea and a package with extra tarts and gingersnaps for those on Plum Point, and we continued our walk toward the shipyard. Unfortunately, Mr.

Chamberlain was bound for the boat dock when he met us on Water Street. He was again pouring over his ledger page, and this time I saw the signature of Governor Charles Eden. Chamberlain had completed Knight's business, but he had a surprise for Lizzy.

"Your Papa Knight asked me to purchase this for you, Miss Glover," he said as he presented two pelicans carved from driftwood.

"They are just right," she said, beaming as she grabbed for the pelicans. "They will fit on my ark."

"May I see?" I asked. She passed one to me and one to Marybeth. The carver had marked both pieces with the double X symbol. Drake studied the mark, and when he shifted his finger to cover the top and then the bottom half of the symbol, I saw it, too. The top half made the letter W, and the bottom half was M. Perhaps the maker was Wallace McNeil.

Lizzy snatched her pelicans back, and during the sail home, she made them dance on the boat's bench, and once we reached Plum Point, she begged the rowers to hurry back to Knight's Landing and her Noah's ark.

When we disembarked, Drake ran to find Ody, and Marybeth changed her pretty yellow dress to work clothes before rushing to the Bride's Tower to look for Edward's sails.

"There was no sign of him," she said, her face as gloomy as a morning fog as she stopped by my room. "But I found this beside Edward's spyglass on the tower. Did you buy it in Bath, Aurora?" she asked,

"I haven't been to the tower yet," I replied. "Henrietta is unwrapping her peach tart, and Drake and Ody aren't in the house. What's in there?" She opened the parcel, revealing a package of sugared orange peel. Of course, that meant nothing to me, but Marybeth's smile lifted the fog.

After supper, the crewmates went to their quarters, and the others of us enjoyed a starry night on the porch. We shared stories of our day, and while we cheered Hetty for her brave speech, the boys were just as interested in our town gossip.

Ody and Drake did not join our game of guessing who might be carving ballast stones into grave ornaments. And when Drake brought up Lizzy's comment that Penelope was Edward's early love interest, Marybeth trembled. So, Ody dragged Drake off for a quick patrol of the yard.

That left us ladies to consider the possibilities of more among Thache's crew settling down with the women of Bath. Of course, any of the ladies might be interested in the wealth and vigor of the town's newest citizens, but who had been there long enough to become acquainted and bring gifts to his lady?

Henrietta guessed that the romance had started before Captain Thache and his crew left on their voyage, but her daughter disagreed.

"Sally said her friend got the new dress only days ago, and all the crew was at sea then, weren't they?" Marybeth asked.

"Perhaps the sailor had a dress made for his girl, but it was delivered only recently. Could that be it?" I asked.

"No one except seamstresses for Governor Eden and Tobias Knight could produce a fine garment like the ones the Captain gave Marybeth," Henrietta said. "And I'd consider it unlikely that any of Thache's crew could hire such work from those households."

"Was no one left in town besides Caesar and the Crow?" I asked.

"Edward needed every man for the voyage," Marybeth replied. "He only left those two to care for us."

"Then could one of them be the mystery beau?" I asked.

"Let's find out tomorrow. 'Tis time for me to get ready for bed," Marybeth replied.

When I started to bed, events in Bath swirled in the darkness. Mr. Moseley had practically branded Captain Thache as a thief. And who was the man who joined Edward Mosely for tea? While Tobias Knight's ledger wasn't my concern, and neither was Chamberlain's business with the other men in town, the matter poked at my curiosity.

And where had I seen those initials, ML?

21 Nagging Doubts

Marybeth Thache

It had been a long, eventful Sunday with all that happened in Bath. But Aurora Saunters wasn't as worn out by it as I. When I went to my room, she was there first, folding the dress I wore to the scripture service.

"Are you looking for me, Aurora?"

"No, my dear, I saw your nice dress lying on the bed and thought I'd put it away for you. But look at this." She unfastened the back laces to show me the letters *M* and *L,* finely embroidered on the facing. "We saw this mark today," she said.

"It's like the mark on Lizzy's scarf."

"Aye, the one that Eden's ward, Penelope, lent to her."

"Do you think my dress and this scarf once belonged to the same woman?" I asked.

"No. The initials are in the wrong place for an owner's mark. 'Tis likely a maker's label, and no plantation seamstress would bother with one."

"So, do you think they came from the same shop? Maybe in Charleston or Williamsburg?" I asked.

"'Tis possible, but your wedding dress looked French to me. Is it marked the same way as this one?"

I dug into the chest at the end of my bed and pulled out the blue dress. The maker's mark was in the same place and identical except for the thread color. "What does this mean?" I asked.

"Only that one seamstress made all three garments," Aurora replied. "And they could have been in the same shop on this side of the ocean."

"And if Edward gave that scarf to Penelope, they were all three in his hands."

"Yes … *if* …," Aurora replied.

"What else could it mean?" I asked.

"Edward might know. Let's save that question for his return, shall we?"

Aurora helped me fold the dresses and return them to the chest, then she patted my hand, saying, "Don't fret over what *might* have been, girl. We have enough troubles that *are*."

The Widow Saunters was right. If Edward had a romantic interest before he met me, it did not affect our marriage. But, the thought of it made me restless again. I needed a moment on the tower to look for the North Star and think of my husband. On my way there, I was surprised to hear Ody and Drake in the Captain's den.

"Are you sure it was in here?" Ody asked.

"I think so, but I'm not positive," Drake replied.

"Do you want me to try to find it?" the older boy asked.

"No, it could be dangerous."

I stepped through the door. "What is dangerous?" I asked. "What are you looking for?"

"Er … hm … it was a shell I dropped. It had sharp knobs on it," Drake replied.

I searched the floor. "Well, I don't see anything dangerous to step on here. Do you need it right now?"

"No. No, ma'am. It's not necessary."

What were those boys up to? I shrugged past them on my way to the tower but turned at the hatch. "Please be careful with Edward's things. They might be important to his travels."

Ody stepped between me and Drake, who still scanned the floor for his elusive shell. "No, Ma'am. We won't touch a thing."

I nodded and continued my climb. The sky was clear enough to find Polaris, but I had to face the other direction to watch for the *Adventure's* sails billowing over the Pamlico River. I wasn't surprised that I had no luck. Edward warned me the voyage would take weeks, but looking for him was my way of wishing him home.

I dropped to my knees to begin my prayer for safety, but when Ody and Drake popped through the hatch, I turned to greet them.

"Sorry to interrupt, Ma'am," Drake said. "Chamberlain brought a note a while ago asking Caesar to row to Knight's landing tonight. Caesar thought you should know in case you saw him from the lookout."

"Oh, yes, Caesar spends some time helping Mr. Knight, but usually not while Edward is away. I hope there is no problem." I said.

"No problem, Ma'am. The jollyboat was at the landing, so Caesar is on his way," Drake replied.

"Where else would the boat be?" I asked.

"Oh, sometimes The Crow has his reasons to row, too," Ody said.

"Usually fishing," Drake added. "Do you think he might be the sweetheart Sal spoke of?"

"Where would he get a dress to deliver to a sweetheart?" I asked. Then I thought of the dresses Edward had given me. Nothing was missing from my chest, but had this new dress in town come from the same source? Weakened by the thought, I dropped to the stool by the lantern.

"What is it, Marybeth?" Ody asked.

Drake knelt by me. "Do you need water? How can we help?"

It took several tries, and the words stuck in my throat, but I finally spit it out. Two garments to me and one to Penelope Golland had likely been gifts from Edward to women he favored. I didn't speak my buried fear, but the boys saw it. *Had Edward shown favor to someone else?*

Ody was the first to try cheering me. "If he had such feelings for Penelope, they are long gone. He's your husband, now."

"And we have no idea where the dress Sal spoke of came from," Drake added.

Tears welled as I replied, "But Sal said she might get a new dress, too. And she has her eye on a captain."

"There's more than one captain in Bath," Ody said. "We met Captain Harding, and ships besides his come to this port."

Drake nodded, "Besides that, Captain Thache is at sea and couldn't deliver anything to anyone in Bath."

Ody offered me his handkerchief, and I wiped my eyes, nodding. The boys were right. I was silly. "Thank you, both. Forgive me for letting emotion cloud my judgment."

But as I returned the handkerchief to Ody, his eyes brightened.

"*Of course*. It must be the Crow. The night before Edward sailed, one of the oarsmen from Knight's boat took a sack up the gut toward the crew shack."

My worry returned as I added, "And when we saw Coleman the other night, he had a sack in his hands. But we checked, and it wasn't from our cellar. And that was after Edward sailed, so where did it come from?"

"Maybe it wasn't inside the cellar," Drake said. "Could it have been inside the tunnel but outside the door?"

"It's possible, but where did he take it?" Ody asked.

"We know he rows to Bath sometimes. He usually claims to be night fishing." Drake snapped his fingers. "He had that sack with him when he rowed to Bath the day after Edward left. That's when he came back wearing the fancy blue coat."

The Crow had said Edward gave him that coat. Could he have given him a dress for his girl, too?

"Do you think The Crow visits a lass?" I asked. "But where would Sal or her friend meet young men at night? The owner doesn't allow the girls to carouse at the Marsh Moon."

Ody scratched his head. "It could be anywhere they agree to meet … if she can escape her family."

"Maybe she's old enough to make her own choices," Drake said.

I nodded. "Aye, the war and the fever left plenty of young widows in Bath."

"We can visit the town and see what we can find out," Ody said. "But how can we spy on The Crow if he has the jollyboat?"

"There's no easy way," I replied. "When Mother and I were forced to run, we had friends to ferry us to the other side of East Creek."

Drake smiled. "I have an idea." He looked at Ody, nodding. "We know a man with a boat."

The boys left me to craft their plan, and I finished my prayer. No matter the circumstances, I wished Edward a safe journey home. We'd work out the rest when he returned—if my trust in him could hold till then.

22 The Hornpipe

Drake Saunters

For a day or so, Marybeth was worried by Sal's gossip in Bath, but she finally shrugged off her doubts. She was cheerful when she shared her sugared orange peel with Ody and me, whispering that it was likely a gift from Wallace. Soon after that, McNeil left another present on the tower, a seashell bracelet, and Marybeth's smile brightened even more.

Wallace's visits worked for us, too. He was just the helper we needed to carry out our plans to spy on The Crow. So, we decided to watch for his next secret visit, and when we met him in the tower, he confirmed what I had suspected. He was the stone carver in Bath under the protection of Captain Harding, his employer.

McNeil suggested we watch the goings-on in the Hornpipe Tavern, where the regular customers were sailors, shipbuilders, and their friends. He agreed to show us how to observe those in the tavern without revealing ourselves. And if we needed it, he would bring us home on one of Captain Harding's tender boats. Ody had been watching The Crow come and go, and he decided Thursday nights might be the best to watch what happened in Bath.

As Ody had predicted, after dinner on Thursday, Coleman said he'd be fishing for red drum at the Towne Point and likely miss supper. So, we asked to ride with him into town.

Once The Crow was out of the house, Grandma cornered us to find out what we were up to. Ody explained that Marybeth had asked us to watch The Crow, so Grandma pulled us aside, whispering, "Remember who you are and *when* you are. Don't forget the dangers."

Ody nodded. "You said I'm the field leader, and we're here to help Drake learn the ropes. Show us a little trust; these are risks we are ready for."

Grandma's face was grim, so I chimed in. "We stayed here to help protect Marybeth and her mother from the trouble coming. In Bath Town, we can find out more about what's brewing. We can do this."

"I wonder," she said, shaking her head. She rested a hand on Ody's shoulder, sighing as she asked, "Will you use your pendants at the first hint of trouble?"

Our heads bobbed, so she sighed as she fished several bits of eight and passed half to me and half to Ody. "Even pirates go to bed early. Be back by dark, do you hear? If I must come to you, I'll be smackdab in the middle of your trouble. So don't make me wait too long."

"We won't," I shouted. Grandma still frowned as my cousin and I flashed wide grins and ran to plan our evening.

***

The Crow didn't say much as he steered us into Bath's Towne Point, but once he waved us off he headed for the East Branch, and we struggled to keep from running on our way to the shipyard.

The workers, busy with their last tasks of sawing, fitting, and shaping, paid no attention to us. So, we finally asked someone who directed us to Captain Thomas Harding's home between the shipyard and the rest of town. A fenced garden by the street nearly hid his townhouse, but luckily, we found Harding bent over pepper plants by the street. Once we waved to get his attention, he stood to greet us.

"I remember you, fellows," he said. "Are you back for another turn with our periaugers?"

Ody checked around for who else might overhear before saying, "Sir, we are here to speak to Carver."

The captain looked left and right, but when he saw no one else nearby, he opened his gate and waved us inside the fence. "What carver do you mean?"

"We mean Wallace no harm, Sir," I said, "but he told us to ask for him as Carver."

"Stay here," he said. Then he turned with a warning finger in the air. "Don't eat my wife's peppers. You'll regret it." Then, after a few minutes, he beckoned us to follow him through the garden and to a tent beside his house. It was Wallace's live-in workshop.

"Be brief," Harding said, then turning to Wallace, he added, "You risk peril on yourself and my family if you don't take care."

Once we were alone, Wallace asked how he could help.

"We are concerned about one of the men at Plum Point, and we want to follow your suggestion and watch for him at the Hornpipe," Ody said.

"We fear there's thieving going on within Thache's crew," I added.

Wallace shrugged. "And why should I care about who steals from Blackbeard?"

"Because right now, if they steal from Thache, they steal from Marybeth," Ody replied.

"More than that, Marybeth can't sort her feelings without the truth," I said. "She must know who to trust. You said you would be happy for her if Thache is a good husband. So, help her find what she needs to know."

From his scowl, I guessed McNeil didn't like his choices, but he finally agreed. "At least you won't have to go far. The Hornpipe is just across the rail fence there," he said, pointing to the south edge of Harding's lot. "I'll help you enter the inn and show you enough ropes to survive."

"It won't be too dangerous for you?" Drake asked.

He shrugged, "With most of Thache's men at sea, there is less danger for me tonight, but don't speak my name. I'll leave if I must, and you'll be on your own."

Once we agreed to his terms, Wallace asked us to meet him in the tent at sunset. "We'll find a corner before the Hornpipe gets crowded. It's just across the next fence," he said, "But enter from the street, just a few paces down the way."

Then he directed us through the garden and back to Water Street. We hadn't gone ten paces when we saw the sign, The *Hornpipe Tavern, Silas Van Horn, Proprietor*. We had missed it before because, like Captain Harding's house, this tavern sat deep in its lot, but now we knew where to look.

The sign on the building entry showed a pipe resembling an ancient, curved clarinet leaning against a tankard. This tavern had no glass windows, but the shutters were open, and a steady stream of shipmen on the path to the inn proved the bar was packed, even at this early hour.

Ody and I had supper at the Marsh Moon, and Sal may have wondered why we kept ordering more cider, but we lingered as long as we dared. After that, we watched the old horse grind grain at the mill, and then we tarried by the creekfront, watching boats come and go until most businesses closed. By the time Tobias Knight's rowboat headed toward his plantation, the sun was setting, and it was time to meet Carver near his tent.

The sky dimmed under cloud cover, and Wallace lent us each a brown poplin cloak to hide our clothes. Then we traded our tricorns for brimmed wool hats like the sailors wore. Wallace, similarly shrouded, joined us. He pointed to a spot where trees shielded the fence, and we climbed over. Then we kept to the trees until we were near a back entry to the Hornpipe.

"Wait here," Wallace said. "Find me inside in five minutes. Don't speak my name."

We found him at a dark table under the stairs, where we could watch without drawing attention. The bar crowd had thinned since supper time, but with the sunset, it began to fill again.

"Here ye are, Jim," the serving girl said as she brought us three glasses and a pitcher of ale. And as I had no experience with ale and didn't know what it would do to me, I was pleased to see that she also sat three ciders on the table.

"You ordered well, … Jim, is it?" Ody asked.

"Every crew has a Jim. Every tavern has a Mary," he replied. "And none of them ask questions if you pay up as you should."

Our corner, well out of the lantern light, grew darker as the sun lowered, and we chatted quietly while the crowd thickened.

These men may not have been pirates, at least not lately, but they were men of the sea: shipbuilders or makers of ships' stores such as tar, pitch, and staves. They sat among the fishermen and old men who had made their living from the sea but could sail no longer. They drank, laughed, and told bawdy stories. And when one salt picked up a hornpipe to play, another did his best at a sailor's jig.

But what surprised me most was the sprinkling of women who joined them. Were these the young widows Marybeth had described? Or were they lonely girls fishing in depleted ponds for a mate? A few of them cast flirting glances at our table, but we sat in the shadows and under the pulled-down brims of our hats. They had no idea what types of men hid in the dim corner, so they soon flitted to the lights of brighter lanterns.

Then, one of the moths found a tall, thin man sitting on a bar stool.

Ody nudged me, whispering, "Coleman."

The Crow turned to the woman, grinning broadly. "There's my Colleen," and he had her spin around to model her new clothes. Her dress was bright and well made, like the ones Thache had given to Marybeth. Could this be the prospective bride and her beau?

"Ah, that green sets off your lovely red hair," Crow said. "Come have a drink with me, girl."

Smoke from a dozen pipes fogged the room, and eyes glazed under one too many ales. Then, the hornpiper picked up his beat. Hands clapped. Sailors sang along if they knew the words and belted out a chorus of *la-la-las* if they did not.

Then two sailors, with glasses held high, began their jigs, and one grabbed a girl to dance with him. She wiggled and twirled as she kicked up her heels to please the dancer and the crowd. Then, the other jigger grabbed Colleen, pulling her to her feet.

With a throaty laugh, she joined him and moved from man to man as they took turns as her partner. But when she began to tire, her spins were less controlled, and she fell against one man as she danced with another. Ale spilled onto her dress, and as she stopped to brush it away, someone else grabbed her, pulling at the laces on the back of her dress.

She spun toward him, loosening the laces even more till the white chemise was all that covered her back. The Crow limped to her rescue, pushing the jiggers aside. "Let her be. You'll ruin her frock."

But the crowd had other ideas. "Let the girl have her fun," they cried. "I prefer her without the laces."

When the blows started, Carver slipped away through some unknown door.

The men forgot dancing as they began bludgeoning each other. Finally, the barman, Silas van Horn, came round the counter, stomping his pegleg against the floor, and when that didn't stop the brawl, he smashed a jug on his bar to get their attention. "Quieten down, you lot," he shouted.

And then, in the lull of the peace he created, Sally appeared, and her face turned red to match her new dress, and she called to the crowd as she pointed to The Crow sprawled on the floor, "What's the matter with you? Don't you know this is Captain Thache's man?"

The room quieted, and as Sal straightened Colleen's laces, we saw the letters *ML* on the facing of her dress.

Then another man shouted, "Who are ye to stop our fun, lass?"

Another whispered his reply. "You better heed that one; Sal belongs to Cap'n Hands."

We hid among the men pushing to get out the door. And then we crawled under the fence and back to Carver's tent, where we dropped his cloaks and hats and retrieved our tricorns.

Then, under the cover of trees, Ody and I found our pendants and commuted safely to Grandma's room.

"Did you find what you wanted to know?" she asked.

Ody spoke first. "The Crow was with Sal's friend, Colleen. It looks like her new dress was a gift from Coleman."

"It had the same initials as on that scarf Lizzy had, too. Israel Hands is the captain Sal has her eye on, and I guess he's stealing from Captain Thache."

"You can't be sure of that," Grandma replied.

"No. But it's still my best guess."

Grandma nodded. "Very well. Tell Marybeth what you learned and see if she agrees with you."

23 The Crow and the Carver

Marybeth Thache

While Caesar and The Crow were busy along the creek, Ody and Drake told us what happened in Bath.

"Are you sure?" Mother asked. "The same seamstress made all these garments? And Thache or his crew gave them to two women outside this house?"

"Yes, ma'am," Drake answered. "Penelope Golland and now Crow's Colleen, and Sal might have had one from Israel Hands."

"Do you reckon Captain Thache gave them as presents?" she asked.

Aurora shook her head. "We have evidence they all came from the same place, but not necessarily as gifts from Captain Thache."

"But what place is that?" Mother asked. "Do you think Blackbeard went shopping for women's clothing? Or does he have a stitcher hidden on that ship?"

"He told us he was in Charleston," Drake said.

Ody looked puzzled. "He did?"

"Yes, that's where Dr. Neuvo joined his crew. Thache was there for medicine. Don't you recall?"

"Edward told me about Charleston," I said. "It's not something he likes talking about, but he didn't just stop in to trade; he and a fleet of ships held Charleston harbor under siege. He stopped ships going in and out and took some of those aboard as captives." I looked at the still faces around me and continued. "He still had the *Queen Anne's Revenge,* and it was before he took the King's pardon. According to Governor Eden, The King's forgiven him for that now."

"The King, maybe," Mother scoffed. "But I reckon there are still a few Charleston merchants with bones to pick."

"So, did he take clothes from a ship trying to reach Charleston?" Ody asked.

"It's a possibility," Aurora replied. "Perhaps the clothes were a shipment for a Charleston clothier or maybe an order for some lady in the town."

"But why would he keep a chest of lady's clothes?" Mother asked.

Ody shrugged. "Perhaps he expected to take a bride."

My eyes teared. "Someone like Penelope Golland," I said.

"Or someone like you, my dear," Aurora replied.

"A chest of dresses doesn't sound like a prize for pirates," Henrietta said, shaking her head.

Ody nodded. "You make a good point there. I can't see why the rest of the crew would choose women's clothes, so maybe Captain Thache took them as part of his share—maybe they belong to him alone."

"Well, if that's the case, that dress we saw in Bath last night was surely stolen from him, and we might have seen The Crow in the act," Ody said.

"That's true," I added. "Twice, we've seen Crow or another sailor move a full sack across our land. And if it's the Captain's property, and someone moved it without Edward's approval, then it's against the ship's rules."

"Do you think that lily-livered Crow has the gumption to do such as that?" Mother asked.

"He would if he had help—someone important watching his back," Drake said. "And that might be Israel Hands. Edward said he was a snake."

"You have a lot to discuss with Edward," Aurora said.

"And in the meantime, we can find out what Caesar knows about it," Ody replied.

The others returned to their chores, but my mind was not on cooking or cleaning. Where was Edward, and how much of this could he explain?

***

When evening came, I found a bouquet on the tower railing. I sniffed the peonies as the sky dimmed, and soon steps knocked against the wall as someone climbed the ladder. Then, with my nose still deep in the flowers, I turned to see Wallace's face at the railing, and despite longing for Edward, I was glad my old friend was there.

As he climbed over the rail to greet me, I fancied I heard more steps against the roof, but if they were real, Wallace's voice drowned them.

"Did your men learn what they were after last night?'" he asked.

"Aye. 'Twas a start," I replied. "But I still have …" *What shuffled on the roof around the tower walls? A squirrel? Maybe a raccoon?*

"You still have what?" Wallace asked.

"I still have questions that only Edward can answer."

"Then ask them as soon as you can," he replied. "Learn the truth about him, and then you'll know the truth about me."

"I like your flowers," I said, smiling, and his return smile was soft and warm in the moonlight.

"I must go before they catch me," he said. "Remember. I'm on your side, and I'll watch over you."

I tossed a peony to him, and then with a wave, he was over the rails and gone. But in less than two minutes, the steps sounded again. *Was Wallace returning?*

No. Someone else had been waiting, and a new voice interrupted the night. This time, The Crow came over the railing and stepped close to me.

"Thache'll want to know the truth about *you*, Missy," he said, hissing into my ear. "He'll want to know the games you're playing."

How much had he heard? I stepped back, "I'm not playing games. But *you* are, and Edward will make you pay for it."

"Thache won't care a fig about me once he finds out you're cheating on him."

He grabbed my arm and pushed his face next to mine, his ear braids sliding against my cheek. Great bruises on his chin and under his eyes had nearly blackened his face.

"There will be nothing left of that face when Edward hears how you speak to me. You forget who my husband is."

"Oh, no. I didn't forget," The Crow said. "But apparently, *you* did. I heard he scared an old beau away from you. Was that him on the tower? Maybe Edward won't care about him anymore … or maybe he'll be rid of you both."

"Maybe."

Ody Saunters rose from the hatch carrying an old cutlass from Edward's den. "Or maybe, he'll just toss *you* off the ship the next chance he gets," he said, flicking the blade to catch the moonlight."Now let her go."

"I don't reckon you know how to handle that, boy," Coleman said as he tightened his grip on my arm.

"I know where the pointy part goes. And I reckon, even though you're spry enough to climb a ladder, you're not up to a sword dance. One blow will do it. Even the old blades stay sharpened among The Captain's gear. 'Tis one of your rules, isn't it?"

"Well, I've got this girl dead to rights now," The Crow said. "I saw her with the stranger who brought flowers, and now you, a man in Thache's own house, stand with her on the tower. It ain't the first time I've seen you with her, either."

"Of course, it isn't," I replied, trying to free my arm. "Edward ordered everyone here to watch me and this house. Ody is following the Captain's orders."

Ody held the sword steady. "We have no reason to fear the Captain. But you've been stealing from him and trading in Bath with the Captain's share of his last prize."

The Crow let go of me and stood facing Ody, fists drawn, feet planted. "You have no proof," he said.

Ody nodded as he shifted between The Crow and me. "Anyone who saw you take those bruises last night knows what he heard. The town is full of eyes and loose tongues, Crow. The Captain will know the truth."

Crow dropped his fist and moved back a step. "Let me tell you what kind of man the Captain is," he said. "And you better both hear me."

"Then, speak up, Crow," Ody said, lowering the sword.

Crow took another baby step backward. "Do you know what happened after the Captain grounded the *Queen*? He sent another pirate, Stede Bonnet, to get his pardon, and while he was gone, Thache stripped Bonnet's ship and moved all the goods and prize gold we had onto a tender boat and then into the belly of what's now *Adventure*. Blimey, for all I know, that dress I gave to Colleen wasn't even Thache's. Bonnet had a wife at home. Maybe that chest was a gift for her."

"I don't believe you," I said.

The Crow shuffled backward toward the ladder at the railing. "Well, it ain't much to his credit, but Thache left Stede's ship for him, even if it was all but empty. But then, he marooned Stede's men on an island. Thache kept his most loyal crew and took them to sail with him. I dared not speak against him then, even though he wrecked the most powerful pirate ship the sea ever saw. And he did it on purpose."

"Why would he ground the *Queen* on purpose?" Ody asked as he moved toward Crow.

"Hands knew it, and I reckon he has the proof. Hands says Captain Thache is to blame for losing the sloop he captained the day we lost the *Queen*, and now Hands is reduced to Mate of *Adventure*. He tried to help Bonnet find Thache to get what was coming to him, but they had no luck. But the Cap'n's slippery and usually gets what he's after." Then as he stepped backward again, he twisted in my direction. "Just like when he was trolling for you, little missy."

I shuddered as I remembered Wallace's abduction story.

"He wanted you and this fine lookout spot you have. So, he got rid of everything in his way, and once he has all he wants from you, he'll ground you and be onto his next prize."

By this time, The Crow was near the ladder. When I stepped toward him, Ody raised the sword, and as quick as flight, the Crow was over the rail, slipping to the ground.

I collapsed on the tower floor, and Ody dropped the blade and rushed to me, holding me as I sobbed.

"Pay him no mind," Ody said. "You know what kind of man he is. He's a proven liar and cheater. Don't let him scare you. You're stronger than that."

Ody was right, and my mother told me many times; we Bellieu women know how to face monsters. Coleman Adler showed what he was made of, but was my husband cut from the same cloth? Was love enough to shield me while standing within Edward's storm?

When would I ever know for sure?

24 Home Harbor

Marybeth Thache

Every night after the confrontation with The Crow, I dreamed of Edward, and while the dreams were comforting, he never visited my dreams alone. Sometimes Israel Hands lurked in the shadows, rifling through my things, and The Crow flew behind Edward's back like a magpie looking for anything that glittered.

Women appeared in my dreams, too. Penelope Golland laughed from the window, hoping Edward would desert me. Sally and the girls from town fished from the rafters in their bright calico and gingham dresses, trying to catch a pirate of their own. But the worst was Mother. She stood between Edward and me, sending me to my room and ordering Edward to the sea.

Then there was the Saunters family. Drake grabbed Edward's coattails while Ody brandished the captain's old cutlass. Aurora watched as she leaned on her walking stick, nodding as if she knew the ending for us all. But if she knew so much, why didn't she tell us?

Waking brought little relief, and Mother noted how tired I was.

"Sleep, eat, take care of business. Then, let fate work out the kinks," she said.

Aurora agreed, saying, "Edward will be home soon." She was right, but to me, the nights dragged by until, at last, Edward's sails floated over the water.

Finally, the morning brought a loaded periauger headed for Knight's landing. I gasped as Edward's beard, longer now, floated past his neck with the breeze, his red sleeve waving from his post at the rudder. Then soon after he disembarked, Knight's assistant, Mr. Chamberlain, rowed to Plum Point, and I hurried to the porch to meet him.

"Good day, Mrs. Thache. The Captain brought the first load of cargo to Tobias Knight, and he asked me to bring you this letter and a satchel for safekeeping."

"Is he well?" I asked, clasping the parchment in my palm.

"He's as fit as always," Chamberlain replied. "He has tallies to review, but even before he passed the ledger to Knight, he asked me to carry this letter to you."

"Thank you," I muttered as I broke the seal, and I was so engrossed in my message that I failed to notice Chamberlain's return to Knight's Landing.

> *"My Dearest Marybeth,*
>
> *I'm Home at last, my Love, and I can hardly wait to hold you again, but Necessities come first. After our long Voyage, we could not leave our Posts till the Ship was sea-ready again. Careening the Hull and Mending the Rigging were our first duties. As much as I long to have you in my Arms, Governor Eden and Tobias Knight await the News of Goods we fetched for Bath.*
>
> *I'm happy to say we met with fair Weather and our share of good Fortune. The town of Bath will not be disappointed.*
>
> *We will secure the Cargo in time for me to return home for supper. I hope you will welcome me then.*
>
> *Yours,*
>
> *Edward"*

With the letter crushed in my hand, I ran to the kitchen, shouting, "Edward will be here for supper. We need a feast to celebrate his return."

"Perhaps Coleman can find fresh game," Aurora said.

"We haven't seen The Crow this morning," Drake replied, "but Caesar can row into town to see what's there."

Mother nodded, adding, "We have plenty of rice and fresh vegetables." Aurora joined the task by volunteering to try her hand at a plum pudding.

The ear-to-ear smile nearly split my face, but I stretched it enough to giggle as I ran to tidy the house.

"Any tasks for us, Ma'am?" Drake asked.

I paused, turning to Ody and Drake. "Ah, yes. Well, fresh eggs and milk, I think. And will one of you carry this pouch to the Captain's den? 'Tis heavier than I expected."

Drake helped with the pouch, and Ody offered to help Caesar in town.

The boys ran off to their tasks, and I laughed to see that their enthusiasm matched mine. Mother and Aurora chuckled too. And even after their laughter faded, smiles replaced Aurora's normal worry over her grandsons and Mother's constant disapproval of Edward.

"Well, go on with ye," Mother said. "Let's ready this place for whatever wind blows in with the Captain."

I hurried to do my work and help with dinner and supper, but I spent every spare moment in the Bride's Tower peering through Edward's spyglass. My husband remained on Tobias Knight's plantation while a second loaded tender brought goods for Knight's cellar. Israel Hands oversaw the unloading of that boat, and when it was empty of goods, it filled again with sailors longing for a bit of shore leave. They must have stayed in Bath for supper because the tender had not returned to Knight's landing when a jollyboat brought Edward and Doctor Asjen Nuevo to Plum Point.

***

The late afternoon breeze was stiff, but within seconds of Edward walking through the door, it slammed shut, and all was still. Edward was the weight-bearing wall that held the roof steady over our heads. Others were in the room, and perhaps they spoke, but no dream ghosts trailed behind. I saw only my husband, and the only sound was my rushing breath as it synced to match the slow rhythm of his chest. Edward shared my air once more. All was well. Of course, doubts still nagged at me, but I trusted they would fly away as soon as Edward explained.

The floorboards groaned as his sack slipped from his shoulder to the floor. I stepped toward him, but he swept me into his arms, holding me, and his kiss sent desire pulsing through every vein. I melted in his kiss, clasping his shoulders. Here was all I had waited for: Edward, home at last.

I couldn't pull myself from him, so he spoke for us both. "Here's my treasure."

With a sweet smile peeking from the black beard and eyes as soft as butterfly wings over the meadow, he gently returned my feet to the floor. "Home, at last, my dear Wife," he said. And even my mother couldn't despise him for that.

"And greetings to all," he said, laughing as he turned to others in the room. "Oh, my, something smells like home."

Then Edward turned to Asjen Nuevo and pulled him in front of him. "Speak up, Asjen," he said. "I hope you're hungry, too."

Nuevo was not a small man, nor one to go unnoticed, but Edward dwarfed him, and in the excitement of Edward's return, I had forgotten him. Mother found her manners first.

"A welcome return to these shores, Dr. Neuvo. May I take your things?"

Asjen passed his hat and coat, and Mother took a small book he carried and placed it on a table by the row of wall pegs. Then she waved us all to the next room, saying, "Please, everyone, let's gather at the table."

"What a fine idea, Mother Bellieu," Edward said. "It has been a few nights since we had roasted meat, and 'tis a welcome change from a sand-pot fire dinner on the deck, don't you think so, Asjen?"

The doctor agreed.

Our supper that night was better than a Christmas feast. There was roast lamb and goose with corn, peas, peppers, and buttered radishes. Ody found a spare loaf of fine wheat bread in Bath, and Aurora's plum pudding didn't turn out half bad.

Edward thought so, too, proclaiming, "'Tis as good as any I ever had as a boy in Bristol."

After we ate, we carried ale, wine, and cider to the porch, where the winds had quieted and fireflies mingled with bright stars to illuminate our happiness.

"How was the voyage?" Ody asked. "Could you find the goods the town wants?"

"We did," Dr. Neuvo replied. "And 'tis mostly to the credit of our Captain." He raised his glass toward Edward.

"Aye, we expected some trouble but found more than we bargained for."

"How so?" Aurora asked.

"Well, for one thing, that dandy, Stede Bonnet, hit the ports ahead of us. Now, he calls himself Captain Thomas or Richards and renamed his ship *Royal James.* And from the stories we heard, he tried his hands at fair trade, but it didn't take him long to raise his black flag."

"Some say he even wore a black beard to instill fear in his targets."

"He pretended to be you?" Drake asked.

"Oh, he probably found a bandy-legged oaf from Yorkshire with a black beard to stand in," Edward said.

Neuvo continued the story. "We know a sloop took a couple of ships heading for Bristol, but Edward doesn't challenge English ships. And then, they captured one loaded with sugar, molasses, rum, and cotton, heading for Philadelphia, and the word around Delaware Bay is that Blackbeard was trolling the seas. But we didn't even see those ships; it must have been Bonnet."

"Aye, I half wanted to chase him and take that cargo for Bath. But worse than that, he robbed a schooner from this colony and for nothing more than a few dozen calfskins. I hope the Governor doesn't blame that one on me."

"Then how did you find what the Governor wants?" Mother asked.

Neuvo answered, "Edward used his wits instead of his frightful beard."

"Frightful? When was I ever frightful?" Edward teased, stroking his be-ribboned chin hair.

"Yes, and it nearly got you into trouble anyway," Nuevo said. Then he turned to us to explain. "Captain Thache has friends of all stripes and knows where to find those willing to part with their stock. But wisely, he sent others in to trade for him. So, I found medicines and spectacles, and Israel Hands closed deals for gunpowder and sugar."

Edward took up the story. "A few plantations dealt with us directly, and I know smugglers and petty robbers, happy to trade their loot away."

"And Captain Thache knew where to find safe harbor. But someone spotted him in the streets of Philadelphia on shore leave. So, then the papers got the wrong idea and wrote how Blackbeard was back to his robbing ways."

"'Tis no matter; we got what we meant to, and the crew got their cut of the silver, and they'll soon have more when we settle with Tobias Knight."

"And now you're home safely," I said, beaming.

"Aye," he said, locking those soft eyes to mine.

"Tell us more, Captain," Drake begged, "What else did you see?"

Edward chuckled. "You sound like me as a boy. So, I'll tell you what my father told me. First, we saw the wide sea with manatees and even a giant whale."

"And dolphins?" I asked.

Edward's eyes twinkled as he replied, "The dolphins followed us, especially when we reached Carolina shores."

"No serpents at the sea's edge?" Ody asked.

"The sea has no edge, boy, and no end to its stories."

"What about its treasures?" Drake asked.

Edward shook his head, "After hunting prizes for these years, I'm afraid there isn't much left for new seekers."

"Or perhaps it lies in corners not yet discovered," Drake said.

Edward chuckled, "Either way, 'tis harder to fish for gold these days." Then he squeezed my fingers, adding, "Perhaps the greatest prize is on dry land, after all."

Then he turned toward Drake, "Asjen can give you a different look at what we found. He takes those pastels of his everywhere."

"I wondered what might be in his book," Mother said.

Nuevo fetched his book from the front room and shared it with Mother. "As I travel to new countries, I fear I may never pass a place again, so I like to remember it with sketches."

"You should see the volume he has on the ship," Edward said. "This is just a bit he can carry."

Aurora, impatient for a turn, peeked over my mother's shoulder, her eyes growing wider with each turned leaf. "Ody, you should see this," she said.

Ody squeezed behind the rocker to look over Mother's shoulder. He watched as several pages flipped. "Each one is signed," he said, pointing to the initials *AN*. Then, with a short gasp, he turned to Aurora. "You were right. 'Tis remarkable, indeed."

After a few more page turns, Aurora asked, "We saw a portrait of Captain Thache's mother displayed in his den. Did you draw that, too?" she asked.

"Aye, I did," he replied. "That was years ago when I tended the elder Mrs. Thache in Jamaica. I'm surprised Edward still carries it."

"'Twas 1699, the year she passed. 'Tis the only likeness I have of Mother, and I treasure it," Edward said.

"She has white hair," Drake said. "Was she quite old?"

"She was only in her forties," Edward said, sighing. "But, she was born to be an English rose and couldn't adjust to the climate of Jamaica. She became sick as soon as we arrived, and she never rallied. Her hair soon turned white, and she failed and began to age before our eyes. I should have insisted Father take her home."

"Oh, my," Oma said. "You must have lovely memories of her in England. But what about you as a boy, Edward?"

I turned to Asjen, "So, you knew Edward as a boy. Do you have a drawing of young Edward?"

The Captain chuckled as Dr. Nuevo shook his head. "If I drew one, 'tis among the sketches on the ship. Oh, wait. I recall. Perhaps I should not speak of it, but I drew a picture of Edward as a young man, about Ody's age, and he was with a lass he was fond of at the time."

It was my turn to smile, even if I reddened at the thought. "I would love to see it, and I'll try not to be jealous of a girl from Edward's past—not one from decades ago, anyway."

Nuevo chuckled, saying, "I was lucky to catch them. They had to steal away for privacy in those days. I went out to sketch the moonrise and turned to find them holding hands among the palm trees by the front porch."

"You drew that?" Edward asked.

Neuvo shrugged, "'Twas a golden opportunity."

"Do you know what became of her?" I asked.

Dr. Neuvo did not answer me directly, but he smiled as he lowered his chin. "I was merely the artist."

"Edward?" I asked, hoping for more.

His smile dimmed as he replied, "My dear, the truth is that when we were of age, that young lady became the first Mrs. Thache."

Drake muttered a name with barely enough air to carry it to my ears.

"Did you say, *Abigail*?" I asked.

Drake raised his head, eyes wide. "Er … No. I just said she must have been … a bonnie gal."

Edward nodded, smiling wistfully. "She was, and you were twice right; her name *was* Abigail. But in those days, a string of catastrophes hit Jamaica. And sadly, when the hurricane of 1712 left sickness in its wake, she did not survive."

"I'm so sorry, Captain," Aurora said. Then she turned to Drake, "Be careful what you mutter, Dear. You'll have Plum Point thinking you know the future … or the past."

I smiled at Drake, saying, "Don't worry about that. Mother already thinks Aurora can see the future. One more prophet won't upset the household."

Dr. Neuvo studied Drake and Aurora with curiosity as he gently closed the book on his lap. "We see many things in our travels, and sometimes we may even catch a glimpse of the past, but you haven't made journeys I'm not aware of, have you, Drake?"

Drake kept his eyes on the floor but quickly snapped his head to say *no*.

"Well, thank Goodness for that," Aurora said, "But even so, we must be careful not to step on old memories, especially when they are sad ones."

"'Tis the way of things, Mrs. Saunters; tragedy is part of living," Edward said. Then he gently took my hand again, adding, "And luckily, life brings new joys and new loves when we are ready to permit it." His smile returned as he squeezed my fingers. "Let's think happier thoughts," he said as he went for the sack he had brought. "I have memories of the voyage for you too."

"Ah, now it feels like Christmas," Aurora said as Edward found gifts for each of us in his sack.

"They are always knitting in the northern colonies," he said as he produced warm hats for Ody and Drake, a yellow shawl for my mother, and he had two pounds of English tea for Aurora. Then he reached into his pocket and presented me with a small parcel. "And here's a trinket for my bride," he said, smiling.

I untied the black velvet parcel to find a mother-of-pearl pendant carved into a star with many points, framed in silver beads.

"Is this …?" I asked.

He nodded. "'Tis Polaris, the North Star."

With tears in my eyes, I picked up the ends of the black velvet ribbon, and he tied it around my neck.

"No more searching for the North Star," he said. "I'll be no trouble to find now; my heart is always home with you."

I held tight to the star, fearing that what he said today might not always be true. But for now, Edward was home, and we were happy.

Then he looked into his sack again. "Ah, I have socks for Caesar and The Crow; I'll speak to them."

"You may not find The Crow," Mother said. "He's been missing lately."

Ody nodded. "The Crow …." The boy hesitated as if might misspeak, but then he stiffened his neck and continued. "While I was in town with Caesar today, we heard that The Crow has been spending more time there than we knew. And the word is he's spreading tales among the sailors."

Edward raised an eyebrow. "Oh? And what tales are The Crow cawing about?"

Ody swallowed again before speaking, "I can't say his exact words, but the gist is that you cheated Stede Bonnet out of his share of a prize."

Edward huffed, shaking his head. "Stede Bonnet had done no ship's work in nearly a year, and he signed no agreement as all the crew members do. Bonnet was one of the men requiring medical help we asked for in Charleston. And he was lucky Dr. Nuevo joined us with his new ideas about treating Bonnet's malady. He was feeling some better by the time we reached Beaufort, and 'twas time for our agreement to end. So he went to find his pardon, and I left his men waiting for him."

"That's not how Coleman tells it," Drake said.

"Bonnet wouldn't tell it right, either, but he's a shifty sort. The Crow was once a man of Bonnet's crew, so maybe what he says leans in Bonnet's direction," Thache said. "Besides, Asjen can vouch for my version. He was there."

Neuvo chuckled. "I was only with Bonnet for days, but everything I saw aligns with the Captain's version."

"There's more than that, Captain," Drake said. "We've seen The Crow carrying loaded sacks around this plantation. He wears a blue silk coat these days and gave his girl a dress as fine as the ones you gave your wife. We reckon those garments came out of the sack he carried. Were those your belongings, Captain?"

Edward nodded, and his eyes turned even blacker. "It sounds like he's found goods I left at the camp under the watch of Israel Hands. I'll see what I can find out. And if we can't locate Crow, Caesar and I will row the good Doctor back to Knight's plantation. After that, he will head to the camp with Israel Hands and the crew, and perhaps the Doctor can worm the truth from my second in command."

They were soon off to investigate, but I feared what else Edward might learn from The Crow. *Should I be the first to tell him about Wallace McNeil?*

25 The Reckoning

Marybeth Thache

I lit the lantern to guide Edward home, but his return to the tower took longer than expected. Polaris sat over Bath Town, and the crew's campfire flickered at the east end of Plum Point Gut. Hopefully, Caesar was there to temper whatever The Crow had to report to my husband. I waited for the better part of an hour, wondering what they would say. Then, three men emerged from the forest. Caesar and Asjen took a path to the landing, and I watched as my husband climbed the rope ladder to join me.

Perhaps the lantern was too dim or the shadows too long, but Edward's beard seemed even blacker, and eyebrows knit to his nose, adding to his dark expression. But the shadowy centers of his eyes glinted white as he straddled the tower rails.

I smiled, but he did not return a pleased look.

"What happened?" I asked.

He took his time to reply, eyeing me before he spoke.

Finally, words came. "Caesar says The Crow has made himself scarce from Plum Point. Coleman follows my orders, all but one. He doesn't see fit to guard *you* anymore."

"Caesar said that?" I asked,

"Aye. Caesar disagrees with The Crow, but 'tis how he tells it."

I swallowed, unsure what to say, but finally muttered, "We had a confrontation."

"Concerning what?"

"He threatened me." I paused, hoping Edward would pay attention to the first part of my story before I told the more damaging part. "He said he'd claim I cheated on him if I told his secrets."

"And what secrets were those?"

"Ody and Drake saw him in town, and he gave his girlfriend a dress with the same maker's mark as on my wedding gown. I suspect he stole the frock from you, maybe with the help of Israel Hands. He wanted to frighten me from telling you."

"Israel Hands was with me on the voyage, so how could that be?"

"Ody saw a man moving a sack cinched with a leather band off the boat that brought Chamberlain and Hands here before you sailed. Then later, we saw Coleman carrying the sack across our land. He appeared to come from our cellar, but it was locked, and nothing was missing."

"How could he claim you weren't faithful? What gave him that suspicion?"

"He's seen me on this tower with Ody, but the boy is helping me watch, that's all."

"Anything else?" He stood closer, and this time it felt more threatening than sweet. "Tell me everything, and I want the truth."

I weighed my words carefully. "Do you remember my mother mentioning a boy named Wallace? He was my suitor before we met."

He nodded. "What about Wallace?"

"What about Penelope Golland?" I asked.

He raised his eyebrows and pushed the hat back from his brow. "Penelope?"

"Did you give her a scarf from the same trunk my dresses came from?"

He nodded. "I did, but that was before I met you. Miss Golland was nothing compared to you. To be true, she didn't care much for me. But don't fiddle with your answers; what about Wallace?"

"He was before I met you and well before we married. I am yours as I vowed—heart, soul, and body. While you were away, I came to find the pole star and look for your sails in the river every night. I feared for you, longed for you. There is no room for anyone else in my heart."

"Is there more?"

"Coleman wants me to fear you, Edward, but fear only separates us. I am willingly bound to you—by more than vows. But I would run if I feared you, and doubt is the tool to break us."

"Did you doubt me over Penelope?"

"No, but there was one other thing, another woman."

"Tell me."

"Sal told me she plans to marry a captain, and for a while, I feared it might be you."

Edward laughed. "Really? Sal?"

I nodded, "But when the boys heard she has her eye on Captain Israel Hands, I worried more that he was helping Crow steal from you. So, then I was afraid for you, not myself."

"And this Wallace? Did you meet with him?"

"Ody found him on Plum Point, and he asked to speak to me. I thought Wallace had fled or might be dead, but he's alive and has my safety at heart."

"And does he want you?"

I looked at his face again. His eyes were no longer hard, but they still questioned. So, I dipped into the deepest part of my heart and told the truth.

"It makes no difference what Wallace wants. 'Tis what *we* want. When we married, we planted seeds of promises and trust and covered them over with official words, but love took root from what we planted. I felt it growing every day as I longed for you. Today you returned, and from the moment you entered Plum Point's door, the love had grown so strong I could barely speak. It jumped from me to hold you tightly and never let you go."

"I felt that, too, my love," he whispered.

"But the Crow wants to break us. Has he succeeded, Edward? Did Coleman break our trust and ruin our happiness?"

The captain was inches from me, and one hand rested on the hilt of his cutlass. It would take nothing for him to throw me from the tower or cleave me with that blade. But I found enough courage to speak.

"If he's broken us, go ahead, end me. I can't live without you now," I said.

I held my breath as his hand slipped from the sword, and both fists clenched as he decided what to do with me. Then he grasped the brass handle, drew his blade, and laid it at my feet.

He pulled me to him, kissing me even more passionately than when he first came home. I exhaled, relieved we still had each other, and I gripped his chest and shoulders, holding him, owning him as I yielded, pressing for my husband's kiss, as regenerating as fresh water. Then he held me inches from his chest as he tenderly reached for the North Star, pretended to pluck it from the sky, and sealed it in the pearl star at the base of my neck.

Then he bent to sheath his sword, and as he rose, he swept me into his arms and to our bed, where the breath and warmth we shared brought us home at last.

***

Just before dawn, Edward woke me. "The sun will rise soon," he said softly.

As I leaned on that sturdy chest, my face resting in his beard. I found every scar on his warm arms and brought a rope-calloused hand to my lips, whispering, "Stay with me."

"As long as I can, my love," he replied. Then he chuckled. "Well, as long as you want me."

"And why would I not want you?" I asked. "You are the answer to my prayers."

He chuckled again, saying, "Some say I'm more born from hell than headed for heaven. And when I tell you my secret, you may say so too."

Fear tried to rise within me at those words, but I put it aside. Our bond had survived doubt and rumors, and our love was stronger. So I snuggled against him again, saying, "Tell me."

"Did you wonder why I had a supply of women's clothes?" he asked.

"The Crow said you may have taken them from Bonnet—that they may have been a gift for the wife he left behind."

"Nothing like that," Edward replied. "I stole nothing from Bonnet. He earned none of our prizes while he lounged on my ship. I even left him his library of books. I relieved that chest of clothes from a prisoner on my ship trying to enter Charleston while we had it under siege."

"Were they for Penelope?" I asked.

"Nay. I had not met her yet." He paused a moment letting his fingers play in my curls. Then, finally, he said, "I kept them for my daughter, Elizabeth."

I raised my head to study his expression. "You have a daughter?"

He nodded. "Her mother was Abigail, the first wife I spoke of."

"The girl still lives?"

"Yes. I rarely see my daughter, but her last letter tells me she has a suitor. I thought she might like a trousseau, so I saved them for her." He ran his arm over my shoulders. "She is about your size and not far from your age. But when I met you, I knew who should own those dresses. So I selected some for your trunk and brought that chest to you. Others I hid on Ocracoke." Then he winked, adding, "For future gifts."

"And what about Elizabeth?"

"Her relatives can buy her dresses. I'll send a dowry."

"But how did The Crow come to have them?"

"'Tis not well known among the crew that I have a daughter, but Hands knew I saved the clothing for her. Of course, Caesar knew about Elizabeth, but he knew nothing of the dresses. I'll have to investigate."

Edward squeezed me tight and kissed me on the forehead. But when he touched my pearly star, he sighed and sat on the edge of our bed. "Perhaps I should confess one thing more," he said.

My stomach tightened, but I could survive one more arrow.

He took my hand, smiling sadly as he said, "While I was in Pennsylvania, I visited a safe harbor for men like me, the town of Marcus Hook."

"And?" I asked, not sure I wanted the answer.

"There is a friend there. Margaret. She was once closer than a friend, and I wanted to tell her about you," he said.

"Was she a lover?" I asked.

"Let's just say we enjoyed each other's company when I was in port. I wanted Margaret to know things had changed for me, and she guessed it as soon as she saw the blue ribbon in my beard."

My throat closed. "What did she say?"

He nodded. "She was sad that our friendship changed—but happy for me. And when I told her I wanted a North Star for you, Margaret found the right shop for me."

His fingers gently brushed the star again. "Margaret wishes us happiness," he said.

He touched my cheek, and his eyes brightened.

"You haven't thrown me out of the room yet. So, are we in good standing?"

"Are there more secrets? More women?" I asked.

He leaned over me, twisting a loose lock of my hair around his finger. Then he flashed the charming grin I loved as he replied, "None that will ever come between us."

"Is that the truth?" I asked.

"Better than true," he replied. "You have my word on it."

Then I kissed the hand in my hair, and he kissed me again. Once, twice, three times, and then the grin beamed as he added, "You're the only woman I'll ever want. But right now, I'd welcome a little breakfast."

I kissed his cheek and smiled as I left to put the kettle on. I don't remember making tea or stirring porridge. My love for Edward erased every chore, but it was hard to fathom; I had a stepdaughter older than I was. Would she marry and have a child soon? Whoever heard of a grandmother under twenty?

After the usual family banter at breakfast, we each moved to our duties on the farm, and I dared hope this would be our future.

But in only a few days, a new storm blew across the Point, and the Saunters family heard about it before I did.

26 Trouble in Paradise

Ody Saunters

The Captain had returned to Plum Point, and love must have worked magic. Edward had resolved Marybeth's doubts, and she had confessed to meeting Wallace, all at the cost of a few tears and without a single drop of spilled blood. Now, Thache's laugh bellowed over the Plum Point grounds, and Marybeth practically walked on air.

But even good things have consequences. Oma began to whisper about returning home, which made me lonely for my own time and place, including my friends—and my phone.

It was a more difficult choice for Drake; he'd become fascinated with Captain Thache. My cousin referred to Edward as *Captain* or *Sir* in the presence of anyone from our current century. But when we were alone, and he caught sight of sails on the creek, Drake's eyes sparkled, and his smile spread to his ears as he whispered, "*Blackbeard*."

Edward had brought laundry ashore with him, and while I helped Oma draw well water for the wash, Drake caught up with us.

"What are you two whispering about?" he asked. "Washing is no secret."

Since there were few times when the three of us were alone, Oma drew us into a huddle by the well. "I think we've been here long enough, boys. We've met our mission, and it's time to go home."

"Not yet," Drake pleaded. "We haven't been on a real ship, and didn't you say trouble was coming?"

"Yes, it is," Oma replied, "and we'd best be out of the way when it does."

Drake shook his head. "Can't we stop it?" he asked. "Thache is a good man as far as I can tell. Why should he die for that?" Then, he turned to me, pushing my Plum Point button.

"What about Marybeth? She'll be heartbroken."

Oma put a hand on his shoulder. "We can't change what's written in history, and it would be wrong to try."

"So, we can't save Edward or Marybeth, either?" Drake asked.

"We don't know what becomes of Marybeth, so helping her won't snap the strings of time for long. But Edward has lived his life, and his choices have etched his path. We can't change his destiny."

"How do you know we can't?" Drake asked. "You said you don't understand how we travel, much less what happens when we do. So how can it hurt to save him?"

I shook my cousin's arm. "It's not what we came here to do, Drake. We came to help you understand traveling out of time, and we've accomplished that. We must leave the rest to history."

Drake gave up on me and turned to Oma, "Well, what about Asjen Nuevo? Shouldn't we learn more from him?"

Oma straightened her head as she eyed Drake. "I've been meaning to ask you about that. You haven't commuted again, have you? You know how dangerous that is."

"I know," he replied, "No, I didn't go anywhere, but shouldn't we stay to find out what Neuvo knows about time travel?"

"He probably knows nothing," I replied. "Even if he *is* Augustus Neumann or one of his relatives, in 1783, Neumann had more questions than answers."

"OK, Neumann told you he can't travel to the past," Drake replied. "but maybe he lied. Oma did … sort of."

"I did not lie," Oma replied. "I can't travel to the future; I can only return to the century I came from."

Drake shrugged, "OK then." But he still grumbled as he helped us fetch water and set big kettles over the fire.

Once or twice, I caught him staring at the attic window, and I wondered if he was thinking about the brief commute he took on his own.

"If you want to travel more, don't worry; I'm sure Oma has more planned for you."

"I guess so," he mumbled. Then after he helped Oma prepare the clothes for their lye soap bath, he left to check the goats.

I tended the fire till Oma and Henrietta came out to finish the clothes, then Marybeth sent me to help Edward check the perimeter fences.

"Ah, good to see ye, lad. Help me set this rail right," he said as he lifted a split log into place. "It seems we're missing a man around here. Maybe you can fill the slack the next time I sail."

I wasn't sure of Oma's plans, but I felt I should give the Captain a fair warning.

"Captain, you might be short a couple more men on your next voyage. So, you'd best find replacements for Drake and me."

"Are you going somewhere?" he asked.

"Oma says it's past time for us to go home. And now that you're back, we can leave."

"Are you in such a hurry?" he asked.

"No, Sir, meeting you has been a privilege, but we must return to our home sometime."

Edward pushed his hat back and studied me with those black, sparkling eyes. Then he nodded, saying, "All right, then. I'll assess the situation and figure out what to do. You and your family have watched over mine in trying times. 'Tis the least I can do to respect your wishes."

"Well, it's not *my* wish," Drake said as he caught up with us at the fence. "I'd like to know you better and sail just once on your ship if possible."

Edward smacked his shoulder, saying. "Who knows what opportunities may come, young sailor." Then he laughed that big belly laugh that rang all over Plum Point.

We finished the patrol together, and Edward's eyes darkened as he saw a man at the landing.

"Chamberlain," he said. "I wonder what Tobias Knight has for us now. If you lads get the chance, tell Mrs. Thache I'll be home directly."

***

Marybeth smiled as we joined her in the dining room. "Just in time, gents," she said. "I need help with chopping and peeling these apples. Mr. Schute blessed us with a barrel full of them—an appreciation gift for Edward's voyage." She passed us each a kitchen knife and pointed to pans for the apples and the peelings.

When we told her of Chamberlain's arrival, she stopped peeling to make a crock of cucumber water for the men on the porch. But then, in a few minutes, she returned to the kitchen, plopped down on a chair between us, and snatched up a knife.

She worked silently, but Drake raised his eyebrows at me, nodding to her slicing the apples as if she were slitting throats. Then, finally, she spoke, her voice deeper than usual, "I think Mr. Chamberlain has a new order for Edward."

"Will he sail again?" Drake asked with a hopeful smile.

She continued peeling as if it were a vendetta, then without looking up, she replied, "It could be so."

Oma and Henrietta had joined the apple party by this time, and we were short a knife.

"There's another by the wash basin," Marybeth said.

"And Ody's blade is dull," Oma added. "Come with me, lad. You know how to use a wheel; there's one in the shed." Then when her whisper was out of earshot, she said, "The details of this trip might help us with our plans."

I nodded, then Oma took my knife to sharpen, and I kept to the house wall till I reached the peony bushes by the front porch. There, I heard Mr. Chamberlain make his case to Edward.

"Governor Eden and Mr. Knight are happy with the goods you brought to town," he said. "The merchants can sell these at half the price other traders charge. But, of course, that's *if* they bother to bring their ships to our harbor."

"Then there's no problem, is there?" Thache asked.

"There are a few problems," Chamberlain replied, "'Tis mostly the behavior of your men in town. They are taking liberties with the ladies, and even though the girls do not complain, the respectable folk in town keep the Governor's ears burning."

"Maybe the men will settle down once they pair up. I want nothing more than to be with my bride as much as possible."

"It's more than the women. It's the drinking, gambling, and general disrespect for the streets of Bath. Everyone is happy to see sailors' coins, but your men behave as the townspeople expect."

"Shall I speak to them about that?" Thache asked.

"Do you rule them on dry land?"

"Our rules govern our voyages for the sea, but I reckon they'll obey me if they want to sail again. I'll find them in town tonight and see what's what."

"As you like, but the Governor would be pleased to move them out of town. Will they stay put at your camp on Ocracoke?" he asked.

"Not happily," the Captain replied. "The best part of a voyage is coming home and enjoying the comforts of a harbor."

"Then take your men south this time. Take them back to the Indies, maybe St. Thomas, and see if they'd prefer to stay there. Trim your crew a bit. Keep just enough men to make trading voyages for Bath if that's what you prefer."

"The bulk of them are a good crew, and I'd hate to part company with them."

Chamberlain nodded. "I understand, but there's trouble here, too, and it's not just in this town or even in this colony alone. Tobias Knight is your friend, Edward, but he suspects there are those looking to oust the Governor and replace him. Knight and Eden have enemies happy to draw targets on their backsides, and they might use you to do it, even if it's not your intention."

I had heard enough. I returned to the kitchen, but Drake stopped me at the corner.

"What kept you so long?" he asked.

"I … I heard something by the porch." I lowered my voice to a whisper. "Marybeth's right. The Captain might be sailing again soon—this time to the Indies. The Governor wants him to get his men out of Bath. So, he could be gone longer this time, and I reckon he'll take The Crow with him."

Drake nodded, "That Crow can be trouble, but Marybeth won't have much protection with only Caesar, although I reckon Wallace will be around."

I shook my head. "I don't know about that. The Captain might not want Wallace visiting her; Edward might scare him away from Plum Point for good. After that, Marybeth and Henrietta will be on their own."

"Caesar might have the answer," Drake said. "I can ask him how he'll fare without a helper."

"Well, I want to speak to Wallace and find out if he will guard Marybeth if we leave. Then, we can compare notes tomorrow."

Drake's eyes brightened. "Maybe we're jumping the gun. Grandma might stay here longer for Marybeth's sake, or maybe I can convince her Blackbeard's worth saving."

"That's a tall order," I replied.

Drake nodded. "I can do that."

"You can? How? No one can stop Oma."

"I know how."

"Are you cooking up more trouble, cousin?" I asked.

"Not for anyone but me," he replied. "Grandma needs to hear the truth, and I know where to find it."

27 Somewhen Else

Drake Saunters

Would those on Plum Point *never* sleep? *I had plans.*

Finally, Henrietta was the first to bed, and soon after that, Marybeth and Edward closed their door.

Nearly there. Only Grandma was left, but she found Ody and me on the tower.

"Are you boys arguing? If staying here puts you at odds, the sooner we go home, the better," she said.

"We're OK, Oma," Ody replied. "Drake idolizes Blackbeard a little more than I do, that's all. But Marybeth seems better now. For a time, she worried about the pirates and the girls in Bath, but you saw her with Thache tonight. They're right as rain."

Oma agreed. "Yes, they managed to wrap up their doubts about each other, but sometimes that comes from wishful thinking."

"At least The Crow will be out of the way," I said. "So his thieving will end, and if he's plotting with Israel Hands, the Captain will handle that on the ship."

"On the ship, yes," Grandma said. "But what happens to Marybeth if he chooses the sea over her?"

"He'd never do that," I said.

Ody disagreed. "He might. He's left women behind before."

"But he only married one other," I replied. "That vow means something to him."

"Will it stand when his crew thirsts for bigger prizes?" Ody asked.

Oma stopped our argument. "Well, we can't stop what happens to Thache, and only history knows what happened to Marybeth; it's not our duty to fix it."

"I guess not," Ody said.

They must have found me silent for too long because Grandma roused me from my thoughts. “Drake? What do you think?”

“Huh? Oh. No, not our duty.”

“Very well, then. Good night, you two.”

We watched the stars and waves till the mosquitoes swarmed, and Ody headed for bed.

“You’d be better off downstairs,” he said. “These bugs will eat you alive.”

“I’m OK. I want to watch the moon rise.”

“Suit yourself.”

Then he disappeared through the hatch, and when he was safely on the guest floor landing, I crept to Thache’s den, where I waited in silence till Ody snored.

***

The first time I commuted alone was by accident. With the blood pounding in my ears, I hardly heard anyone speak, so I returned to Grandma. But, this time, I had a purpose—to learn more about the young Blackbeard.

I was sure of the commutator, a gold star pendant hanging over the corner of Mrs. Thache’s portrait. But before I touched it, I reviewed what I knew. I’d arrive precisely when and where I had on my first trip, in the shadows behind the hinged mirror in Mrs. Thache’s sick room. Edward would be there, and through openings between the hinged panels, I’d witness the mother giving the star to her son. Dr. Neuvo and the young nurse would come and go. But, of course, none of them saw me then, and I meant to stay invisible. I assumed everything would happen as before, but I’d pay attention to what was said this time.

After double-checking my ticket home, the pendant with Grandma’s hair, I stood close enough to grab the star. But, according to Oma and Ody, the star would not commute with me; it would fall from my hand. So, I held the pendant by the chain, letting the star dangle behind the pastel portrait.

Then, I prepared myself for the shock and disorientation of travel. I vowed to neither move nor make a sound when I landed and took the star tightly in my fingers.

The charm froze midway to the tabletop, and the sounds, lights, and patterns, now familiar in a commute, whirled through my head till the pixels dissolved and reappeared. Then I opened my eyes to shadows, focusing on lacy curtains fluttering over a glass globe lamp by the bedside of Elizabeth Thache.

I first saw only her pale face, framed by disheveled white hair that had come loose from two silver combs. Her eyes were closed, but one hand clasped the star at her neck, and the fingers of the other hand intertwined with those of a large, masculine hand.

"Mother," the young man whispered. "Guess who is here."

Her eyes remained closed, but the white lips turned up at the corners as she stroked his fist. "Is it a conch shell?" she asked.

There was a deep chuckle as the man replied. "No, Mother. 'Tis your Neddie."

Young Ned was not as tall as the Captain Thache I knew, and although bigger than Ody, he was not quite as slim nor old as my cousin. But his limbs were still lean, and although his skin showed damage from the heat and storms of Jamaica, this young Thache was not yet as weathered by the open sea as was the Captain in Bath.

She opened one eye. "Neddie. So, it is."

"How do you feel, Mother?" he asked.

"Like an old woman. Too weak to live much longer but never too weak to wish for my son."

"Don't say that, Mother," he said, reaching his free hand to tuck a lock of hair behind her ear.

"I have something for you," she said. "Please take this from me. Keep it." And she opened her fist to offer the star.

"No, Mother. It was a gift from Father. He should be here. He should have been with you more."

She nodded. "My Edward does his duty to keep me safe and make a home for me, and sometimes that means he must be away."

Ned shook his head as he stroked her cheek. "But he brought you from a home you loved to an island that has weakened you from the moment you came here. He should take you home, Mother. I'll do that someday. I'll take you home."

She smiled and raised the star. "Edward gave this to me to find his way home from his travels. Now you need it so your father can find his way to you, and you can find your way home, too. Please take it. Remember me."

A tear fell down his cheek as she fiddled with the clasp. His big thumbs were clumsy, and hers were weak, but together they opened the latch, and Neddie took the star, pressing her hand around it, and then he clenched his fist around hers.

"There is no home to find without you, Mother," he said, tears streaming.

She closed her eyes again, saying, "Home is where you find love, and love always grows in a good heart."

"My heart isn't that good, Mother. I'm more like Father, brash and demanding."

She rested quietly for a moment before whispering. "You look like your father. Big. Strong. Masterful. He gave you that."

Ned nodded and squeezed her hand harder.

"It will be easy for the world to see him in you. You will be his legacy, but I want to live on in you, too. So be my legacy, as well, son."

"How can I do that, Mother?"

"My heart is in you. Let it show. Be fair. Merciful. Good. Let the world see that, too. Then …"

"Then, what, Mother?"

"Then the best part of me will live on, and when you come home, I'll be waiting."

After those words, Mrs. Thache fell back to her pillow and was too weak to say more.

Ned's eyes widened, and he rushed to the door. "Call the Doctor. Mother needs him." Then Ned Thache hurried back to her side until a younger Dr. Asjen Neuvo came to check her.

Nuevo put a horn to her chest, listening to her heart and lungs. "She is failing," he whispered. "'Tis a matter of weeks. I wish to speak to her nurse. Will you call her?"

Again, Ned stepped to the door, calling, "Abby. Mother needs you."

A beautiful young woman with honey-colored hair swept into the room. "May I help?"

Doctor Nuevo gave her his instructions for comfort and care, warning all in the room that Mrs. Thache did not have much time left. Then he went to report to Elizabeth Thache's husband.

Abigail nodded her understanding, and when Ned asked her to tidy his mother's hair, she removed Elizabeth's shawl and the loose silver combs and placed them in a drawer containing a brush and other combs of silver and shell. She selected the brush and two tortoiseshell combs to arrange Mrs. Thache's hair.

"These shells will be easier for sleeping than the silver ones," she said.

When his mother slept easily, Ned escorted the young woman out of the room. Then, through the window curtain, I saw the two of them holding hands under the palm trees by the porch columns below me, and although it was bad manners, I was curious about what they said to each other. I was tempted to leave this room and walk to the porch to listen, but even though the sun was setting behind the palms, moving that far over unknown terrain was risky.

I had accomplished what I came to do; pay attention to the man Ned Thache had been. That was a win, so I dared another small risk. I crept to the bed and whispered to the sleeping lady. “I believe your son has your good heart.”

She may have opened one eye. And that reminded me that anyone who took risks might lose the gamble. So, I teleported to Grandma, who was sound asleep in Bath.

28 Second Chances

Drake Saunters

My commute convinced me that Edward Thache was not the kind of man to hurt Marybeth. But, if I told Ody what I witnessed, would he have more faith in the Captain? And if he did, would that help us persuade Grandma to stay in Bath longer? Maybe not. Thache wouldn't hurt her, but would he leave her in greater danger with fewer men to protect her?

We'd have more information after Ody talked to Wallace McNeil. But what about Caesar? If Thache sailed to St. Thomas, would Caesar go too? And if he stayed with Marybeth, could he be enough to keep Plum Point safe and supplied? And would it mess with history to use that angle as leverage for my argument?

Ody interfered in Bath's history more than I did. It was my cousin who reported that stolen sack to Edward, causing the Crow to flee, and Ody was the one who set up a meeting between Marybeth and Wallace. What if Edward chased Carver away, too? Even Grandma would agree that we couldn't go home if the women on Plum Point died because of us.

After supper, we patrolled the upper perimeter with Edward, and on our way back along Plum Point Gut, we found Caesar fishing behind the crew hut.

"Yo, Caesar! Has The Crow given up on his fishing duty, too?" Edward asked.

"Aye, Cap'n. I ain't seen him for days now. He has a girl in town, and I reckon he spends time with her."

"Did he take his gear, too?"

"Aye, most of it, anyway. Coleman cleared out the day after you returned. Since then, he brought deer and a few rabbits, but that's all the provisioning he does now. 'Tis good I can both fish and farm from here."

"Don't fret; I'll find The Crow and set him straight."

"Aye, ye will, Cap'n. No doubt of that."

Edward checked the hut to see if Coleman left anything behind and returned carrying an empty canvas sack, cinched by a flat leather strap that Ody and Edward recognized.

"Ye were right, Lads. This sea sack belongs to Israel Hands, and from this pine rosin on the side, it may have been near a pine tree for a time. If he carried dresses to Bath in it, he's been stealing from me. Only Israel Hands knew where to find them. So, either The Crow's a better finder than I knew, or they conspired to rob me. Did he tell you about this sack, Caesar?"

"No, Sir. But I feared it meant no good. What will you do with him?"

"He'll get what he deserves," Thache replied. Then he folded the sack and passed it to Ody. "Hold this for me if ye will, Lad."

Then he squatted beside Caesar and took off his hat to talk to his old friend. "I thank 'e for coverin' The Crow's duties and keeping up with your tasks, but be honest with me, can you manage this place with only the women to help you?"

"I believe so, but I can't say what might come up over weeks and months. Are ye' sailin' again?"

Thache scratched his head as he studied the campfire, then turned to Caesar. "Looks like the Governor has another voyage in mind for us. We'll be shoving off in a few days, and with The Crow leaving his post, I can't trust him to help here. You're another matter. I've trusted you with my blood before; now, I must do it again. On or off the ship, you're a good crewmate."

"What will become of The Crow?" I asked.

"Like it or not, he'll ship out with me, and I'll watch him on the voyage and find a good spot for him while we're away. I doubt he'll be back—not here anyway."

"Should I tell him that if he shows up again?" Caesar asked.

"I'm sure I'll find him first. But you must consider if you can handle this post alone or if I need to find a new man to help. Think about that, and we'll speak again tomorrow."

"Aye, Captain," he replied.

He slipped a glass flask from his jacket and passed it to Caesar. "Take it easy with this now. We need you with your eyes peeled more than ever."

"Aye, aye, Sir," Caesar said with a nod. "I won't let you down."

Thache beckoned us to walk on, but I figured Ody was enough company. So, I said, "If you don't need me, Captain, I'll help Caesar catch tomorrow's fish."

"Fishin' is a pleasure," Thache replied, his beard waving as his grin spread. "Ody will be enough help for me. You carry on here."

Once Ody and the Captain started toward the house, Caesar passed me his line and rigged up another for himself. "I'll keep the hooks on; you handle the bait," he said, pointing to a crock of nightcrawlers.

Our conversation moved from fishing to other things we liked to do. Since a pirate crewman wouldn't have heard about baseball or video games, and we didn't have much common ground in swimming or diving, the topic turned to girls.

"Do you have a favorite girl back home?"

I grinned. "I like one or two better than most," I replied.

"Well, how do you entertain them girls?" he asked.

I cocked my head. "We talk. Most of them like to talk a lot. And I ask questions." Then, I chuckled, adding, "Sometimes I listen, too, but Grandma says I don't do enough of that."

Caesar swept his line back and forth as he asked, "So, what do you like to talk about?"

"Mostly whatever they choose," I replied.

His chuckle turned to a belly laugh. "Sounds like the women I know, too. Only most of them work for a living, and they don't have much time for talking."

"Dr. Neuvo said Edward had a girl when he was young. He drew a picture of them together; did you ever see it?"

"Never saw any picture, but I saw the girl."

"You did? What was she like?"

"Well, she was young, but then, so was Edward—both about Mrs. Marybeth's age. She was a pretty thing, and young master Thache was near struck dumb by his love of her."

"How did he meet her?"

"She worked at the house, and when Old Mrs. Thache began to fail, Abigail became her serving girl. Edward liked how she comforted his mother and finally loved her enough to want her for his wife."

"I heard the Captain say she was the first Mrs. Thache. Did you see their wedding?"

"No. Ned and Miss Abigail ran away to marry. It wasn't smooth sailin' for them two. The old Captain wanted better for his boy. Only a lady was good enough for his Ned; a lady's maid wouldn't do. But Abigail was the only woman in the world for young Edward."

My next question was more delicate. "Do you think the Captain loved Abigail more than our Mrs. Thache—Marybeth?"

"That's a hard question, and it took years of searching the seas before Edward found his answer. Things are easier now, I'd say. When he and

Abigail married, those were hard days. Things got so bad between Ned and the Old Captain that the son left his father's farm."

"What did he do then?" I asked.

"Edward knew a little farming but more about the sea, so he signed onto the *Barbados Merchant*, a hired ship out of Plymouth. The farms in Jamaica were still struggling, so it was the best way he had to provide for his wife."

"Is that when you left, too?"

"Soon after. Working the *Merchant*, he figured he'd be in England as much as Jamaica, so he settled his wife in London and settled me there, too, to watch after them."

"Did that work out?"

"For a time. Edward paid the bills, and he came ashore when he could. He was there when his baby girl was born. Ned named her Elizabeth after his mother. He considered staying ashore, but he finally decided his wife and baby needed his pay as much as he and Abigail wanted to be together."

"So, did Elizabeth grow up in England?"

"Not for long. Queen Anne's War was raging, and the Royal Navy needed men. So, they pressed Edward and some crewmates into service aboard the H.S.S. Windsor. Then later that year, old Captain Thache, Ned's father, died, and he had hardly left enough money to pay for his funeral, and what else there was went to Edward. But he couldn't keep it."

"Why not?"

"Because the older Edward left a widow and two children without support. So, Edward signed his inheritance to them, and since he now needed to support two families, he moved Abigail and baby Elizabeth back to Jamaica. That way, he had only one household needing his money."

"And did you go to Jamaica again, too?"

"Well, yes. 'Twas mostly more slaves that Edward inherited, so the Jamaica house had family for Elizabeth and hands to work. But while Edward stayed in the navy, I helped Lucretia and Abigail till a worse tragedy struck. Abigail fell sick and died. Edward blamed himself. He hadn't sent enough money, and the navy wouldn't pay him more. Edward's heart broke till it would work no more. He never got over being at sea when she died. That's when he left the navy, and that's when I sailed with Edward again."

"So, he lost his wife and his child at the same time?"

"Aye, he did. The family thought he'd be a bad influence on little Beth. Maybe Edward thought so, too. He was plunderin' Spanish wrecks by then. He sent money when he could, but he stayed away from his child after that."

When we had eight nice trout in the tub, Caesar figured that was enough, so I gathered our fishing kit while he added more creek water and covered the tub.

"Were there other Mrs. Thaches?" I asked.

Caesar chuckled again. "There were other women, and some called him husband, but it wasn't so. Edward's a brawny man; he likes the ladies, and they like him, too. But he's what you might call a one-woman man, and for a time, they might have seemed like wives, but none of them were his Abigail. He told me he'd never promise himself to another woman who'd have to share him with the sea."

"Then is Marybeth just another of those women? Will he leave her when he ships out?"

"Oh, no. Marybeth—she's the end of that. This is the first time he's let himself love again, and he says the sea can't take him from her. So no, I don't think he loved Abigail more than Marybeth. He couldn't be there for Abigail when she needed him, but now he can devote himself to Marybeth. She's his second chance to love a woman the way she deserves. That never happened to him between his two wives. They are the clamshells around his heart, first love, and final love. But with Marybeth, he can live the life he planned—the one he wanted with Abigail. He even hints at new children to come."

"But he must sail at least one more time, Caesar. Can you keep her safe alone?"

"I'll die trying if it comes to that."

"I'll stay by you if I can," I said. "But it depends on what Grandma thinks is best."

"Will she stay?" he asked.

"I think I can convince her," I replied. "But let's see what the Captain figures out. He won't let you down."

"Come back in the morning, I'll clean these, and you can help me tote 'em to the house," Caesar said as he waved me goodbye.

It was nearly night when I got home, and the house was silent. Ody was not in his bed, and that was too bad. Surely, he'd believe Captain Thache's good intentions after hearing Abigail's story. He'd be on my side to stay at Plum Point so that we could protect Marybeth and her mother. I tried to stay awake to hear about his visit with Wallace and why he was out so late, but my eyes wouldn't cooperate. Ody's story could wait till morning.

29 Articles for Sea

Ody Saunters

After we left Caesar's fishing hole, the Captain told me he planned to row to Bath for the evening, and I asked to ride with him.

He grinned as he asked, "Meeting with a lass in town, are ye?" But before I could answer, he added, "Well, I must warn ye, the business I have in mind tonight might take some time. Would that trouble ye?" he asked.

"I reckon I can find a fisherman sailing this way who'll bring me home."

He raised his eyebrows as he rubbed his chin. Then he said, "You're man enough to mind yourself. But if things don't work out as you plan, you can rest in the jollyboat till I'm ready to shove off. If you're not there when I get to the boat, I'll reckon you found your way."

"Fair enough."

We stopped at the farmhouse long enough for the Captain to say goodnight to Marybeth. Then while he visited his den, I explained to Oma that Drake was fishing and that I'd be in Bath with the Captain.

Cocking an eyebrow, she asked, "What business do you have in Bath?"

"While the Captain does his work, I'll catch up with Wallace."

"Hm," she whispered, and she moved closer. "Be careful," she said. "You know the stakes, so I'll say no more than that."

Edward returned wearing his red Captain's jacket. The sack he carried, the same duffel he had taken from Caesar, was no longer empty, and it partially covered the sword scabbard hanging to his knee. After a last peck on the cheek to Marybeth, he donned his broad-brimmed hat, and we were off.

Once we shoved off the landing, Edward took the oars.

"So, is it a lass you're after, Lad, or are ye just fishing for one?"

"Not that," I replied. "I met a fellow here who watches over the shipyard at night; I'll keep him company with a few dice games."

"Well, watch your coins; gaming can make a man poor in a hurry. 'Tis probably happening right now with some of the crew. That's my business tonight. I'll see what they're up to and pass the word that we will sail again soon."

"Where will you find them?" I asked.

"Wherever they be."

He was silent for a while, probably pondering where to look for mischievous crewmen, but then he turned to me again. "You know I never asked; where is this home you want to return to?"

Too many questions about home could lead to trouble, so I stuck to simple words, "east of here," and then quickly changed the subject. "Mrs. Thache was lonely for you while you were at sea before. 'Tis a shame you must sail again so quickly."

His lips thinned, and his chin dropped to his chest as he replied, "This trip shouldn't be so long. I hope to return within a week or two. Things should be better for us after that." Then after a pause, "But you never know how the winds will blow."

I nodded, "Aye, you never know."

When we rowed into the Towne Point landing, Edward waited for me to go ashore and waved me on. "Be about your business, boy. I'll tie us off."

I nodded and hurried north to the shipyard, where I found Wallace.

"Back again?" he asked.

"Yes, I have business in town, but I must ask you a question."

Wallace put down his chisel. "Speak up, then,"

"Very well. The Captain will be sailing again soon," I said, "And I'm not sure how much longer my cousin and I can stay in Bath."

"What does that have to do with me?"

My throat went dry, but I said, "I'd feel better leaving if I knew you'd keep watch over Marybeth."

"Well, 'tis not much of your business," he replied, "but the truth is, I'll protect Marybeth as long as she needs me to."

"Even though she loves Captain Thache?" I asked.

"I told you—as long as she needs me."

"All right, then. That's good to know."

"Is that all you need of me?" he asked as he picked up his chisel again.

"Well, some of the crew are in town tonight, and a couple of them have been stealing behind the Captain's back. Can I borrow your cloak and hat again? I want to watch them for a while."

He shrugged as he worked. "They're on the pegs on the tent posts."

So I swapped my tricorn for the wool hat and covered the rest of me with the cloak.

"Thank you. I'll return these tonight."

He grunted as I left for town.

Lucky for me, my shadowy table under the stairs was empty even though the Hornpipe was already filling up. I wasn't hungry, but I figured eating was a good excuse, so I ordered the supper stew with cider to drink and an ale to hide behind.

The Tavern room was thick with pipe smoke, and the peg-legged barman, Silas Van Horn, opened the doors to catch a cross breeze. I reckoned it was his job to keep an eye on the patrons, and while he couldn't get across the room quickly, the cross breeze helped with the smoke so he could at least keep an eye out for trouble brewing.

Two women shared a table with three of the men. Other men sat grouped around the piper's spot, and one man sat alone in a dark corner near the door. Anyone entering might have missed him in their rush to find the barman or join a table near the piper, and this shadowed man preferred solitude.

The chatter was generally pleasant, with giggling girls and saucy quips from the servers. But the night was early and the drinking light, except for the shadowed man who called for his third round.

I recognized the girl who brought my stew, even though she was new at this job.

"Beg pardon, Sir," she said when she bumped the table and spilled a bit of gravy. She quickly grabbed a towel to wipe the mess.

"Colleen, is it?" I asked.

"Aye, Sir. Have I served 'e before?"

"No, I saw you once, dancing among the sailors. There was a bit of a scuffle that time."

She grimaced. "'Tis nothing unusual here, Sir—not when the men start feeling what's in their cups." Then she wiped her hands on her apron and smoothed the skirt as she stood. "Will there be anything else, Sir?"

"Can you tell me the name of that fellow near the door? He might be a big chap when he stands, and if he's going to feel his cups, I will keep out of his path."

"By the look of 'im, just a sailor or a fisherman, Sir. 'Tis all I know."

The quiet man beckoned to Colleen, and while he spoke to her, I risked studying him more closely. It was hard to gauge his height while sitting, but he must have been tall. His bent knees would have scraped the table had he not extended his legs, and I could see the toe of his boots leaning against the rungs of the chair opposite him. A wool hat like mine covered his hair, and the brim hung over his face. He wore a salt-crusted fisherman's cloak with the collar buttoned up to his chin as if he expected a squall.

Colleen had far more to say to this stranger than she had to me, and from their expressions, it was not flirting. She must have had news for this man because she brought him no food or drink, but he passed her two bits when she left his table.

In a moment, Colleen brought the fisherman his new round and carried a fresh cider to my table, laying one of the bits beside it. "From the gentleman you asked about, Sir. He says not to give him away. I thought you didn't know him."

"He must be mistaken," I said, "but I'll take the cider all the same. You keep the coin."

When she left, I tipped my glass to the stranger, hoping to recognize him. The tip of a sword hung from beneath the cloak, scraping the floor, and when he tilted his head to sip ale, wavy black hair escaped from his collar. The man was Captain Thache, wearing his version of the cloak and hat disguise.

I nursed my stew, and Edward watched the crowd. The Crow was not among them yet, but there were a few who looked like men I had seen from afar. The only one I recognized was the oarsman who had ferried Edmund Chamberlain to Plum Point on the night of the meeting—the man who had carried Hands' sack up Plum Point Gut.

Edward ordered ale for one of the patrons and had Colleen direct him to the shadowy table near the door. There was only one table between Edward and me, and the room's din made them speak louder than they might have preferred, so I stirred my stew and listened.

"Pippa Morton," Edward said as the man sat.

"Aye, Cap'n Thache. What brings you here?"

"I've news for my crew, and I wanted to tell a few of 'e first to see how the wind blows. We have the chance at a new voyage," Edward replied.

"Tradin' up the coast again?" he asked.

"Nay, to the islands this time. The Governor is asking for more rum, molasses, sugar, and indigo, which is easier to find in the Indies. Can I count on you, Morton? You're the best gunner I ever sailed with."

Pippa leaned back and clasped his hands on the table. "Same articles of sailin'?" he asked.

"Should be," Thache replied, "but you know how it goes; the crew votes on what they want. If the others are satisfied with the rules we signed after losing *Queen Anne*, so am I. Is there one you want to see changed?"

Morton leaned over the table. "Well, it's like you say, Cap'n, I'm your best gunner, and if we sail to the Indies, we'd better have enough firepower."

"Put your oars in, man," Thache said. "Say what you mean."

"I want plenty of powder and help to keep the guns ready. And on top of that, I want a bigger share. One and a quarter ain't worth the risk. If Hands gets one and a half, I'm due closer to that."

"You're worth every penny of that," Edward replied, "but we must bring it before the crew and agree. How do you reckon the men will take that? More for you means less for them."

"Some others will want more, too, but I'd wager they want to keep a good gunner in the crew. It'll pass."

"Very well, then. We might not have time for a new vote till we get to St. Thomas, but you have my word, we'll have a vote then."

"Fair enough, Captain. Is there anything else?"

"First, I'm pleased to keep you on the crew. How are things with the other men? Do they like it here, or do they wish for wider seas?"

"'Tis a mix, Cap'n, but most are wid 'e no matter where."

"Then spread the word among them closest to ye. Let 'em know we may shove off at short notice."

Pippa nodded.

"And tell them this, too. There are complaints about rowdiness in town, and they should mind what they do and how they treat the ladies if we want to keep a home port here."

"I know you'd prefer that, Cap'n. I'll spread the word."

Edward called others to his table, and they spoke of their hoped-for changes.

Jonah Kursey, a deckhand, was one of the men at the table with women. He was ready to find a wife and give up the sea. Thache reminded him of the standing rule that no one left the group till he had shares totaling 1000 pounds. But then the Captain suggested a compromise.

"We're in unusual circumstances here. How about if we make this voyage an exception? Anyone who prefers to stay in Bath can leave our company now, or they can choose to leave or stay once we reach the islands. Sailin' will give you plenty of time to decide, not to mention a cut of our profits."

"'Tis only if the crew approves the rule, right?" Jonah asked.

"Aye, if they do. Of course, staying here will be an agreement between the crewman and me, and those of us reaching St. Thomas will vote on general changes there."

Jonah bobbed his head. "Agreed, Cap'n."

"And remember this, Jonah," Thache said, nodding toward the women at the table Jonah had left, "the rule about disrespecting prudent women—that stands."

"I hear ye, Sir. Death to any who violates a woman without her consent."

Jonah hurried back to his table, and I wondered if he proposed marriage then and there. But soon, another cluster of men came to talk to Thache.

These three wanted better conditions onboard the ship. Jerky Husk, the sailor who carried Hand's sack across Plum Point, wanted more drink; Gibby Garote, a boatswain, asked for better food; and Timmy Tyler wanted a higher limit for onboard gaming.

Captain Thache had a similar reply to each. "Food has always been all you want from our provisions unless we have a shortage, then we vote on rationing or not. I can't think of a sweeter deal than that, but we can begin the voyage with better provisions if we find 'em."

"That'd be a start, Cap'n," Gibby replied.

"Strong drink goes by the same rule, except drinking ends at 8:00 of the evening when we move to night watch, and we can't do better than that, either. As to gaming, same as drinking, none after 8:00, and Captain's choice of punishment to any man taking more than a pound's value off a man in gaming."

Tyler petitioned for up to five pounds, and the Captain said he'd allow a vote, but we'll maroon any man found cheating, and any dispute will be settled with pistols on shore, same as always.

When Tyler seemed disappointed, Edward said, "I tell 'e what. You can gamble for five pounds, but it must be agin me. If you can win gold from me, you're welcome to it."

"Fair enough, Cap'n," Tyler said, grinning.

"Remember the no cheatin' part too, Matey," Edward warned.

When Garote and Husk mingled with the crowd again, The Hornpipe was soon buzzing about the rules the men wanted to change, but Timmy Tyler was still at the Captain's table when Israel Hands walked in with The Crow.

"Watch Israel Hands, Captain," Tyler whispered. "He's been telling the men he wants to be captain, and when we next vote, he may have won some of them over."

"Then I may be looking for a new Quarter Master, Tyler. Are you interested?"

"Won't the men vote on that, too, Captain?" Tyler asked.

"They will, but I believe these two latecomers have broken one of our other rules. The one that says you can't cheat the crew or any man among them for a value great than a pound. I believe I can prove that those two stole from me. So, who knows? They may not live long enough to see a vote."

Tyler's eyes widened, and he hurried back to his friends.

Word spread quickly that Thache was there, and Israel Hands scanned the room till he found Edward. Then he stood to address the crowd.

"Well, is the Captain spying on us?" he asked loudly.

"This establishment's open to any seaman, as I recall," Thache replied, ignoring the accusation. Then, standing taller than anyone in the room, he pulled the seabag from his feet to the tabletop. Perhaps no one besides The Crow and Hands knew the sack with the leather band, but those two got Thache's message—the Captain had caught them.

Thache dropped the cloak and hat, fluffed out his black beard, and let the hair swirl over the shoulders of his white shirt. Then he pulled his broad-brimmed hat from the sack, and with the crown of the hat and feather from the rim, he reached the ceiling.

Last, he pulled the sword from his scabbard and faced the two thieves before him. Then, shifting the sack with the edge of his sword, he asked, "How did this get to Plum Point, Hands? And Crow, how did a dress from this sack find its way to Colleen's back?"

Hands face hardened as he took a couple of deep breaths before replying, "You gave that sack to me, Thache. 'Tis mine for caring for the crew on that forsaken island you put us on."

"You were to protect the contents of that sack for me, Hands. And you violated my trust. On top of that, I hear you're petitioning to be our next Captain. Is that so? I believe I can produce witnesses."

When Hands drew his sword, Silas made his skip and hop to the door and hurried all who were not part of the crew outside. Most patrons didn't know me, so I left, too, but I loitered around the open back window to witness what was said.

"You know I don't want to draw on you, Captain," Hands said, adjusting his eyepatch with the free hand.

"I never figured you for an idjit, Basilisk."

"Then, shall we take this matter to the beach, Edward? Or should I wait for you to fetch your pistols?"

Edward lowered his head like a bull ready to charge, his eyes sparking like flint on steel. "I reckon I can handle the two of you with my sword—maybe my bare hands will do."

The Crow stood wide-eyed, partly protected behind Hands' shoulder. Then he stammered, "Wait. I had no idea that the sack belonged to the Captain. And Hands told me I could use the clothing as I liked." The room fell silent, and Coleman shook like a flag in a gale before adding, "Do … do we need a trial?"

"No," Thache replied. "I know who stole from me, and punishment is by the Captain's choice. I didn't come here for satisfaction, though. That'll keep. Tonight, I came for two purposes. The first is to see if my crew perplexes the town of Bath and the Governor himself. The second is to inform the crew of a voyage we must soon take on Eden's behalf and to ask them their pleasure concerning changes to our ship's articles."

"Changes?" Hands asked.

Edward took a step closer and lifted the tip of his sword to his shoulder. "So, tell me, Basilisk, what rules do you want to be changed when we get to St. Thomas? And what about you, Crow?"

Hands stood firm. "I want what the crew always wants, and the crew knows I'll give it to them. Bigger prizes for all of us—bigger than we can find out of Ocracoke." The muttering from the crew showed they liked that idea.

The Captain turned to The Crow. "And you?"

Coleman was nervous; he swallowed hard to get enough spit to speak. But the murmurs blowing through the crowd gave him courage. "I … I believe …." His voice cracked as the last words rushed out. "I believe we need a new Captain."

This time the crowd was less favorable, so Coleman turned to them as he added, "You all know he cheated Bonnet, and he'll cheat us, too."

Thache strode toward Crow and came so close that he trod on the toe of Israel Hand's boot. "Careful, boy," he said, although fewer than ten years were between their ages. "We already have a rule about disputes on land. But if you want a new captain, you can vote for one when we get to St. Thomas. Then you can live or die with your vote."

"Let the men speak," Hands said. "I call for a voice vote now."

The Crow took up the cry, "All for Israel Hands for the captain, say *aye*." When the room remained silent, not even The Crow dared vote for Hands.

"The men are too cowed by you to vote their wishes," Hands said. "We can have a proper vote on the island."

"Oh. Let's finish what we started," Timmy Tyler said. "Who's for Captain Thache?"

There was a roar of ayes in support of Edward.

The Captain laughed as he said, "'Tis settled then. Time to turn in, Mates. We have a voyage to prepare for."

As the men rushed to wherever their beds lay, Edward had the last word to Israel Hands. "We'll settle this when the time is right. But, until then, make ready to sail, *Master* Hands."

And even while crouching outside the backdoor, I heard the sarcasm as he spoke the word *master*. And from the flop sweats on The Crow's brow, I figured we'd never see him on Plum Point again.

30 Articles for Land

Ody Saunters

Once Captain Thache gave the order to turn in, I hurried back to Wallace's tent. The ringing peal of metal on stone reached me before I left the street, and I wondered if he pulverized rock to gravel.

Carving memorial stones was not all Wallace did for Captain Harding. He used his carving skills to fit pieces of periaugers together, and an unfinished wood carving, as long as a good-sized canal boat, lay along one side of the tent.

He nodded but said nothing as I returned his cloak and swapped his hat for mine. He was too busy striking chisel to stone with such power that I thought his bones would break if the stone did not.

I was wrong. It was the chisel that snapped.

"Dang it all," he shouted, throwing the pieces to the floor.

"Can that be repaired?" I asked.

If he muttered a word, we didn't hear it amid clanking metal as he rummaged through his tools.

"Is something wrong?" I asked.

"Of course, there is. Thache is in town," he spat. "Or was. Is he still here?"

"Could be," I replied. "Did you break your chisel because of Captain Thache?"

He turned to me, chisel raised, and I thought he might pound me instead of the ballast rock on his table.

"I'd like to break him," he said.

"Then give it a try, boy."

Captain Thache's voice was soft but clear, but hissing of danger.

It took a moment for Wallace McNeil to rein his anger, but when his teeth stopped grinding, he asked, "What are you doing in my shop?"

"What have you been doing at my house?" Thache replied.

"Plum Point is not yours," Wallace bellowed. Then he slumped to his work stool, barely whispering, "Maybe Marybeth is, but Plum Point is not." Wallace blinked to deny the tears that washed over the name of Thache's wife. Then he asked, "If you come to finish me, get on with it."

"Not yet," Edward said, and he walked around the shop, examining the carver's work, and found a partly built periauger to use as a seat.

As the Captain toured the shop, Wallace watched his every move, gripping his chisel so tightly that his fingers turned white. Maybe he was bracing for the sword or picking his moment to strike as he watched silently.

Finally, Edward spoke. "I believe we need parley. We might both benefit."

"Parley?" I asked, not expecting to hear French from Edward. "You want to talk?"

"Aye, if the lad is willing. Or we can take up arms if he'd rather. A good battle might be relaxing. It seems we need to settle things one way or another."

I was all for talking. The Captain's blade was sharp, and I didn't want to see Wallace skinned like a rabbit. McNeil dropped his chisel and ripped the scarf from his head. His hair was returning, but the scar was still visible.

"Do as you like," he said. "Talk or fight." He wiped his bare hands on his breeches as he waited.

Edward stood and examined the work of his henchmen on Wallace's scalp. "Whoever gave you that scar did a poor job of scratching out a skull," he said.

"Then you should train your men better," Wallace replied.

"My men, eh?" Edward tapped the blade of his cutlass against his hand as he studied the scar. "I reckon they used the wrong knife. I bet you have a better one here."

Even though the feather tickled the canopy, Edward kept his hat on as he strode through the tent, rifling the work blades. Finally, he chose a sharp knife, about ten inches long, then sheathed his sword, and with the dagger in hand, he returned to Wallace. Standing with the knife's point at McNeil's eyes, he said, "Your weapon. Now, there's a fair fight."

I wasn't sure if this side of the Captain frightened Wallace, but it sent shivers through me, so I asked, "Aren't you going to talk?"

Thache flicked the knife point to the air. "He hasn't agreed to it," he replied.

"For goodness' sake, Wallace, tell the Captain you'll listen."

"Speak your piece," the carver replied.

"Very well. Article 1: I want you to tell me face-to-face that you accept that Marybeth is my wife, and I want you to promise you'll never try to slither between us."

Wallace summoned his voice. "She married you and told me she loves you and wants to stay with you. And even though I'll always wish for her, I honor her vows."

Thache nodded as he sat against the boat and rested the knife on his knee. "She loves me, and I trust her. 'Tis you I want assurance from. I must be sure you won't bother her while I'm at sea."

"Well," Wallace said, venom in his eyes. "I agreed to that. So, what else do you want?"

"Oh, I want more, but now 'tis your turn. What do you want of me? Besides, of course, me letting you have my wife."

Wallace clenched his fists, shaking his head. "I want you to admit you mistreated me," he said, pointing to his head.

Again, Thache nodded. "In this case, my men acted on what they thought I wanted, but I admit, I kept no secrets about wishing her to be my wife. I'm not sorry about that, but I regret your assault and will take responsibility for it. Name your price."

"I don't want your stolen money," he said. "You won the woman I wanted, but you spirited me away to do it. That's on your soul, and you can't pay that back—not to me. So, what else do you want?"

Thache pursed his lips. "I'm a man short at the Point, and I must sail again for the sake of Bath Town. I want you to keep Marybeth safe. I'll pay you for your trouble. Whatever you think is fair."

Wallace stood up, feet squared, fists at his side. "I'd give my life for Marybeth because she is worth it. This world would be less of a place without her breathing its air. I'll do whatever I can to keep her well, but I won't take your money for that."

Thache stood, too. He matched McNeil's swagger but let the knife drop as he towered over Wallace, his massive fists rock-hard and ready to throw blows if that's what McNeil wanted. Instead, he inched forward, neither slowing nor stopping, till he forced Wallace to his stool.

Then, with his opponent cowed, Edward, jaw stiff and eyes narrowed, turned from Wallace and patrolled the shop again.

"It may happen that you'll need gold to protect her," he said.

"I'll find what I need."

Thache looked out the tent door toward the boats in progress. "I could use a second periauger. Plum Point needs more than a jollyboat, especially to ferry goods. Marybeth will be safer with another boat; the men I leave with her can row it if she needs it. Are any of these for sale?" he asked.

"Captain Harding approves the twenty-footer at the far end for sale as soon as we test it. You can talk to him about it."

Thache turned back to Wallace. "Buy it for me. The trade will go smoother if you handle it. I'll give you the coin when you bring the boat to Plum Point landing."

"I can do that," Wallace said. "Is that it?"

Edward's face showed no emotion as he shook his head at McNeil. He huffed as he paced, examining each project. Finally, he spoke softly. "'Tis like leaving a fox in my hen house. You love my wife a little too much."

"So it may be," Wallace replied, "but I won't dishonor her, and no one will protect her better than I."

"What's this thing here?" Edward asked, pointing to the enormous wooden carving.

"'Tis a figurehead. Surely, you've seen those."

"Aye, but never on the ground—always on the bow of a ship."

Wallace nodded. "This one's for a sloop Captain Harding is building. 'Tis a dolphin, or it will be."

"Can you make a smaller statue?" Thache asked. "One the size of a person standing on Plum Point tower?"

"As a favor?" Wallace asked.

Thache turned to face him. "No, not a favor, as a pledge."

"What pledge?"

"Make it for me, and I promise to pay you twice the wages you get for this one. Do you agree?"

"Yes, I'd agree to that. Money helps me start my own business. But now I have another thing to ask of you."

"Say it," Thache replied.

"I want to be able to work in the open and stop hiding in Bath. I want you and your men out of my way."

"That's fair."

"Then what carving do you want?"

"I want a likeness of Marybeth watching the waves as she waits for me to return. And as you make her likeness, remember what I say, then you'll know what she means to me and what I'd do to anyone who takes her from me."

Wallace sat stiff, his face swept with emotions changing like clouds before a hurricane. Finally, with teeth clenched, he said, "I'm listening."

The Captain nodded. "Make her look as soft and sweet as she is in the flesh. And dress her in a gown that flows as if tossed in the ocean breeze. Make her hair tickle her shoulders and brighten her eyes as if she's lighting a safe path to lead me home. And make her laugh with pleasure as she does when she sees me coming to the porch."

Wallace gripped his seat as he listened to the torture Thache had brought to him. He blinked back tears as he replied. "I agree."

"Then we have a pact. Ody, write this down."

I searched for pen and ink to record the agreement, and each man read it aloud.

"Article 1: Captain Edward Thache admits his actions and those of his crew brought hardship and distress to Wallace McNeil. Edward Thache promises to cease further measures against McNeil or his business endeavors. And in return, Wallace McNeil vows to respect the love between Thache and his wife, Marybeth Bellieu Thache, and will never interfere between them as long as they live. Instead, he will do whatever he can to keep Marybeth Thache and her Plum Point property safe from harm or distress, whether Thache be home or abroad.

"Side Agreement 2: Wallace McNeil promises to acquire a periauger for the Plum Point plantation. Thache is to render species sufficient to cover the price set by the owner, Captain Thomas Harding.

"Agreement 3: Wallace McNeil will carve a statue in the likeness of Marybeth Thache of appropriate size and shape to stand on the tower of Plum Point plantation. In return, Edward Thache promises to pay twice the wages earned by McNeil for the production of the Dolphin figurehead he is now making for Captain Thomas Harding."

We made two signed copies of the document, one for each of the two men. Wallace threw his copy into his toolbox, and Thache tapped the brim of his hat before beckoning me to leave.

When we reached Plum Point, the Captain gave his copy to me for safekeeping. So I acquired the key, and he followed me to the hiding hole, where I dropped it in the same bottle as the contract he had given Marybeth before his first voyage.

So, Thache saw the secret tunnel and where we hid the bottle. As to the key, he asked me to let him hold it for a time, but he promised to hide it in a safe place for Marybeth, should she need it. And after hearing his bargain with Wallace, I had no doubt he'd do what he said.

31 Putting Plum Point in Order

Marybeth Thache

Word of a new voyage spread like streak lightning from Bath to Ocracoke. And since the men had done their duty in careening, repairing, and mending *Adventure*'s sails, the day for Edward to ship out was coming too quickly to suit me.

The men looked forward to this new voyage far into the open sea. They hummed sailor tunes as their periauger stopped at our landing on their way to Bath. Some spoke of reunions with family or mates they hoped to see in the islands, and Edward said some begged him for a stop in Jamaica, or better, New Providence.

"Will you allow it?" I asked.

"Jamaica is my old home, but there's nothing for me there now."

"Well, there's your daughter. And didn't you mean to give these dresses you captured to her?"

"She has a family to provide for her, and I doubt she'd want to see me again. My showing up might put a wedge between her and her husband-to-be. I'd likely do more harm than good."

"I can't say about that," I said. "But I'd love to see my father again, and his blessing on my wedding would have meant a lot."

Edward nodded. "But your father didn't have my reputation. And while I provide some service to Bath, those in Jamaica haven't heard it. So, I'd probably do best for my Elizabeth by sending a letter."

"Send her my wedding dress with your note and give her our best wishes."

"You're a treasure, my darling. I'll send the note to my stepmother. She will know how Elizabeth will receive it and make the best choice. Otherwise, I'll steer clear of there."

"And what about New Providence?"

"That town was once a pirate stronghold—a perfect place for pirate hunters like Hornigold to find us and give chase."

"But you aren't a pirate now, Edward. You took the King's pardon."

"Aye, but some, like Bonnet, took the pardon and returned to the pirate way, making it worse for us all. Some of the crew might slip back to it. 'Tis safer to stay clear of old haunts."

Between boat runs with the crew for provisions in Bath, the Captain ensured Plum Point had full larders and that our fences and walls were well-mended. Then, with Mother and me at the table, we listed every possible need.

"You should plan provisions for a month," Edward said. "Write anything missing on this page, and I'll find it." Then, when he saw my disappointment, he assured me it shouldn't be that long. He just wanted to be safe.

The Crow was to ship out with the others, but we had Caesar, and he made room for a new sailor to move into the hut. "Jonah Kursey says he plans to be a landlubber now. Kursey wants to marry a girl here. So, he's no longer on my crew, but he'll learn farming here while I'm gone and make a fair wage for it. I'll leave coins enough for you to pay him and run the house, too."

"Who will make him listen?" Mother asked.

"You will, good Mother. You run the crew; let Mrs. Thache watch the pennies. Neither Jonah nor any other man will face my wrath if you're not well-treated."

Mother smiled at Edward despite herself.

"What of the widow Saunters and the lads?" he asked. "Do we know if they'll stay here?"

I nodded toward the summer house. "They're discussing it now. I believe the boys are trying to convince her."

"They need to decide soon," Edward said. "We may need to ask Knight to have his men watch our landing."

Mother stood, fists to her hips. "I can use Bert's gun, and Marybeth practically lives on that tower while you're away. We can manage."

"But what if the unexpected happens? What if the Indians rise again?" Edward asked.

Mother twitched her lips a few times before replying, "Aurora and her grandsons are resourceful, but they have soft hands. I doubt they want to fight the Tuscarora. So, your men will have to do."

"Is there word of an uprising?" I asked, fear rising in my chest.

"No," he replied. "Just thinking of the worst. But I've arranged for a new periauger for Plum Point. My men can row it, and so can the Saunters boys if they stay. It will carry what you need, but you must promise to go to the fort if trouble comes."

Mother spoke up. "I'll see that Marybeth escapes if need be, but I won't leave my home."

"Well, you ladies have your parley over the details while I see what Aurora has decided."

32 Stuck in Bath

Drake Saunters

Ody and I sat on the rock walls of the summer house while Grandma paced the floorboards, ticking off the points of her argument. We had heard it all before. Our time was running out, and we had been away from home too long. And now that Hetty's health had mended and the Captain was on hand to protect Plum Point, it was time to go home.

That's what Oma said, but I disagreed.

"We're time travelers," I said. "Asjen Nuevo might be one of the few people on this planet who know anything about our secret. Shouldn't we want to learn more while we're here?"

Ody didn't buy my argument. "We don't know if he has any answers. Augustus Neumann sure didn't know much."

"I agree with Ody," Grandma said. "If we found two chances for answers, we will surely find more. So, this decision should be one of safety, not taking risks for the improbable."

Ody shook his head, "But I have a different reason for staying; Marybeth is my worry. I've seen Captain Thache angry, and it's not pretty."

Grandma shrugged. "Captain Thache might blow his stack occasionally, but we've never seen him be anything but kind to the ladies of Plum Point."

"There's another good reason to stay," I said. "We could set the record straight. Everyone thinks Blackbeard was such a bad guy—murderous and scary. I don't think he's like that—not to those he cares about, anyway."

"Grandma put a hand on our shoulders. You make good points, boys, but we aren't here to correct the perceptions of history or to change it. When we go home, we'll be part of a family, and we must tuck all that happens here deep inside us till the rest of the Saunters clan is ready to learn about it. And we should probably go before we see things we can't tuck away."

She kept her hands on us, waiting for a response. I went first.

"Thache is a good man," I said. "I've seen it."

"I believe he means well for Marybeth, but he's a bully, too," Ody replied.

Grandma sighed. She sat on the rocky wall opposite us, saying. "We are getting nowhere, and when we can't all agree, someone must decide, and this time that is *me*."

"Uh oh," Ody said. His attention shifted as he watched a freshly painted and polished periauger pulling into Plum Point landing; Wallace McNeil was at the helm.

Grandma strained to see the new arrival. "Oh, this can't be good. I'd better head this off," she muttered, leading the way to the landing with Ody and me on her heels.

"Wow, Wallace. That was fast. She's a beauty!" Ody said.

"You knew about this?" I asked. "Couldn't it wait till the Captain sailed?"

"The Captain ordered it," he said, grinning.

"And here he comes now," Grandma said, pointing to Edward striding down the boardwalk. "I hope you're right about this, Ody."

Captain Thache stopped at the landing and eyed the boat from all sides. "'Tis as good as I hoped," he said. And he chuckled as he added, "You named it *PlumMary*. Excellent choice. Now name your price."

Wallace was not smiling when he replied, "Captain Harding asks this sum, and he signed it to prove the value." He handed Edward a paper with a price written on it, and Edward found the amount in his pocket.

"Here 'tis, and four pounds more," he said.

"I don't require extra," McNeil replied.

"'Tis for the extra duty you might do for the Point. Keep it."

Grandma's eyebrow raised. "Have you two become friends?" she asked.

"No," Wallace replied. "But we've come to terms."

Ody nodded. "They signed articles, and this boat is part of the deal."

"What's the other part?" I asked, but he didn't need to reply as we were about to find out. Jonah Kursey ran to the dock, and Marybeth was close behind.

"Your lady fetched me, Captain. What's this here?" Jonah asked.

"'Tis a spare boat I ordered for Plum Point in case we need to ferry more people or goods. We needed more than a jollyboat here," Thache replied.

I agreed with Ody, the boat made perfect sense to me, and I expected the truce would suit Oma and be better for Plum Point. But things never go that smoothly.

Wallace McNeil jumped from the boat with a knife and grabbed Jonah, saying, "Do you remember me?"

Jonah sucked in his breath, shocked, as he wiggled to get free from Wallace. Then, finally, he gasped, "Is this some kind of trap?"

"If it is, I'm ready for it," Wallace said, turning to the Captain. "Is this your idea of a bargain?"

"It ain't my idea of how to buy a boat; I can tell you that," Edward said. "What's the matter with you two?"

Wallace jerked off his headscarf. "This toady was among the gang that carved up my head and left me to die."

The sound out of Jonah's throat was more of a gurgle than words. "'Tis what the Captain wanted," he spurted.

Marybeth gasped. "What?"

When the Captain had each of the fighters in hand, he dragged them to the summer house, where he held one man to the left wall and the other to the right. "Come down here, all of you," he shouted, and we followed to the little arena.

"McNeil, is this one of the men who attacked you?" Thache growled.

"Aye, just as I said."

"And, Jonah, did you do this?"

"Well, I didn't do the cuttin', Sir, but I was with the crew who swore 'twas your order."

"And who told you it was my order?" Thache asked, shaking Jonah till his bones rattled.

"'Tain't clear, Sir. I was just selected to be in the crew who handled McNeil."

"Very well. McNeil and I have come to terms with this matter. He accepts that Marybeth is my wife, and I accepted responsibility for his attack." He turned to Marybeth, mouth agape and palms clasped to her cheeks. "I did not order it, but I reckon the men guessed what I wanted, and I accept responsibility."

"How did you make up for that?" I asked.

Ody knew the answer. "Wallace's price was that the Captain vow none of his men would bother the Carver again and that he could do business openly in Bath."

Marybeth's palms dropped. "You agreed to that?" Marybeth asked.

Wallace stared at his boot. "I did. The Captain is your husband, and I can't change that, so he wanted to make amends, and we bargained as to how."

"Did he offer you anything else?" I asked.

Wallace nodded his head. "He offered me money, but he can't pay for a heart lost, so he allowed me the thing next most precious. He will let me protect Marybeth and her family, which eases my pain."

Tears streamed over Marybeth's cheeks as Edward spoke.

"Now, you men made deals with me, and I had no idea you had strife with each other. Let me clear that up now. Jonah wants to give up the sea and live in Bath. He will help my wife run the farm while I'm gone. He's a fit sailor and might use the periauger for trading."

Then he turned to Wallace. "Wallace will help guard Plum Point, and while he will keep a respectful distance from my wife, he will help provide for her and my mother-in-law." He nodded toward Ody and me. "He'll also work with the Saunters family if they decide to stay."

Then he turned to Jonah. "Now I'll let loose of you two if you can promise to work by these articles and stop fighting on my land. I've bargained with 'e for help, not more trouble. Do I have your word?"

Once they agreed, Edward set them loose, and Jonah returned to the hut. Then we watched as Edward rowed Wallace to Bath, arguing for as long as we could tell, but neither struck a blow. Then Marybeth went to the house to dry her eyes.

I turned to my family, "See, I told you he was a fair man."

Ody scoffed. "You call that fair? They had to give their word, or Thache would have drowned them both in the creek. What else could they do?"

"He'd never do that," I said.

"Oh, good grief! Hush, you two," Grandma said. "Good man or not, we have no choice now. We must stay here. We can't leave Marybeth with one helper and two ready to murder each other on her land. If we did, there would be no need to worry about a war to come; there'd be one right here already." She stomped her foot.

"We're staying."

With that issue settled, I was happily stuck in Bath as I had hoped. Now I'd have time to learn more about Neuvo and get proof about Captain Thache.

33 Articles of Love

Mary Beth Thache

Surely … *surely* Edward had set his men straight, and there'd be no more fighting.

I wouldn't say it out loud, but the worry spun like a spider's silk in the wind, gathering into knots when housework didn't keep me busy. And now my husband was late returning home, so I had more webs to untangle and sweep away.

When Caesar came for the crew's supper, I couldn't resist asking the question that burned inside me. "Have you heard word from the Captain?"

"Well, no, Mum," Caesar replied as if the missing captain was of little concern. And he was right; Captain Thache was absent more than present on Plum Point. But then he sniffed the covered trencher and, with a broad smile, said, "Supper smells good, Miz Thache. I reckon this will be better than Jonah's normal fare of late."

I tried to force a smile, but I wasn't sure it cracked through my worries. "Do you know Jonah well?" I asked.

"Not as well as some crewmen, but he was no trouble to the Cap'n or anyone else, as I recall. I trust Jonah will do the best he can here, and he'd be wise to study farmin' if he aims to make his living that way."

"Well, I hope you both enjoy your supper," I said, but he stopped me before I turned to the porch.

"Ma'am, are ye worried about the Cap'n?"

A heavy sigh poured over my fears. "Edward has been gone for hours, and now he'll miss supper. The last I saw of him was when he rowed our new periauger to town. He said nothing about having late business in Bath. And the last time I saw him, he was arguing with Wallace."

"I wouldn't fret. Some of the men are probably having a night out before they sail, and 'tis my understanding that he's keepin' an eye on their behavior." Then with a sharp and sure nod, he added, "He'll be along soon. You'll see."

His words, though well-intended, were of small comfort, but even a bit was better than none.

Edward did not make it home in time for the meal, and after the widows cleared things away, the Saunters family and Mother kept me company on the porch.

"I reckon the Captain sets his hours by the clock inside him," Mother said.

"I suppose."

Ody leaned toward me, saying, "He had other work for Wallace. So maybe they're talking about that."

"What other work?" I asked.

"Uh … I can't rightly say. Maybe he needs a ship fitting. The Carver is good at that kind of thing."

Drake leaned on the porch post, fiddling with his knife. "My guess is his men begged him to join him at the Hornpipe, and they are having a high old time swapping tales and throwing back ales."

"Drake!" Aurora shouted. "That is *not* helpful. The Captain is a grown man, and if he didn't get lost in the middle of the ocean, he isn't likely to lose his way in Old Towne Creek. So, you boys take a look from the tower to ensure all is right on the point, then off to bed with you. I'll wait with Marybeth a while longer. The mosquitoes will run us all in soon enough."

"Don't bother, Aurora," I said. "I have a few things to do in my room. You're right. Edward will find the path home."

"Well, don't tarry, Girl," Mother said. "Watching that dock is like waiting for water to boil. Things happen when they happen."

I sat for a few minutes longer, watching the current splash toward the river and the jollyboat bounce against its mooring. But no matter how hard I strained to see the periauger upstream, I couldn't conjure it out of the mist, so I finally went to my room.

I looked again from my front window, but the jollyboat rocked alone at the landing. There was no Edward. Where was he? And where was he going on this voyage? Would he see his daughter, Elizabeth?

I opened the little chest at the foot of my bed. And for the first time, I noticed the letters *ML* carved in a medallion inside the lid. Smaller painted letters read *Maison LaVonne*. I had seen the initials before, of course, but I had paid them no mind, but now they had meaning. The chest carried the same mark as the dresses Edward had given me. It made sense. The trunk had once held a shipment from a French clothier to Charleston, and the man who would become my husband had pirated it.

I folded my gown, lovingly touching the blue roses and creamy satin. Then I found enough tow cloth to make a package and lay the folded garment in the center for one last look before I wrapped it out of sight.

'Twas then boots stamped up the porch steps. Edward was home.

He quietly stepped into our room and closed the door behind him. "What are you doing, my love?" he asked. "Does your gown need such care?"

I caressed the fabric once more, then turned to my husband. "I thought I'd make a package for Elizabeth. Then you can hand it to her or send it by someone else."

"Your offer is generous, Marybeth, but I can't give that dress to Elizabeth," he said.

"Because you stole it?"

He raised his eyebrows and took me by the shoulders. "No. Of course not. I can't give it to Elizabeth because I'll always remember it on my bride. You wore it while waiting for me to stand beside you before the Governor." Then he pulled me closer. "And I remember helping you loosen the laces on our wedding night. Such memories are not for my daughter; they are for my wife."

I bent my forehead to his chest, and he caressed my back. "Why are you so worried, Marybeth?"

"Because you must leave me again. And so much of you is a mystery. I learned only days ago that you had a daughter. I fear that your past will capture you, and then one night, you won't return."

He held me tighter. Then after a kiss to the top of my head, he said, "No one knows what storms may lie ahead, so I can't promise there won't be a storm too big for me to survive."

I couldn't hold back my tears, so he held me close and led me to the edge of our bed, where he wiped my eyes.

Once the tears stopped flowing, he said, "There are promises I *can* keep, though. First, I promise to be faithful to you while I'm away, and I vow that my intention will always be to return to you. And as soon as I can settle my debts with ship and crew, we shall share every night."

Then he touched the pearl star at my neck. "This is where my home is," he said. "This is the home I'll return to as long as I live."

"But what debts must you settle?" I asked, looking into his eyes.

"I should help my men find a course that suits them," he said. "Most of 'em signed on to follow me. But, while a few of them will live nicely here in Bath, some can never be so tame. So, I'll give them every chance to choose their future on this voyage. Some, like Jonah, already mean to live here, but Israel Hands won't be satisfied till he has his own ship. Others will want the old lands in the islands or to return to their homes."

"But won't you need a crew?" I asked.

"A few of the lads may follow me back here and sail with me as traders, but some won't be able to give up their lust for the pirating days. I loved that too. And I'm part of what put that love in them, and it's doubtful I can convince them out of it."

"Stop sailing for a time and let them find their ways."

"They can't run free here in Bath. And we don't have enough ships coming and going to take them where they want to go. So, they need a place to work the wild out of 'em, and that ain't here."

I lay my head against his chest, crying again. "The sea is so big, Edward, with storms, wild creatures, and wilder men. Can you beat them all? Are you strong enough to fight your way back?"

I felt the chuckle rattle his chest as he held me tight. "Do you doubt it?" he asked. But then he stroked my hair, whispering, "I've always been strong enough to meet my challenges. I reckon I have that much fight left in me."

Then he looked at the open chest at the foot of my bed and remembered something else. He kissed my cheek and took my hand as he stood. "Come with me."

Edward led me to his den, where he examined every item on the wall and looked into every shelf. Then he sat me down on another chest. "I intend to return to you. You are the best of my life now, but I must promise one more thing. I must protect you from the worst of me."

"What do you mean?"

"You make me the man I always wanted to be. I've been a pirate, and it's not enough to be good and true now. I must protect you from the danger that may come because of the man I was."

"How can the man you once were hurt me now?" I asked. "You are my husband, and I'd want no better than you."

"Some men may want revenge. Others may want to use me to gain power over their enemies, and some may want to hurt the ones I love. So, it's not enough that I ensure you have enough food, gold, and help on the farm. I must worry about my enemies coming for you."

"What do you mean?"

"Some things here are tools to find paths in the sea. Any navigator might have them. There's a bit of gold and silver, too, and while someone may try to take that from you, coins alone don't prove I was pirating. The papers are the danger—especially any paper showing agreement about prizes or articles of piracy. I won't leave them in this room for someone to plunder. I'll go through the room tomorrow and clear out anything that might cause you grief if the worst happens to me. That's my third promise, Marybeth. I promise not to shoulder you with the burden of my thieving past."

"What about my dresses? Aren't they proof of piracy?"

"Aye, they are. I'm guilty of taking them, but Eden granted me the King's pardon. So, if thieves come to take your gifts, they will be the guilty ones, not anyone at Plum Point."

"Then are we safe from trouble?" I asked.

"The one thing they might steal for profit and not get the noose is evidence against someone else." He looked around. "What a mess I have here. I've barely had time to drop a sack and pick it up to go again. But I'll wade through these things tomorrow and make sure nothing is left to bring you grief."

"Edward, you sound as if you won't come back."

"Such a short memory?" he asked. "What did I promise?"

I smiled as I recited his pledge. "You promised to return to me from every venture as long as you live."

"Perfect, my love."

"But is it true?" I asked.

"'Tis better than true. You have my word on it." He held my hands in his, "As you say, the sea is big, and the world is wild, but so far, it's been no match for Edward Thache. But, I'll take care of this mess, settle my crew, and then I'll be back." Then he turned his head to one side, showing me the best version of his coy smile, and when he winked, I couldn't hold back a giggle.

My laugh stretched his smile. Then he raised eyebrows over the mischievous grin, saying, "I have an idea. Let's see you in that blue gown once more." Then as we walked down to our room, he added, "I'd love to help you loosen those laces one more time."

I laughed, pulling away from him till he gave chase and caught up with me in our room.

34 Partitioning Blackbeard

Mary Beth Thache

When I finished my morning duties, I found Edward in his den pushing chests and sorting sacks into three groups—the three facets of my husband.

Captain Thache needed his charts, sextants, and dividers. But he looked over the maps to ensure no markings tied him to ships he had once plundered. He was pardoned of the deeds done in those days, but he said it was prudent to leave no evidence of those piracies that might injure men who had not taken the pardon.

Edward, my husband, had personal effects, chests of clothes, packets of letters, and drawings of people and places he loved.

"Look at this old girl," Edward said, showing me a sketch of *Queen Anne's Revenge*.

"Asjen drew it as we sailed from Charleston," he said. "She was an awesome beast with sails at the full and guns at the ready."

"Who is this?" I asked.

Edward's face softened as he looked at the pastel drawing of a man who might have been an older Edward riding a black stallion.

"Is that your father?" I asked. Then noting the initials *AN*, I added, "Did Asjen Nuevo make this?"

"Aye. The doctor tended to my father when he was ill, as he had my mother. And when we met again in Charleston, he gave this to me." He smiled and tenderly tucked that sketch into a leather pouch that he had left in the desk drawer with the framed drawing of his mother and her star pendant.

His spare clothes went into a chest that he pushed near the attic door, next to his old boots and under a few pegs holding some hats and a scabbard with an aged sword, thin from years of sharpening.

"That was my first warrior's blade," he said, pointing to the sword. "'Twas a gift from Benjamin Hornigold."

"How did *this* get here?" I asked, lifting a sack like the one I had seen The Crow carry across our plantation.

"Caesar found it among The Crow's things. 'Twas used to shift some of the ladies' clothes I had from the island to the girls in Bath. When I took it back, I placed a few dresses I saved for you to store here."

"Why would you do that?" I asked.

"Well, my Love, I gave up pirating, so who knows when or how I'll get new finery for you. I'd better save back a few surprises." He started to open the sack and pull out a skirt to show me, but he paused, asking, "Would you like them all now? In case things don't go well."

I put my hand on his. "If these are for me, I will wait till you return. Leave them here."

He smiled, saying, "As you wish."

Then we came to the third face of Edward—the pirate, Blackbeard. This group contained ships' logs, correspondence, ledgers of prizes taken, and their distribution.

"Some of these, I must destroy or hide," he said. "Not every crewman has asked for a pardon, and some of these mates ride under other sails now. If they signed articles of piracy for old voyages, this could prove they were pirates, and they'd risk the noose. Those pages, I'll burn. The correspondence and agreements I'll keep hidden. They could prove useful to my current crew and me."

"What about the distribution of prizes? Isn't that as damning as signatures on the Acts of Piracy? Should you burn those, too?"

He scratched his beard, "Hm. I am not sure how the men would feel about that, but as for me, I'd like to keep a list of my prizes."

"Why?" I asked.

"Well, sometimes items of value end up in odd places, such as the dresses Hands took from me. Of course, the clothing won't matter much, but I have a few rare pieces like that silver cup on the top shelf. I'd rather keep a record of the cup because I've been pardoned for taking that prize. No one can accuse me of stealing it again."

So by the day's end, we had put the three faces of my husband against three walls. Some would accompany him to the ship, while others would remain in his den. The third part, he'd burn or hide should prying eyes invade Plum Point.

It pricked me to think of the third set because if men invaded our plantation to look for those, my family, life, and livelihood would be in as much peril as Edward at sea.

The day soon came when Edward boarded *Adventure* and was off to the islands. The town expected him to return with sugar, cocoa, molasses, and rum. Governor Eden and Tobias Knight hoped he'd return with a much-reduced crew.

At that moment, I believed that when Edward returned on *Adventure*, I'd be satisfied.

35 Masking Sadness

Ody Saunters

The morning after Captain Thache sailed for St. Thomas, I found Marybeth sobbing in the Bride's Tower. So, I quickly reversed my steps and tried to tiptoe down the blocks without intruding on her sorrow. It didn't work.

Barely recognizable words escaped the grieving girl's sniffles. "Who's there?"

I stuck my head through to the tower to reply. "Just me, Mrs. Thache. I'm sorry to disturb you."

After a few more sniffs, she wiped her eyes and waved me to the bell tower. "It's all right," she said. "It's just that the Captain's empty den makes the house feel lonely."

"Yes, I see he's shifted his belongings. Maybe you shouldn't go there," I said. But the words weren't off my lips before I realized Marybeth couldn't stand vigil on the tower without passing through the Captain's den. "It does appear more vacant. Did he take more with him this time, or did he just tidy up?" I asked.

"Some of each. I was with Edward when he sorted his belongings to determine what he should leave there. Some things he needed on the voyage, and others he wanted in a safer place, and he had little time to put the rest back." She dropped her chin as she added, "There's too much space now; too much of him is gone."

"Maybe I can help with that. I can rearrange what's left if that would help."

She nodded. "It might. Edward has already moved anything valuable or dangerous. But, if you can, try to organize these boxes and crates so he won't have to search for things when he returns. And can you make it look more like before he left?"

"Sure. Drake can help me. He spent more time in that room than I did. He'll probably remember where things should go."

She liked the idea, so I presented the project to Drake at dinner. He was happy to help, probably because it gave him more chances to look through Captain Thache's belongings. Whatever his motivation, my cousin joined me on the bare floor in the center of the Captain's attic room that afternoon.

"Marybeth is right," he said. "It looks different with all these boxes pushed against the walls."

"Yes. And Mrs. Thache wants us to make it look less lonely. Is there anything you remember?" I asked.

"There are too many empty pegs by the door now. Wearables should go with hats, coats, and belts. There must be spares somewhere; I'll find them."

I nodded, adding, "He left some maps on the wall by the east window. The desk is there, too, so we can keep papers and charts there."

"Yes," Drake said. "That was his writing desk as near as I recall."

"Let's start with that, and then we'll see what's left for the other two walls."

Drake agreed. "But if this place makes Marybeth sad, let's try to make it look the same as before."

"Cluttered and crowded?" I asked.

He nodded. "Like a captain's cabin."

"Good idea," I said. "I'll start with the papers and books, and you look through the chests and sacks for wearables."

The desk's center drawer had clean paper, sealing wax, and a wooden stamp marked *B o' P P*—Bellieu of Plum Point. Next to the carved seal were a pen knife and a supply of quills. So, I placed one or two trimmed quills beside the ink well on the desktop. And I replaced the pastel of Elizabeth Thache at the back of the desk and carefully dropped the chain of her gold pendant over the corner.

The top drawers on the left and right had correspondence, ledgers, and journals with *Edward Thache* written on them, but the bottom drawers had papers belonging to Bert Bellieu.

"Hey, Drake," I called. "If you find anything with papers or charts, set them over here, OK?"

When he didn't answer me, I turned to find him prancing around in one of the Captain's older coats. "Having fun?" I asked.

"What do you think?" he asked as he turned to show off each side.

"I think I'd give my eyeteeth for a smartphone with a camera," I said. Then, when Drake threw a glove at me, I added, "It swallows you whole and drags nearly to the ground."

"Well, it won't look much better on you," my cousin said as he retrieved the glove.

"Hm .... Let me try."

It wasn't the braided silk coat he wore on his wedding day, nor the black leather sea coat or silk captain's coat we had seen him wear to his ship. Instead, this brown leather jacket was older and less refined. And even though it was smaller than the others, it still didn't fit us.

"At least the coat doesn't drag the ground on me," I said, modeling the jacket.

"No, but it hangs below your knees. Neither of us is anywhere near the Captain's height."

"Let me try the belt and scabbard," I said. "Maybe that will shorten it."

It didn't. Not by enough. But soon, I was swaggering around the room in Blackbeard's coat. Drake laughed at how the old sword banged my shins, but he looked just as silly with the broad-brimmed hat sliding to one side of his head. His leather gloves were so oversized that he could hardly right the feather bobbing on top.

"Hurry, put these back," I whispered as we heard someone coming up the stairs.

We had not pegged all the evidence before Oma peeked into the room.

"What are you boys giggling about?" she asked. But when her mouth fell open at our costume parade, we hurried to hide the evidence. "Are you two supposed to be here?" she asked.

"Yes, Ma'am," Drake replied. "We're doing a favor for Marybeth."

"Hm." She wasn't convinced. "Well, stop playing and get it done. We're going to need more firewood for cooking."

We replied in unison, "Aye, aye, Cap'n."

We soon decided that unidentified wooden tools would go to the south wall, right of the shelves holding personal mementos. That left the west window and wall for miscellaneous, anything that didn't fit our designated categories.

As we sorted and arranged, we quizzed each other about things we didn't find.

"Wonder where his pistols are?" Drake asked.

"He probably needs them for the voyage. I want to know where he keeps the pirate flags. Does he dare keep them on the ship while under pardon?"

"Well, they aren't here," Drake replied. "Do you think he might need them on this trip?"

I shrugged. "Whether here or on the ship, I'm sure the Captain has them under lock and key."

The reorganization went quickly, but in the end, Drake had another question.

"If the Captain took everything valuable or dangerous, why did he display his mother's portrait and gold star necklace? That gold pendant must be worth a lot."

"I reckon he wanted it there," I replied, "But should we hide the gold star?"

"I'll get it," Drake replied. He still wore Thache's gloves as he reached for the pendant and dropped it in a basket of seashells on the shelf below. "I'll put the portrait over here too. I'll tuck it in the back, but it should go with the other personal things."

When I handed him the coat, he stuffed the leather gloves into the Captain's pocket, then looked at the rest of the clothing. "Where should I put this?" he asked, pulling a flowered sleeve from the sack.

"Don't these belong to Marybeth?" I asked.

"That looks like the sack Thache took from The Crow's hammock. If he wanted Marybeth to have them, he'd have left them with her. Should we ask?"

"No. Let it be. If Mrs. Thache looks for them, we know where to find them. Just stick them behind the Captain's boxes under the coat pegs." I spun around to admire our handiwork and asked, "Does this look like the old den?"

Drake scanned the room. "I reckon he took his gold dust and coins with him, but what happened to the cup?" Then he found it, nearly hidden on the top shelf. "Oh. Here it is."

I nodded. "So, the Captain took his gold dust. Do you think he doesn't trust us?"

"I reckon he might need gold for trading. He trusts us," Drake replied. "Otherwise, we'd be on that ship with The Crow. The Captain keeps those he suspects under watch."

Then Marybeth came to see our progress. "You've done very well, Lads. There are differences, but not ones that jar me with Edward's absence." She lay a hand on each of our shoulders, saying, "You're good crewmen for the Captain and good friends to me."

"Just not crewmen on his ship," Drake said.

"No, but you're securing his home port," she replied. "I reckon that means more to him while he's on this voyage."

Drake's chest puffed up. He was proud of crewing for the Captain, whether on sea or land. However, I was more honored by the kind words of the Captain's wife and the touch of her hand on my shoulder.

Marybeth depended on me more as the days passed. I stood beside her as she checked for traffic on Old Towne Creek and marked each day of the voyage on the tower railing. When a week had passed, we figured *Adventure* had not yet reached St. Thomas. She prayed for Edward every evening, and even though her husband wasn't halfway through his voyage, she found Polaris every time the sky was clear enough. She asked God, the sky, and the seas to keep Edward safe and bring him home quickly.

We were indeed closer, but my role was a shoulder to lean on and an advisor when the opinion of a man might matter. I cherished even that role, but there was no room in her heart for anyone else. Captain Thache held that space, and if there had been just a smidgeon more room for matters of the heart, that would belong to her first sweetheart, Wallace McNeil.

Act Three: Squall on the Horizon

36 Inland Pirates

Ody Saunters

Before he sailed for the Indies, Captain Thache did everything possible to make Plum Point safe, but Marybeth was more than an object of his care. She and Hetty were critical parts of the plan—surrogate captains of the plantation.

Since the death of Bert Bellieu, his widow had run the farm. But now it was Marybeth's turn. She had two prime examples of how to handle adversity. At sea, Edward was in a constant battle to conquer the waves, and at home, he braced for a fight, too—a struggle to make something new of himself while helping those in his home port. Captain Thache was vigilant and ready to face situations head-on. Marybeth, young and eager to succeed as a captain's wife, did her best to follow his lead. Hetty was her on-site partner, and, of course, Oma, Drake, and I were there to help as she dealt with any foul winds that reached Plum Point.

Wallace McNeil was a helper, too. But he knew his place with young Mrs. Thache and his bargain with the Captain. There were no more visits to the Bride's Tower nor favors to remind her of their young love. His regular Tuesday visits to Plum Point were to deliver goods to Hetty and nothing more than polite greetings to her daughter.

McNeil usually discussed security with me—routine things about the crews' helpfulness and perimeter security. But one day, Wallace beckoned me to the summer house for a talk about mischief in Bath. After a few curious questions about when the Captain might return and what his crewmates did in their spare time, I urged him to get to the point.

Wallace bent closer. "Some plantation owners complain of men stealing goods between their farms and the town port, and so far, no one can figure out who's responsible."

"Farmers stealing from farmers—how can that be?" I asked.

"I suppose it could be shipyard workers or sailors coming in and out of port. But whoever they are, groups of men are surprising plantation boats at night. They strike when there's cloud cover or no moon, and they seem to know when something of value is going to the market."

"Sounds like a bunch of creek pirates," I said.

He nodded. "You don't reckon Captain Thache left a crew of robbers to take prizes here, do you?"

After seeing how Captain Thache took such good care of Marybeth, I preferred to think the best of him, so I replied, "No, he doesn't have that many crewmen to spare. And why would he bother with Bath farm goods when he has plenty of that to trade? If the robbers know when a crop is coming in, I reckon farmhands or their families might be suspect."

"In a place the size of Bath, they're all connected—farmers, their hands, shipbuilders, and sailors; all are of the same blood. But 'tis unlikely anyone who puts his sweat into a field would want the harvest stolen before it makes it to market. And we've seen nothing suspicious with the men in the shipyard. Has anything gone missing here?" Wallace asked.

I shook my head, "No, not that we've noticed. But we don't usually grow crops for the market. Gathering from farm, forest, and sea keeps us busy, and even with that, we barely gather enough extra to put by for the winter."

Wallace bent his head to whisper. "Some of the plantation storehouses have been robbed, too. With the shortages in town, they've lost rum, sugar, cured meat, and grain. Captain Harding has asked me to look into it. So, let me know if you find anything, and I'll report it."

"Does your captain have any suspects?" I asked.

Wallace cocked his head. "Not Harding, no, but some of those in high places suspect Captain Thache's men."

"Why the Captain's men? They're at sea. And they'd never stop for anything as small as a creek canoe. And what man in Bath County doesn't know his way around a periauger?"

Wallace nodded. "Those are good points, but I reckon if a man is into thieving, he'd take any target he found."

"Since you work in Bath, you see more than we do, but Drake and I will keep our ears to the ground, and we can take a look in town."

***

When I told Drake about the thieving, we decided to question Caesar and Jonah. Unfortunately, all Caesar could report was what he heard from his duties at Knight's Landing. Knight felt the shortages, too. Without much rum, even his high and mighty guests made do with Kill Devil punch or straight whiskey.

When we spoke to Jonah, he wrung his hat and replied, "I give half my wages to Alice's father as payment toward my promise to her. And I do chores on their farm to pay for my supper on Friday nights. All my news comes from the family table and the men who help me slop the hogs."

"Is there no clue as to who's thieving?" I asked.

"They don't even mention it. Mostly, they talk about whether I am good enough for Alice. Right now, she's a bit miffed with me. After seeing the dresses Colleen and Sal wear, she's wonderin' why she has no frock from her sailor. But I don't know where Hands and The Crow found dresses. So, the best I can do is give her my silver pay bits to carry to her father. When he's satisfied, so is Alice."

"Do you see any of your old mates in town?" Drake asked.

"Nary a one," he replied. "Never even heard rumor of any of the crew in Bath."

***

Friday was Jonah's regular night to visit Alice, and Drake rowed with us in the jollyboat. But once we let Jonah off at Towne Point and he ran down Front Street toward Alice's farm, Drake had plenty to say about the rumors regarding Captain Thache's crew.

"We know how to find Jonah and Caesar, and no one else on the crew is in the county. Someone's tryin' to hurt Thache's reputation," he said.

"Well, if he lets his mates run as bandits, that's as bad as pirating, isn't it?"

"Thache runs a tight ship and means to do well in Bath. I'd bet he's not behind any bandits in town. Besides, you heard Jonah; he's breaking his back and emptying his pockets to impress his future father-in-law."

I nodded. "But Alice wants more from him, and don't underestimate the Captain. He usually thinks a few steps ahead and might have found a way to rob while at a distance."

Drake shook his head, "Well, let's not condemn Jonah nor Thache till we know more. Shall we try the Hornpipe?"

"The Marsh Moon," I said. "Nobody keeps up with Bath better than Sal."

Drake was all for a good supper, so we stopped in to find Sal and ordered two servings of pork pie.

When she returned with a trencher of pork with corn cakes on the side, I said, "Things must be going well around here, Sal. The Marsh Moon never seems to have trouble putting dinner on the table."

"'Tis more challenging than you think," she replied. "Crops start from the plantations, but some don't make it to town. Good thing those creek robbers are picky, though. They take all the corn, rye, beans, and apples they can get, but at least they leave us the melons and berries."

"Odd things to pick," Drake said. "Does that make any sense to you?"

She shrugged. "Not really. No idea why they don't take all if they take anything,"

"Have any girls in town been wearing new dresses like the one Hands gave you?" I asked.

"Not so far. Not while the crew is at sea."

When the front bell jingled, Sal turned to two new customers. "Edward Moseley and Maurice Moore," she whispered. "They're staying in Bath for a few days and won't be happy to hear we are out of rum, so, I'd better hurry to tend them."

"The Captain will help with that," Drake said. "He means to return from the Indies with more rum and molasses."

Sal paused to reply, "Then I hope he hurries. Our only hope of rum is when one of the farmers sells his cache for silver. Unfortunately, that doesn't happen often, and Marsh Moon is nearly out of coins, too."

Drake sipped his cider before asking, "Is it the same at the Hornpipe?"

Sal made a face and shrugged. "'Tis the same everywhere in Bath. Folks out of supplies and thieves around every corner."

***

While we waited for Jonah to return from Alice's farm, we stopped to ask Wallace his opinion on the stolen goods. "Why take corn, rye, and apples but not melons and berries?"

Wallace peeked around his work screen, shrugging as he replied, "All I know is, you can make whiskey from rye, and apples store longer than berries."

Drake removed his hat and twisted the rim, saying, "It couldn't be Thache's men; they're all at sea." Then he paused. "Shh. Listen," he said, beckoning us to the tent flap.

A split rail fence divided a stand of oaks as it ran toward Water Street, separating Thache's lot from the grounds of the Hornpipe Inn. A female voice, garbled, but understandable, came from the oak grove.

"It's Colleen," I whispered.

Then we spotted her and watched as she entered the Hornpipe's side door with a flask half-hidden beneath her fluttering apron. A moment later, she returned to the dark grove and spoke to a stranger hidden there,

"Is that all he'd give ye?" A man's voice whispered.

"'Tis all," she said.

Jonah stood by the Hornpipe, and we didn't want to lose him, so Drake wound through Harding's garden and met Jonah on the street.

Wallace and I kept to the cover of trees as we crept a little closer to listen. Someone spoke to Silas Van Horn, asking. "Have ye any rum, barkeep?"

Then, after coins scraped across the counter, a cork popped, and liquid filled a small glass.

"Well, there's rum in there," Wallace whispered. "I wonder where it came from."

"From someone who'd rather have silver than drink," I replied. "But who would have rum to spare?"

When we listened to voices in the grove, the man's words were low and raspy, and though the girl muttered, I recognized Colleen's voice. Wallace and I tried to see the man better but couldn't make out much through the trees and sassafras stands. But Jonah left Drake at the fence and wandered into the grove.

Then, while Drake waited at the street and I hid among Harding's oaks, Wallace sneaked from tree to tree to follow folks moving in the grove, but he had no luck.

"I didn't find them," he said, shrugging as he returned.

"Did you see the man she was with?" I asked.

He shook his head. "Not clearly, but I don't believe it was The Crow. The bloke had more the bearing of a farm hand than a seafarer."

Then Jonah returned to Drake, so I said farewell to Wallace and hurried through the garden to meet my cousin on the street.

Jonah panted from struggling through the brush, but he didn't catch up with the pair in the grove.

"I called to Colleen," he said. "I wanted to ask how I might get a new dress for Alice, but she didn't reply, and I couldn't catch her."

"Well, no matter. Drake will solve the puzzle. That steam coming from his ears is him cooking up an explanation that will clear Captain Thache."

Drake pushed my shoulder as he said, "I'll figure it out, and you'll see. The Captain is not behind any robbery."

I snickered at him. "Yes, who'd believe a pirate would stoop to robbery?"

When we reached Plum Point, Drake went to bed, and Jonah went to the crew shed. I checked the grounds from the tower alone. Drake was quiet as I climbed into bed. Could he be conjuring another explanation for the robberies? Was he sleeping—or just pretending to be?

37 A Bumpy Ride

Drake Saunters

I was still fuming when Ody came to bed. *How could I convince him to trust Captain Thache?* By the time he snored, I had resolved to learn more about young Blackbeard, and that meant taking drastic measures—like a quick trip to Jamaica.

I grabbed my clothes and slipped into the landing. But Grandma was a light sleeper, so I carefully tested for creaking boards as I climbed the narrow stairs to the Captain's den.

The window light was enough to brighten the gold star in the bowl of seashells, so I slipped on a glove, fished out the pendant, and dropped it into my vest pocket. So far, so good. But I had one more stop to make.

If Grandma woke while I was gone, she might press my hair charm to come to me, and her sudden arrival would be a disaster where I was going. I needed her braided circle pendant. So, by the light from her window, I separated my hair pendant from Ody's and slipped mine into my vest pocket.

Then, after closing Grandma's door gently, I crept down one more flight and took a path midway between the rooms of Hattie and Marybeth to grab my boots.

When the lantern clock struck ten, I froze. Marybeth stirred, but instead of entering the parlor, she poured a sip of water from her pitcher, and the bed ropes screeched as she returned to her pillow.

Then, when all was quiet, I slipped out the front door and down to the summer house. There I sat, letting my heart slow as I pondered the act I had in mind. *Could this time turn out worse than the first?* What could I expect?

If things happened as they had for Ody in Salem, I'd land behind the hinged mirror screen as I had before. I'd see the same people in the room, but they wouldn't see me behind the mirror. This time, I wanted more than simple eavesdropping, but I'd have to be cautious at each new step.

Grandma couldn't rescue me on this trip; I had her hair charm. The risk swelled in my lungs, and I nearly gave up the idea. But Ody had been alone in Old Salem, and if he could survive, so could I. He might be the mission's captain, but I was the sole commuter to Jamaica. And who more than I should be the captain of my fate?

I dangled the gold star, as I considered the risk. If I gripped it with my bare hand, the commute would begin. *And there was problem one.*

The star would fall to the summer house floor, and someone might find it there and follow me. So, I'd better be careful about where that pendant fell. *Ah. Under the floor.* That would be safe.

Before I launched, I took a final inventory—*Grandma's hair pendant.* Check. It was around my neck; I'd need that to get home. *The charm made of my hair.* Check. In my vest pocket to prevent Grandma from following me. I was set.

The star spun on the gold chain in my right hand, and I crouched to dangle it inside the hole exposed by the fallen ballast stone. Then, with a deep breath, I dropped the pendant and star into my left hand, squeezing it inside my fist.

There was the usual rush of time and space around me. Then the last thing I saw was the pendant frozen mid-fall as the vista around me turned to pixels. Then everything was charcoal gray before colors burst around me again. I held my breath tight as the back of Mother Thache's mirrored dressing screen appeared before me. I was in Jamaica. It worked.

Then it didn't.

I landed behind the mirror. And while straightening from the crouch, I stumbled, toppling the screen. It crashed to the floorboards, and glass shattered across the planks and under the bed.

Edward turned to me, wide-eyed, fists clenching as he stepped between his mother and the intruder.

"Who are *you*?" he demanded.

"Err."

Young Edward didn't think it was much of an answer, either. He stepped toward me, head down like a charging bull, fingers reaching for my throat. My hand flew to my neck, probably an instinct to save me from those choking fingers, but instead, I found Grandma's pendant and landed in Bath by her bed.

***

"Drake?" she murmured. "Is that you?"

The clock struck eleven.

"Got to pee, Grandma," I gasped, running from the room. *But to where?* The summer house.

But what now? Did I dare try the commute again?

I sat in the gazebo, trying to figure it out. What had I done? When Edward returned from his voyage, would he remember me from that mess in his mother's room?

Then I had the answer. Ned wouldn't remember me if I never broke the mirror. So, I'd go back and *not* break it.

Could that be right?

It had to be.

But this time, there'd be no crouching.

So, I used a handkerchief to recover the star and crept up the stairs to Edward's den. There, I held the gold chain over the basket of seashells before I began the commute. Then, with my breath still and eyes shut tight, I landed behind the unbroken mirror. The sigh of relief was slow and silent.

I watched again as Neddie spoke to his mother and called for Dr. Neuvo, who came and left. Then Abigail tidied Elizabeth Thache's hair. And finally, while Mother Thache slept, the sun set behind the palms, and I watched as Neddie held Abigail's hand.

Phew! All was well. Somehow time allowed me to write over my mistake. But did I dare to follow the lovers?

On this trip, sunset in Jamaica was near midnight in Bath, and Hetty Bellieu would be up at five. How much had time travel disoriented me? Surely, I could judge when five hours passed.

I had to risk the task I came to do. How else could I get evidence about the heart of Edward Thache?

38 Dubbin Delight

Drake Saunters

Luckily for me, no servants were in the hall, and it was quieter and quicker to slide down the banister. On the lower landing, I hid behind a potted plant and checked the entry. Good. No prying eyes.

Through the window, I saw Ned and Abby, their backs to me as they enjoyed the sunset. I slipped through the door, and from the bushes bordering the porch, I could hear their whispers.

"Your father doesn't like to see us together, Ned. I should be with your mother when he arrives." Abby moved to slide her hand from his, but Edward held it fast.

"Stay till the sun drops." He brushed her cheek with his hand, saying, "Let me watch the sun's roses on your cheeks and the darkening sky ignite the diamonds in your eyes."

"Someone will hear," she said, stepping back from him. "I should go."

Ned sighed, and his hand slid down her arm as he said, "I should go, too. McGruder is having trouble with Father's friend, Benjamin Rostan. I should watch how he treats Caesar when he brings his horse to the stable."

"But it's his right. Isn't any gentleman allowed to treat a servant as he wishes?" she asked. "Your father certainly feels that way about me."

"My father will not always treat you that way. And besides, you are a free citizen, a paid lady's maid. And someday, you will be the lady of this house."

"But not today," she replied. Then she cocked her head. "Did you hear Rostan mistreating Caesar, or is it just gossip?"

"I didn't witness it, and Caesar hasn't said much, either, but the men don't hide rumors from me. You're right, though; I should see for myself."

"Then, go. I'll see to your mother."

Ned grabbed her shoulders. "Will you grant me one kiss?" he asked.

She dropped her chin, but Ned lifted it again, and she closed her eyes as he pulled her chest to his. Their lips met briefly, and she pressed closer to him for a few seconds before pulling away. Then she smiled as she touched his stubbly black beard before hurrying to her Lady.

Ned watched her through the partly open door as she trotted up the stairs. Then young Blackbeard settled his hat and turned toward the stable path.

Caesar told me of the encounter with a gentleman and how Ned had taken his part. If I saw that, I'd have proof of Ned's character. Surely, if I witnessed that, I could find some detail that would convince Ody. I'd follow.

But before Ned left the courtyard, he encountered Dr. Nuevo and asked, "Have you been sketching again?"

Neuvo smiled. "'Twas a beautiful sunset, and I couldn't help noticing you enjoyed it too."

Edward took his hat in both hands as if to beg a favor of the doctor.

"Oh, no worry, lad," Nuevo said. "Your secret is safe with me."

Ned went on his way, and I waited till Dr. Nuevo put his pastels away. He was near enough to touch me as he passed into the house and to Mother Thache's room. Then I sneaked through the trees along the path, fearing to meet the older Captain Thache. But, when I heard him chatting with Ned as they walked homeward, I hid deeper among the bushes till they passed.

"I suppose Benjamin wants to see the plantation by the light of a full moon," the Captain said. "He'll probably ride back in an hour or so."

"Very well, Father," Ned replied. "I had hoped to speak with him, but another time will do."

They continued to the house, and I followed the path to the stable. Finding a hiding place with a view would be a safe way to watch what happened there. I looked forward to meeting Caesar as a boy, and I had time, since, by my reckoning, barely more than an hour had passed since I arrived behind the mirror.

As the twilight dimmed, white blossoms opened, and the forest grew more fragrant. But scents of manure and saddle soap overpowered the night flowers. When I walked through the stable door, mares neighed as they shifted against the stall rails. Then the rhythmic slap of brushes against leather halted, and Caesar peeked from the tack room door.

Even with nearly two decades of difference in time, he was not much shorter than the man of thirty I knew in Bath, and when he turned toward me, his face had the same pecan-shell hue. But the creases were not as deep; he had not yet spent years squinting across the waves with Blackbeard. I was still fifteen, but in this century, he was a year or two younger than I was.

"May I help ye, Sir?" he asked.

"I'm here on business for Edward Thache," I replied.

Caesar nodded and returned to his work, and I followed him to his worktable. As he had said, he was already as stout as a stump. First, the lad gave a vigorous buffing to the saddle and then slung it over a rail to await the next rider. Then, as he lifted a second saddle to clean, he turned and seemed surprised to find me still there.

"May I help ye with your business, Sir?"

"Err. No. Thache is looking for a man named Rostan."

"Oh," Caesar grimaced as he scrubbed mud from the saddle. "The Captain said he's still an hour out; I'm to stay here to care for his horse when he returns."

"Well, maybe I can help you til then."

"Are you part of the plantation, Sir? Are you a new hand?"

"Uh. No. I'm here for Rostan."

"Well, I reckon you can wait by the well if you want to." Then when we heard footsteps, he added, "Maybe that's him coming now."

"I'll go see," I said and hurried out of the room to avoid exposing my lie. I had no idea who Rostan was; he didn't know me either. But as I passed through the stable door, I bumped into Asjen Nuevo.

"Oh, excuse me, Sir," I said.

"'Tis no matter," he replied. "I'm here to borrow a bit of dubbin for my boots. I hoped the stableboy might have a dab."

"Aye, Sir. I've heard 'tis hard to keep black leather black," I replied.

He stepped back and looked me up and down. "Well, you do a good job with those boots."

"'Tis the fault of my Grandmother, Sir. She knows a woman who makes polish. And as a matter of fact, Edward asked me to clean his."

"I don't suppose you have a bit of boot wax, do you?"

"No. But I have an oilcloth full of Grandma's shiner in my pocket."

"Follow me, then, Lad. I'll show ye where the household drops boots for cleaning."

I wasn't sure about following Neuvo. After all, what I wanted was to see Ned Thache in action. But I was curious. If this man knew something about time travel, this could be my only chance to learn it. How long could it take to brush a pair of boots?

I followed him to a service shed near the large front porch, and inside it was a table with at least six pairs of men's boots in various shades of brown leather.

"Sir, the master here sent me to the stable to do a job for him. And my polish is for black leather only."

"Very well, Lad." He fished two bits from his purse, saying, "Please do mine; they are a sorry sight."

I chuckled as I stared at his boots. "You have a good eye for that, Sir."

"I tell you what," he said, removing his black boots. "Clean these first and bring them to me in the house." He pointed toward a service door across from the shed. “I’m second to the left at the top of the stairs through that door. Then you may be on with your task. ’Twill be our secret.”

He left me to work, and the boots were as good as new in half an hour. And now Nuevo had given me a reason to be inside the house.

I crossed the yard unobserved, and no one was on the stairs or in the hallway to Dr. Neuvo’s room. But when I dropped the boots by his door, another room opened, and Abigail emerged.

“What are you doing here, lad?” she asked, although I wasn’t much younger than the nurse.

While I stumbled for an answer, Neuvo opened his door.

“Ah, dubbin delight! Fine job, lad.” He picked up the boots, Abby turned to her original destination, and I sneaked along the stable path again. Caesar was in the corral, so I climbed to the hayloft, where I had a good view of everything. Oh, how I wished for my smartphone to record what happened next.

39 Confrontation

Drake Saunters

Doubts gathered as I waited for the scene to unfold. What if this were not the abusive gentlemen Caesar had described? Was it so important to convince Ody of Thache's character? Surely proving myself right and Ody wrong was not worth risking my health, the happiness of my family, and the path of history.

I might have commuted back to Grandmother then, but Rostan's voice stopped me. And, since Rostan and I were both there, I might as well see what happened.

Rostan stopped at the well, and while the horse drank from the trough, the stablemaster greeted him.

"Mauvis McGruder at your service, Sir. Does your horse require special care tonight?"

"A good brushing down for Spirit and a cleaning for my saddle should do it," Rostan replied.

"Very well, Sir," McGruder said, beckoning Caesar to take charge of the stallion. Then he latched the corral gate and drew fresh water for the drinking pail and trough by the well.

Caesar brought Spirit to a stall, and from the attic hatch, I watched him collect his grooming tools and return to service the horse.

The stallion was one of the tallest I had seen, and Caesar barely stood as high as the saddle horn, but it was no trouble for the boy to remove the saddle and fling it over the stall railing. He did a fine job on the hooves, too. I doubted I'd be strong enough to prompt the horse to lift his foot, but Caesar was as skilled as he was stout.

With the help of a small stool, the currying and brushing went well, but then he came to the mane, a higher reach. Caesar used the bottom rails of the stall fence to give himself a few more inches, and as he reached his fingers to detangle the mane, Spirit shifted. Then Caesar lost his balance and fell into Spirit's side.

The horse reared, creating more of a tug on his mane, and amid the neighing and pounding of hooves that followed, Rostan ran to the corral. He wrestled with the gate latch, yelling, "McGruder, what's happening to my horse?"

The stablemaster rushed to the stall to find an agitated stallion and Caesar cowering for cover against the stall walls.

Rostan shouted, "What kind of stable do you run here?"

While the owner settled his horse, McGruder grabbed Caesar by the collar, and when he laid hold of a riding whip, he smacked at Caesars's back as he drove the boy from the stable to the corral.

That's when Ned arrived.

Young Thache grabbed the whip from McGruder, and with the other hand, he shook the stablemaster's fist till he let go of Caesar. Then he pulled McGruder into the stable to see what had happened in the stall.

"He could have damaged my stallion," Rostan shouted. "I'll spread the word about the lax manner of treating animals here."

A shadow covered the stable door, blocking the moonlight.

"And what's wrong in my stable?" a deep voice boomed.

"Ca … Captain Thache," McGruder gasped.

"Just look how your man cowed my stallion," Rostan shouted. "If you don't make this right, I'll spread word of your business, Thache. I fear you'll make few sales of the stock kept here."

Captain Thache fumed as he turned toward McGruder. "What's happened here?" He kicked the stableman, who was still held fast in Ned's grip. "Speak up."

McGruder wiggled free but cowered before Captain Thache. "'Twas that boy, Caesar. He fell and excited the gentleman's mount."

"And isn't it your job to train him?" Ned asked.

As Rostan soothed Spirit, he said, "It seems you have trouble with your family, staff, and servants, too, Captain. I hope you did a better job of being a shipmaster. You may need to return to that profession."

Thache growled as he turned toward McGruder. "*You*. Take care of this gentleman's horse and see that he is satisfied." He grabbed Caesar by the collar and turned to Ned. "*You*. Follow me."

Then he dragged Caesar to the corral with Ned at his heels.

"What did you have to do with all this?" he asked his son.

"I had nothing to do with this; I just stopped the master from beating this lad. Accidents happen."

Thache huffed, "You stopped my man from correcting a servant?"

Ned clenched his fists and squared off to his father. "Caesar does good work, but McGruder gave him the wrong job this time. He had no choice nor chance of servicing a stallion of that size, but he did his best, and an accident happened."

The captain's snarl grew more sour. "Are you sayin' this boy ain't fit for the job we gave him? If he ain't, why should we keep him here? Do you think we should sell him for a taller man?"

"What I'm sayin' is that when McGruder saw the size of that horse, he could have called another servant to do the job. And he sure had no reason to beat him over an accident he could have prevented."

The Captain jerked Caesar to his feet, saying, "Go on with ye. Get to your quarters; you'll get your punishment in the morning."

When Caesar was gone, he turned toward Ned, shaking his head. "You'll never be the master of men," he said. "Haven't you learned to hold the stick over their heads? 'Tis the way of keeping them in line. Whether it be a ship's crew, plantation slaves, or a pack of vandals at your door, if you want to master the situation, they must fear ye."

"So, I need to manage with a whip? Is that it?" Ned asked. "Should I whip them no matter who is right?"

"Whether it's the master with the whip or the Captain with a ship, any who cross him should fear him."

"So, you get your way with fear even when there's a case to make for leniency. Would you punish a good navigator for a mistake?"

"I would. The mistake of a navigator could cost all on board their lives. And the mistake of a servant could cost us our livelihood."

"And who will direct the ship if you toss your navigator overboard? And who will do the work of a plantation if you can't forgive the mistake of an otherwise good man?"

The Captain growled. "Your mother has made you too weak. Get a spine, boy. Otherwise, I cannot see you ever being the master here."

For a moment, the two were mirror images glaring at each other, squared to fight with jaws set like steel. Then the old Captain spoke again.

"When the morning comes, you will lay the whip to Caesar's back. Then the men will know who's master."

Ned ripped off his shirt, then turned his back to his father, saying, "You'll have trouble putting fear in me, Father. If lashes must be given, lash me. After all, Caesar did his best; 'tis I who have disappointed you."

Captain Thache's face grew as black as a thunderhead, and he gripped the riding crop till his knuckles were white. Ned stood braced against the rail, ready for the lash.

The Captain heaved his breath, letting the storm build inside him till it was ready to blow. He stepped toward his son, and with the crack of lighting, he slashed the whip against Ned's back. Blood streamed. Ned stood silent, bracing for more.

But Captain Thache's rage was not satisfied by that lash. After glancing at his wife's bedroom window, he stomped past his son, growling, "Your punishment will come in the morning, too."

"If you have more lashes, lay them now," Ned said.

"I'll teach you a lesson without more lashes," he replied.

The Captain went to his quarters, and Ned poured water over his back to wash away the blood before donning his shirt. Then he left too.

I returned to Plum Point to reset my visit to 1699. I pinched the star, returned to my spot behind the hinged mirror, and the scene began to play again. After I returned my hair charm to Grandma's pouch, I spent the rest of the night on the tower, reliving what I saw in Jamaica. *Was the whip lash still visible on Edward's back? Would he tell Ody the story behind the scar?* Maybe that would convince my cousin of the nature of Captain Edward Thache, Jr.

40 Winds of Suspicion

Ody Saunters

It was the first of September, but the widow Bellieu wrapped the shawl around her shoulders as Drake handed her the egg basket.

"'Fall is nippin'," she said. "Ody, if you're obliging, we might need more wood for these chilly nights."

I dumped my armful of logs in the porch bin, and by the time I gathered another load, Hetty and Oma had breakfast on the table.

Marybeth shivered as she reached for corncakes and jam. "The summer is nearly gone," she said. "Surely Edward will return soon. I hope his voyage has been smooth."

"The weather here has been calm enough," Oma said. "And summer isn't over yet. Give him time; he'll be here."

Mrs. Bellieu set a plate of bacon on the table and wiped her hands on her apron. "Yes, daughter. Get that crease off your brow. You act as if you doubt the Captain's abilities at sea."

Marybeth straightened her back and put on a brave face as she added an egg to her plate. "Of course I don't. The sea is where he shines brightest. I'm just missing him, is all."

Drake swallowed a mouthful of breakfast as he reached to pat the young wife's hand. "Aye, now you have it right. You know better than most; the Captain is up to handling whatever he meets."

Marybeth nodded but turned her head down to hide her worry.

"Now, stop your frettin', girl," Mrs. Bellieu said. "The Captain is doin' his work; we should be doin' ours. Here's an example," she said, pointing to the open jam jar. "We've put back more fig preserves than we need this season, and we'd be amiss if we don't try sellin' the rest."

"Are you short of money?" Oma asked.

"No, we are not," Marybeth replied. "Edward left enough to care for us."

"Well, wise women do what they can for themselves," Hetty said. "This farm used to be our bread and butter, and we need to make of it what we can. So, if these lads are willing, perhaps they will row you to Bath, and you can see if anyone will take these for coin or trade."

Oma agreed. "What a fine idea. You can ask your friend Sal if the tavern needs jam, and maybe she'll have time for a chin wag. That will brighten your day, won't it?"

Marybeth gave us her first smile of the morning. "That does sound nice."

"Then, let's do it!" I replied.

***

Marybeth huddled under a quilt and kept the jars steady as Drake and I rowed. Then we each took a basket and followed Mrs. Thache up the shell path to The Marsh Moon Tavern. Sal greeted us and took one of Drake's jars to examine in the light.

"These are lovely and bright," she said. But when she carried a jar to the manager to see if he would take the trade, she returned with mixed news.

"Martin says we spent our last spare coins on sugar, and the best we can do is barter."

Marybeth had learned bargaining from her mom, so she had a twist to her offer. "These figs are full of sugar; we had plenty when we made them. So can't you use them to sweeten breads and cakes?"

"I never thought of that," Sal said. "While I put that idea past our cook, take a seat, and I'll bring a pot of tea."

Marybeth beamed in the light streaming through the bottle-glass window. "'Tis sweet of Sal to take such bother for us. This time of day, she's usually up to her ears chopping and stewing for dinner."

But it wasn't Sal who returned to discuss the trade; it was the tavern master, Martin Malone.

"Them's fine figs," he said, "and my cook says she can use 'em in cookin'. I reckon we can sell some outright, too. But times are hard, so here's me best offer."

Malone bent his big belly over our table, and we leaned in to listen.

"Mrs. Thache, your ma was a good cook when she worked here …."

Marybeth raised her palm to interrupt. "My mother is happy at home," she said. "She doesn't want to cook for customers now."

Martin nodded as he cocked his head. "'Tain't precisely what I'm askin'. As I recall, she made excellent fig puddings. If I can provide the flour, eggs, and spices, will she make puddings for us to serve here?"

Marybeth leaned back in her chair and peered through the green glass, considering the offer. Then after a deep breath, she turned to Martin and nodded. "I believe she might do that, but only if there's more to the trade."

Martin squished his thick lips together, making dimples roll on one cheek. Then, finally, he said, "Very well, for the lot you gave me, less three jars returned to make the pudding, I have extra dried beef, a couple dozen fresh clams, and a peck of apples. Will that do?"

Marybeth ticked her fingers. "So, you provide cake ingredients, beef, clams, and apples, and our end is these jars plus three homemade fig cakes?" she asked.

"That's my offer," he replied.

Marybeth must have known Oma's trading rule: never take the first offer. "I want one more thing," she said.

Marty rolled his eyes, "And what would that be?"

"Give Sal a few minutes to have tea with us. I'd love a chat with my friend."

"I can do that," he replied. "But you're lucky I have an extra girl working this morning."

"Make it two pecks of apples," she replied. "'Tis you who's lucky that my mother had a good crop of figs."

Martin chuckled, but then he had a new question. "Do you know if Captain Thache is back?" he asked. "I hope he might return with more sugar … and coins, too."

Marybeth's smile faded. "Sadly, I've heard no word of his return."

"Well, no worry. He'll get here when the waves bring him."

We sipped tea as we waited, but it was only minutes till Mrs. Thache smiled as Sal joined us.

"Glory be, you're a good friend, Marybeth. Marty never wants to see us sittin'. How did you get him to give in?" she asked.

"'Tis part of a good trade," Marybeth giggled.

"And it doesn't hurt when the trader is the wife of a powerful man, either," Sal replied. Then she added, "Malone says the Captain's not back yet, but I heard rumors that he might be."

The three of us from Plum Point perked up our ears. "What kind of rumors?" I asked.

"For one thing, we've heard about more trades for sugar and rum, and not many in town can spare that."

Marybeth shook her head. "Maybe it's the robbers we heard of," she said. "Have you learned anything else about them?"

"Well, Colleen told me Alice has been bragging that she'll get a new dress soon. And we all thought maybe Captain Thache would bring it."

"That's Alice being wishful," Drake replied.

"You folks would know better than most," she said. "I'm sure the Captain will find his wife first thing when he returns to these shores."

Drake and I agreed.

Marybeth smiled but added a caution. "When he comes to land, his first job is to clean and repair his ship. The rules say no one can leave the camp till that's done. But you're right. He will send word as soon as he can."

"I'm sure of it," Sal said as she patted Marybeth's hand. "But now Martin is glaring at me. You finish your tea; I have work waiting."

I also had a task, so I turned to Drake. "Will you wait with Marybeth till we can collect our trade? I want to speak to Wallace for a moment."

Drake pulled his lips to one cheek. He didn't like being left out of the action. But when I promised to hurry, he didn't argue.

***

Wallace was working hard, as usual, and none too happy to see me. When I asked him about news from the Hornpipe, he balked at first but gave in.

"The deal I made with Thache is working out so far. 'Tis nice to walk around town without worry, but I steer clear of that lot in the Hornpipe. I never know what they might do when they get deep in their cups."

But when I asked him if he had heard anything about Captain Thache's return, he bent over the worktable, beckoning me to come closer as he shared his news.

"One night when I passed the Hornpipe, I heard Quincy Underwood conversing with another man about a trade. At first, I suspected Underwood had caught a rum thief, but they were talking about a dress, and Quincey was pressing the man with the same question everyone else in Bath asks—was Thache back from his voyage? The other man had no idea, but Underwood promised trouble if the man didn't let him know when Thache was back in Pamlico."

***

While sailing back to Plum Point, I told Marybeth and Drake what I had heard.

"Why would this man, Underwood, care about finding the Captain?" Drake asked.

"Your guess is as good as mine," I said, shrugging. "And what would Underwood know about Edward and dresses?"

Marybeth had a clue about that.

"Quincy Underwood looks after Moseley's property in Bath. Sal says that when Moseley commented once on her pretty frock, and she told him it was a gift from Israel Hands. So maybe that's the connection—Underwood thinks Hands is back in town and assumes Edward and his crew have returned."

Drake looked over his shoulder. "But Moseley isn't a trader and is rich enough to buy what he wants. So why would he care about dresses and Captain Thache?"

"Good question," I replied. And once we had our goods safely stored and Marybeth went to the Bride's Tower, I asked my cousin, "Do you think Oma knows what this is about?"

We agreed to ask her as soon as possible but didn't get the chance that day.

I joined Marybeth on the tower before I went to bed.

"Are you all right?" I asked. "You don't think the Captain is back in Pamlico, do you?"

She shook her head. "I don't know."

"But if he's here, wouldn't he get a message to you?"

"I believe he would, but 'tis hard to say. I can only judge by the one time he sailed away from me. He said he chose me over the waves, but the sea pulls on him like the moon on the tides. So maybe it's pulling so hard he can't break free."

I shook my head. "I've seen how he looks at you; the sea can't put that glow on his face."

"When he returned from his last voyage, he sent a message by those bringing goods to Tobias Knight. I've watched that landing every night since he left, and there's been no sign of him or goods coming to Knight's Landing." She turned north, away from Knight's Landing and toward Polaris. "Look there," she said.

One dark cloud after another sailed passed Polaris so that the star was a tiny flash amid the rush of what looked like a fleet of gray ghostships zipping through the sky.

"They are only clouds," I said. "The North Star shines, whether we can see it or not."

Marybeth didn't smile, but she nodded. "Edward will find his way or die trying."

"He will," I said. And despite the chilly winds and the shiver the ghost clouds sent down my spine, I knew Edward would make it home—at least this time.

41 Family Magic

Drake Saunters

Ody and I knew better than to ask Grandma what she knew about Thache's future, especially if anyone else might hear it. So, lucky for us, Marybeth asked instead. The following day at breakfast, she couldn't hold her question long enough for the kettle to boil.

"Widow Saunters, my mother believes you are a seer. If that's true, will you tell me when Edward will return?" she asked.

"I cannot speak about what your mother believes," Aurora said.

Hetty slapped her dish towel to the table. "Then I'll speak for myself. Aurora Saunters knows things she has no cause to know. That makes her a seer, in my book."

Grandma put her hand on Mrs. Bellieu's wrist to stop her speech. Then she turned to Marybeth. "I see, hear, and learn as you do, dear. Perhaps I put it all together a little better than some. But that doesn't make me a seer—a good puzzler, maybe. But there is no magic in that."

I nearly coughed up my biscuit. *Was Grandma lying?* If time travel wasn't magic, what was? But then I remembered; Grandma always said that what appears to be magic is only something missing an explanation. She constantly searched for a cause for time travel, so she met her definition and wasn't lying about being magical.

Oma put her arm around Marybeth. "We all know you are worried about Edward's return, so does that make us seers?"

"Well, answer me, then; will he return soon?"

"I'll give you an answer, but 'tis based on how I put things together and nothing else. Yes, Edward will return because he said he would. It will be soon because that was his estimate, and he is our expert. I can't predict the weather, but Edward knows how to read the wind and waves. Since he said he'd be back before the end of summer, he will likely do that. See," she said, spreading open palms. "No magic."

Marybeth smiled. "It makes me feel better, anyway."

With her worries lessened, Marybeth went about her work. And Grandma asked Drake and me to help pick late berries on the south side of the point. I suspected it was an excuse to speak to us privately, and I hoped she would tell us what was to come, but she started a different conversation.

"Boys, we must go home soon. Things are beginning to boil here, and we shouldn't be in the middle of it."

"You told us Edward's days would soon end, is there worse than that?"

"There are forces at work that will bring about his end, you need to know some of it to keep out of trouble. But you must never tell anyone what will happen or when. Meddling in time that way can be dangerous."

"Did you tell the truth to Marybeth? Will Edward return soon?" Drake asked.

"Yes, we will see him by the end of the month, and it could be as soon as a week."

"Aren't you sure?" I asked.

"Some things history records, other information is implied, and it's difficult to measure what truth comes from someone else's reasoning."

"Well, what can you tell us?" I asked.

"And what should we be careful not to repeat?" Drake added.

She crouched by the blackberry vines and looked around for listeners. When she found none, she whispered, "Enemies of Tobias Knight and Governor Eden are using Edward to steal power from the Governor."

"But they don't succeed," I said. "They can't. Edenton gets its name from Governor Eden, so he's honored, not disgraced."

"You are right, and I'm proud you remember your history enough to puzzle that out. Eden's enemies fail, but sadly, Blackbeard is caught in the middle."

"Who are his enemies?" Drake asked.

"A group wants to replace Eden to change the politics in North Carolina."

"Is this something you know for sure?" I asked. "Or are you piecing it together?"

She sat down beside her bucket in the berry thicket. "Here is a fact. In December of this year, some men of this group will invade the home of an official, looking for evidence that Governor Eden and Tobias Knight are involved in Blackbeard's piracy. If Eden has broken the law, his enemies have grounds to replace him."

"Shouldn't we warn him?" Drake asked.

"The Governor will get his warning," Oma said. "But not from us. We must leave the facts as history knows them."

"So, what should we do?" I asked. "How do we stay out of the way?"

"Well, for one thing, interact as little as you can with Eden, Knight, Edward Moseley, Maurice Moore, and Jeremiah Veil."

"Moseley is an enemy?" I asked.

"Don't interfere," Grandma replied. "Let history take its course."

"Then maybe we should leave now," Ody said. "We can't mess anything up if we aren't here."

"My main reason for staying is Marybeth," Oma replied. "History doesn't know what becomes of her; there are no facts for us to ruin by tampering."

"And didn't that guy back home tell you what happens happens? If we are here now, we were always here, so we can't mess up anything, can we?" I asked.

"That's a working theory; perhaps our being in her century protects the girl. There is so much we don't know, but one thing strikes me as true; we shouldn't change the facts that made it to our time," she replied.

I felt it was time to confess, so I rose from our huddle and backed up a few feet to address my family.

Ody stepped toward me. "Drake, are you going somewhere?"

I shook my head. "No. I'm sticking here. I have something to say." And with a deep inhale, I began. "Grandma, I learned something new about traveling that I didn't tell you."

Ody punched my shoulder. "And what is that?" he asked. "And why didn't you tell me?"

I ignored him. Grandma stood too, probably trying to puzzle me out, but her expression was grim. "Go on with it then. What did you discover?"

When I hesitated to speak, Ody moved toward Grandma, and they stood like two judges, ready to hang me. "We're listening," Ody said.

With a deep sigh to clear the butterflies from my stomach, I blurted it out. "It's possible to rewrite what we do in time."

"How could you know that?" Oma asked.

"Because I did it. I teleported back to Jamaica and broke a mirror, but when I came home and tried again, I stopped my stumble, and the mirror was whole again."

"That's dangerous stuff, Drake," she replied. "Are you absolutely sure?"

"Yes, Ma'am. I watched the exact thing happen on my first commute. After that, everything was the same, except that the mirror I broke on trip two was all back together on trip three just as it had been the first time."

"Why did you go again?" Ody asked.

"I wanted to see the measure of Edward's character, to convince you he's a good man at heart. I saw him take a lash intended for Caesar because the punishment was unfair," I said. "Edward is a man who stands up for what he believes."

"He's a pirate," Ody said.

"Pirates are thieves, but they can be good men, too—like Robin Hood," I replied.

But Grandma stopped our argument. "That may be so, Drake, But meddling in time is dangerous. Not just for you, but for all of us."

"Did you go to find out more about time travel?" Ody asked.

"No, that wasn't my intention, but I spoke to Asjen Nuevo this time, and I'd like to speak to him again. I have questions."

Ody shrugged. "We all have questions. But getting the chance to ask them depends on when we leave. When will that be, Grandma?"

Oma took a deep breath. "If we avoid the major players in the drama brewing here, we will be safe for now. However, things get more critical in late September. We can wait till Edward comes home without causing damage. But know this; when Edward returns, he will bring a secret with him—a big one. One he won't be able to handle on his own."

"What secret?" I asked.

"I can't tell you that; Marybeth can't know it ahead of time, and neither can Edward's enemies."

"Then why tell us about it at all?" Ody asked.

"Because knowing about it might help you be wary of trouble. If we are here when Edward returns, you must avoid his enemies and the secret. Otherwise, we could tip the conflict."

Instead of listening to more, I plucked a blade of grass and twisted it into a knot as I considered what was said. *If we left within a week—before the secret arrived—would I have time to revisit Jamaica?*

"Stay on your best behavior, Drake," Oma said. "We walk a tightrope here."

"I understand, Grandma."

Ody put his hands on his hips. "I reckon he understands, but he probably won't listen."

As it turned out, we didn't have weeks till Thache returned. Marybeth heard from him before the next week passed.

42 A Bit of Bother

Marybeth Thache

Nights passed, but no boat came to Tobias Knight's dock, and there was no message. But after a few days more, a small sailboat pulled to Plum Point Landing. The lone man was not tall enough to be my husband, but perhaps he carried word from Edward.

I buckled my shoes, wrapped the shawl around me, and was nearly out the door when I remembered we had thieves in Bath County, and this might be one of them. So, I ran up the steps and called Ody.

"Wake up. Come with me. Someone is on the landing."

Then I hurried to meet the stranger, and luckily Ody was with me by the time I reached him.

"Mrs. Thache?" he asked.

I nodded, too breathless to speak.

"I be Olwyn Finch, and I have a message from your husband."

I had never met the messenger, but he clearly belonged to the sea. His hat, coat, and even his eyes reflected the deep bluish-slate of the ocean waves under a cloud-covered sky. But while frothy white caps broke blue waves, the pale spots on Finch's coat and hat were salt crusts. His voice cracked like waves slapping a rocky shore, and the hand that passed the note from my husband was thick with callouses from oars and fishing nets.

"Edward. At last," I said, holding the note close. Even folded, the letter dwarfed my palm, but it would fit perfectly in Edward's hand. The stamp on the wax was from his signet ring, but I wanted answers before breaking the seal.

"Where is Edward? Why didn't he come himself?" Then cold reality hit. "Is he hurt? Is he ...."

"I saw him, Ma'am, and he seemed quite well, but he has business at his camp that keeps him there. So, he found me at Swan's Quarter and trusted me to get word to you."

"Swan's Quarter, that's not so far to row," I said.

He nodded.

"So, how do you know my husband?" I asked.

Ody added, "Were you with him on the *Queen Anne's Revenge*?"

The stranger knit his brows. "And who might *you* be, lad?"

I put a hand on Ody's chest and stood between them. "He's a trusted friend who watches out for me during Edward's absence. Do you sail with Edward?"

"No, Missus," he said. "There was a time, but not lately. We sailed along this shore years before he returned to Bath. But good mates never forget who stays true to 'em while fightin' the waves."

"Please, come in, Mr. Finch," I said.

He shook his head. "Edward took a risk coming to me. Even at Swan's Quarter, he has enemies and doesn't want them to know he's returned. Everything you need is in the note. 'Tis all I can tell you, Mrs. Thache, and now I must return. 'Tis still a long row home, and I've only this little boat this evening."

Marybeth gripped his wrist. "Thank you, Sir. Your message means the world to me. May I offer you refreshment?"

"I came with provisions, Ma'am." Olwyn tipped his hat as he shoved off our landing and headed toward the Pamlico River. Ody watched with me, then held my arm to steady me as we walked toward the porch and parlor.

Once behind the safety of my bolted front door, he settled me on Edward's favorite chair and took the nearby rocker. "Do you wish for privacy to read the letter, Marybeth?" he asked.

I shook my head but said, "I can't say till I read what's in it."

"Then I'll wait till you know what you prefer," he said.

I nodded, ripped open the seal, and my sobs woke Mother, and tears blurred the words I tried to read.

"What is happening here?" she shouted. "Why is my girl crying?"

"She has a message from the Captain," Ody said.

By then, the house was up, and the others sat silently among the sounds of the ticking clock and my intermittent sobs. Finally, I dried my tears enough to read what Edward had written while the others sat breathless, waiting for the news.

I read the letter silently, once from eagerness and again for understanding. Then I lay the page in my lap, swapping it for a handkerchief to wipe my eyes again.

"Go on, girl," Mother said. "Tell us what you will or tell us to leave you."

Aurora was more patient. "Take your time, dear. How can we help you?"

I took a deep breath. "Edward is busy at his camp on Ocracoke." Then I looked up to explain, "'Tis not in his note, but before he left, he promised the crew to establish new sailors' rules once they reached the islands."

"Yes," Drake said, "We heard something of that when we visited the Hornpipe."

I nodded, "Now, he writes that the men had trouble agreeing, and as he expected, some of the crew chose to stay in the Indies. Then they met with what he calls a 'bit of bother' on the voyage home."

"What happened?" Ody asked.

"He hasn't given me the details, but apparently, there is extra work and fewer crewmen to take care of the ship, so he can't leave yet."

Mother's eyebrows raised at that puzzle as she asked, "Well, how long has he been back?"

"He didn't say, but it must have been a few days. He couldn't have left immediately, not even to get a message to me," I said.

Aurora Saunters sat with her back straight and chin up—a picture of composure that might have given me the strength to hold myself together. But then she placed one hand over the other, slightly kneading the knuckles of her right hand. She was nervous, too. "So, when will he come home?" she asked.

Drake leaned forward, adding, "Does he give you any idea?"

I swallowed as I looked at the words again. "Edward says he'll be here within a week, but I shouldn't watch for him as it will likely be late at night when he comes to the house."

"A week from when?" Aurora asked.

I checked again. "The letter is dated today."

"Well then, maybe you can get a few nights' sleep," Mother said. "You should look better than dog tired for your husband, my dear."

When did Mother start caring how I looked for Edward? That was a change. But I repressed a chuckle as I reread the note.

Aurora tilted her shoulders toward me. "Does it say more?" she asked.

I read the words repeatedly but couldn't understand the last part. Maybe the others had an answer. "Edward says I should burn this note. But why? Could it be the enemies the messenger mentioned?"

Now Aurora's eyes grew darker. "Did the messenger mention enemies?" she asked.

Ody and Drake, both grimly alert, looked at their grandmother, and once Mother saw where they focused, she studied Aurora's face.

"What do you see, Aurora?" Mother asked.

Aurora took a deep sigh, then bent the corners of her lips upward. "I see that Edward wants you to follow his instructions. So, I suspect you should do as he wishes for whatever reason."

Mother pointed to the fire. “Do as she says.”

I reread the page, caressing each letter and each spot where his fingers may have rested. Then I kissed his signature before dropping the page into the flames. Mother stirred the ashes till no sign of the message remained.

Aurora patted my shoulder. “Go to bed, Dear. ’Tis late, and sleep will salve your worries.”

As I turned to my bed, Aurora chatted as she helped Mother settle into hers, and then Mrs. Saunters walked up the steps to the rooms where her family slept.

After their doors closed, I tried to sleep, but I yearned for Edward. He was near. He was safe, but I couldn’t reach him.

I rose to pour a sip of water and caught sight of my face in the mirror. Now I saw why Mother worried about how I looked. I was no longer a blushing bride but the troubled wife of a sea captain who often faced a bit of bother.

Then there was another sound—a few halting steps.

Creaking boards.

A door swung open. *Was it Edward?*

“Who’s there?” I called.

I splashed my face and pinched my cheeks before running toward the sounds at the back of the house. A man ran across our yard and into the forest. I shouted for him to stop, but the man kept running.

Ody reached me first. “Who was that?” he asked.

“It wasn't Edward,” I replied.

“What’s this mess on the floor?” Mother asked.

Aurora bent to wipe the spill. “’Tis rum,” she said.

“Those sounds were from the cellar. Someone’s been in our rum.”

“Drake. Let’s go find out who that was,” Ody said. Aurora protested, but the boys gathered shoes and jackets to follow the thief. Then before they could leave the porch, Caesar stumbled into the yard dragging Jonah behind him, shouting, “Look what I found.”

Jonah still had hold of the neck of a broken rum flask.

Mother took it from him. “This is ours.”

“Are you stealing from us?” I asked. “Edward pays you good silver, and you steal from us?”

Jonah hung his head but said no more.

“What shall we do with him, Mis’ress?” Caesar asked.

Mother had the answer. “Let him sleep with the hens. Bolt him in, and we’ll figure him out in the morning. There’s been enough trouble tonight.”

She was right, but how could I sleep now?

Drake went to help Caesar confine Jonah and returned with a report that our thief was secure for the night. Ody checked the doors and combed the cellar while I looked around the bell tower. But other than a tapped keg and an open sugar barrel, there was nothing unusual to report.

Then Aurora came for me with a toddy of herb tea, honey, and rum. She tucked me in like my mother did when I was a child, and she was still rocking beside my bed as I fell asleep.

My last thought was of seeing Edward within a week. Yes. Even after a bit of bother of my own, I could sleep. Edward would be with me again soon.

***

When we woke, Caesar and Drake let the chickens out, leaving Jonah to have his breakfast in the hen house. After we ate, the lads set Jonah on the porch edge, hands tied behind him, while the rest of us gathered in a circle of chairs.

Mother started us off. "Well, Jonah, you go first. What do you have to say for yourself?"

"I'm sorry, Widow Bellieu, Mrs. Thache. What I did was wrong, but I was up against a rock with Alice. 'Tis why I took the rum."

"Were you so hard up for a drink?" Caesar asked. "I keep a swaller or two in the shed. You know that."

"'Tweren't for me," Jonah replied. "It was to trade for Alice's dress. She's been after me to get one for her—like those she saw on Mrs. Thache and the other crewmen's girls."

"Couldn't you use the silver Edward gives you for that?" I asked.

"I give that to her father, so he'll let me keep company with Alice. I figured I had no choice but to disappoint her. But then someone, he might have been a farm hand, came along with a trade. He claimed to have a dress that would fit Alice, but he'd take only rum for it. He figured the Capt'n left some here, and I could get it. I helped the Capt'n unload once or twice, so I knew where to look."

Ody shook his head. "Some of our sugar is gone, too. Did you steal that?"

"No, Ody, I swear I didn't take anything else. No sugar. No other rum. Just last night, and you caught me at it."

"So, who put up the trade? And how did he come by a woman's garment?" Mother asked.

"I don't know the *how*, Ma'am, and as to *who,* the man who spoke to me said it would mean his neck to tell," Jonah replied.

I stood up and walked toward the culprit. "What will the Captain do with you when he returns? Who would you rather face, some petty thief or Captain Edward Thache? What will he do with a man who violated his trust and stole from his family?"

Jonah gulped as he shook his head violently.

"Let me go, Ma'am. I took no rum out of your house. And now Alice is unhappy; the men of Bath are after me on one side and the Captain on the other. Let me go. The best chance I have is to run."

Ody stood in front of me. "The only reason you didn't take rum out of this house is that you broke the bottle. That's precious little to recommend you."

Jonah, cornered as he was, made a play for sympathy. He bent over his knees, face to the floor, begging for mercy.

"You're right, Mistress Thache. I'm a low-down scoundrel. And after the Capt'n granted my plea to stay here and win Alice, I dishonored him. I ain't worth the feed you give the chickens. So let me go, and you'll never see me again."

"What would you do then?" Aurora asked.

He looked up, face puffy and red as he scanned the point for an idea. Then, finally, he said, "I'll go to Alice and see if she still loves me. Maybe her Papa will let me live in his hay barn till I learn enough farming to suit him."

"What do you think, Caesar?" Aurora asked. "We caught this man stealing. Have you found any part of him trustworthy?"

Jonah tugged at his ropes as he hollered, "You can't let Caesar testify against me. He ain't allowed to tell on a white man in a court of law."

Now Mother stood up. "This ain't a court of law; we will listen to whomever we choose." She turned to Caesar. "What say ye, Caesar?"

Caesar cleared his throat and said, "Well, I must say he worked hard as he tried to learn farmin'. But, night and day, all he ever talked about was Alice. If he cared that much for rum, I would know. He'd've been after mine first."

"Do you have any idea who was into our sugar?" Drake asked.

"No. And I can tell you Jonah never brought any to the shed."

Ody agreed. "He never had anything like that in the boat when we took him to town, either."

"Did he ever go missing from the shed? Could he have been thieving elsewhere? Did anyone else meet him here?" Aurora asked.

Caesar shook his head. "I don't recall him ever being long gone without reason. I'd never have pegged him as dishonest before last night."

The widow Bellieu turned to Marybeth. "Girl, you've heard the same as me. What would you do with him?"

The others returned to their chairs, and Jonah looked at me, pleading. I was the unwilling mistress of this house, but everyone waited for me to speak, so I did.

"He stole the rum. There's no doubt of that. But he might be telling the truth about trouble with his girl."

Jonah raised his head, nodding in hope. "That's the truth, Mrs. Thache. I just wanted to make her happy, and I knew no one here was drinking much with the Captain gone. He'll likely bring more rum when he comes, so I figured it wouldn't hurt anyone."

"That doesn't change that you broke the Captain's trust."

"No, Ma'am," he said, head lowered. "What will ye do with me?"

"I will allow you to stay here, but with no further payments and no overnight visits to Alice until the Captain returns. You will be under the guard of Caesar while you are here, and Ody will be in charge of you when you go off the Point." I turned to the group. "What do the rest of you think?"

They all nodded and agreed the plan sounded fair—all except Jonah.

"But Mrs. Thache, what will Alice think? She won't know what's become of me?"

"Can you write?" I asked.

"I can."

"Then write your note. After that, Ody will deliver your letter to explain to Alice."

"She will want to know when I can be there again to help her father—when he might get more silver from me."

"'Twill be when Captain Thache returns and decides this matter. More than that, I can't say."

***

On Jonah's usual day to visit Alice, Ody delivered the letter to her instead. We went to Scripture reading on Sunday, and Sal told us that Alice had gotten her dress. Her story was that one of the farmhands brought it to Alice, expecting rum for the trade. At first, he refused to give it to the girl. But when Alice showed him the letter Jonah sent, the trader grinned from ear to ear and stuffed the letter into his pocket as payment.

Now I was bothered again. What value could Jonah's plea to Alice have to a farmhand?

43 Knight Visit

Ody Saunters

"Jonah's gone—probably for good. So, only breakfast for one today," Caesar said as he came for his trencher.

"He fled?" I asked.

"Yep, he's been frettin' over the Cap'n's return, and last night he was more skittish than usual. And, when he went out to take care of nature's business, he didn't return. Didn't take his duffle nor nothin' else."

"Did he give you any clue he was going?"

"Nary a word. He wanted to take a leak, and I heard him stumbling in the brush. He hollered once, and I thought he yelled *cap*, but I reckon it might have been a less polite word if he fell."

We tried tracking Jonah's path, but with all the deer and wild boar that passed through the woods, we had no luck. And when we reported the news to Marybeth, she thought Jonah's return to Alice made the most sense.

She shrugged, saying, "Well, if that's what he did, we will find out soon enough, and Edward can settle with Jonah when he gets here. I wonder how he got over East Creek, though. The ferryman wouldn't be there at night."

"That doesn't matter much with all the boats in the creeks at night. Someone would be near enough to ferry him," I said.

The widow Bellieu didn't worry about Jonah. She was glad it was the end of the growing season, not planting time. And she had Caesar and three from the Saunters clan to help with the harvest that was left.

Despite the extra work from being a man short, there was an additional duty for Drake and me. The Captain's note said he'd come at night and for Marybeth not to bother watching for him. But that didn't suit Mrs. Thache; if she had her way, she'd stand on that tower night and day. So, to give her some rest, Drake and I split the night shift so there would be someone on the point to watch for Edward. Lucky for us, we didn't have to watch for long.

There was no moon the night the Captain returned, not at midnight, anyway, and there was enough haze to hide the stars. With nothing but a candle's warmth, I buttoned my coat and kept a shawl around me as I peered over the blackness of Old Towne Creek. The flutter of batwings and the call of night birds wouldn't keep me awake for long. Thank goodness for the tea and biscuits.

For four hours, it was my duty to watch the house and keep an eye out for Captain Thache. Drake and I were happy enough to do it. My cousin would never disappoint the Captain, and I'd do anything for Marybeth.

In less than an hour, I spotted the *Black Sam Bellamy*. I lit the lantern as a signal and a brief, dim glow returned from the boat's stern. I could see little of the deck, but there was light from windows at Knight's Landing. As the *Bellamy* pulled to shore, I watched through the spyglass as four men secured the ropes and began carrying boxes and barrels into Knight's dockside tunnel. Then the taller man, Captain Thache, by his silhouette, disappeared into the shadows around the side of the house.

'Twas then I woke Marybeth, and as the tower offered a better view than the porch, she followed me to the belfry.

"Are you sure 'tis Edward?" she asked.

"It looks to be Edward, and he's at Knight's farm like the Captain said he would be."

She watched the men moving crates and barrels for a while and then said, "He must have done well on his voyage. He's bringing goods from the islands."

I nodded, "Aye, Knight will be pleased."

"Not as pleased as I am," she said.

"He hasn't been there long, and I reckon he must report what's happened to Knight or one of his men."

She nodded and pointed to my cup. "I'll fetch more tea."

I tried counting the boxes and trips to the cellar, but the light wasn't on my side.

Finally, when I gave up counting, Drake popped his head up the hatch. "What are you doing here?" I asked. "It isn't time for your watch yet."

Drake sat a cozy-covered teapot at my feet, saying, "Well, what am I supposed to do; wait till the excitement has passed?"

Marybeth followed him with more cups and a basket of biscuits, and the three of us sat staring at shadows across the creek, wondering when Edward would come home.

Then, when the pot was empty, Drake saw a small boat rowing toward our landing with only one tall man aboard.

"'Tis Edward," Marybeth whispered, and then she sprang from her chair, shouting, "Edward is here."

Then we all hushed as we hurried to the parlor to greet him. Not that Drake and I had much to do with that greeting. The captain pegged his hat and pistol holster, and then it was all hugs and kisses as the couple reunited.

Hetty stood frozen at the romantic display, but Oma chuckled and went for another kettle.

Captain Thache dragged Marybeth to the rocker beside Bert Bellieu's chair and held her hand as he explained.

"I can't stay long, but I had to see you, my dear."

"Is it the bit of bother you mentioned?" she asked.

He nodded somberly. "Things got out of hand on the voyage home."

"Why do you have your guns?" she asked, pointing to the pegs. "Is everyone all right?"

"We brought goods for Bath, and such cargo needs guarding. But everyone is hale and hardy—nearly everyone. Dr. Neuvo has a few patients on the island, but none of that should bother you. 'Tis part of sailing," he said.

"Then, why all the secrecy? Why would you have me burn my letter?" she asked.

He sighed as he lowered his eyes.

With a hand on his shoulder, she asked, "'Tis the bother again, isn't it?"

"Aye," he replied. "I must get things in order; that was part of my visit to Knight, but 'twill take time. And Tobias says I should keep my return a secret for a few more days. He needs to summon the Admiralty Council, and until he does, there should be no connection between our farm and his. Do you understand? No one should know I was there, so keep that news within these walls."

We all nodded, but the Captain had more bad news. He took Marybeth's hands as he told her, "I won't be able to visit again until Knight gets a ruling from the Council."

Marybeth buried her face in Edward's chest as Drake spoke for all of us. "That sounds serious," he said.

Hetty's eyes widened as she turned to Oma, who sat with brows knit and lips white. "'Tis true, isn't it?" she said. "I can see it in Aurora's eyes. 'Tis grave, indeed."

Thache patted his wife's back as he replied, "Mother Bellieu, I assure you, Widow Saunters could know nothing of my situation. But 'tis in the hands of friends now, so all will be well."

The Captain peered out the window. "My men will finish their work soon, and I must join them. But, quickly, tell me about you and the farm. Has everything worked out as expected?"

Marybeth told him about Jonah, trying to make as little of it as possible.

"He stole rum from us?" Thache bellowed.

In the hopes of smoothing it over, I said. "It was just the one time. There's been some petty thieving around town, and Jonah swears he didn't take the sugar."

This time the Captain stood, fists clenched in rage. "Someone stole sugar, too? From our cellar? How did they get in?"

"Jonah came through the back door, but I have no idea when or how anyone else came in," Hetty replied.

"Why would he do that?" Thache asked.

Drake replied, "It had to do with that girl, Alice. She wanted a dress, and someone offered to trade one to Jonah for rum, figuring there would be a flask wherever Thache lived."

"What kind of dress?"

Marybeth shrugged, "Sal said it was like the ones you gave me."

"But those are in my den," Edward replied. "Remember? You told me to leave them there."

"I did. No one disturbed that sack, as far as I know."

"Did Jonah ever go to the tower?" Edward asked.

Drake replied, "No. Never. No one passed through that room besides us, and after we helped Mrs. Thache put things in order, we only passed through on the way to the tower."

I added, "Caesar swears he knows Jonah's comings and goings. And we keep watch. We've had no visitors besides Wallace and the messenger you sent."

"Wallace? He climbed that tower before, didn't he?"

"It wasn't Wallace," I said. "He comes on Harding's tender, and he's with one of us all the time he's here."

"Well, then who … Oh no." Edward flopped into the chair.

"What is it?" Marybeth asked. "You don't suspect Wallace, do you?"

He shook his head and cleared his throat. "The Crow. I knew that scalawag would cause trouble. The Crow didn't show up for the launch to St. Thomas. Have you seen him here?"

"No," Drake replied. "We thought he sailed with you."

Edward nodded. "Well, he was wise not to show his face, but I'd wager he's been here. And I bet we'll find at least one dress missing when we check that sack. The Crow's had time to heal, and even with a gamey leg, a barrel man could scale the roof ladder quickly and quietly so no one would hear him."

Marybeth started for the Captain's den, but Thache said, "Please wait, my Dear. The chest will keep. Stay with me a moment."

Edward rechecked the window. "My men are nearly done. I must return to them, but once we're all aboard *Bellamy* and headed for Ocracoke, I'll stop again for a quick goodbye." He took Marybeth's hand. "I brought you something from my voyage." Then with a quick kiss on the cheek, he grabbed his hat and holster and was out the door.

Marybeth followed him as far as the porch and watched til the rowboat reached Knight's landing. Her eyes were glued to the dock until the crew boarded the *Bellamy* and rowed for Plum Point. Then while four black crewmen waited at the oars, Thache bounded to the porch with a box in his hands.

"Sweets for my sweetie," he said.

As Marybeth tore open the box, Thache had another question.

"Did you tell anyone I've returned from the voyage?"

"No," she replied. "Not a soul other than those with me when I got your message."

"What about Jonah?" I asked. "He was in the cellar when Marybeth read your letter. If he heard how you promised to visit within the week, we can't say who he may have told."

Thache made a noise close to growling. "I must get back to Ocracoke. The sun will be up in an hour, and we should push on to the sound. Unfortunately, there may be more trouble waiting when I reach the island."

"What about your men?" Marybeth asked, pointing to *Bellamy's* crew. "They must be tired. Do they need refreshment?"

"No, Knight's men helped them unload, And they ate and rested while I visited you. They are eager to get to the camp, I'm sure."

After a last loving embrace, he turned to leave.

Oma stopped him. "Captain," she asked, "Is your sword in good repair."

"Of course, me lady. None of my men rest without a good look at their weapons—'tis part of our rules. My sword is as sharp and good as new. Why do you ask?"

"All Bath is bothered, Captain. First, your voyage, Jonah at Plum Point, and traders report robberies, too. So, we should all keep eyes open and wits sharp."

"Wits and weapons, too," he replied, grinning as he tapped his scabbard.

He turned, but Oma stopped him once more. "Captain, you won't have reason to stop between here and Ocracoke, will you?"

"No, indeed, widow. 'Tis a long row, but we're rested and will catch the wind in the sound. My men are home on the waves, even at night, but they'll hurry to our camp. Besides, as I said, I'm not ready to let Bath know I'm home." Then with a wink, he added, "Thank the stars that I can trust you to keep my secret."

I was pretty sure we wouldn't tell anyone. Not anyone else, anyway.

Grandmother was silent, but her pursed lips spoke for her. When Marybeth and the widow Bellieu closed the house, Drake and I followed Oma to her room.

"What's wrong, Grandma?" Drake asked.

"It's starting," she said.

"Is the Captain in trouble?" I asked.

She nodded. "It will get worse."

Drake sat beside her on the edge of her bed. "What can we do?"

With a sad face, Oma looked first at Ody, then me, as she shook her head. "It's too late, and it's history. We can't change it, nor should we."

"But you warned him," Drake said. "Will that change history?"

"No," I replied. "Grandma says we were always part of this equation, even though we arrived here from our future."

"So, did you lead Edward to danger or keep him from it when you suggested he sail straight to Ocracoke?" Drake asked. "Does it even matter which?"

"That's three questions, and I have no answers to any of them," she replied. "I'm as green as you are about some aspects of time travel."

"Then why worry?" Ody asked.

After a great sigh, she replied, "Because I don't like to think about the trouble Captain Thache faces nor the possible unhappy fate of Marybeth and her mother."

None of us liked that thought. So we went to bed tired and still uneasy about what we may have caused.

44 The Trouble Begins

Ody Saunters

Wallace McNeil usually brought Hetty's goods and the gossip from Bath on Tuesdays. But this was Thursday, and I suspected McNeil might carry troubling news about the Captain's secrets. I wasn't wrong.

Wallace bounced out of his boat as Drake and I ran down the boardwalk to meet him.

"Have you heard?" he called. "I figured this house ought to hear it from a friend." Then he gave us the gist of what had happened.

While Thache and his crew of four rowed for Ocracoke, five men on a periauger accosted a county trader, William Bell, at Chester's Landing.

Could it have been the Captain and his men?

"Who was the robber?" I asked.

Drake's words nearly stepped on mine. "And when did it happen?"

Wallace looked around the yard and then at the bell tower. "Where is Marybeth?" he asked. "Maybe she should hear this."

The last thing Marybeth needed was more to upset her.

"Tell us first, and then we will decide if it's worth troubling her," I said. "When did this happen?"

"I wasn't there," Wallace replied, "And 'tis hard to say precisely when, but Bell knocked on the Governor's door before Eden was out of bed. The servant sent him back to Knight's Landing, and Tobias was barely up himself. 'Twas half past seven, I reckon." Then paused, adding, "Come to think of it, Bell said the robber approached when it was dark—about an hour before dawn, 4:30, maybe."

"That's when Thache left us," Drake whispered.

I covered Drake's whisper with a quick question. "Chester's Landing? Where is that?"

"'Tis near the mouth of North Creek, about three leagues from here, nearly three hours by boat, I reckon," Wallace said.

"Who robbed Bell?" I repeated.

"He wasn't sure. Bell said a white man jumped into his boat looking for a drink, but it was too dark to pour, so the leader demanded drink, money, and guns, and when Bell didn't oblige, the robber called for his sword."

The attacker couldn't be Edward. He left Plum Point with his sword and pistols, and even if he took them off once his crew unloaded the cargo, why would he attack a boat with no weapon?

"The sword must not have done much damage," I said. "After all, Bell couldn't have been hurt much if he could sail his boat to the Governor's house in Bath and then back to Knight's Landing within a few hours. Was anyone with him?"

"Only his young son and an Indian servant. But even with his sword, the attacker couldn't overcome them alone. So, the leader called for his men, and the five managed to subdue Bell and his passengers. But the leader broke the end of his sword in the fight and left a piece of it on Bell's boat."

"But wasn't Bell bleeding?" Drake asked.

"After he reported the robbery to Tobias Knight, Bell spent the morning at the Marsh Moon drinking cider and retelling his story. But no one said anything about blood or injuries."

Five robbers left Bell uninjured and able to row to Bath to report the attack. The story made no sense to me.

"So, if the robbery started about 4:30, and Bell rowed to Bath afterward, did the robbers grab the loot and run?" I asked.

"Well, it took a while. After the bandits tied Bell's hands, they rowed his boat to the middle of North Creek, robbed it, threw the oars and sails overboard, and rowed away. It would take time to get his boat back and his sails re-rigged before he could row to see Eden," Wallace said.

Drake nodded. "Unless somebody else helped him get to Bath. "

"I don't think so," Wallace replied. "Such a man would be the main one spreading the gossip, and no one else was with Bell in the Marsh Moon. I pieced the story from Bell, the men at Knight's plantation, and anyone at the tavern."

"Did Bell know any of them—the leader or the crew?" I asked.

"Bell suspects Thomas Undey or Fittery Dick, two men who'd stoop to robbery," Wallace replied. "And the others he described as black men—or maybe men disguised as black. He said it was too dark to pour rum, so I reckon it was too dark to see the men clearly."

"But if it takes over two hours to reach Chester's Landing and even more time to rob Bell, Wouldn't it be well past dawn by then? How was it still too dark to tell if a man was black?" Drake asked.

"No one said, but I reckon he either waited to meet someone or packed up his cargo and waited for enough light to sail," Wallace said, shrugging.

"What was stolen?" I asked.

"Some money—over £50. Besides that, Bell says they took a box of cloth, a tray of pipes, half a barrel of brandy, and some other boxes."

"Other boxes? What was in them?" I asked, but Wallace couldn't be sure.

"No one said. Maybe Bell didn't know. He was mostly worried over the money and who might have said he had it on the boat."

"Hm. If Bell carried cargo for someone else, that might explain why he was waiting on the landing and didn't report what was in the boxes," I said.

Drake jumped in, "And maybe that money was his payment to deliver the goods."

Wallace leaned in, saying, "But you haven't heard the worst of it?"

"There's worse?" I asked, holding my breath, unsure I wanted to hear more.

Wallace nodded, "The word going around is that the leader was Captain Thache."

We couldn't tell Wallace that the Captain was at Plum Point an hour before dawn and so couldn't have been at Chester's Landing for the robbery, but Drake had a different angle that made the same point.

"It couldn't be the Captain. Why would he attack a boat? And if he wanted a prize from it, why would he attack without his weapon?" Drake shook his head again as he asked, "Does anyone in Bath think Edward Thache couldn't take a man, a boy, and an Indian with his bare hands, much less with a sword?" he asked.

"It makes no sense to me, either," Wallace said.

I added, "And the Captain keeps that sword like new. He even told us once that it was one of his ships' rules—no one rests till his weapon is clean and ready for battle."

The excitement faded from Wallace's face as he added, "You're right about that, for sure." He shook his head as he scanned the bell tower. "There is no reason for Marybeth to hear this. It will only serve to upset her with no purpose."

I shook my head. "It won't matter; gossip finds its way. She'll hear it sooner or later and feel the grief then."

He shuffled his boot in the sand. "I don't believe the rumors, and neither does Captain Harding. But there is another mystery to solve."

"Like what?" I asked.

Wallace leaned in again. "No one comes or goes from Bath Harbor without Harding or his men knowing it, and one of the ships sailed passed

Ocracoke on the way to our port. Their crew reported seeing a ship's topsail on the island. The vessel was not a sloop, and according to the description, it must have been twice the size of Thache's *Adventure*."

"Do you mean to tell that to Marybeth?" I asked.

Wallace shook his head. "Well, I'm the last to want to trouble her without cause." He shook the dust from his hat and then shrugged, saying, "I'll see what Hetty needs before I go."

As Wallace trudged up the boardwalk to the porch, I turned to Drake. "That robber couldn't be Edward. And I'm sure if Knight hears those rumors, he'll dismiss them out of hand."

"Tobias must have other things on his mind, like gathering the Admirals' Council," Drake said.

I was thinking the same thing. The tall ship at Ocracoke must have dwarfed the problem of William Bell's robbery.

"Grandma says trouble is due to find the Captain. So maybe this is it," Drake said.

"Maybe," I replied. "But I'd better find out what Wallace tells Marybeth."

After Wallace heard what Hetty needed for the farm and gave his respects to Mrs. Thache and Grandma, he left without passing on his news of the robbery or the tall ship.

After he left, Marybeth joined Drake and me to look for evidence that the Crow had visited Thache's Den. It wasn't hard to find. The dress sack was open, and Marybeth recalled at least one missing item, a dress of rose linen. Drake and I planned to track it through Jonah and his mysterious trader. But now there was a suspect—The Crow.

But other items were missing from the pegs behind the attic door. There was the Captain's old brown coat, hat, and a sword sharpened so many times it was thin in the middle—a gift from Benjamin Hornigold.

"Why didn't we notice this before?" I asked.

"We often pass through this room at twilight going to the tower and again at night when we return," Marybeth replied. "And we aren't looking for what isn't there."

"The coat and sword are behind the open door," I said. "So, we didn't see those things on our way up the hatch. And when we returned, the door was open and lying against the pegs. It was dark then, too."

"But at night, anyone entering from the tower hatch would see things hanging beside the closed door," Drake replied. "There's no telling what else he took from here."

"I reckon he came for rum and sugar first and only came through here to get to the cellar," I said.

Drake nodded, "He must have dallied here longer when he searched for a dress to persuade Jonah to do his thieving for him."

"But why would he take Edward's old clothes?" Marybeth asked.

I shrugged, "Maybe he needed a change, and the sack only holds women's clothes."

Drake had a different idea. "Or maybe he got another offer—like payment to make Edward look guilty of a robbery."

"Thank goodness Edward removed his valuable papers. Who would guess a thief would want old clothes?" Marybeth asked.

Drake walked to the shelves on the south wall to check for anything missing. He shifted the basket of seashells and looked behind all the objects resting there. "No one took anything from here," he said.

But then Marybeth put her hands to her cheeks. "Oh, yes, they did," she said. "Our wedding cup is gone. Edward gave it to me as a gift on our wedding day; it was a prize taken from the *Great Allen*. The ship's Captain, Mr. Taylor, gave Edward particular grief in that encounter. So, Edward made Mr. Taylor's treasure his own. But, of course, that was long before he took the King's Pardon in Bath."

"I remember that old thing," I said. It looked like it had a cup on both ends.

She nodded, "Yes, it was a game for us after our wedding. We had to drink from both cups at the same time without spilling. Edward knew how to do it. He said he and his officers used it after a successful mission, wagering to win treasure from each other."

"Did The Crow play that game?" I asked.

"I don't think so. The men used the cup when the Captain had *Queen Anne's Revenge*, and his officers joined him in his quarters to celebrate. I doubt The Crow was part of that."

"But maybe he heard about it from Stede Bonnet and stole it for himself when he had the chance," Drake said.

"When Edward returns, I'll tell him. He'll know what to do," Marybeth replied.

45 Time Riddles

Drake Saunters

A fake robbery and a mysterious ship on Ocracoke signaled danger for Edward Thache. Maybe Marybeth was headed for trouble, too. And Grandma said we could not stop it.

But hadn't I changed the past in Jamaica?

I pondered the matter all day but didn't dare discuss it with Grandma or Ody. They would stop me before I could try to find answers, and if I *could* change events in the past to protect Edward and his family, they'd stop me from doing it.

Maybe they should. Maybe changing things would be wrong.

But I had not changed any events from happening except my coming and going. I had not made anyone turn right when they had turned left before, but I had written over a short, temporary portion of history. I erased the events after I broke the mirror when I returned to the exact moment of my first arrival. I didn't break the mirror then, so Edward's reactions to it breaking never happened.

Was that right? Did anyone know how that worked?

There was only one person I knew who might have answers, but I didn't have the means nor the time to row the better part of a day to reach him in Ocracoke. And even if I could get there, the Captain wouldn't welcome me to a port where he harbored a mysterious ship. But I *could* talk to Asjen Nuevo in Jamaica without anyone knowing.

By the time Oma and Ody were in bed, I had decided to try. There was time to go to Jamaica and return before anyone woke.

I didn't bother to fetch Grandma's pendant this time. Waking her was too risky. But I sneaked to the Captain's den, grabbed the star charm, and soon found myself behind the hinged mirror again.

Still as a mouse, I watched Edward speak to his mother, and then after Dr. Neuvo came and Abigail left, I crept down the stairs and hid behind the stone wall. I met Asjen as we passed on the path, and once he noticed my black books, he led me to the workroom. This time, after I polished his boots, I knocked on his door, and instead of dropping the shoes, I handed them to him.

"Ah, that's a fine job, young man. You're a master of dubbin. What shall I call you?"

"Dubbin is fine, Sir. Do you have more for me to do?"

"Well, there is another pair if you'd care to work on those for me," he said. "I'll bring them to the workroom."

He walked with me to the door, still admiring the polish of the boots. "Dubbin delight," he said with a smile as Abigail left her room and walked down the hall.

No one else saw me as I returned to the shop, and no one else dropped off shoes while I was there. Soon Neuvo arrived carrying a pair of grimy, black boots and a sack with a bound book sticking out the top.

"I will not keep you longer than needed," he said. I'll finish my sketch while you work. Then I can carry the boots back myself.

"That's quite a large book," I remarked as he chose a loose section of over a dozen pages. He opened it to his last sketch, the one of young Edward with Abigail. Several other *chapters* slid from the covers when he laid the bound book aside.

"Aye. That's better," Nuevo said as he looked up from sketching. "Do you draw?" he asked.

"No, not very well, but my family traveled, and my father made sketches of our destinations."

"Ahh." He continued touching up his sketch as he spoke. "Since I was a young man, I've been a wanderer myself—first as a journeyman artisan, then with warriors, but sometimes I studied among men who spent their days reading, writing, and thinking. I may have enjoyed those times the most. The group benefited from my perspective as a traveler. They felt the same as I; 'tis as intriguing to think of what *might* be as much as recording what *is*."

"I admit, I enjoy puzzling over such matters myself," I said.

"Oh, what puzzle intrigues you?" he asked.

"I don't know," I said, scraping mud from his boot. "Did you ever think about the future? Or how it would be to visit the past? Maybe to the time before Europeans found this land?"

He chuckled. "I may think about that more than any other man on Earth."

"Was it part of your work?" I asked.

"Well, I once lived in a colony of great thinkers. And occasionally, to change the topic from those of Earth, morality, and their travels, they considered the matter of time," he replied.

"Did they think about traveling through time? What did they decide?"

"Most thought it impossible, but some were brave enough to ask *what if*," he replied.

"What if?" I asked.

"What if it *were* possible? But most concluded if a man could go back in time, no such person has revealed himself, not publicly, anyway."

"Perhaps such a man would hide his secret from those he met," I replied.

"My friends thought time travel produced too many puzzles. For example, if a man traveled to meet his father as a lad, could he prevent himself from being born?"

"Did anyone have an answer?" I asked. "If a time traveler killed his father accidentally, what would happen then?"

"They called that a paradox—an impossible riddle. Yet, some found a theory to solve it. They claimed if a man born in the year 1000, for example, traveled to the year 900, he was always there. And what he did in a time before his birth was always done because he was there to do it."

"Sounds like a vicious circle of reasoning," I said.

Asjen sighed, "The premise was unresolved, but others argued as you did—that it might always be desirable to return to the past undetected. So, one might come in disguise or purposefully stay away from relatives or friends who may have known him in another time."

"But what about over a shorter time? Could a man come back to avoid a mistake he made? For example, if a man found himself on a ship headed for a wreck, could he return to the time before he sailed and avoid going aboard?"

"Hmm. My friends didn't get that far. We gave up the discussion because we couldn't imagine a time travel mechanism other than the nonsense of magic wands or incantations. So that's what we discussed more—*how* would one go to a time before he was born? We never had a suggestion better than magic."

"Do *you* think time travel is impossible?"

Asjen stared at the ceiling, then answered, "Well, in one sense, we are all time travelers. We proceed from day to day as we move forward through time. You've moved more than a decade through it, I'd say. For me, it has been considerably longer. The difference is that you and I don't move without everyone else moving too. We are all on the same ship, so to speak."

"Right. I wondered how to move through time apart from my own reality, not with it."

"I'm sorry that I have no answers for you. The farthest my friends ever got was to suppose that to hide his secret, a time traveler must move far enough distance or time away from those who know him."

"So, hundreds of miles or years," I said.

"Perhaps," he said. "It would depend on the availability of faster travel and the span of life. Those things might change over time. For example, these days, ships commonly sail to the new world. It wasn't always so. That would make it easier for a time traveler to hide in a new land where no one knew him."

The conversation reminded me that I wanted to hurry without anyone else seeing me. The sooner I left, the less I could disrupt time. So Asjen returned to his sketches, and I buffed the boots more rapidly.

"I've finished these, Sir," I said, holding up my work.

He dropped his current sketch and toppled the other sections he had brought with him in his hurry to take the shoes from me. "These beauties will make quite an impression at tonight's meeting," he said.

As he swapped his footwear, I tidied his sketches, flipped through the bound book, and found the drawing Grandma and Ody had described. It was undoubtedly Grandma in Europe. Her ring was one of a kind, and the setting was just as she had described Cadiz, Spain. That couldn't be a coincidence. Despite the riddle of how old he appeared, this must be the same man with a new name. Augustus Neuman was Asjen Neuvo. The dates were a puzzle, but even the questions were telling.

I had another theory, too. Rewriting time was possible because I had the mechanism Asjen's thinkers missed. I could control where and when I landed and leave without being noticed because I could revisit an exact moment and reset the clock.

Ody could have done that in Old Salem, but he stayed too long and met too many people. Grandma could return to the moment she left her house, but on her next trip out, she'd return to a new moment, not the same one.

She'd have to help me untangle that logical knot, but for now, I needed to erase Asjen Nuevo's memories of our chat. So, once Asjen left me, I returned to Bath, pressed the gold star, and arrived once more behind the hinged mirror near sunset. Edward spoke to his mother just as before, but I left before the rest of the scenario played out. The mirror didn't break, Edward never knew I was hiding there, and I left before anything else could go wrong.

Later that 1699 evening, Edward spoke softly to his Abigail as always. I didn't talk to young Caesar this time, but he had a dispute with the stable master, and Edward interceded. Those events were part of 1699 without my interference. And this time, Asjen Neuvo did not learn of impossible boot polish, nor did he meet Dubbin Delight and discuss time travel.

I could overwrite time after a brief visit, but it was tricky. And it was only possible because I could repeat traveling to the same instance in history, and I had control over when to travel to a specific moment and when I returned.

It wasn't much, and it was only my best guess, but it added to the little we knew of our family's ability to commute through time.

But unfortunately, it did not help us avoid our current danger. So far, the Saunters time travelers could not slide into a moment of our choosing—only ones allowed by the accidental find of a commutator. I had no way to change the time our messenger brought us the news that Thache would return within the week, so I could not prevent Jonah from hearing it nor from him tipping off Thache's enemies about his return.

I could not prevent those events from happening, but maybe Grandma, Ody, and I could tamp down the trouble they caused.

46 Decisions at Sea

Ody Saunters

Edward returned to Bath only once before the Admirals' Council met. But the first thing he did was to send Caesar to meet Jonah and get answers about who acquired Alice's dress.

Caesar got his answers, and to no one's surprise, The Crow was behind the theft. A farmhand first told Jonah he had access to a dress, and then Alice found out. But he was only a go-between with The Crow pulling his strings. And instead of rum, The Crow was happy to get the information everyone in Bath wanted—when Captain Thache would return.

"Why did he care about that? Was it to keep hidden from the Captain?" Drake asked.

"That makes as much sense as anything," Caesar replied.

I nodded, adding, "Or maybe someone else was willing to pay for that information, and the Crow knew who to sell it to."

Through Alice and Colleen, Jonah learned that The Crow slept in the rafters of the Hornpipe, paying for his keep with stolen sugar and rum. But when Wallace and I searched his quarters, The Crow had flown. None of the Captain's clothing was there, and the silver cup was missing, too.

When word spread that the Captain sometimes lurked in Bath's shadows and his hands were on the pulse of what happened there, rumors of his involvement in Bell's petty robbery dissipated like a morning fog. But more ill winds stirred as the time came for the admirals to meet.

Edward and his ship's master, Israel Hands, were called to testify. After the hearing, Hands rowed to Bath for supplies, and Captain Thache came to Plum Point, where he told us what happened.

It was the second time Captain Thache and Master Hands stood before Tobias Knight and the Admiralty Council. On both occasions, the matter was the dispensation of a ship acquired by questionable means.

Thache's *Adventure* was granted to the Captain when he first came to Bath because the King's Pardon forgave him for that crime. No one else claimed ownership, and the ship was necessary to help Thache maintain a livelihood of legal means.

But it was after his pardon that the Captain brought this second ship, the *Rose Emelye*, to Ocracoke. If the vessel proved to be a pirate's prize, Thache, Hands, and most of the crew would lose the protection of the King and Governor Eden.

"How did you get that ship?" Marybeth asked. "Surely you wouldn't risk our lives here by stealing it."

"Oh, no, no, my Dear. 'Twas not like that. We had no luck trading in St. Thomas, and some of our men chose to stay there. Others hoped to return to New Providence, but there's an English governor there now. So, we decided against the Bahamas too."

"And where was the *Rose Emelye*?" she asked.

"We had contacts in Turks and Caicos and could get part of the cargo Eden wanted, plus provisions for our voyage home. So, figuring we'd do no better, we followed the currents toward home and found the *Rose*. But, we were short-staffed and in no position to take a ship as big as the one we met."

"Did the men want to try it?" Drake asked.

"Being on the waves made the men itch for prizes, and I admit it tempted me, too. But I tried to put them off the idea and convince them of the pleasures of home."

"So, how did you end up with the *Rose Emelye*?" I asked.

"The men kept a watch on the ship, and Israel Hands commented on how low it rode and how it seemed to follow the whim of the waves instead of keeping a straight course. So, we figured it was either abandoned or the crew disabled. And after we voted, we decided to investigate."

"That sounds dangerous," Marybeth said.

"Well, not so dangerous with no men aboard," Thache replied. "We boarded it and found it abandoned with a full load of sugar, sweetmeats, cocoa, and cotton. 'Twas one of the biggest prizes we found in the last year. What were we to do? We couldn't leave that sugar for the sharks, could we?"

"What became of *Rose's* crew?" she asked.

"That, I cannot say," he replied. "We found no signs of what drove them away. Perhaps they had another ship and chose to sail away in that, but 'tis hard to imagine why they'd leave the cargo behind."

"Perhaps they had a bigger treasure on the ship they kept," Drake said.

Thache shrugged. "One of the sea's mysteries, I reckon."

"But how did you get it back here?" I asked.

"We bound that ship to our'n, and with a steering crew on the *Rose*, slow but sure, we brought her home."

"So why was there such secrecy?" Drake asked.

"Well, on the way back, it occurred to us what it might look like to the folks here, so we brought her to the camp, and after we fit the *Adventure* for the sea again, I came to Bath to explain to Tobias Knight and leave him a sampling of the cargo. We convinced him of how we happened to bring the *Rose* home, but to stay on the right side of the law, he called in the Admiralty Council."

"And what did they decide?" Marybeth asked.

"They considered Knight's faith in us and what the cargo would mean to Bath. They asked to examine the *Rose*, but once Nuevo helped us get two injured men to shore, we sheltered the load and scrapped the ship for rigging. After that, there wasn't much left to see. In the end, the Council proclaimed it a prize fairly taken, especially since we had delivered the Governor his share and promised more."

"How were the men injured? Was there a storm?" Marybeth asked.

"No, not that. The *Rose* had some damage, which could explain why her crew left her, but we had little choice but to try to float her home. That cargo was too much for *Adventure*. Then, during our sail home, we found more leaks, signs of worm damage, and some loose cannons. One of them burst from its bolts, injuring two men. That disappointed Israel Hands; he wanted the ship for himself. But it proved too damaged to mend, so Knight and the Admirals agreed we should scrap it for parts and burn the rest."

"Guess that made Israel Hands none too happy," Drake said.

"No, he was not best pleased, but we no longer have a crew to man a ship of that size, especially one crumbling."

"When will she burn?" I asked.

"I'll go back to camp today, so tomorrow, I reckon. 'Twill be dark under a new moon," Thache said.

Drake's eyes glistened as he said, "You'll brighten it up, then. Can we see it?"

"Maybe so," Thache replied. "You're capable lads. You can help if you want to."

"Really?"

"Well, we have no cabin boys as of late, and we used to give the boys a quarter share for setting the charges to burn a ship. Do you reckon you boys could do that?"

Oma stood tall as she faced the Captain, nearly shouting, "They could not! 'Tis far too dangerous, and I cannot take them home in pieces."

"'Tis a pity," Thache replied.

"Maybe Jonah would like the cut," Marybeth said. "He has been living without income for some time now and hopes for the pay you promised him. Maybe he can earn it by setting the burn."

"Can you trust him?" I asked.

The Captain pulled at his beard. "Maybe not. He'd need a watcher. Or I could give him a test."

"What kind of test?" Drake asked.

"Do ye reckon he could find my silver cup by morning? That might square us. Why don't you lads see how Jonah feels about that while I visit with my lovely wife? Tell him to be at Ocracoke before sunset if he wants the job."

***

Jonah might not have wanted the job, but he needed the money from a quarter share. And while he could no longer lead us to The Crow, he knew Thache's former barrel-man did not have the silver cup. Alice heard it from Colleen, and she heard it from Sal. The Crow used the cup to escape his latest bout of trouble. Who held it now was a mystery, but not the problem at the top of our list.

We needed a bigger crew to get our periauger to Ocracoke. Jonah was a sailor, as was Caesar, but Plum Point would need a guard if Caesar sailed. So, we stopped by to see Wallace for advice and were surprised to find Tobias Knight at Captain Harding's shipyard.

Captain Harding agreed to let Wallace navigate for us for a report on the burning, but Tobias Knight wanted a witness, too, and since Caesar had worked on both sides of the creek, he was the best choice.

Knight agreed that Caesar would be a witness and a sailor, and he promised to leave a lookout on his dock to watch for any sign that Plum Point was in trouble. But McNeil, Jonah, and Caesar were still not enough.

Before *Bellamy* headed for Ocracoke, Drake and I needed Oma's permission to sail with the others. So, on the way home, we tried and failed to figure out a strategy to get our grandmother's approval, But as it turned out, Oma's questions about what we learned in Bath did the trick.

***

"I wonder who The Crow stole from this time," she said.

Drake shrugged, "No one has told us that. Someone with rum, I reckon, but probably not a tavern owner. Crow was using rum to buy his bed at the Hornpipe. Could it be one of the wealthy planters or a man in town?"

"Hm," she replied. "That narrows it down."

I put my hand on her shoulder. "Tell us what you know, Oma. We can keep a secret; the more we know, the safer we will be."

She studied our faces and the tips of her shoes before beckoning us to the Bride's Tower. We crouched beside her as she whispered the information she carried from our century.

"I don't know for sure who is in league with The Crow, but Edward Moseley means no good for Captain Thache or Tobias Knight. Moseley has a house in Bath, and if the Crow is obligated to Moseley or his kin, he will do what they want to bring trouble for the Captain."

"Can we help?" I asked.

She shook her head. "I don't think so. The die is cast."

"So, may we go?" I asked.

"We want to see the pirate ship," Drake added.

She nodded, "I know you do. And it's a once-in-a-lifetime opportunity." Then she took our hands in hers. "Will you promise to stay in the periauger? You'll have to get close to shore to get Jonah there but stay out of danger and take your …." She paused to look around again before finishing the sentence. "Take your lucky charms."

"As always," Drake replied, tapping his neck. I nodded.

"Is there anything else we should know?" I asked. "What else can you tell us?"

She looked for anyone near the hatch or the rail ladder before whispering, "That ship … *Rose Emelye* … it wasn't deserted. The Captain and his men captured it."

Drake gasped. "What happened to the crew?"

"They sailed away on *Rose*'s companion ship and headed for France. But you mustn't tell anyone or ask too many questions. Just go; stay quiet; see what you can see and come home safe."

We all turned to the Captain's hatch as another voice squeaked like a creaking door.

"Are you telling me that the Captain lied to my daughter?"

Henrietta Bellieu's head popped from the attic hatch. She climbed to the tower and thrust a package at me while waiting for an answer.

"Err … I wasn't telling you anything, Hetty," Grandma said. "I was cautioning my grandsons. This trip will be their most dangerous task. So, they must be careful."

"What shall I do with this package?" I asked.

We weren't sure how long Hetty had listened, but she tilted her chin to one side, puzzled over what she had heard. Her breathing was ragged, and she blinked a few times before she replied.

"Marybeth baked a pumpkin tart for Edward. 'Tis his favorite, but he could not wait for it to bake. She wants you to deliver it to him."

"What a lovely thought," Oma said. "Does she want to enclose a note? Perhaps I will send one, too, a reminder to watch over my grandsons."

Hetty pressed her lips to a thin line so that her words barely escaped. "She put in a note already, and I have a few words for him as well," she said. Then she tightened her fists till the knuckles were white.

"Shall we wait for you to write something?" Oma asked.

"No," Hetty replied. "I'll tell him next time he dares enter my house." Then she returned to her kitchen.

"Here's your chance, boys," she said. "Write on Marybeth's note. Tell him The Crow gave the cup away to get out of trouble. We aren't sure of the trouble or who has the cup now."

"Are you changing history?" I asked.

"I don't think I can," Oma replied.

Drake nodded as if he agreed.

"Well, we surely will not change anything by rowing to Ocracoke," I said. "Not when we only watch from a safe distance. We can't harm the universe by that. At least, I don't think so."

Oma sighed and shook her head, asking the question we all had.

"Who knows? The universe is older than we are; perhaps it knows best how to care for itself."

47 Burning the Rose

Drake Saunters

The voyage to Ocracoke was more rowing than I ever wanted. And even though farming had built our muscles, Ody and I would never have made it without the real sailors, including Wallace. Captain Harding had made a sailor of his stone mason, and now McNeil matched Caesar and Jonah at pushing *Bellamy* through the waves.

During the first part of the trip, those three found their working rhythm. After that, they brought Ody and me along as part of the team. And by the time we passed Chester's Landing, we Saunters lads could pull our weight too.

"There 'tis," Wallace said, pointing to a spit of land to the port side. "'Tis where someone robbed William Bell."

"Someone?" Jonah asked. "Don't you think it was Captain Thache?"

"I am sure it was not him."

"'Tis further than I thought," Jonah replied. "And if the robbery happened before dawn, 'tis hard to see how Bell could have made it to Tobias Knight's house not long after first light."

"I was on Knight's dock and helped Bell to shore at the landing," Caesar replied, "but I have no idea when he was robbed."

"I wonder why Bell was sitting in his boat in the dark with a boy and an Indian. It was like he was waiting for a robber," I said.

Jonah eyed the distance from shore and the houses set back into the trees. "Did he have relatives here?" he asked.

"I never heard such," Wallace replied. "Isaac Jacobs lived here, his daughter married John Chester, but I never heard that Bell was attached to any of them. There's talk of a smugglers' den up this creek, though."

"That makes it even more curious that he'd choose to camp here in his boat," I added.

Jonah spoke up. "The only time I sat on a landing at night was when the crew camped there, but we'd only sit in a boat to guard it. We might go fishing in one if the red spots were running."

Wallace shook his head. "Bell was loaded up to trade, as I heard it, so maybe he was waiting for someone to bring the cargo, or maybe he was waiting out the dawn to deliver it."

"Where would he be taking half a barrel of rum, pipes, and 58 yards of crepe?" Jonah asked. "The merchants of Bath would be in no hurry for such a load."

Caesar replied, "Bell said he was taking cargo to Bath Town, but he said nothing about where it would be delivered."

"The story he told in town was that there were other boxes, too," Wallace said.

"Might have been so," Caesar added, "but he didn't tell Tobias Knight what was in those. Maybe the cargo wasn't for resale. We get deliveries for Mis'ress Catherine and little Lizzy at Knight's Landing often enough."

I shrugged. "Maybe Bell didn't know what was in the boxes. Maybe he just agreed to get a shipment to Bath and was guarding it till daylight."

"It was dark, you say?" Jonah asked.

Wallace nodded, "Aye. Bell said it was too dark to pour rum."

Jonah knit his brows and turned to Wallace again. "And how did Bell describe the robber?"

"Said he was a white man who jumped in his boat with no weapon. He had four crewmen with him, but Bell couldn't say if they were black or disguised to be."

"Is something wrong with that man's eyes?" Caesar asked.

"But he could see the first attacker was white," Jonah repeated.

"Aye. The attacker was in the boat with Bell. The others jumped in to help him after a while, too."

Jonah pulled his lips to his cheek, shaking his head. "And he still couldn't tell if they were black or made up to look like it?"

Wallace shook his head.

"Did he mention a long black beard or that his attacker was uncommonly tall?" Caesar asked.

Wallace raised his eyebrows and grinned as he shook his head no.

"Hm," Jonah replied. "I've been on the water enough to know that even with a black sky and the air full of pea fog, I could see Captain Thache's beard if he sat that close to me. If you've got eyes, you'll not miss that beard."

"You're right on that one," Caesar replied.

Wallace snickered as he agreed. Then with a chuckle, he added, "Let's get on with it, lads." And we left the mysteries of Chester's Landing behind.

When we reached the sound, we caught the wind, allowing us to rest the oars for a time, which was good for me. However, tacking around the shoals made the ride rougher, and I spent part of the voyage with my head over the railing.

"Feeding the fish, are you, lad?" Jonah joked.

The others laughed at me as they reached into the sack Grandma sent with us. But after I got my stomach back in place, I could tolerate a bit of cider, cheese, and even potted venison on a corncake.

When Wallace announced that Ocracoke wasn't much further, Ody and I exchanged glances. *How would we mix with actual pirates in their camp?* At least they'd never suspect our biggest secret. Sailors and landlubbers were different enough, and with luck, no one would notice a bit of time travel added to the mix.

There were other treacherous pits to avoid, though. Wallace and Edward had made an uneasy peace, but they loved the same woman, and a wrong glance or a word misspoken could set them on opposite sides of a fight.

We weren't sure of Jonah's allegiance to the Captain. And Israel Hands was another question. So, before we sailed, Ody and I agreed; we wouldn't discuss anything vital as we rowed. Instead, we'd let the others drive the chatter.

Once at Ocracoke, we would get our message to the Captain and then keep our eyes open for whatever we could see from *Bellamy*. Maybe Thache could figure out which crew members were on his side, and perhaps we could see things he did not—things that might help him or Marybeth.

"Will we go so far as the Captain's camp?" I asked.

"Oma wouldn't like that," Ody replied.

Wallace spoke up. "Our job is to get Jonah to the shore and report what happens. But I doubt we'll sail to the camp; we'll watch from a safe distance."

"Is there more food in that parcel?" Jonah asked, pointing to the package by my feet.

"Yes, but not for us. Mrs. Thache made that for the Captain," Wallace replied.

Caesar chuckled. "Don't worry, Lads. If there's fish in the sea or wild boar on the land, the Cap'n will feed us."

I wondered what we might find on Ocracoke, but the mystery was solved when we spied a great ship's hull rocking on the waves not far offshore.

"There she is," Wallace said. "I bet she was a grand lady with her masts up and the sails flying full."

Ody knelt by the edge of the bow to get a better look. “How will they get her into the water? She’s too close to burn there, isn't she?”

Jonah nodded. “I reckon they’ll tow her out before setting her alight.”

“You mean before *you* set her alight,” Ody replied.

“Aye. Me and someone else. ’Tis too big a job for one man.”

A shadow crossed Ody’s face. “The Captain isn’t still angry with you, is he?” he asked.

Jonah buried his chuckle. “Are ye worried he’ll let me burn with the ship?”

“I don’t know. You let him down. How does the Captain treat someone who disappoints him?” Ody asked.

“Well, I’ve seen him storming mad many a time, but he’s never burnt a man alive. Not even his worst enemy,” Jonah replied. “He was full of fire and fury when he burned *Protestant Caesar* last spring, but he warned the ship’s Captain that he’d do it and then gave the crew time to reach shore before he fired it up.”

Caesar agreed. “The Captain is a man worth fearin’, but he’s no cold-blooded killer.”

“Why did the *Protestant Caesar* rile him so?” I asked.

“Mainly because it was from Boston, and after Sam Bellamy and his crew drowned when the *Whydah* sank, only nine souls made it to shore. Six of ’em confessed to being pirates, but even after the sea spat them out and the lads repented of their crimes, the men of Massachusetts hanged ’em.”

“So, was Captain Thache mad because Sam Bellamy was his friend?” I asked.

“’Tis part of it,” Caesar replied, “but Captain agreed with Sam Bellamy that most freebootin’ men had no better choice in life than being sea rogues, and Sam loved his men like sons. From what I saw aboard Edward Thache’s ship, the Captain always valued a man’s right to live. ’Tis why, whenever he took a ship, he sent the crew sailing safely for home.”

“But the stories they tell make him sound like the Devil,” Ody said.

Wallace chuckled, “People love a good story, but I’ve seen the Captain’s wicked side, and it ain’t all tall tales.”

“You saw what he wanted you to see,” Caesar said. “He makes good use of fear.”

Ody asked again, “Are you sure he wouldn’t let you go down with that ship, Jonah?”

“I sailed with Thache long enough to trust him with me life, yes,” Jonah replied. “My only danger is not doing my part right, and I reckon I’ll take care to get off that ship.”

I poked Ody’s ribs. “I told you he was a good man.”

Wallace snickered, and Jonah added, "I'm not sure *good* is the right word, but he's fair with his crew."

Thache spotted us and rowed a jollyboat to meet us in the channel. Jonah jumped in with him, and I had to agree. Even with no moon, there was no mistaking Edward's beard.

"From Mrs. Thache," I said as I passed him the parcel.

He opened it, grinning. "Oh, my pumpkin tart," he said. "And a note."

He broke the Plum Point seal and smiled as he read Marybeth's good wishes. Then he reached the words I had added; *The Crow used your cup to escape trouble,* and his smile faded. But when he looked to us for an explanation, all we could offer was a shrug. Then he snorted as he turned to the job at hand.

"Well, Jonah, 'tis time to get to work. The rest of you lads can stand by the well if you like, but you'd be wise to keep your boat clear of this ship. She might take a bad turn," Thache said.

"I'll keep to the water till the burn is over, Captain," Wallace replied.

"Then, here, take my spyglass. I have another in camp."

We pulled to a safe distance and dropped anchor to watch the end of *Rose Emelye.*

"'Tis good the night is clear," Caesar said. "A ship burning is a sight to behold."

"You've seen this before?" I asked.

He nodded. "Many times. Perhaps too many."

Two large tenders tied to her hull. And even though she creaked and moaned, they pulled the *Rose* halfway to us in the sound. Jonah and another crewman climbed aboard, where explosive charges with long fuses stood ready for a spark. First, Jonah and his mate checked that one end of each fuse was far from the powder sack and the other securely inside it. Then, they waved the OK to the Captain. Thache gave the order, and when Jonah and his mate struck fire, the tow boats cut their ropes.

As Caesar said, Jonah may not have been much of a swimmer, but he was a better-than-average diver. So, with the fuses alight, he and the other fireman jumped from the hull and swam for the boats headed for shore.

Shooters stood on the shore to fire on the charges should the fuses fail, and the *Adventure*'s cannons stood ready as a third resort. But Jonah and his mate had done well with their jobs.

Soon, a ring of flickering fuses circled the deck of the *Rose*. Then the powder blasted, and smoke rose from the hull. Fire reached other charges below deck, and the ship, now a flaming shell, moved eerily with the current. Then, without a rudder man or Captain, the fiery vessel groaned as it moved over the sound, and I wondered if it might return to shore or come into the path of one of the boats—maybe ours.

"Uh oh," Ody said.

"What do you see?" I asked as I grabbed the spyglass.

"Just kidding," he replied.

I smacked his arm with the glass.

There was no worry about flames sailing for us because the hull was no longer seaworthy. Instead, with great hisses and sputters, the planks fell from the ship and into the sea. A few boards floated, and some made it to shore. But within hours, the *Rose Emelye* was nothing but a memory. The Council had ruled that Thache did not pirate the *Rose*, and hopefully, the secret Thache had concealed from the admirals would now disappear like the stench of gunpowder hovering over the ship's hull.

48 The Captain's Camp

Drake Saunters

The Captain pointed us to a safe landing near Ocracoke's well, and his cook delivered a feast of roast pork, apples, and corn, but Captain Thache spent the night celebrating with his crew.

Even from a quarter mile away, we heard the music and laughter, and when tipsy men came to the well, it was clear that rum flowed through the camp. These men recounted a few bawdy stories and complained of their gambling losses. No wonder Grandma wanted us to stay on the boat.

But Ody, Wallace, and I were tired and sore from rowing, so we spread bed rolls around a campfire by the well while Jonah and Caesar mingled with their pirate friends.

I opened one eye when a sailor in a striped headscarf led Jonah to collect water.

"So ye found a woman who'd take ye," The swabby said, slapping Jonah on the back. "Where did you find one blind in both eyes?"

"Oh, she's too good for me, fer sure. But I was a good choice among the few men left in Bath these days." Jonah gulped at his ale, then tripped over the well's rope as he lifted a pail.

"Oh, Blimey, I'll get that. Ye'll be waterin' down the whiskey," the crewman said. And the two of them stumbled back to the party.

Then after a bit, two more sailors crept toward us.

"Look at the sleepin' lambs," one whispered.

"Lambs to the slaughter," the other one said, chuckling.

A rumbling voice sounded from the roll across the fire.

"Hold!"

It was Wallace.

One man drew a knife, and Wallace showed his pistol, locked and loaded. "Ye might be good with that knife, but I reckon I can bring you down before you cut me."

The knife man snorted. "But we're two men here, and your mates will be easy pickin's in their sleep."

"I reckon the Captain won't be happy to hear you say that. These lads are kin of his wife. That makes 'em as good as family to Thache."

Wallace was stretching the truth, but we figured he had reason for it. Unless we counted whittling knives, Ody and I had no weapons. But whether we could fight or not, three lads made a better show of strength than Wallace alone, so we stood by him.

Thache was fast, and coming from the shadows as he was, we didn't see or hear him until he pushed the knife-wielding man, who stumbled forward.

"Whar's your manners, Bolwith?" Thache asked, shoving him toward Caesar.

"Oh, we were just playin', Cap'n. We thought these lads might want to join the party since we're about to toast young Jonah."

Thache nodded. "Would you care to join us, lads?" he asked.

The knifeman's friend, Rogers, spoke up. "Maybe the Cap'n will let you drink from his wedding cup."

Now back on his feet, Bolwith added, "Yeah, come try it. We can win wagers on the likes of you, for sure."

They were still giggling as Caesar dragged them back to the bonfire. But the Captain winked at us before he followed. "Bolwith 'as one thing right," he said, nodding to me. "I'd better see what I can find out about that cup."

After that, we took shifts standing guard, but the men who came for water treated us with respect other than the mildest of jabs at the young landlubbers.

Just before dawn, I woke to relieve Wallace. The ruckus had settled, and McNeil was wrapped in his bedroll with his back to the fire. I shook Ody awake and motioned for him to follow.

"Where are you going?" he asked.

"I want to see the camp," I said, tugging at his sleeve.

"We can't leave Wallace alone here," he said.

I stepped toward the third bedroll, and after a gentle shove, we found it empty. "No worrying about Wallace. He had no qualms about leaving us here," I said.

"Yeah, look," Ody said. "He's sleeping in the boat with his gun."

We followed a path from the well to Thache's Hole, a slough deep enough for a sloop to navigate. When we reached the stream, water barrels separated the way to the well from the banks of the slough where Thache made his camp. Sleeping tents were to our right, and the Captain's *Adventure* bobbed to our left, ready for a new voyage. A few crewmen were on the deck. Some scanned the horizon or the mouth of the slough. Others played a dice game.

Beyond the ship, one canopy covered a beach-side kitchen. Barrels, sacks, and crocks of camp provisions sat beside a wood stove. Clean pots, pans, and huge scoops hung from a cross beam nearby. There we found Jonah sleeping with his head propped on a mast timber.

"Morning, Jonah," I said.

He rolled over, rousing just enough to say, "If you're lookin' for Cap'n Thache, you might check his camp." He pointed toward the camp we passed.

Ody shook him again.

"Not yet," he moaned. "I ain't heard no bells."

I wondered what he meant till a bell on *Adventure* rang four times.

"'Tis only four," Jonah said. "Leave me be."

"Are ye lookin' fer me, lads?" Captain Thache said, grinning as he strode toward us.

"We're exploring, Captain," Ody said.

"Well, this here's our mess tent, and quarters for my officers are at the stern of my ship. My quarters are west of that with tents for the crew when they're off-shift."

"Is that what the bells were, Captain?" I asked. "Something to do with shifts?"

"Aye, shifts change when eight bells sound. That's every four hours, including bells on the half hour."

And I added, "We hoped to see your ship up close."

"Today might not be the best day for it. We'll be busy cleaning up the mess left from Rose's burnin', and we have some cargo to shift to Bath, too. But we'll get you on board soon; you have my word."

I grinned at that.

Thache added, "Find Wallace; I'll rouse Jonah and bring your breakfast. I'm afraid you lads will need to be on the water soon. It's another long row back to Plum Point, and I need ye there."

Then he turned to Jonah and gave him a good shake.

"Shh. Don't wake the cook. He'll boil me alive if you do."

"And I'll boil you if you don't get up," the Captain said. When Jonah found his legs, Edward hollered for the cook to start his breakfast and stomped off to find him.

Jonah rubbed his eyes, "Oh well, so much for my last fling with the lads. But with the cash from the burn, Alice will marry me soon, fer certain."

"You didn't lose it to the gamblers, did you?" I asked.

"Nay, I know this lot better than that. I kept me silver to meself. But thar's a bit more silver for the men who carry a ghost tale to the others who may come here," he said.

"What story is that?" Ody asked.

"Well, the Captain figures someone saw the *Rose* burning, and he wants the crew to give a new reason to what they saw."

"What's the point of that?" I asked.

"Once folks spread the story, any who saw the burning will blame ghosts instead of Edward Thache."

"Ghosts, you say?" I asked.

"Aye, the Cap'n loves his ghost tales. They put fear into most folk, and the Cap'n knows the value of tradin' in fear. It might even keep folks from venturing to Ocracoke and finding this sugar load before we get it sold."

"Don't you recall when Caesar told us about the ghost of Sir Henry Morgan?" Ody asked.

I nodded. "I think of that every time I walk the shore."

"Well, this one ain't that old," Jonah said. "'Tis a story of the murder of French settlers trying to make it ashore. As it goes, the passengers were killed and robbed on the night of a new moon in September, but their burning ship overtook the robbers, and they sank with the settlers and the loot."

Thache chuckled as he caught up with us. "The cook's firing up the skillet, and he's waiting for Jonah to fetch more firewood. But you'd be safer back at the well, lads. Find Wallace, and I'll get breakfast to you."

Thache soon joined us with breakfast, but Jonah had been persuaded to have a few more ales and was in no shape to eat. So, when it came time to shove off, Thache poured him into our periauger and put the oars in his hands.

"Don't mind him, lads. He may be four sheets to the wind now, but he'll rally when the spray hits his face."

Thache threw a sack with cold chicken and hardtack in after Jonah. "For your journey home," he said.

"Will you be back in Bath soon, Captain? Your wife will want to know," Ody asked.

"You tell Mis'ress Marybeth, I'll be quick to return."

"Did you find your cup, Captain?" Jonah asked.

"Not yet, but it can't crawl off this island alone. If 'tis here, I'll catch up with it."

When Caesar arrived with a jug of cider, he and Edward gave us a mighty push toward the sound, and Caesar jumped in to help row.

"Off with ye, now, and smooth sailin'," Thache called.

As we sailed into the sound, we passed a couple dozen blackened planks bouncing against our hull, and I couldn't help imagining *Adventure* as blackened as the *Rose* had been. And if that happened, what would be the fate of Edward Thache?

49 Almost the Truth

Marybeth Thache

I hoped Edward and a boat full of happy lads would arrive in time for dinner, but, just in case, I chose recipes that would keep till suppertime. And, as I feared, the sun was setting when the boat returned, and worse, Edward was not aboard.

After dropping the others at the dock, Caesar rowed to report to Tobias Knight, but Wallace and Jonah stayed for supper. All the lads were weary from rowing, with more need of rest than food, but they dug into the chowder and corncakes to please us while Aurora tried to coax supper conversation from the group.

"Lads, we want to hear about *Rose Emelye*, but first, tell this young lady what she wants to know. How is Captain Thache, and when will he come to Plum Point?"

"Yes, please, tell me about Edward," I said.

Ody leaned across the table, "He said to tell you he'd be here as quick as possible."

"He's very well and happy to have that ship burnt," Jonah said, "and he paid me well for my part. So, Alice shan't be able to say no to me now."

Then all the lads took turns telling us of the sight of the ship flaring up like a giant bonfire on the sound before it spent its fuel and sunk beneath the waves.

"So, it's burned and gone with the approval of the Admirals," I said, smiling broadly. "Things will be better on Plum Point now. At last, Edward can trade without so many whispers against him, and maybe I'll have a better notion of when he can be home with me."

Mother held her tongue till supper was over. But when Wallace and Jonah took the jollyboat back to Bath, and we had finished the evening chores, she dimmed my hopes for our happy future on the plantation.

"You may imagine things will be better if it pleases you, daughter. But I fear we have more shallows to cross regarding your Captain Thache. What stories will go 'round about that ship he burned? And if the Bath folk do not know the facts, you can rest assured the tales they weave will not put Blackbeard in a good light."

"You won't need to worry about that this time, Mrs. Bellieu," Ody said.

Drake spoke up. "The Captain has the crew spreading tales of French Huguenot settlers murdered on the way here, and their bodies burnt with the ship before it reached the mainland."

Ody nodded, adding, "And after their ship sunk in flame, it rose again as a ghost ship that sails past Ocracoke each time this year. The Cap'n reckons if anyone saw the *Rose* burn, they'll think it was the ghost ship, and a ghost might keep them out of Ocracoke, too."

"What French settlers would those be?" Mother asked. "Bert and I kept in touch with the Huguenots of New Bern, and there was no story of a shipload of them robbed and murdered. I'd have heard of such a thing."

Aurora tried to calm flaring tempers. "Perhaps Edward invented the story to cover the suspicion that might follow."

"Another lie, then," Mother said, brushing crumbs from her apron. "Just like the one I heard you speak of the other day, Aurora."

I turned to Aurora and then back to Mother. "What lie was that?"

"Why, the one about Edward finding that sugar ship abandoned," Mother said. Then turning to Aurora, she added, "You told your grandsons he pirated it."

"I was whispering to the boys while the wind whistled around the tower, Hetty. You must have misunderstood me."

"Misunderstanding or not, when it comes down to it, that man is more comfortable with lies than the truth," Mother replied.

My temper rose amidst her accusation. "It was an abandoned ship. Edward said so. And how could Aurora possibly know what happened near Bermuda? Besides, I've spoken with Edward about his loose hold on the truth, and he doesn't lie to me. The Captain doesn't mind embroidering a story with a good exaggeration, but when he fibs to others, he usually has a good reason."

Aurora patted my hand, "Then ask him to tell you the truth about the *Rose* when he returns. Don't fret about it till he can speak for himself," she said.

The boys were falling asleep in their chairs and soon went to bed. Not long after, I wished everyone a good night and blew out my lantern. Mother and Aurora shared a final elderberry cordial on the porch outside my window, and thankfully, they did not speak of the *Rose Emelye*.

Perhaps Aurora was right. The fall air had weakened me. I could barely climb under the covers, but, tired as I was, I couldn't sleep. Edward and I had argued more than once about his keeping secrets from me. If I couldn't trust him to tell me the truth, I couldn't trust him at all. Surely, he wasn't hiding things from me again.

There was no way to untangle the riddle, so I clutched my North Star and tried to shut the problem from my head. I finally fell asleep, weary from the battle of reconciling Edward's promises with the truth.

***

Mother and Aurora let me sleep till noon the next day, but even after a long sleep, walking to the kitchen was a strenuous task. Food didn't sit well, either, but luckily, I made it to the back porch before my porridge traveled the wrong way, spilling to the ground.

"Back to bed with ye," Mother said. "I'll fetch the tea."

After I held a bit of bread and tea in my stomach, the widows left me to rest, and I slept till Edward bent to kiss my cheek.

"What's the matter with my little sparrow?" he asked, tickling my neck with his beard.

Despite my worry, it revived me to feel his arms around me, and I couldn't resist pulling him closer. Then I could relax, surrounded by his strength.

He chuckled as he kissed me again, then moved away to hang his coat on the pegs by the door and remove his boots. When I sat on the edge of the bed, he called me to him.

"Come sit by me," he said, patting the armchair beside him. "Tell me what's wrong wid 'e."

The chair was only a few steps away, but I moved slowly, holding the bedpost as I rose to go to him.

"I'm glad you're here," I said. "Is the trouble over? Will you be home for a while?"

Even though he squeezed my hand, the sadness on his face held my answer.

"So, there's still no peace."

"All didn't go as planned on the voyage," he said.

"But you came home with cargo, didn't you? Surely the Governor is pleased."

He nodded and took my hand as he answered, "Yes and no."

"But the Admirals approved your keeping the *Rose*, and they agreed with the burning," I said. "What problem could there be?"

"Well, to start, I had problems with the crew that we couldn't settle in St. Thomas."

"Couldn't they agree on new rules? You promised to listen to their wishes, didn't you?"

"Aye, I did. But there were changes in the Islands, too. The crew who wished to return to free-bootin' didn't have the choices they expected. Some in our old haunts did not welcome us as before. Ye see, the English took charge of Nassau a few months back. 'Tis no longer a republic for crews like mine."

"Like yours? But aren't you all under the pardon now? Free traders?"

"England sent a governor to New Providence, and Woodes Rogers came with a mandate to make Nassau subject to the rules of the Crown. So, he's pushing out the pirates and privateers. He even got the best of Charles Vane, and that's no easy task."

"Charles Vane?"

"Aye, Vane promised to take the King's pardon, but promises don't take for men like him, so he's back to pirating. Only a few of my men found new paths in the islands. Most returned with me, and they won't likely behave much better than before, so there's still work to bring peace between the men and the town."

I left my hand in his but leaned back in the chair. "And what about you, Edward? Can Blackbeard be satisfied on a plantation?"

He smiled as he replied, "You satisfy me, my dear. My greatest wish is to make my little bird sing with happiness."

"But is that the truth, Edward? Can you be happy here with me if your men are unhappy and unruly?"

He dropped my hand as his chin fell to his chest, and the great beard wobbled back and forth as he pondered his next move.

I reached to pat his knee, saying, "The truth, please, Edward. We can't exist without honesty between us."

Finally, he looked me in the eye, still shaking his head at the hard truth. "You are my beloved, the source of my hope. But I must do two things at once," he said. "I must care for the men who have followed me to and through danger, and I must care for you. But how to do that is a quandary."

"Is that all?" I asked. "Have you told everything now?"

He clasped his hands against his chest. "Almost," he whispered. "Almost all."

I sat up straight. "What else is there?"

He shook his head at the floor as if it were the source of his troubles. Then finally said, "There is Israel Hands. When we were in St. Thomas, Hands made a play to be captain of *Adventure.* We promised to make new rules there, and the crew voted on who'd be captain. We had fewer than three dozen men when we left for St. Thomas, but Hands had lured some to his side when he was in Ocracoke and I here. And when they brought up the idea of a new captain, only twenty voted for me."

"Couldn't you leave him and his faithful in St. Thomas?" I asked.

"'Twould have been a dangerous voyage home with so few. We could have made it, though. But since Hands and his minions had no ship, they vowed to follow me—at least, they said so. No one besides me could captain as well as Hands, and even with good winds, sometimes it takes the skill of all crewmen to cross the mighty current near Florida."

"So, now that he's back on land, can you boot him?" I asked.

"He's back in the nest with me, so we can't be shed of him yet. Besides. That's not all there is to tell about Hands and the trip home."

"What else?" I asked, bracing to hear it.

Edward drew a deep breath. "It has to do with *Rose Emelye.*"

The air locked in my chest. "Tell me," I said, even though I feared the reply.

"It started as I told you before. Almost."

"Almost?"

"Aye. Hands watched the ship we found, but the *Rose* had a companion, two ships together—one weighed down, the other floating high."

"Two abandoned together? What could have caused that?" I asked, guessing such a situation was unlikely.

"They were not abandoned," he said.

"So, you lied to me about that," I said, my voice raising with disappointment.

"Hear me out," he said.

"Hands wanted us to take the ships as prizes. He figured he'd take one to captain with the crew who voted for him. I told him it was too risky for our small sloop to try for two, twice as big, but he boasted he could do it."

"He dared you. Did you give in to that dare?" I asked.

"Hands said if the great Blackbeard couldn't do it, he'd show me how. So, I knocked him to the deck, and he stood, shouting for a vote. The men were hungry for prizes, so even those who wanted me to be captain wanted to take that ship."

"And you did?"

"Aye," he said, shaking his head. "The vote carried, so I gave in to the crew's will. The *Adventure* was more agile than the big slavers, so we took the French ships by surprise, and when I pulled close to one of them, I ordered Hands and part of the crew to jump aboard. Then we had two ships on one, and the crew of the *Rose* surrendered."

"You risked your life and our safety here because of a vote?" I asked, rising from my chair.

He pulled me back to my seat. "We were successful in the take. We kept the *Rose* with its cargo—sugar, cocoa, cotton—much of what Eden wanted. And we put the French crew on the other boat to sail for France, their home."

"And you lied to Tobias Knight and me."

"I couldn't tell you the truth till I knew how the Admirals would decide the issue. If anyone came to question you and suspected you knew the truth, your life would be in danger, too."

I stood, pacing the room, raging. "But Israel Hands and all your crew know the truth. Won't they betray you? It could mean your neck, Edward. How do you think I'd live after losing you that way? I would be disgraced in Bath and Mother along with me." Then my mouth dropped. "Will they hang me, too? Will they hang my mother?"

Edward rushed to put his arms around me. "They will never harm you nor any of our family. I won't allow it."

I pushed away from him, crying as I asked, "Why didn't you let Hands sail with the cargo? Why did you bring that ship here?"

"Because the *Rose* was leaky, and we didn't have enough men for the ships to sail alone. He couldn't be sure to get anywhere safe in it, and he had no idea where safety was. Graveyard of the Atlantic, or not, the safest harbor was here." He held out both hands to me. "So, we came home."

He held me tight again; this time, I had no strength to resist. He kissed the back of my neck as he whispered into my ear. "Where else would I go but to you—my North Star? Who will keep you safe if I do not?" He turned me to face him, saying, "'Tis done, my love. Knight and I dealt with the Admirals, and I will keep my thumb on Hands."

"It's still a lie, Edward," I said, tears building.

"'Tis the last one. I promise, my darling. We will find a way to deal with the crew, and I will be with you here. No more lies. Only love."

"But how can I be sure? How can I know when you are telling me the truth?" I asked.

He paused momentarily, twirling a beard curl around his finger. Then he turned to me.

"My dear, I told you *Rose* was abandoned to protect you, and when I stand before an enemy vowing to strike him down with no purpose other than encouraging him to yield, you might call that a lie. However, those words are a means to an end. The purpose is true, even if the words are not."

"But if you use your words that way, how will I ever know the truth?" I asked.

"Here is how we shall fix that," he said, taking my hands. "I will offer you something dearer to me than truth. When I give you my word, by my heart and my mother's heart, you may rely on it."

"How do you mean?" I asked.

"If I say to you, 'The *Rose* was abandoned,' take that to mean it's better for everyone concerned if they believe it. But if I say, 'You have my word; we found the *Rose* abandoned,' there is no doubting it. It was so. My word is my bond."

"What if you say, 'I'll be home for dinner on time?'"

"Then plan around that, expect that, and I'll do my best to make it true."

"But if you say, 'You have my word; I'll be home for dinner on time.' How will that be different?" I asked.

"In that event, if I'm not home for dinner on time, I'm likely dead. But I won't be that specific about dinner in most cases," he said with a grin.

"So, when you offer me something better than the truth, what will that mean?" I asked.

"It will mean you have my word on it," he replied.

Suddenly weak again, I fell against his chest, and he held me tight, perhaps a little too tightly, as he said, "I'll never let anyone hurt you, and I'll never let you go. You have my word on it."

I heard him.

He meant what he said.

But I threw up on his bare feet anyway.

50 Broken Promises and Broken Blades

Drake Saunters

Ody and I did not see the Captain the night he returned from burning the *Rose*, but he was at the breakfast table when we came down.

Edward offered to take tea to Marybeth's bedside, but the Widow Bellieu wouldn't hear of it.

"Sit down, Cap'n; a mother's touch will be the right remedy here." And soon, Mrs. Bellieu made her way through the parlor, balancing a plate of boiled eggs in one hand and a teapot in the other. But she glanced over her shoulder long enough to call, "Aurora, if you have any remedies for a sick stomach, share 'em with Marybeth before dinner."

Grandma followed and helped Hetty through the bedroom door. But once the clatter of crockery settled, the door snapped shut, and our grandmother returned to our table.

"Is all well with your bride, Captain?" she asked, pouring her second cup of tea.

"Hm?" Edward looked up from stirring his porridge. "Oh. Yes, just an upset stomach, I believe. Perhaps nerves over my being away so long. Nothing to worry about."

Grandma watched as Edward dipped the spoon in his bowl half a dozen times without taking a bite and then finally forgot his oatmeal and raised the teacup to touch his lips. Then, without a sip, he slapped the cup to the table.

"Is something on your mind, Edward?" Grandma asked.

This time he lifted the cup and drank it in two gulps, and after snapping it to the tabletop again, he turned to Grandma.

"Israel Hands," he said. "Israel Hands is on my mind. What's that man up to?" he asked.

"You know him as well as anyone. What does he want most?" Ody asked.

"Well, he wants a ship of his own, but I'm not sure anyone in Bath can get that for him, and by the hairs on my beard, he'll not have *Adventure*."

I shrugged. "Who else can help Hands get a ship?"

Thache shook his head, "He doesn't have the gold to hire Captain Harding's men to build one, but he's been wheedling my crew to choose him as captain. He nearly won the vote while we were in St. Thomas. Maybe he'll try again."

I sat up straight. "They'd never vote for Hands over you, would they?"

Thache shrugged. "He didn't win in the Islands but might have better luck next time. He only needs to turn a few more to his side." Then Edward rested his chin on his clasped fists, bouncing the beard against his signet ring. Then with a new light in his eyes, he pushed back from the table and stood.

"Good questions need answers, lads, and I reckon we should go find some."

"Are we going back to Ocracoke, Captain?" I asked.

"Not this time. Hands rowed in with me to get supplies in Bath, so 'e's still here, and I reckon he'll be chartin' his next move."

Grandma raised an eyebrow. "Do you mean to ask him directly? Is he likely to tell you what's on his mind?"

Edward sat back down. "Not at all likely," he muttered, drumming his fingers on the table.

"Who might know?" she asked.

Edward cocked his chin to one side as he continued drumming. Then he nodded again, slapping his hands on the table. "Suit up, lads," he said. "We're going Crow hunting."

"Where?" Ody asked.

"In Bath, for a start. Get ready to row."

***

"What now, Captain?" I asked when we dragged the boat ashore at Towne Point.

Edward tugged on his beard. "Drake, come with me to the Hornpipe. Ody, try the Marsh Moon; see what Sal knows about where The Crow might be."

Thache pushed the Hornpipe's wooden door open and pointed me to Colleen scrubbing a table. Then the feather in the Captain's hat tickled the rafters as he strode to the bar to speak to the owner, Silas Van Horn.

Soapy water dripped onto Colleen's no-longer-new frock as she paused to push her hair back.

"What's on yer mind, lad?" she asked. "See Silas if you want somat from here."

"Thank you, Miss Colleen," I replied. "I'm here to find a friend of yours, Coleman Adler. We know him as The Crow."

"Well, The Crow's long gone from 'ere," she replied. "I ain't seen nor heard from him in days. I reckon he's hiding from all the trouble he made."

"What kind of trouble could take him away from someone as pretty as you?" I asked.

The corners of her mouth turned up a twitch at the compliment. "Well, I reckon you know pirates as well as any around here, and like most of 'em, he couldn't stop thieving. So, he finally had to run from it."

"I won't agree that's true about all pirates, but you pegged The Crow well. We found he'd been stealing from Plum Point. I reckon that's why the Captain wants to find him."

"Well, Captain Thache will have to stand in line. Plum Point wasn't the only place he stole from."

"But with no money, where could he go?" I asked. "You don't reckon the law found him, do you?"

"I reckon worse than that has found him. Thieving ain't never a good idea, and with the hard times we've had round here, folks might kill ye over a boiled egg."

She dropped her brush in the bucket and leaned on the table as she turned to me. "You're wasting your time here. When Crow couldn't find more rum for the bar, Van Horn kicked him out, and I'm working at half wages to pay for what he still owes. Talk to Silas if you want to know more. Now waste your time somewhere else. I'm busy."

Thache, probably due to his fearsome reputation, got more from Van Horn than Colleen told me. When I reached his side, Edward leaned over to question Van Horn, forcing the barkeep to step back.

"You say he offered you my cup?"

Silas wrung his bar cloth into a nervous knot as he replied. "Well, he offered me a silver cup, Captain. I had no idea it came from you."

"And you didn't know he took my rum and sugar, either?" Thache asked.

"Times are hard, Cap'n. We need rum to keep the customers happy, and we don't ask where it comes from. But I reckon he ran afoul of someone he robbed; he cleared out of here days ago."

"Where would he go if he left Bath?" I asked. "He ain't practiced in living in the wild."

"I think he might still be around. Sometimes Colleen sneaks out of here early, like she's got a meetin' planned. But I have no idea where The Crow's hiding."

"Do you know what he did with my cup?" Thache asked.

"I had no use for it," Van Horn replied. "But he might have found a buyer. Colleen seemed happy enough with him for a few days. Perhaps he shared a few pence with her."

"Could he be hiding at her house?" I asked.

"No, I wouldn't think so. The girl's been sour on him mostly as of late."

"Come on, lad," Thache said as he dropped a Spanish dollar on the counter. "Let's find your cousin." Then he turned back to Van Horn and tapped his sheath, saying, "You get word to me if The Crow shows up. Else you'll find steel rather than silver on your counter."

"Err … I heard you broke your sword, Cap'n," Silas squeaked.

Edward turned with a face like thunder and drew his blade. "Does it look broken to you?" he asked, brandishing the blade in Van Horn's face.

"No, Sir. No, Sir," Silas replied.

Thache bent closer, scowling. "And what kind of captain would I be with a sword that ain't ready for a fight? Where would you have heard such a thing as that?"

"Nowhere special. Just people talking," Silas replied.

"Well, you set them talkin' folks straight. Tell 'em if they need to see my blade up close, I'll be happy to oblige." Edward sheathed his sword and strode from the room.

Even taking double steps, I only caught up to Edward when he paused his fuming parade at the Marsh Moon door.

There, he bent to whisper, "Go speak to Wallace McNeil. Tell him I want to know where The Crow might be hiding these days and who else caught him stealing."

Then I turned toward Harding's shop, and the Captain entered the tavern to meet Ody.

51 The Hunt for Silver

Ody Saunters

Once in the Marsh Moon, I chose a table by the window. But when Sal arrived to take my order, she was not in her usual good spirits.

"What'll it be?" she asked, a fist to her hip.

"Tea and biscuits, please," I replied. "Is something wrong, Sal?"

"You might know better than I do," she said, her brow puckering. "Has something happened to Israel Hands? Did Thache threaten him somehow? He seems to have forgotten all his promises to me. He doesn't even bother being friendly and without a word to explain the change. What happened on that voyage?"

"I didn't sail with the Captain, so I can't say for sure, but maybe Hands didn't come back as rich a man as he hoped."

"Well, all I can say is that he hasn't passed a penny to me, neither as a gift nor for service. He's not the man I once knew."

I shrugged. "Disgruntled, I guess."

Sal stood, her right toe tapping rapidly. "And why should Israel Hands be disgruntled? I know it was not on *my* account, and if he wants any favors from me, he'd better take care not to let me down."

Given her stormy emotions, I hesitated to reply. But when she tapped her pencil on the table, scowling, I muttered, "Just tea then. No biscuits."

With a disgusted growl, she turned and stomped toward the kitchen.

My thumbs were red from twiddling when I saw silhouettes of the Captain and Drake outside the bottle-glass windows. Then Drake returned toward the Hornpipe, and Edward joined me in the tavern.

"Any luck with Sal?" he asked as he removed his hat and stretched his long legs under the table.

"Not good luck," I replied. "Sally's angry with Israel Hands for some reason."

Edward stroked his beard, but his eyes twinkled as he replied, "That might work to our advantage."

"The enemy of my enemy is my friend. Is that it?" I asked.

Thache chuckled. "I don't know where ye heard that one, but I might just write it down." Then he winked at me, saying, "Now, here's one for you to remember. Catch flies with honey, not vinegar." He beamed his most charming smile as Sal returned.

She slapped the teapot and cup on the table and asked, "So, tea for you, too?"

Edward settled the crockery as he replied, "Tea will be fine, Sal, if you please. Take your time. We're in no hurry." He removed his hat from the table, set it on the chair beside him, and flashed a happy grin at our waitress.

She took a deep breath, and even though her furrowed brow hung over her squinting eyes, the sun peeked through the storm as her lips twitched upward at the corners. She hurried to the kitchen, and in less than two minutes, she returned with another cup, saucer, and a plate of honey biscuits. Then she asked calmly, "Will you need anything else, Captain?" Then nodding at me, "Ody?"

"Nothing else for me, Sal," I said, reaching for a biscuit.

But Edward raised a finger. "Sal, I have a question if you have time. I've been trying to locate The Crow. I hear he ran into trouble with someone in town and isn't at the Hornpipe. He has something of mine, and I'd like to get it back."

Sal's face nearly went sour again. "Pirates!" she said as if the word burned her lips.

"Beg pardon?" Edward replied.

Sal waved her words away, "Oh, don't mind me. I'm afraid things are not going well with Mr. Hands and me."

"Ah," Edward replied, his eyes growing softer. "Then we share a worry. He and I are not exactly chartin' the same course, either. But such things pass. Perhaps all will be well with you soon."

"Doubtful," she replied. "But tell me what The Crow has filched now. Perhaps I'll hear something that will help."

Edward nodded. "'Tis a silly thing—a silver cup shaped like a woman. I gave it to my wife on our wedding night. Unfortunately, it's missing, and we hear the Crow has it. Marybeth isn't feeling her best these days, and 'twould be my pleasure to cheer her by returning her gift."

Tears rose on Sal's lower lids. "'Tis so nice to hear of a man who cares for his lady. Our Mary has a treasure in you, Captain."

He smiled, and he may have blushed under that beard.

"Anything to make my little sparrow happy," he replied.

Sal bent to whisper. "I did see such a cup. But it wasn't with The Crow."

"Oh?" Edward cocked his head.

"'Twas in the hands of Edward Moseley. He was here with his houseman, Quincy Underwood. The two of them often dine here when Moseley is in town."

Oma had warned us about Edward Moseley, but what was he doing with Edward's cup? Hoping Sal knew more, I asked, "Isn't bringing a cup to the tavern like bringing salt to the sea?"

Sal nodded. "Believe it or not, they brought it to show to Israel Hands. Was he trying to recover it for you, Captain Thache?"

I shook my head. "I sincerely doubt that."

"Perhaps he wanted to buy it to patch up your quarrel, Sal," Edward said.

Sal clenched her fists. "We didn't quarrel. Not yet. He's been too busy to bother speaking at all. No. That cup was not for me."

"Did Hands buy it?" I asked.

Sal shook her head. "I don't think so. Those men had a long discussion, and at the end, they shook hands as if they had agreed. After that, Underwood passed the cup to Israel."

"Underwood," Thache said, "Red-haired man … thick Scots accent?" After Sal nodded, he continued, "He's crossed my path a time or two, but I haven't met him properly. Isn't he the caretaker of Moseley's townhouse and office here?"

Sal nodded. "I can't say what job Underwood has, but houseman fits what I've seen."

"I wonder what they agreed to," I asked.

Sal shrugged, "They passed by me as they left the tavern, and Israel said, 'There's some satisfaction in this. It shall be *my* prize now.'" Then she grimaced as she smoothed her apron. "I'm sorry, that's all I know."

As Thache paid twice the price for our tea, he said, "You've been accommodating, Sal, and now I know where to find my wife's cup. This news will make her feel much better."

"Is Marybeth unwell?" Sal asked as she collected the coins.

"'Tis nothing serious," he said. "A bit of tummy trouble, especially in the mornings."

"In the mornings, you say?" Sal asked.

Thache nodded.

Sal chuckled, saying, "Then you may find that your little bride has a gift for you, too." Then she tapped a finger beside her nose and returned to her work.

When we reached the street, Thache turned to me. "Go find Wallace. Drake may still be with him. Ask Wallace if he's heard anything about The Crow hovering around Edward Moseley's house."

The Captain didn't speak much as we started down Old Towne Creek, but before we passed the mouth of East Branch, he had solved part of the puzzle. He leaned forward from his rudder seat to explain.

"Moseley is an important man in government, as I understand it. He's a wealthy one, too, and since he's away from that townhouse more than he's there, The Crow might have thought that house a plum for the takin'."

Drake let his oar drift as he replied, "But he didn't count on a houseman—Underwood."

I looked over my shoulder. "So, do you think Underwood caught him stealing and took the cup as payment not to report him?" I asked.

Thache nodded. "It sounds reasonable. But it doesn't explain why Israel Hands met with them."

"Perhaps he heard Coleman was in trouble and was trying to help him," Drake said.

"Maybe," Edward replied, cocking his head. "But in my years with Hands, I've never known him to be helpful unless it puts treasure in his pocket. 'Tis more likely Moseley wanted something of Hands and offered my cup to pay for it."

"So, the cup was a payoff. That fits; Hands said it would be his prize."

"Seems a lot of trouble for a cup. But who knows?" Edward replied. "Maybe Wallace can tell us more when he comes for his next visit."

52 The Crow Flies

Aurora Saunters

When Hetty Bellieu was at full tilt, as usual, she was difficult to help and hard to follow. She fluttered around the house, moving from chore to chore, stopping only briefly to add to her list of plantation needs. But around 2:00, just after our dinner meal, she came to a standstill and then rushed to me, holding her list.

"Today's Tuesday. What's become of Wallace?"

"Hm," I replied, "I wonder if Edward gave him new orders the last time he was in Bath. Since the Captain is on Plum Point again, perhaps he or the boys will gather our needs."

"Maybe," the widow replied. "Or maybe that young man doesn't care to see Captain Thache at home with our Marybeth. The lad barely speaks, either to her or about her, since he and Edward came to their agreement."

"We'll have to ask Wallace—either that or be content to guess," I said.

We were both happy to see Marybeth feeling better. She and Edward spent hours strolling over the plantation. The Captain checked crops, fences, and the strength of locked doors, while his wife was happy to walk holding his arm. While in the fields and forests, they left their cares behind them, enjoying each other's company amid late golden blooms nodding in the early fall sunshine. But once they were under the farmhouse roof, conversations often led to more troubling topics.

For example, Israel Hands and Edward Moseley had been meeting. Moseley, Hands, and even the silver cup were parts of documented history in my century, so to keep from inadvertently leaking details of events yet to happen, I wouldn't mention them. But unfortunately, I wasn't always successful in that plan.

Since Wallace missed his visit with us, it was natural that his name came up at supper. And it seemed that Hetty Bellieu, perhaps because she thought of me as a seer, often poked me for more information on sensitive topics.

Hetty brought the final platter of biscuits and set them on the table as she asked Edward about Wallace's absence.

"He's done a lot of rowing lately," Edward replied as he covered his goose pie with gravy. "I reckon he's tired."

Hetty wouldn't let it go. "I wonder if he heard anything about The Crow. You asked him to find out where Adler might be, didn't you?" she asked.

"I did. And Wallace will do his best," Edward replied.

"He said he'd look into it," Drake said, adding a double dollop of stewed apples to his plate.

"Adler's probably long gone," Ody said. "With Colleen mad at him, why would he hang out around here?"

"Where would he go? That's the question," Drake added.

"Inland to find work, maybe," I said.

Hetty scowled. "The Crow's stay at Plum Point proved he's not going to look hard for honest work."

Edward paused before gulping a bit of pie. "Starvin' will teach him otherwise."

"Do you think he's working at Edward Moseley's place?" Drake asked. "He seems connected to Moseley somehow. After all, Sal saw him with the silver cup The Crow stole." Then his eyes widened as he hollered, "Ouch!"

"Beg pardon," Ody replied, "I didn't mean to kick you."

Drake rubbed his shin and returned to eating supper, but Marybeth was not distracted by Ody's diversion.

"Did you say that Sal saw the cup?" Marybeth asked.

Edward nodded. "Aye, but Sal sees lots of things. She thought your sickness might mean something, Mary. Do you have anything to tell me?"

"No, no, Edward. I ate too many muscadines. That's all." She took a bite of corn cake and chewed it slowly before asking, "Why would Quincy Underwood have your cup? What does he have to do with The Crow?"

"'Tis hard to say," Edward replied, "but the boys and I reckon he may have tried to steal from Moseley's house, and Underwood caught him. Maybe The Crow offered the cup to as a payment to keep out of trouble."

I tried again to change the topic from Moseley. "Did Wallace have any other news, Drake?"

"Not much," he replied. "He says many folks asked him about what he saw when the ship burned. You know how folks are. They like a bit of gossip and make their guesses about how you came to have the ship. Most say 'tis hard to believe all that sugar was left floating in the ocean."

Marybeth looked up in shock, searching Edward's eyes. "What stories are they spreading now?" she asked.

Edward took his wife's hand. "It doesn't matter what they say. The Admirals did their duty about that ship. We burned it with their blessing, and that's the end of the matter."

"Of course," she replied, nodding. But she dropped her hands to her lap and kept her eyes on her plate.

"Well, at least they don't think you stole cloth from William Bell," Drake said.

Marybeth looked up, brow furrowing. "Did they think that?"

Edward leaned back in his chair. "'Tis no matter what anyone says or thinks. Most who heard that story know it couldn't have been me who robbed Bell's boat. Even Bell himself suspects others."

"Wallace is on your side," Drake added. "He convinced some of those who brought it up, too. It just doesn't add up that that thief could be you and four of your men."

"Did you say a leader with a crew of four?" Marybeth asked. Then she turned to Edward, "Who else could it have been?"

"You're not to worry, my love. The truth will come out in the wash."

Mary Beth gripped the edge of the table. "And the truth is on your side, right, Edward?" she asked.

"Yes, it is. Sooner or later, everyone will see that."

She sighed, saying, "I'll hope for sooner."

Supper was becoming more trouble than pleasure. And with stumbling blocks like the pirated ship, William Bell's robbery, and now the odd association of The Crow with Moseley's man, Quincy Underwood, I was ready for the meal to end.

"'Tis such a lovely evening. Why don't we settle on the porch?" I asked. "I'll clear the dishes and bring out cider and cucumber water, and we can let the night birds ease us to sleep."

"That sounds like a good idea," Drake said. "I want to hear more about Henry Morgan's ghost."

Hetty helped me clear the dinner, and when we joined the others on the porch, Captain Thache had them captivated by another tale of his favorite adventurer, Black Sam Bellamy. But sadly, the peace was short-lived when a rattling like thunder in January sounded inside the house.

We ran to the parlor.

"Stay here," the Captain bellowed, grabbing his sword to run up the stairs with Ody and Drake on his heels. But they paused on the bedroom landing when a man rolled down the stairs, followed by another man shouting.

"Stay put, you varmint," Wallace yelled. And he reached under Adler's arm to yank him up by the shoulder. Then as The Crow got his feet underneath him, McNeil explained, "He's been staying in Edward

Moseley's stable since Underwood caught Crow stealing from the townhouse. I saw him slipping off Moseley's place, so I followed him, and he led me here."

Edward jerked Crow's arm from Wallace and dragged him to the parlor, where our invader cowered on the floor as we gathered around.

"What was he up to?" Thache asked. "Did he find something else to steal?"

"Not yet, but he was looking," Wallace said.

"If you stole from Moseley, then why aren't you in the pillory, Adler?" Thache asked.

"'Tis Moseley's fault," Crow whined. "He put me up to it. He promised not to send me to jail if I did favors for him."

"Favors like stealing my rum and sugar?" Thache bellowed, brandishing his sword.

"No. Moseley had nothing to do with that," Adler said, covering his head to dodge a feared strike.

Hetty stepped between The Crow and Captain Thache. "What favors? Why did they send you to my house? What favor could they want from here?"

"Those men—Moseley, Underwood, and some of Moseley's kin—when they found out I was on the Captain's crew, they put their heads together, figuring they could use me."

"And what worth did you have?" Hetty asked.

The Crow crawled behind Thache's favorite chair. Crouching there, he replied, "They found out I stole your old coat, sword, and hat, and they figured I could pass for you in the dark."

Edward moved to threaten Adler's new shelter. "So, you've been robbing the creeks pretending to be me?"

"Well, I didn't start out pretending to be you. That was Underwood's idea."

"Who would believe such a thing?"

The Crow squirmed back a few inches before replying. "No one. No one did—not much, anyway. Not even William Bell thought I was you; he was the one they wanted me to convince. I did you no harm, Captain."

Thache let the sword hang to his side, but he stood over The Crow with feet planted and the free fist to his hip. "Maybe you didn't succeed, but you tried, didn't ye?" He grunted, watching as The Crow covered his eyes. "Well, you already had my hat and coat, so why are you back tonight? Did you mean to try again with my real sword this time?"

The Crow clasped his hands behind his neck, whimpering as he replied, "No, Sir, Captain. Moseley gave up on me being useful. But he couldn't give me to the law because I know what he and his mates are up to."

Thache dug a booted toe into The Crow's side. "Get up from there and talk to me like a man." And when Coleman Adler rose as far as his knees, Edward asked, "And what exactly are they up to?"

The first attempt to speak didn't make it from The Crow's mouth, so he swallowed and tried again. "Get … getting dirt on you and Tobias Knight," he said.

Thache rubbed his head. The sword in his other hand flickered in the candlelight as he paced the room, and occasionally a reflection from the blade slashed at The Crow's face. Then he paused, turning to the Crow. "Well, I can give you up to the law right now. Knight is only across the creek, and I have a few able-bodied men to hold you while I row."

Even though cornered, The Crow dredged up a bit of courage as he knelt with one foot on the floor. He struggled but finally placed his bets with the following bold words. "You don't want to do that, Edward."

"And why not?" Thache said, shrugging with one open hand and the sword arm spread wide.

"Because," he said, pausing to gulp. "Because I know all your secrets, and you wouldn't want Bath to know most of them. And there's worse that you don't know yet."

Thache pulled a chair before the kneeling man and sat like a judge with the sword crossed over his arm. "I'll take you to Knight, and he'll hang ye. You'll spill your guts with a noose around your neck."

"Then, I'll spew secrets to end you, Marybeth, and most of your crew."

"I'll take my chances," Thache said.

"You'd better hear my deal first," he said.

Edward looked down his nose, studying the Crow. "I'm listening."

"I want a ticket out of here. Enough silver to get me out of Bath forever and out of the reach of the law."

Edward chuckled. "And what do I get for my silver?" he asked.

"I'll tell you what I came for. Then you can destroy or hide it. If your enemies never find it, they can't touch you and your missus. So, you'll be safe to live the life you wanted."

"How can knowing what you came for solve my worries?"

Marybeth touched her husband's arm. "Maybe he knows something, Edward. Please, listen to him."

The Crow's courage grew. "Ten pieces of silver to tell you what they want. Ten pieces to get your cup back and ten more for me to leave and never return."

Thache turned to his wife, grimacing as she mouthed, *please*, but then the Captain turned back to The Crow, nodding. "Your news better be worth it, or I'll run you through right here, and they'll never find your body."

"I can meet that test," he said. "It's worth it."

"Speak up then."

"Promise you won't kill me."

"If what you know is worth it, I swear I will not kill you today."

"There are witnesses here. Everyone here heard you agree."

"We all heard you," Ody said. "Tell what you know."

The Crow stood and said the following words.

"Moseley wants Governor Eden more than you. Your only worth to him is to discredit Eden. Moseley wants to *be* Governor or at least to *control* who's governor."

Thache stood, towering over The Crow. Again, he shrugged. "What do I care who's the governor? What does that have to do with me?"

"'Twas Hands who convinced him you had something worth the bother. He claims before you set sail on that first voyage out of here, you signed a paper with Eden and Tobias Knight that proved you were working together. That you'd pirate for their benefit and bring them the goods."

Marybeth gasped, her eyes darting to the cellar door.

"That contract said no such thing," Ody said.

Crow smiled. "Then there *is* such a paper. That's what I was looking for. Where is it?"

"Where you'll never find it," Edward said, grinning.

"Well, knowing it's here to find is worth something. Maybe my neck won't stretch after all. Pay me my first ten pieces of silver, and I won't tell Moseley it's here."

"If I kill you, you won't tell Moseley about it either."

"No, but your wife and the other witnesses heard your promise. So, give me my first ten pieces of silver, and I'll stay out of your way while I retrieve the cup."

Thache tossed the silver at his feet, one coin at a time.

"And where is my cup?"

"Israel Hands has it."

"You said you'd find it."

"Well, I only know he has it, so my end of the bargain will be to go through his things."

That sounded like a bad bargain to me, and Edward must have had the same doubts because he gave the matter some thought.

"What did Moseley promise to pay you for my signed contract?"

"For me? Nothing, But Underwood claimed he could deliver a ship to Israel Hands."

"In that case, I'll take care of Israel Hands and find my own cup."

"If I find it first, can I get the second ten pieces?"

Edward grunted as he nodded. "I'm nothing if not a man of my word. Now take your silver and get out of my house."

The Crow gathered his first ten pieces and fled to the shadows of the yard.

"Shall I follow him, Captain?" Wallace asked.

"No, let him go. Maybe ten pieces will take him far enough from us. But, if you will, keep an eye on Israel Hands and Edward Moseley should you see them in Bath."

"Aye, Captain," Wallace replied. He moved to leave, but Marybeth stopped him with a hand on his shoulder.

McNeil's back went stiff, and when he turned, his eyes were closed, relishing the darkness. Then, when he forced his eyes open, they softened on the contours of Marybeth's face, and he said, "Yes, Mrs. Thache? How can I be of service?"

When Thache gripped his sword and shifted to square his stance with Wallace, Marybeth pulled her hand from McNeil and glanced toward Edward. Then she turned to Wallace again.

"Thank you, Wallace. You are a dear friend, and you've alerted our house to a danger that could ruin us. Thank you for helping keep my family safe."

Wallace nodded, "'Tis my honor to serve this house, Ma'am." His eyes glistened as he turned toward the porch and vanished into the night.

Marybeth turned to face us. "What shall we do now, Edward?" she asked.

Edward sheathed his sword. "Well, for a start, I'll speak to Tobias Knight. Then we will see where things lead."

53 More Trouble on the Home Front

Marybeth Thache

After breakfast, Edward walked me to the summer house, where the creek glittered in the rising sun.

As was his routine, when Caesar finished his early chores for us, he left for his daytime duties at Knight's plantation. But today, as he reached the landing, Edward beckoned him to our little pavilion. My husband had a message for Tobias Knight that he dared not write down.

"Aye, Capt'n, how can I help ye?"

"When you can find a private minute with Mr. Knight, tell him I request a meeting between us alone."

"Knight's feelin' poorly, you know," Caesar said. "He leaves as much as he can to his man, Chamberlain, and only rises for government business when no one else can do it."

Edward nodded. "He's growing weaker. I saw that at the meeting of Admirals. I wish I could help him, but this matter is important to him and me, too. We should put our heads together."

"I'll tell him what you said, Captain. You'll have his answer as soon as I do."

Once Caesar was underway, Edward sat with his arm around my shoulder.

"Are you any better, my dear?" he asked.

I nodded. "Sometimes. But this morning, my stomach won't stop rolling."

"Sounds like seasickness," he replied.

"I haven't been sailing lately." I ruffled his beard as I added, "My captain has been away."

He smiled and pulled me closer.

"Will you be home more often now?" I asked.

"You know I want to be. But you heard The Crow. There are many squalls on the horizon. I can't say how I'll have to navigate 'em."

When I rested my head on his shoulder, he added, "But right now, you are most important. We must get you feeling better."

"I'll be fine, Edward. You mustn't worry."

"I met Olwyn Finch in Bath. He's to get word to Dr. Nuevo and tell him to come to see you. Maybe he'll know what to do."

"If I'm fixable, he'll be the one who knows how to do it."

"Do you still think it's muscadines?" he asked. "If 'tis, I'll tear those vines down with me bare hands."

"I don't think so. Those spewed out of me some time back. I'm surely mending by now."

We sat silently for a moment, feeling the breeze and the nearness of each other. But the Crow's words swirled in my head, forcing me to break our peace.

"What will you do about Israel Hands?" I asked.

"I don't know," he replied, "but if I don't act, he'll have my crew, my ship, and your silver cup, too. Ye can't let snakes lie, especially not that basilisk. That's another good thing about Neuvo coming here. He'll let me know what's happening on Ocracoke."

"And what about here in Bath? The Crow and Edward Moseley?" I asked.

He watched a flock of gulls flying toward the sound and shook his head. "I hope Tobias Knight can help me with that. He knows the ways of townsmen better than I do."

He was restless beside me, ready to fly like those gulls or at least to confront his enemies, and his restlessness made me uneasy, too. So, I patted his hand, "I should get busy. Mother must need me for something."

"As you wish, my sparrow," he said. "I hate to quote the scoundrel, but The Crow was right about one thing; my papers could stand another read-through. Maybe I left something unsecured. Ody can help me with that."

We walked back to the house, arm in arm, and the world was better with Edward beside me, but the many aggravations attacking from all sides made things worse, too.

When we reached the porch, Edward called for Ody and Drake. The lads helped Edward go through the rest of his papers to be sure nothing dangerous was lying about in his den, and they double-checked other hiding places. The sugar kegs and rum casks that Jonah and The Crow had rifled were sealed again and moved to darker spots. As Edward said, "If they're gonna rob me, at least we can make 'em work for it."

When Caesar returned around noon, my husband and I were busy with chores on the front porch.

"Come with me now, if you can, Captain," Caesar said. "I'll show you where Knight wants to meet. We'll need the lads."

My husband found Ody and Drake, and they hurried to our dock to row to Knight's landing.

Mother joined me on the porch. "So where are they off to now?" she asked. The men were barely more than dark specks to me at that distance, but I pointed them out to Mother. We watched as the dots skirted around the main entrance, followed the sideyard, and disappeared into the garden bordering Thistleworth.

"It still surprises me that Edward can shift so quickly from being an attentive husband to a warrior running toward a fight."

Mother turned toward me with an eyebrow raised. "Then you don't remember much about your father, do ye?" she asked. "He kept one eye out for us and one arm around us. But when that bell rang and danger was at hand, he shoved us into the attic and called all hands to the tower. 'Tis the way of men, daughter, and while Edward may be bigger than most, he isn't much different."

Soon Aurora joined us to help with the mending, and our chat turned to easier puzzles than the mysteries of men. But as dinner time approached, the widows left me to watch on the porch, and they worked to put a meal on the table. It was a little past two when the men rowed toward home.

Caesar turned the boat around to row back to Tobias Knight, but the other three lumbered up the boardwalk to the house. They did their best to wash up but sat at the table, sweaty and exhausted.

"I'm glad we didn't have to do that alone," Drake said as he dropped into his chair.

Mother glowered at the damp heads around her table. "What in the world did Knight have you do?" she asked.

"'Twas the sugar," Edward said. "After I told Knight what The Crow said, he was eager to shift it to a new hiding place."

"The sugar you took to him soon after you returned?" I asked.

"Aye. That, and since then, the rest from Ocracoke too. 'Twas twenty barrels to Knight, sixty to Eden and the town, and the rest for the crew. We had nowhere to store it on the island except under tents, which isn't the best place for sugar. So, we moved it to the tunnel under Governor Eden's old plantation house. And now that we've settled the matter of *Rose Emelye*, we'll get it where it belongs in town and sell the rest."

"Governor Eden's old plantation? But didn't he sell that?" I asked.

"The men who bought it are mariners and friends of mine. Eden, Knight, and I trust those fellows. They'll help us turn sugar into gold, silver, or whatever suits us. Maybe wheat, tea, and hair ribbons," he winked. "Then we can give the men their cut. But if Edward Moseley means to give the Governor trouble, we must sell part of it and distribute the rest quickly.

That's why we shifted what was still in the tunnel away from Eden's former land."

"Where did you put it?" Aurora asked.

Ody replied, "We stuffed it in Knight's old barn. It's safe enough for now, and Mr. Knight says the Governor will find a better place for it until the town needs it."

"It was sure a lot of work," Drake said as he paused from stuffing his face.

Aurora nodded, "And you two are worse for the wear of it. Once you eat, find a good spot in the creek to clean up."

Edward jumped in the creek with the lads, and I waited for him to join me on the tower where the breeze could dry his hair and beard. And there he told me about Tobias Knight.

"Knight isn't well at all," he said. "It's as Caesar said; he barely gets out of bed. I met with him in a wine cupboard by his garden. When I arrived, he was perched in a soft chair, sipping nothing more than ginger water. Even in that dim room, I could see he was pale and breathing with difficulty."

"Did he know about Underwood's arrangement with The Crow? That he meant to make you appear guilty of robbery in Bath?" I asked.

"He remembered that Bell reported a robbery, but no one claimed I did it. And it was news to him that The Crow and his creek pirates were working with Moseley's men."

"Does he trust Moseley, then?" I asked.

Edward chuckled, "Knight treats all men here with respect, but he has suspicions about Moseley and his friends. So, he wasn't surprised to hear that his family meant to harm Governor Eden's reputation. Knight had no idea of the lengths they'd go to, though. So now, he will clear his and the Governor's offices of any damaging records. And he asked me to ensure that the contract we signed at Plum Point is safe—he wants me to return it so he can destroy it."

"Why would he want to do that? It was a legitimate business arrangement, wasn't it?" I asked.

"It was. But Knight didn't ask questions about where I found the goods during my first voyage out of Bath, and knowing all the details would not have been in his best interest."

"So, will you return it to him?"

"No. Moseley means harm to Eden and Knight, but we could take the blame for anything they lay at Eden's feet. That contract was to protect you, so I assured Tobias it was safe unless we needed it."

"And he accepted that?"

Edward shrugged. "I reckon he trusts me more than most do."

"So, is the problem solved? Are we safe?"

He took my hand in both his. “I cannot promise we’ve seen the end of trouble, but we are on the side of the men with the most power, and for now, that’s the best position we can be in.”

I rested my hand against Edward’s shoulder, feeling more at ease until he whispered, “But Knight shared another problem.”

My head rose in alarm. “What’s that?”

“You mustn’t fret,” he said, convincing me his news would be fret-worthy. Then he gripped both my shoulders. “You’re safe with me. I have this in hand.”

“You’re frightening me. Just say it,” I said.

Edward tightened his grip on me and said, “Knight has reports that the Indians may rise again. He fears more attacks.”

I stiffened. My stomach pulled to my back, and I gasped, “Here? In Bath?”

Then I stepped back from Edward and turned toward the attic hatch. *Where could I hide?*

“They are not here, my love,” he said.

He put his arms around me for shelter, but the constraint didn’t suit me. I had to run. *But where?*

“I’ll be here to protect you if it happens, but Knight has no proof yet,” he said. “’Tis only rumors.”

I was sobbing then and suddenly nauseous, so I ran to the railing where my dinner gave a curious decoration to the fig trees below. Then, pressing my stomach to the tower wall, I leaned over it, weak, empty, and mouth like dry sand.

“Hetty!” Edward yelled.

But Mother was already at the hatch. “Hurry down here, you two. Your doctor is nearly at the landing.”

Edward ran to the creek side of the tower. “She’s right. It’s Olwyn Finch’s boat. He’s brought the doctor.”

“Of course it is; do you think I’m blind?” Mother said as she rushed to my side. “What a sorry state you’re in; we’ll never get you down that block ladder.”

Edward clung to my other side. “I can carry her down.”

“What? Like a sack of potatoes over your shoulder?” Mother said. “You keep her from falling over the side, and I’ll fetch the doctor.”

Edward lifted me to a chair. “I’ll go. You tend to her.”

Mother patted my shoulder as she wiped my face with her apron. “All will be well, me girl. Don’t fret.”

Gasping, I locked to Mother’s eyes. “The Indians. Tobias Knight says the Indians might return,” I said, digging my nails into her palms.

She squeezed my hand as terror flashed over her face. But the moment faded, and her determination replaced fear.

"It will be fine, Mary. No one is invading yet. And despite my misgivings, you've brought us Captain Thache. He and his men will guard us. You've done well by us, girl."

Tears streamed, but Mother found a clean corner of her apron. "Now straighten up. The doctor is on his way."

54 Creekside Revelations

Aurora Saunters

With all the shouting, I followed Edward to Plum Point's landing to see what the fuss was about. There Edward greeted his old friend. But even as they clasped forearms, Nuevo's expression turned from happily greeting a friend to a physician's search for symptoms. First, he assessed Edward's state—in control as usual but approaching panic.

"Come, old friend," Edward said. "My little flower needs you more than I do. Losing half the food she eats can't be good for her." Edward grabbed Asjen's arm, ushering him to the tower, and I followed.

Asjen nodded to Edward and pulled his arm free to address his patient.

"Good day, Mrs. Thache. Tell me your symptoms, and let's see if we can fix what bothers you."

While Marybeth explained her recurring nausea, Dr. Neuvo asked what she had eaten and when she was likely to be ill.

Witnessing his exam felt like déjà vu to me. I had watched Augustus Neumann at work in Salem, and I always considered him above the eighteenth-century curve of medical understanding. Asjen Neuvo gave me the same impression. I had seen it when he cared for Hetty Bellieu and now again in examining Marybeth.

There was no suggestion of bleeding or purging, and other differences were more subtle. Nuevo looked at the balance of body systems, not just the collection and dispelling of blood, water, and bile.

Despite the contradictory dates, I couldn't argue with the conclusion drawn by Ody and Drake—Asjen Neuvo and Augustus Neumann might be the same man.

"Has your vision changed?" Neuvo asked as he counted her pulse. "Has there been any dizziness or blurring?"

Marybeth shook her head no.

Nuevo brought out his long, brass ear horn to listen to her heart but found nothing abnormal. And although the girl was tired and queasy, she carried on a rational conversation and was strong enough to stand, sit, and hold Asjen's cane at arm's length while sand passed through the doctor's minute glass.

"Very well," he said and turned to Edward. "Captain Thache, do you think the two of us can get Mrs. Thache to her bed? Then perhaps these ladies will help me with a further examination."

"'Tis no problem for me, doctor. If I can climb a rope, I can get my wife down a ladder. But is she well?"

"Well, if I were a betting man, I'd wager she will feel much better soon."

Thache lifted Marybeth into his arms and asked her to grab round his neck, then, as deftly as an acrobat, he held the rail beside the ladder with one hand and tightly to his wife with the other,

While Thache carried Mary downstairs, the doctor whispered to Hetty, and I wondered if his diagnosis was the same condition Hetty and I had discussed.

Downstairs, we found Marybeth comfortably propped on her pillow. Neuvo closed the door on Edward and me while Hetty assisted with the bedside examination. Marybeth gasped as they shared the news. Then they called Edward and me in to hear it as well; Marybeth had a baby on the way.

We left the couple laughing and crying as they absorbed this change in their family and how it might fit into this worrisome time of their lives. But there were more giggles than grieving as they yielded to the joy of a new child coming.

Then, reinvigorated by their news, the couple joined us in the parlor.

"Congratulations, Marybeth. What a pleasure to think of new life in this house," I said.

Hetty hugged her daughter again and embraced the Captain for the first time. She touched each of them on the arm, saying, "We've had so much loss and tribulation. Now, I can only imagine little knees crawling over my rug and sticky fingerprints on the walls." She moved both palms to her face, crushing her cheeks around her smile. "I can hardly wait!"

"But what if he grows to have a long, black beard?" Edward asked, grinning.

Marybeth laughed. "Never fear, Mother. He won't be born with it, will he?"

"No, indeed," Edward replied. "Especially not if the babe is a girl." We chuckled as Edward touched his wife's smooth face. "She'll be pretty as a peach," he said.

Dr. Neuvo slapped Edward on the back. "Congratulations, my friend. It has been quite a while since you held a baby. I believe it will be good for your soul."

"So, you think a little fluff is what it takes to tame me?" Edward asked.

"Well, you should see that *Marybeth* stays tame for a while. See that she eats right and gets enough sleep. Try to keep her calm and happy. She has a few months to grow this child and needs to take care of herself."

"I'll see to that, doctor," Hetty said. "And the rest of the household will watch over her, too."

"Now, as to nausea, the best I can offer is ginger tea. So here is my gift to the new mother." He reached into his pocket and pulled out a tin of candied ginger root.

"Oh, ginger!" Hetty said. "This has been hard to come by lately."

"Aye, 'tis so. But I was able to gather some while we were in the Indies. This should be enough to get her through the early days. Ginger tea sweetened with honey, as needed," he said, handing the tin to Hetty. "That should help."

"Thank you for making the trip, Asjen. There aren't many I'd trust with the care of my sparrow. You are as skilled today as you were with my mother those years ago."

Ody and Drake surprised us by coming in the front door. "We've been to see what Olwyn brings," Ody said. "He has a barrel of crabs on his boat. Should we fetch some?"

Marybeth paled at the thought, but Edward thought it was just the thing.

"Let's go see, lads. We'll have a celebration feast tonight."

We followed him to the landing to see for ourselves.

"Just in time, Captain," he called. "I was about to take this bounty into town."

Marybeth stood on the wooden walk as Edward boarded the boat to peek into the barrel.

"What do you think, Hetty?" he shouted, beckoning Mrs. Bellieu aboard.

"They look fine," she said. Then she turned to Edward, "Enough to fill my pot would suit me."

Edward nodded, "Ten of yer biggest, I think, Mr. Finch."

One of Olwyn's oarsmen found a pail to hold the crabs, and as he passed it to Edward, he whispered, "Hurry back if you can. I'll need to move on to Bath soon, and I've news for you."

I feared his news might upset Marybeth, so I beckoned the others to come to the house. Unfortunately, my plan failed when Hetty caught sight of Wallace returning to our landing.

Marybeth moved to greet him as he pulled his jollyboat to the floating dock and tied off opposite Olwyn's boat, *Bounty*.

"Good morning, Wallace," Hetty called. "Have you more news about The Crow?"

"I have a word for the Captain," he replied.

Olwyn Finch stepped to the rail of his boat, saying, "Have you need of crabs today, Sir?" he asked.

Wallace froze as their eyes met. "No crabs, thank ye," he said. McNeil studied the yellow and white boat and the weathered face that peered from behind its sail. Then he looked at the *Bounty* again before speaking. "I recognize the face but not the craft. Have we met, Sir?"

"'Tis possible," Finch replied, "I have more than the one vessel, and 'tis my business to supply the needs of sailors hereabouts."

"Is one of them called Jolly Bum?" he asked.

Olwyn's brow wrinkled. "Aye, 'tis indeed. Do you know my rower?"

Wallace's face went dark. He squeezed his eyes shut and shook his head as he remembered. Then he opened his eyes. "You're the one who saved me," he gasped. "You saved me from where they left me."

"Oh, aye. I remember ye. Stranded on some island, ye were. You were a right mess with that bleeding head. Little Porpoise Island, it was. Not far from Brant Island Shoals."

Marybeth gasped and stepped toward the sea peddler, "Is this the man who rescued you after the pirates stranded you?"

"Aye," Wallace replied. "I had nearly put that out of my mind." He turned, scowling, as Thache strode down the boardwalk with silver and an empty pail for Finch.

"Ah, Wallace," he called. "Have ye news so soon?"

Wallace clenched his fists. "I brought news, aye," he replied.

Edward clapped him on the back, "Well, speak up then, lad. We're all friends here."

Wallace pulled away from Edward's hand, and with a stony face, he replied, "It'll keep."

The Captain noted the slight but only scratched his beard and then turned to Finch. "Mr. Finch, you had a spot of news for me, too. What's happ'nin' on Ocracoke?"

Olwyn eyed Wallace and the unfamiliar faces of Ody and Drake and then stepped closer to Edward. "'Tis for your ears only, Captain. It comes from the whisperers."

Edward shrugged. "Well, I have two men bringing me news, and neither is ready to speak it. So, one of you tell me what you came to say."

Wallace stepped up. "This man, here, Captain. He did me a great favor on an occasion you might recall. Not long after you came to Bath, a group of your crewmen grabbed me, tortured me, and left me on an island to die."

Edward took a deep breath, and his chest swelled as he faced Wallace. But before he could speak, McNeil continued.

“This man is a witness to the state they left me in. I would have surely starved without his help.”

“Is this the one who brought ’e back to Bath?” Edward asked.

“He did. But he took me to Captain Harding, who cared for me and kept me out of the way of your men. He saved my life. Your crew meant for me to die on that island, Captain.”

“Is that what you think?” Thache asked.

“I do.”

“And do you use that as cause to break our agreement?”

“No, Sir. I’m a man of my word, as I thought you were.”

Marybeth moved to stand between the two men, but Hetty pulled her back. “Be safe, girl. Think of the child.”

Thache shifted to block Marybeth from her old friend.

“I recall our agreement, and I shall honor it,” he replied. “And I will trust you to do the same.”

Wallace stepped back. “For now, I will. And when I change my mind, you’ll be the first to know.”

Thache nodded, standing like a ship, with the flag of his black beard flying in the wind. “We’ll cross that matter when we come to it, then. I’ll be ready when you are,” he replied. “But until that day comes, tell me the news of this one.”

Wallace stepped back, and Thache turned to the ladies and pointed up the boardwalk. “All is well here, Ladies. There will be no trouble here today, and you won’t miss anything by enjoying the safety of the parlor.”

None of us moved.

Thache shrugged, “Very well. State your news, McNeil.”

Wallace twitched his jaw before replying. “Silas Van Horn sends word that The Crow is no longer at the Moseley house. He doesn’t know if he’s on the run or has found new shelter.”

“Running from me?” Thache asked.

“Maybe from you, maybe the Tuscarora warriors—or maybe he’s running from whoever’s mad at him, and that’s about everybody in Bath. ’Tis all I know.”

“Very well,” Thache said. “I thank you for the news.”

Salty water splashed on the boards as Olwyn Finch stepped forward with a pail with four crabs. "Take this," he said, handing the bucket to Wallace.

Thache begged Hetty to get Marybeth off her feet. But Mrs. Thache wouldn’t budge. First, it was Edward, now Olwyn, and Thache’s bride strained to hear what passed between them as eagerly as I did.

Finch said, "I’m glad we met under better circumstances than the first time, and these fightin’ fellows might make a good dinner for ye. Rest easy, my friend." Then as he passed the bucket to McNeil, their hands touched, and Finch nodded toward the Captain, whispering, "Who do you think sent me to find you on that island?"

Wallace's face eased. Then he nodded before shoving his boat into the creek. "Thank you again, friend."

When the jollyboat pulled away, Edward was insistent that his wife rest. As Hetty and I helped Marybeth back to the porch, Thache shooed Ody and Drake off Finch's boat, pushing them to follow us to the house. But the boys lingered under the cypress trees at the landing long enough to hear Finch's news.

Finally, Olwyn's *Bounty* pulled away, and I passed Captain Thache as he hurried to the porch to check on Marybeth. I rushed to the boardwalk to fetch my grandsons. Drake beckoned us to the summer house, and once we three settled on the benches there, he shared Finch's news.

"Someone named Charles Vane wants to meet with Edward."

"Who's Charles Vane?" Ody asked. "Is he in the records?"

"He is," I replied. "Another pirate friend of Edwards. But Vane's a different animal. This pirate is mean to the core."

55 Ticket to Ocracoke

Drake Saunters

Ody and I were awake till the wee hours as we speculated about Charles Vane's visit to Ocracoke. What news would he bring? What did he want from Edward? Then, finally, at dawn, Ody shook me awake, saying, "We've got to get Captain Thache to tell us more."

When we caught the Captain alone, he seemed eager to talk about the man who would soon visit our shores but not with Marybeth around. Mrs. Thache didn't relish stories of the Captain when he plundered with his pirate band, so Edward picked the place and time.

"Lads, I hear there's good fishing in the East Branch. Why don't we catch a mess of striped bass? 'Twill be no bother for the ladies. Caesar can soak 'em for us, and we can roast 'em over his fire."

Ody was always ready for fishing, and I was just as glad to have time with the Captain. And between casting, catching, and gutting, Thache told us Vane's story.

"So ye want to hear about Charles Vane? The best way to sum him up is to call him a fox—smart, sly, and mean. There ain't none better at navigation nor trickin' an enemy, but he has no regard for our rules. He knows 'em, but he makes no bones about breakin' 'em neither."

"Is he a better sailor than you, Captain?" I asked.

Thache gave me his cock-headed grin. "Well," he said with a wink. "Maybe we're about equal. 'Tis hard to say."

"Is he stronger than you?" Ody asked.

Thache chuckled. "Are ye thinking of jumping ship, lad? Do you think he's a better captain than I am?" He scratched through his beard, then added, "He might come with a bigger crew than mine, but I reckon I'd win hand-to-hand."

Caesar lowered his gutting knife as he snickered. "You don't need to worry about that. The Captain can stand on his own against Charles Vane."

"So, did you sail together?" Ody asked.

"I'd say 'tis more like we passed in the waters, but we both started on the Spanish treasure wrecks and fared well with those. Even though we were in different camps, I saw him more in Nassau. I sailed with Benjamin Hornigold, and Vane was with Henry Jennings' Flying Gang."

"Was he born in Nassau?" I asked.

"No one knows where Vane was born, but we reckon he's English. He doesn't hold much allegiance to any country, though. Hornigold and I struck at England's enemies, Sam Bellamy took any prize he found fair, but Vane took any ship he could best if he figured there was a prize aboard."

"So, what does he want with you, Captain?" Ody asked. "Why is he coming to Ocracoke?"

"It probably has to do with Nassau; 'twas the pirate's safe haven for a time. Hornigold governed it. I tried my hand at keeping it peaceful for a while, but Vane was the governor when Woodes Rogers took it back for England. I reckon Vane wants Nassau again; that'd be my guess. But we'll see when he gets here."

Caesar added a little to the story.

"If Vane's coming to Ocracoke, you better steer clear of him, lads. The Capt'n already told you how vicious Vane is."

"How was he vicious?" Ody asked.

"Well, for one thing, he'd cheat his crewmates as easily as his enemies. And he had no qualms about torturing crews on the ships he took. Why, I heard tell he even keel-hauled his own mates when it suited him. I'd wager that Captain Thache could outwit him on the waves, but 'tis hard to have a fair fight with a man who doesn't know what fair is."

"Is his ship bigger than yours, Captain?"

Thache nodded. "Not as big as *Queen Anne*, but bigger than *Adven*ture. The last time I saw him, his ship was *Ranger*, a Brigantine with thirty guns. I reckon that's still his flagship."

"When's he coming, Captain?" I asked.

"The message I got said by the end of the month, so days or weeks, I reckon."

I couldn't hold back. "Can we go to your meeting?"

"You need to stay clear of Vane," Caesar said. "He'd as soon skin ye alive as look at ye."

"We could stay out of his way," I begged. "Won't you need us to help do chores for all those men?"

"I've plenty of men for that, and your Grandmother would not approve," Thache said. "Besides, I need you here with Marybeth. She'll keep you busy, and you might not like being on Ocracoke with Vane and his gang. So ye best stay here, lads."

"He's right, Drake; that meeting won't be for the likes of us," Ody replied.

Maybe Ody was right. But even if the Captain wouldn't take us with him, Ody and I might have other ways to get there.

We made a tasty meal of roasted bass, and Hetty added parsnips, corncakes, and boiled cabbage to round it out. Marybeth ate tiny bites, but she managed to keep her supper down. Then after a cup of ginger tea, she turned in early, and the others soon followed to their beds.

That night, after Ody went to sleep, I had some figuring to do. Ody and I could travel in ways others couldn't, but could we pull off a trip to Ocracoke?

It was not an easy riddle to solve, and I couldn't talk to Grandma about it. She'd stop me from going to a pirate gathering for sure. But seeing pirates in action was the chance of a lifetime, and I couldn't miss it. Charles Vane and Blackbeard with their ships, *Ranger* and *Adventure,* in the camp—it was as good as going backstage at a rock concert or meeting in the dugout with an all-star baseball team. Then, when my buddies started crowing about their home runs and triple plays, even though I couldn't tell them about it, I'd know I spent my vacation in Blackbeard's camp. That would trump anyone else's summer.

I didn't know enough about commuting, but something tickled my brain—like a time-travel answer trapped there, fighting for freedom. I couldn't connect to it, though. Maybe if I talked to Ody, I'd find the path. There must be a way.

***

After breakfast the following day, I asked Ody to help me check fences, but I pounded him with questions when we were at a safe distance.

"Ody, what do we know about how we commute?" I asked.

"Grandma told you all that before we left Cooper's Peak," he replied.

"Yeah, but I wasn't listening. So why and how does all that work?"

"Well, she doesn't know, but she thinks the ability to commute is inherited. Her dad had the gift, but not her mom. But outside of Grandma and her father, no one else besides me and you have it as far as we know."

"So, is it something she passed to us, like blue eyes?" I asked.

"No, there's a little more than that. We need the right object for it to work—like Oma's walking stick. But it doesn't work for all our relatives, just some of us. The ancestral connection isn't enough to explain it, but Oma guesses strong emotions, like love, hate, or fear, play a part, too."

"Yes, I recall that part. Grandma told you the stick didn't work for you because you were too young to know her father well, so you didn't have the chance to bond with him, and the stick couldn't move you to him."

"That's right."

"So, we can't go home by the stick, but we can commute to each other with our hair charms. My pendant with Grandma's hair takes me to her, as does yours. And she can come to me when she holds *my* hair charm."

"Right. The hair circles have enough of our gene magic to make that happen."

"Is she sure of all this?"

"Of course not. How often must I tell you we don't know how it works? She's theorizing based on what she's observed."

"You mean guessing."

"OK, guessing. And commuting evolves, too. So, it could change for us."

"What about the bugle and the prayer book?"

"The way Oma figures it, they involve genetics and emotion, too."

I nodded, "Elizabeth Glover's prayer book brought us to Bath at the marriage of the Captain and Marybeth. Then I transported to Thache and his sick mother near the time she died."

"Right. Those events were full of love, grief, fear, dread, joy, excitement, and who knows what else—strong emotions."

"So, who was the ancestor? Elizabeth Glover?"

"It's hard to say. Her prayerbook brought us here, but the emotion was Mrs. Bellieu fainting at her daughter's wedding. Edward was there to assist her."

So instead of Lizzy, our ancestor could be someone else at the wedding. There was a lot of tension going on that day, so besides Lizzy, it could be Tobias Knight, his wife, Captain Thache, Widow Bellieu, or even Governor Eden. Any of them would be exciting ancestors, but one stood out. Could Blackbeard be my Grandpa?

"What's that goofy grin about?" Ody asked.

I chuckled. "Just considering the possibilities."

"Oma thinks Elizabeth Glover is the ancestor, but she wasn't nearby when we teleported, just Mrs. Bellieu and Captain Thache. I suppose the relative could be any of those three."

"Hm … Thache, his mother, or Hetty Bellieu. If Hetty is our ancestor, so is Marybeth. As to Thache's mother, she had other children, and his father did, too, so *they* might be our ancestors. But it can't be Edward; Oma said his daughter doesn't have children." Then Ody's eyes flashed open. Did he have the same thought I did?

No. Ody had a different brainstorm with the same conclusion.

"It *must* be Edward!" he said. "That's the only explanation for Asjen Neuvo being in Jamaica and now here. Augustus Neumann was following up on a family mystery with the man with the bugle—our ancestor. Now,

Neuvo is following Edward Thache, and you traveled there with Elizabeth Thache's gold star."

The wiggling idea finally made it to daylight. "Edward is our ancestor, too."

Then Ody turned toward me with eyes wider than I'd ever seen them. "And if *our* mystery connects to the one Neuvo is trying to solve, Neuvo is part of our family, too. That explains why we've crossed his path twice."

"Then Marybeth's baby might be our ancestor, so he must survive, or we wouldn't be here," I said. "And maybe we're the ones who save him."

"Don't be daft, Drake. You said the baby *might* be our ancestor. But if he is, he or she will survive because here we are. So, it's a done deal. You just want an excuse to go to Ocracoke."

He was right. I wanted to go to Ocracoke, and maybe I *needed* to be there.

"Can I get there by commuting?" I asked.

"I don't know that you can, and I'm pretty sure you shouldn't go anyway."

"What if I made a charm of Edward's hair? If he's an ancestor, maybe I can teleport to him wherever he is, just like I teleport to you or Grandma."

"He might not be an ancestor. Or it might be in the wrong century, or maybe the power doesn't work with him like it hasn't worked on our fathers. So, please don't jump the gun; test it. See if Edward's hair tingles for you. That's the tip-off that it can move you. But I don't think it will work; those genetic charms require an emotional bond."

"Are you kidding me? I'm sure wired with excitement. He's our some-number-of-greats grandpa." I stopped, breathless, as the idea hit the light of day. Then I yelled, "Oh my goodness, we're sons of pirates! Descendants of Blackbeard."

"OK. Any more talk of that, and I'm bringing in Oma."

That crimped my plans. If I didn't stop myself, Grandma would do it for me, even if she had to yank me back home.

But wait. Grandma couldn't do that. I was the one with the choice. I was the one who had to press the charm to go to her. She couldn't make me go unless she came to me and dragged me by the elbow off Ocracoke. That would be embarrassing.

And I might have given up on it. But later, I found a lock of Edward's beard that Marybeth tied up in a ribbon when he left on his voyage north. It was so matted when he returned that she had to cut it off him. And when I touched it, it tingled.

When I showed the ribbon to Ody, he knew I meant to go to Ocracoke, and maybe he wanted to go with me. He picked up the lock of Blackbeard's hair, letting the strands brush his finger. But I saw from his expression that there was no tingle. That black curl wasn't taking Ody anywhere.

"See, no buzz," he said. "You wasted your time."

I didn't tell Ody that the lock of hair tingled for me. The thought of being Blackbeard's descendant sure fired me up. Edward was near the end of his days, with my baby grandpa or grandma on the way. None of the boys I left behind in Burke County were doing anything half as exciting as fighting for Blackbeard. There were many things I didn't understand, but that lock of hair definitely buzzed.

Now to test it. How could I commute to Edward when he wouldn't notice me? He should either be asleep or near a solid object like a wall. The universe wouldn't send me into a wall—Grandma said so.

I waited till Edward was working in the cellar. It was dim in there, and there were lots of solid barrels and crates to get between him and me. When I heard him wrestling with one of the hogshead barrels, I pinched his hair, and with all the usual fanfare of flickering lights and wind, I ended up on the outside of the cellar wall, near the barrels. It worked—at least that time, it did. So, I repeated my experiment twice—once when Edward was in the shed and once while he mended a hole under the summer house.

I didn't know how or why it worked, but it worked, and that's all I needed to know. First, I'd find a safe time and place to see the pirates gather on Ocracoke. What a story that would be! But as it turned out, I had a more important reason than that to visit the pirate banyan.

56 Pirate Run

Drake Saunters

Captain Thache didn't tell us when he expected Vane to arrive, but the time was near. Everyone in Bath saw signs of it.

More crew came in from the island to gather supplies for Ocracoke. Luckily Thache's camp had a well with enough water, but the crew bought more barrels to ensure a sufficient supply, and Edward sent a keg of rum. There were rumors of pirates hunting wild boar beyond the fields, and Old Clark butchered a cow that Hands and his men took to the pirate camp. So it must be for the banyan.

Hetty fussed about her missing strings of dried apples, leather breeches, and jerky. More than once, I heard her railing about the excess.

"We'll starve this winter and all because of a pirate party. Captain Thache needs to worry about his family, not that wild gang." But she didn't fuss loud or long, as she didn't want to upset Marybeth. None of us did, especially Captain Thache.

Even while he ordered stock for Ocracoke and insured the security of Plum Point, he was at Marybeth's side every minute possible. They ended each evening on the Bride's Tower gazing at the sky, as was Marybeth's habit.

I met them there one evening, and when I passed through the hatch, he asked me to stand guard.

"Keep my lovely wife company, if you will; I saw something that needs a closer look."

I took the spot by Mary's side, but she wasn't watching the stars then. Instead, her eyes were closed, and she looked like she might cry.

"Is something wrong, Mrs. Thache?" I asked.

"'Tis Edward. Even when his arm is around me, his thoughts are on Ocracoke."

"The company coming must be on his mind."

She nodded. Edward clenched his fist when I asked if he was thinking of Israel Hands. Then he gripped the tower rail and hissed, "I'm thinking about my ship and what Hands might do to it." Then, he peered through the fog as if he could see what happened in the camp just by willing it.

"He's trying to be two places at once, Marybeth."

She nodded. "But even when Edward is here, he's more there."

I distracted her with guessing nightbird calls until the Captain returned.

"Did you find anything?" I asked.

"I saw movement. Someone was out there, but I couldn't find him. Caesar will keep looking," he replied.

"I'll get Ody; we'll help search.

As I entered the hatch, I turned back toward the Captain. Marybeth rested her head on his shoulder, and he stood with an arm around her, but she was right. He studied the eastern sky over Ocracoke. It was impossible to see the island from the tower, but maybe he was looking for Charles Vane, anyway."

That night, on the far perimeter of the plantation, near the headwaters of Plum Point Gut, Caesar, Ody, and I found evidence that someone had been hiding on Hetty Bellieu's land. Charred fishbones left from meals dotted the cold campfire ring, and the ground had been disturbed by at least one bed roll.

After we found those signs, Caesar checked the spot each evening before he went to sleep and again before he left for Tobias Knight's plantation each morning. My cousin and I were less diligent, but for safety, we patrolled together whenever we had cause to go that far. But we never caught our unwelcome guest in the woods until just hours before Thache left Bath to prepare for Charles Vane. One of Edward's last duties for Plum Point was patrolling the farm with Caesar and me to point out weaker positions in our perimeter. Finally, around 4:00, the Captain left us to collect extra firewood for the house. Soon after that, Caesar put a hand to my chest.

"Shh," he mouthed, listening to voices in the woods. By then, the sun was low, and Caesar bent, motioning for me to do the same. Then we listened to two voices I knew as well as he did: Coleman Adler and Israel Hands.

"My mission is to find out how he lives. Where he might hide things," the third voice said. This man was an outsider, unknown to Caesar or me.

"Well, you know where the house is, and I've told you the entrances and hiding spots, but I've looked that place over, and you won't find what you seek there," said The Crow.

Then Israel Hands spoke up. "I know Thache. He keeps what he needs. I've looked everywhere on the Island, so it must be here."

Caesar cocked an eyebrow at me, wondering what they could be looking for. I'd explain about the contract later.

The Crow spoke again. "If 'tis on this farm, it's either buried or hung from a tree like that sack of dresses you left for me. I've done more here than show the paths to Mr. Houston. I've looked for caves, clefts, and fresh digs but found nothing like that in these woods."

Mr. Houston, the third man, replied, "Well, once Thache clears out, I'll bring my men. They are experts in hunting for caches like that. They're trackers, and they'll find what we want."

"Looks like you've finished your job, Crow," said Israel Hands. "Here's the silver I promised you. You can let Houston's men take over in the morning."

"And then where will I go?" The Crow asked. "I can't go backwoods through Indian lands. I hear they are ready to attack. Take me to Ocracoke with you," he said.

"I'm afraid the Captain won't have that. Now, when I become Captain, it will be a different matter. Maybe if you hide out a little longer, I can return for you."

"I don't think I can last much longer in Bath," Crow replied.

"Well, you're a clever man. You have your silver. You'll figure it out," Hands said. Then he must have addressed Houston. "Captain Thache will sail with me tomorrow. You'll have the woods to yourself during the day, except for those two Saunters lads. They should be no trouble for you and your men."

"Then let's head back to Bath Town, Mr. Hands."

"A good idea. The last ferry over the East Branch will be leaving soon."

"I'll walk wid 'e," The Crow said. "This ain't enough silver to leave this county; maybe you can give me enough to hire a ride clear of Bath."

"What about those farmer pirates of yours?" Hands asked. "Can't they row you far enough?"

"They don't have boats of their own. Besides, they're off me now that we can't rob anymore," Crow replied.

"Do ye know, Crow? I might have another idea for 'e to get out of here. We can speak of it at the ferry," Hands said.

Houston added, "I'm finished, too; I only need to check orders with Underwood."

We kept still as stones as the men pushed through the underbrush on their way to East Branch. Then, as we slipped toward the farmhouse to report what we heard, I was both fearful and relieved. Ody and I would have our work cut out for us, keeping clear of Houston, but I figured we'd all be glad to see the backside of The Crow. But the worst thing was the lingering doubt that Adler might be lying again. Was he running from Bath or just plotting his next move?

That night, Caesar took guard duty, and my bet was he didn't sleep a wink as he watched every forest path that led to the house.

I waited in Thache's den, hoping to have a chance to tell him what we heard, but he spent every minute of the evening reassuring Marybeth that all was well.

"Vane won't stay long, and the boys and I have checked everything on the farm; you'll be safe here," he said.

"'Tis no difference if you go or stay, Edward," Marybeth replied. "Your thoughts are on that island, and I reckon your body may as go where your head is."

"My thoughts are always with you, my love. Just let me set the affairs of the crew in order, and I'll be yours."

Their discussion didn't become an argument, but it continued till dawn when Edward said farewell.

"Don't fret, my dear. Captain Vane and I respect each other, and he might bring helpful news. Who knows? Maybe Vane will take all my crew. If they want to go, that's one solution for us."

Thache tried to help his wife focus on happier things, such as how he loved her and the promise of their growing family. Neither Caesar nor I could tell him what we heard in the woods. It probably didn't matter. Caesar, Ody, and I could protect the farm, and if the intruders were after documents, Edward had hidden those where no one could find them. He'd leave nothing to trap Marybeth or endanger their child.

Near dawn, all Plum Point followed Edward to the porch for his farewell. Then, after the couple shared hugs, kisses, and promises, Thache sailed on *Bellamy* with Israel Hands.

A couple hours later, Olwyn Finch stopped at our landing. He had a barrel of apples for us and more fruit to take to Ocracoke. Ody and I rolled the barrels up the boardwalk while Hetty took stock of the delivery.

She met us in the house with a list of the things Finch left us and where to store them. But she passed on a bit of information.

"Mr. Finch says he's to pick up Coleman Adler when he stops at Chester's Landing."

"I reckon Olwyn remembers The Crow from when they sailed in the Captain's fleet," Marybeth said. "But is he taking him to Ocracoke?"

"No, according to Olwyn, some men around Chester's Point owe The Crow money, so he's hoping he'll end up with enough to go to sea. He doesn't mind where he goes as long as it's toward the water and not the woods. I reckon he wants to sign up as a sailor again."

"I suppose that could be a good thing," Marybeth said. "Edward wants him out of Bath, and he surely does not want him on *Adventure*."

I didn't say so, but I had my doubts. The Crow's latest associates were crooks and scoundrels like he was, so he might get an unpleasant surprise if he expected fair payment from them. They'd more likely end up with Crow's silver instead of giving him more. Though I doubted a good outcome, I agreed with Marybeth; Crow could only bring trouble to Ocracoke.

I wanted to go there, though. But I needed a good reason to take the risk.

57 A Good Reason

Ody Saunters

With the Captain away, Tobias Knight agreed to give us more of Caesar's time. So, he was with us for part of each day and through the night. Marybeth spent hours on the bell tower, and Hetty was never far from her shotgun. But from the ground, guarding the plantation was up to Caesar, Drake, and me. And on top of that, we had our usual farm chores, too.

There was plenty to keep us busy, and Grandma kept an eye out to see that our work satisfied Hetty Bellieu. And neither Drake nor I would dare disappoint Captain Thache.

The forest canopy was less of an obstruction since leaves had fallen, so we each took a turn under the bell, watching the land from on high. Wallace brought supplies as needed, leaving the rest of us to guard the farm. While Drake or I watched from the tower, Caesar took the other cousin with him to patrol the woods. We looked for camps and listened for strange voices, but our main target was to find sites where someone dug or shifted rocks as they searched for Edward's hidden treasure—documents connecting him to Tobias Knight or Governor Eden.

The first day passed with no signs of trouble.

On the second day, Caesar rowed to Tobias Knight to see if there was news of Charles Vane, and when he returned, he beckoned Drake and me to follow as he carried his word to Mrs. Thache and Hetty.

"Quincey Underwood has been complaining to Knight. He says a shipment meant for Moseley's townhouse never made it there. Part of it was yards of crepe meant for draperies, and he claims there was also a fancy silver cup in the shipment that never made it to Bath."

While Hetty and Marybeth questioned Caesar about the report, Oma directed us to the goat shed, where we could whisper privately about this news.

"It's beginning to make sense now," she said.

"You said the silver cup was part of the records, but we haven't heard anything about it around town before now," I said.

"Exactly," Drake said, "If Moseley had a cup other than the one he took from Crow, why not complain about it being missing before today? How does this make sense?"

Oma peeked out the shed door to be sure no one else could hear. "Here's what I know about the cup from the records," she said. "After Captain Thache meets his end, there is a trial, and of course, the Captain isn't there to defend himself. The claim is that the Captain stole the cup from William Bell, and they use that as evidence to prove Edward was guilty of inland robbery—a crime not subject to the ruling by the Admiralty Council. If Tobias Knight knew of that crime and did nothing about it, that proves they worked together."

"But we heard the word folks spread about the robbery. As I recall, the bandits robbed Bell of cloth, brandy, and money. No one said anything about a cup," I said.

Grandma nodded. "Underwood took Edward's cup from Crow and gave it to Israel Hands. I reckon he means for Israel Hands to put it where it can be evidence of guilt."

"Oh, I get it," I said. "Moseley claims the shipment of cloth also had a cup in it, which gives Bell a reason to believe the cup was part of the robbery."

Drake picked up the thought. "Edward won't be alive for the trial, and he isn't here right now, so he has no chance to defend himself. Most of the town has heard he's meeting with Charles Vane. So, it's the perfect time to start more rumors against him."

"But I thought Bell claimed other men were the robbers," I said. "He has never claimed it was Captain Thache."

"Moseley and his minions are crafty, for sure," Oma said. "By the time of the trial, Eden's enemies will convince Bell that Blackbeard was the robber, just as they'll convince him he had a silver cup along with the cloth on his boat. Moseley has seen the cup, so he can plant a detailed description in Bell's head."

"Edward should know this," Drake said. "He needs to get that cup away from Israel Hands."

"Well, there's nothing we can do about that till he returns," Oma said. "And since those lies are part of the historical record, perhaps we shouldn't tell him."

Drake's face went dark, and his fingers twitched to do something about that cup. Once Grandma left us, I cautioned him. "What you're thinking is too dangerous, and you heard Oma. It's not our place to warn him."

He turned to me, red-faced and ready for action. "Don't you think this is a good enough reason?" he asked.

"Oma calls the shots. She says we shouldn't tell him," I replied.

Drake shook his head. "OK then. You're the captain; she's the mastermind. So have it your way."

"Look, Drake," I said, "Even if Oma is wrong, we should listen to her. She knows more than we do about time-travel traps."

Drake said he wouldn't tell Thache, but I knew him better than anyone. He wouldn't give up so easily. Oma and I may have stopped him from commuting, but I couldn't keep him from plotting a way to get to Ocracoke.

But then, on the third day, something else happened. Caesar and I found signs of a camp and several dig sites.

"Houston's trackers," Caesar said, pointing to skinned bark on several trees near the fishbone camp.

Caesar shushed me, then whispered, "Can you climb that tree?"

The tall pine was about ten feet from the camp and had only a few low limbs. While I didn't relish grappling with pine resin, I could shinny up the trunk. So, I nodded yes, and he pointed upward, telling me to climb.

The tree was sturdy, so I had no trouble reaching a high point without disturbing the canopy. From there, I peered through the needles and soon found the trackers. One was busy going through a dirt pile, looking for signs of paper treasure, and the other perched on a tree branch, nearly hidden in the brown leaves that still clung to the oak.

They wore wool hats, and their black hair hung long and straight. Then the man on the ground turned to hold the object he found to the sun, and my eyes popped. His face was painted. One eye was white, one black—Tuscarora eyepatch paint.

Nearly bursting to shout, I looked down at Caesar. But even if I whispered, the forest breezes might carry my words to the trackers. So I bent my face so Caesar could see me clearly as I mouthed one word, *Tuscarora.*

Caesar planted himself at the foot of the tree, musket ready to fire. Then he circled a fist, signaling me to call for the bell.

I shouted at the top of my lungs so Drake could hear me. "Indians! Sound the bell!"

The man in the oak turned, and I was face-to-face with the other tracker. He let out a war whoop as he spotted me, and Caesar stood guard as I shinnied and dropped from the tree. He raised his musket, fired into the air, and swapped the empty gun for his pistol. Then I grabbed the musket and led the way to the house as he walked behind me backward, his pistol to the enemy.

The bell clanged, and Marybeth wailed as we ran for home. Oma met us on the porch, and Hetty stood guard as I rushed inside and bolted the front door. Then with both doors closed and barred, we all ran to the tower. Hetty aimed her gun toward the landing, and Caesar watched the forest while Oma stood ready to reload for them. Drake faced south, leaving me the north wall. Marybeth stood under the bell, clanging it constantly as she wept.

Within half an hour, Tobias Knight's men responded to the alarm. When Caesar joined those men to explain what we saw, Hetty wrenched Marybeth's hand from the bell rope. Then, she and Oma helped Mary to her room and settled her with reassurances and a cup of tea.

Drake and I were left alone to watch the grounds from the tower. And when all remained still, he turned to me, saying, "Do I have a good enough reason now?"

I shook my head no.

But later, when Marybeth held her tummy, moaning with cramps, and Caesar rowed across the creek for help, Oma left Hetty's side and paused beside us in the parlor.

"The baby might be in danger," she said before running to the kitchen.

Drake's lips were white and thin as he turned to me.

"How about now?" he asked.

I slumped into Thache's chair, shoulders trembling. Then, with a deep sigh, I shook my head.

"Do you still say no?" Drake asked.

"I don't know," I replied.

Drake kept silent till Oma returned to Marybeth's room. Then he turned to me with that determined look that meant I couldn't change his mind.

"I'm going," he said. "Thache won't forgive us if anything happens to the baby and he isn't here with his wife."

"You know I can't go with you," I replied.

Drake nodded. Then he said, "Being Captain is rotten sometimes, isn't it? Sometimes the Captain must give the fun jobs to the underlings."

I nodded.

Then Drake added, "But being the underling is worse. You get the rotten deal more often, I think. But you can help me make a safe plan."

While Tobias Knight's men followed Caesar to the dig site, Ody and I said we'd watch the landing. And there, we worked out what to do.

58 A Reasonable Plan

Ody Saunters

"I'm your captain," I said. "I shouldn't let you go without me."

"The genes say otherwise," Drake replied. "That lock of hair doesn't work for you."

"But I could commute to you once you're there," I said. "You'd be safer with me."

"How is that safer?" Drake asked. "We'd both be in danger, and fewer people would be here on Plum Point." He put his hand on my shoulder. "It has to be me, Ody. You know that."

I tried to talk him out of it but got nowhere. Drake clammed up on the boardwalk's edge, chewing on a grass reed with his back to me. I couldn't risk him going without us at least discussing it, but I had to be careful.

"If you did go to Ocracoke … and I said *if* … we'd need a plan for a commute that's short and as safe as possible."

He tossed the reed to the ground and turned his head toward me. "That makes sense."

"We have information to work with; after all, we slept at the camp the night *Rose Emelye* burned. And we know the Captain's habits here on Plum Point. So, we could use what we know to pick the safest time to go. *If* you go."

"Aye," he said, with much respect as when he spoke to Thache.

We spent a few moments reviewing how the shift bells worked in Ocracoke. An officer set the ship's close to noon, when the sun was highest, and the rest of the day matched that time. Shifts changed at 4:00, 8:00, and 12:00, and eight bells rang as a signal. Then from one to seven bells chimed every half hour till the following shift change."

"A commute by Edward's beard would take you directly to him. So, you'd have to go when he's likely to be asleep," I said.

Drake nodded, adding, "And it might be good to arrive or move between bells since they may wake sleeping sailors."

Then we reviewed the night after the *Rose* burned. He slept the night shift that night, 8:00 till midnight. But his habits at Plum Point were to have dinner around six and storytelling after that, and he was in bed no later than ten and often up at dawn. We concluded our best time to find Thache asleep was between ten and midnight; that was our best commute target.

"It might not be the same every night at the camp," I warned.

"No, but we're looking for the best chance, not the perfect chance, right?"

"I guess. But we're just talking, aren't we? We've made no decision."

Drake's smile fell, but he finally echoed, "Right."

"Other crewmen will be stirring," I said. "They'll have guards up around the clock. And we have no idea what habits Vane follows."

Drake nodded, "But if I teleport to the Captain, and he's in his tent, no one will see me."

"Vane might be there. They might parley at any hour." I replied.

"Best. Not perfect," Drake reminded me.

So, then we considered the worst case. Vane and the Captain might parley anytime, or what if they were playing cards or dice in the wee hours?

I put that question to Drake. "What would you do if you commute and appear right in front of Charles Vane?"

"I'd have to do some fast talking, I guess. But I'm pretty good at that. You've said so."

"Yes, you are. But it's never meant your life before. This time it might."

"But I'll be with Captain Thache. He won't hurt me. He'll want to know what I have to say."

That answer wasn't perfect, either, but it was reasonable. So, I moved to the next matter. What should Drake accomplish, and how could it be done quickly?

Drake thought for a minute.

"The most important thing is to tell the Captain that Marybeth and the baby are in trouble. But if he finds that out, he might sail straight home."

"He might," I replied, "but probably not with Charles Vane there. He'll need Vane's news; he'll send Asjen Neuvo to check on her, and he'll expect you to leave then, too. So, what else must you do before you return home?"

"I'll tell the Captain we found trackers on the farm, and they look like Tuscarora braves," Drake said.

"But maybe they are just men working with Edward Moseley," I replied. "Anyone can paint their face.'

"I'll tell him that, then. If they are Indians and there aren't more than two, surely Bath can handle that."

"Ok, tell him and let him decide what to do. Anything else?" I asked.

"I want to find the Captain's silver cup and get it out of Israel Hands' clutches."

"Grandma said not to mess with the cup."

Drake nodded. "You're right. She did. OK. I'll leave the cup."

"Good. We're agreed. Two objectives. Get them done, and head for home. Don't dally. Do you promise?" I asked.

Drake's grin spread. "So, you're agreeing?"

I knitted my brows and spoke distinctly. "Do. You. Promise?"

Drake's nod was almost a blur. "I can promise. I mean … I absolutely promise."

"You have your pendant, right?" Ody asked.

"Yes, I can teleport to Grandma. But we need to get my pendant from her. If she finds me missing, she may try to come for me, and she won't be safe on an island full of pirates."

"Oma might surprise you, but I get what you mean. I'll do it. Do you need food or water?"

"Naa, there's plenty of food on the island; I'll be fine."

"Other clothes then. Wear those things Jonah left. You'll blend in better if someone should see you."

"Good plan," Drake said, beaming. And he ran to Caesar's shed to find Jonah's pants, shirt, and hat.

At 10:30, we headed for the landing, as that seemed a fitting place to launch our mission. Fifteen minutes later, Drake was ready to go.

"It's nearly 10:45. Between five and six bells as planned," he said.

"Aye," I replied. But I was nervous, too. "This feels wrong. Maybe you shouldn't go."

"Fortune favors the brave. Isn't that a saying?" he asked.

"Yeah, there's one about fools rushing in, too," I replied.

Drake grinned. He was going whether I approved or not. But his eyes twinkled as he landed a last jab. "Without me here, you'd better learn to think on your feet." Then he clenched the fist holding Thache's whiskers and vanished without another word.

The breeze of his transport blew my hat away, and as I fished it from the water's edge, I wondered what *my* plan should be. Until he returned, I had to carry on at Plum Point as if Drake weren't missing. How could I explain where he was?

Maybe I could think on my feet enough to avoid the question.

Act Four: Batten Down the Hatches

Drake and Ody Saunters

59 To Ocracoke

Drake Saunters

I chuckled, thinking of Ody staring after me as I vanished without a word. Yet twisting to look over my shoulder was not the best pose for a landing.

When my feet materialized on sloped ground, I tipped forward, and crockery rattled as I bumped against Thache's bedside table. So, I settled the saucers and prayed the Captain wouldn't wake as I recovered from the commute. Luckily, he grunted, rolled toward the tent wall, and snored again.

After I stowed the beard-ribbon in my vest pocket, I had only minutes to decide what to do next. People might rouse when six bells sounded at 11:00 PM, and I should be somewhere safe when that happened. Maybe I should stay here. Only Captain Thache and I were in his tent, and we could speak privately about Marybeth. Did I dare wake him?

No. The Captain might be grumpy, and I had time to wait.

In Blackbeard's camp, the ship's bell sounded eight times to announce a shift of four hours, with bells ringing on the half hour. I arrived between five and six bells, so his cabin was safe for me until the shift changed again at midnight. That left me an hour to look around with time to spare to tell the Captain about Marybeth.

I peeked around the tent flap. No one moved, but muffled snores and lapping waves mingled with the whine of a distant fiddle amid laughter and raucous singing.

The music-makers were crewmen relaxing from duty, but others would be sharp-eyed at lookout spots. So, I pulled Jonah's headscarf over my eyebrows and grabbed a water bucket beside the tent door. Then, if anyone stopped me, I could say I was off to the well for Cap'n Thache.

Thache's camp lay on the beaches of a narrow cove. Unlike the Captain's tent, most others had only a top covering with no flaps for privacy for the eight bedrolls inside. Half the beds were empty, and crewmen sprawled on the others. Some snorted, others snored, and a few snuggled beside a rum bottle.

I should move before the next bell woke them, and the officer's tent was handy. The Captain had pointed it out to me the night we burned *Rose.* When I peeked in, the leather-strapped seabag of Israel Hands confirmed he shared those quarters. And since Thache recently finished a shift, it made sense that Hands would be up to watch over the next. But he'd soon return if the first mate's shift ended at midnight.

Here was my chance to search Hands' belongings and find the Captain's cup. And if I were lucky enough to recover it, I could give it to the Captain and explain the trouble it might bring. Regardless of what Ody said, I had time, and I wanted to give it a try.

So, I took my chance. I dropped the water bucket outside the mate's tent and quickly slipped inside. But it wasn't empty. Someone else prowled through Hands' things while the mate was on duty. A man in striped breeches bent over a trunk, his head deep inside, searching. He quietly pulled items from the chest, set them on the sandy floor, and then plowed for more. Instead of opening each bundle, he took stock of its shape to gauge the contents, and then he shook it, listening before discarding that one and trying again.

Surely Hands didn't leave his coins in a chest in his tent.

When six bells sounded, the man paused a few seconds, and his ear braids twirled as he turned to listen for footsteps, light glinted off his gold tooth. It was The Crow. He knew the camp, too. Those who slept in the mate's tent were on duty for another hour. He had time to look, but I did not.

Then, he found something wrapped in a headscarf. It jingled like silver as he removed the binding, and he cackled when he saw what he had.

The Crow had found Thache's wager cup. I couldn't let him take it.

He gathered the cup, wrapped it hastily, and dropped the bundle beside the chest. Then he began to replace the items he had examined.

"Do you need more time before Hands comes after you, Crow?" I asked.

He whirled, grabbed the bound cup, and scrambled to run. I tripped him on his way, and he dropped the bundle but kicked at me as he reached to recover it and crawl out the door. But I grabbed him from behind and pulled him down on top of me. Then I slid from under him and pinned him with an arm across his chest while I reached for the cup with the other.

He wound up a fist and socked me in the jaw. When I reeled back, he was up again, and this time he made it through the canvas flap but tripped over a tent stake. I grabbed the water bucket, slung it around, and popped him in the head. This time he stayed down long enough for me to snatch the cup.

But when I turned, a long arm pulled The Crow to his feet.

"So, who's this interferin' with me sleep? And why the blazes are you wrestlin' around outside me tent?"

It was Blackbeard, groggy but ready to blow.

"Speak up and be quick about it. What's going on here?"

"Captain," I said, eyes to the ground. I held out the bundle. "This is yours, Sir."

"Drake?" he asked. He took the cup, then pushed The Crow into his tent and jerked an arm, motioning me in.

"How and why are you here?" he asked.

"I'm here with news, Sir," I said. "But I ran across The Crow rifling through Hands' chest. I wanted to return your cup, Captain."

Thache motioned to a crewman who peered into his tent. "Take this sneak thief," he said. "Restrain him till I figure out what to do with him."

"Aye, Sir," the crewman replied, and he grabbed The Crow by both elbows and pushed him till he stumbled forward on the path the crewman chose.

Thache poured water into his rum cup and swirled it in his mouth. Then he sat on the edge of his hammock and asked, "What's this all about?"

"There's talk of this cup in Bath town, Sir. Quincy Underwood complained that it was Moseley's—stolen along with cloth from William Bell."

His first sounds were more grumbles than words, but then he roared, "What's Moseley up to now? Why is he claiming this cup is his, and what does Bell have to do with it?"

"Sir, they're reviving the rumor that you are the one who stole this from William Bell."

"By Neptune and Davy Jones, why would I steal my own cup from someone who never had it?"

"It's a story told by Edward Moseley's men, and they've been using The Crow and Israel Hands to bring it to life."

"And what does Crow get out of this?" he asked.

"He'll get silver, for sure, and I reckon Moseley will use his sway to keep him out of trouble for thieving, too."

"And Israel Hands?"

"Well, he might get a pass from his own troubles, plus he's after a ship."

"I see. Well, 'tis time I dealt with the snakes in my den. Fetch me water, boy. You know where the well is. I'll pull on my boots, and we'll see what's what."

"Aye, Sir," I replied. Then I grabbed the bucket and headed for the well, a little less worried about being seen now that the Captain knew I was on the island. After all, only three people in camp knew me well, and one of them was under guard. Besides, two crews mixed on the island, and Vane's men didn't likely know all Thache's. So, I'd be harder to peg as a stranger.

Most of the crewmen I passed on the path paid me no mind. They were too busy laughing at each other and giving the occasional shove to the shoulder as they staggered along the way. But then, I tried to squeeze by a pair of mates, each at least half a head taller than I. The older of the two bumped into my pail and decided poking fun of me might be a good game.

I tried stepping off the path and hurrying past the two men, but that didn't work.

"Well, look ye here, Davis," he said as he grabbed my shoulder and spun me around. "Do 'e reckon this half-a-man rides the waves with Blackbeard?"

"I couldna say, Riles," the mate replied. "But if e's the Cap'n's boy, he must be on the wrong side of 'im. Look at that black jaw." Then he turned to grin at his friend. "Do 'e reckon Blackbeard leaves black marks when he strikes a blow? I've heard worse about Ed Thache."

Riles found his friend's joke funny, but I figured I'd get into less trouble if I didn't laugh with them. As it turned out, they didn't care for my silence, either.

"What's the matter, minnow? Did Cap'n Thache wallop 'e? Come wid us. We'll show ye how to give him a fight," Riles said.

Davis' eyes glistened at the thought of a bit of fun. "Aye. Ye'll need to fight better than that if ye wanna be a freebooter."

My insides froze, and my head nearly did, too. My jaw still ached when I wiggled it, and I wanted no more punches. But how could I get away from these two?

I could commute somewhere, but what would they say if I vanished? Besides, I couldn't travel to Grandma with my mission unfinished, and if I returned to Edward, he'd have more questions than I could handle. So, I pulled the bucket closer and bent my head to make a smaller target.

"Another time," I said. "Cap'n Thache wants his water brought."

"Oh? So ye carry water for the Cap'n?" Davis asked. "P'raps we should press him to our crew, Riles. Maybe Cap'n Vane will take him on, and we can show 'im 'ow to take a proper beatin'."

"What's this?"

It was a new voice. And a push to my chest shoved me away from the crewmen, leaving me to face the back of a man of middle height with thighs like tree trunks and muscled arms leading to coconut-sized fists on his hips. Even though he was not as tall as the sailors, they stepped back when they saw him, and their grins faded.

"We're up to naught 'ere, Cap'n," Davis said.

Riles' words tripped over those of his buddy. "Nay, Cap'n. We're just showin' the lad where to fetch water for Cap'n Thache."

"I see. Move on widje then," he said. And when Riles and Davis followed his orders, the man turned to me. His deep-set eyes took a measure of me, and I read what I could from his face.

The eyes were steel beads, hiding under brows tilted toward his nose. And from the corners, deep lines streamed like rays arching toward his forehead—wrinkles born of frowning at the sun. There were no laugh lines, and I could not imagine this man ever being merry.

"Is Cap'n Thache awake, then?" he asked.

I nodded yes.

"Very well. I'll find Blackbeard, and you do as Thache asked. Fetch his water."

"Aye, Sir." I mustered enough courage to ask, "Sir, are you the Captain's friend? Are ye Captain Charles Vane?"

"Trust me; no one else wants that name." He studied me, waiting for more. "Do ye have something to say about that?" he asked.

I shook my head, "No, Sir. I've often heard of Charles Vane and wondered if you might be he."

He snorted as he lifted his chin. "Well, now ye have your answer, so be off."

It was a quarter of a mile to the well, and lugging a full pail on the return trip slowed me. I returned to the Captain's tent, where his voice and Vane's mingled inside. I was curious but didn't want to disturb their parley, so I set the pail down to listen.

"So, did you hear what's happened to Stede Bonnet?" Vane asked. "Pirate hunters caught him on the Cape Fear. But they were after *me*, Edward, and they're still comin'."

"Was it Hornigold?" Thache asked.

"No. It was ships sent by merchants of Charleston, and if they were after me, they're after *you*, too."

"I reckon so," Thache replied. Then after a pause. "Did they hang Stede?"

"Not yet. But soon enough, I'd say. The hunters are coming after us, Edward. So, we need safer shores."

"Stay here, then. We could use more good men."

"Do you think you're safe here?" Vane asked.

In the silhouette of candlelight, I saw Edward shake his mane. "I cannot say that. Even Governor Eden is not safe. They're trying to link him to me, putting a target on my back. See this cup? I've got men trying to set me up for stealing my own cup."

"Who's against you, Edward?" Vane asked.

"Edward Moseley, for one. He's joined with the Virginia governor and wants to get rid of the one here. They mean to claim Eden's in with pirates and use me to do it. They're using my men against me, too."

"You have traitors, then. How will you deal with them, Edward?" Vane asked. "Ye know you have to root 'em out. Ye can't sail knowin' there are rats aboard your ship."

Thache growled. "I'm workin' on that."

Vane pounded his fist on the table. "Get rid of them rats and join with me, Edward. Let's take Nassau back. Then we'll have our pirate republic again. I'll try it alone, but we're better together, and you know it."

Thache nodded. "I'll think on it, but I have irons in the fire here, and I reckon I'll have to figure out what to do about them first."

Vane laughed, "More irons than scrappin' *Queen Anne*?" But when Thache didn't laugh with him, he added, "I heard you married."

"I did," Edward spoke, and his voice lightened as he thought of his wife.

"I reckon she's a beauty. I meant to marry, too. But my woman's back in Nassau."

"Is that why you want to take it back?"

"'Tis part of it. Is a woman your reason to stay here?" Vane asked.

Thache hung his head toward his hands but lifted it, looking into Vane's face as he replied. "She gives me what I lost long ago. She's the treasure I've searched for without knowing what it was."

"Then, I reckon she'll come with you, Edward. There's room in Nassau for her."

"Aye, but I'm not sure she has the heart for Nassau," Thache replied.

Eight bells sounded; the first shift had ended, and the middle hours began. Men would be moving to their stations, and the men who walked past next would see me lurking outside the Captain's tent, so I lifted the pail and made a scene of dragging it inside.

Edward saw me stumbling by his tent flap. "Ah, the water, at last. What took you so long, boy?"

"There was a bit of bother, Sir, but here it is."

"So, was it you lurking by the tent?" Vane asked, half rising from his seat. "I thought someone was out there. Spyin' were you?"

"Not spyin', Sir. I lingered but a minute so as not to interrupt your parley. Captain Thache doesn't like me to interfere with his business."

Thache waved Vane back to his chair. "'Tis no worry, lad. But head on over to the cook's tent. He'll feed 'e. Captain Vane and I will finish here shortly."

"Aye, aye, Sir."

Israel Hands would be back in his tent soon. So, I stuck to the tree line, staying out of sight as best I could. There was a small lookout camp on the rise behind Hand's tent where men gambled as they took turns watching for ships on the sound. Tents were scattered along a beach bending right from the cove, probably Vane's camp.

Adventure, cleaned and guns ready, was moored beyond the open end of the cove, guarding the slough, and on the south bank, *Ranger* stood tall, but except for guards, that station was empty in those wee hours of midnight till 4 AM, as there wasn't light to work on repairs.

Past *Adventure*, I followed the path to the cooking tent where men grabbed corncakes and fish chowder. I was uneasy about mixing with hardened sailors, so I took my food and returned to the trees. From there, I watched the men gather around small fires to rouse each other with tall tales and bawdy songs.

Some had a work shift next, but the ones who would be off duty drank freely. There was no shortage of rum at those tables.

When two bells sounded at 1:00 AM, Thache and Vane joined the group and fell in with the party. The only difference was that the men, wild as they were, feared the two captains. So, they tempered their unruly behavior till they saw that neither Vane nor Blackbeard was bothered by it. In this man's banyan, no one cared about polite manners, and unless the Captain chose to do it, no one took the edge off rowdy.

But then Captain Thache moved to the mess table, and when the cook pointed toward me, Edward came to find me.

"You don't like our banyan, boy?" he asked, sitting beside me on the sand.

"They're having a good time, Sir," I replied.

"Aye. For the miserable way they live, they deserve it."

Then he clasped his hands, rested forearms to knees, and whispered, "For some, the party's about over. 'Tis time to get rid of a few rats."

I looked up, shocked. "Sir?" I asked, hoping I wasn't one of the rats.

"'Tis as must be. Sleep in my tent. No one will bother you there. I'll see you at the next shift."

I had till eight bells rang for the morning watch at 4 AM. I followed the Captain's instructions, but sleep didn't come quickly. I heard three and four bells but didn't notice again till seven bells sounded, rousing me. Thache would soon return. So, I washed my face, ran my fingers through my hair, and straightened Jonah's clothes over my legs and arms.

Then, with time to kill, I sneaked around for another snack. And there in the mess tent was Olwyn Finch, with two baskets of fresh eggs and four crocks of potted venison for the crew.

"How long have you been here?" I asked.

"Not long," he said. "We caught a few winks before unloading. I didn't know you'd be here, though."

"Right. I had news for the Captain."

"Well, if you finished with your news, you can ride back with the crew and me if you like."

"Thanks, I'll catch up with you on that. There's more to pass between the Captain and me," I said.

Olwyn nodded, "I have messages for him, too." Then he pointed across the camp. "Ah, there he is, now."

Olwyn started for the Captain, and when eight bells sounded, they were still talking, so I went back to the Captain's tent to wait. And it was a good thing I did. I no sooner closed the tent flap than Ody teleported to me.

"What are you doing here?" I asked. "Didn't we agree that you shouldn't come?"

"Oma found out you were gone, and she wants you back right now."

"Home?" I asked.

"Well, Bath," he replied.

"I can't go yet. I haven't told Thache about the Indians."

"Well, get on with it. We've got to get out of here."

"I'll tell him as soon as he finishes with the rats," I replied.

"Rats?"

"Yeah, I don't know either. We'll see."

60 Rats

Drake Saunters

Ody flinched as he heard men approach Blackbeard's tent, but there was nowhere to hide.

"The time is right, don't you think so, Thache?"

Ody jerked his head toward me, mouthing, *"Who is that?"*

I vice-gripped his elbow and moved inches from him.

"That's Charles Vane," I whispered.

He stiffened and plopped down, gripping the cane bottom of his chair.

I wanted to tell him not to worry, but if there was ever a time for fretting, this was it.

Then Thache flung back his tent flap, and the two captains strode in—Thache bending to keep from knocking his tent over and Vane, wide-eyed at the sight of Ody and me.

"What's this all about?" Vane asked.

"Ody? Where did you come from?" Thache asked.

"I … err …"

I shoved Ody to rescue him. "Wake up, Ody." Then I turned to the Captain. "He came with Olwyn Finch, same as me. He's been napping with Olwyn's crew."

Ody followed my lead. "Yes. That's it."

"So, do you boys have news for me?" Thache asked. "Something besides that rubbish about my cup?"

Ody nodded.

"Yes, Sir," I replied.

"Did these boys know about Hands and his treachery?" Vane asked.

"Aye. Besides what I heard from The Crow, they told me most of it."

"And he's locked up now?" Vane asked.

"'Twas my orders," Thache replied.

"Good. Then between the rats and these lads, we can settle this matter. 'Tis time for an officers' parley."

"Very well," Thache replied. "I'll set the room, and you bring the rats."

Vane nodded and left the tent.

Thache turned to Ody. "I've seen you shoot, lad. Can you load a gun as well as your grandmother?" he asked.

"Aye, Sir. She taught me how."

Thache brought two small pistols from his belongings. "They're clean, but I want you to load 'em. Can you do what I ask with no mistakes?" he asked.

"Aye, Sir. As you order."

"Very well. Drake, round up more seats and one more table. You can get them from Hands' tent. He won't miss 'em."

Thache supervised as Ody loaded, and I brought an extra chair and two kegs to serve as stools. As I was in and out, carrying seats, Ody and the Captain whispered about how he wanted the loading done. Finally, on my last trip, the Captain holstered the pistols into the belts hanging across his chest.

Thache arranged the two square tables to make one twice as long. He sat three chairs to face the back of the tent, two toward the door. The Captain pointed to the end seats for Ody and me. Soon Charles Vane, armed with two pistols, returned with three men: Israel Hands, The Crow, and a man wearing a calico shirt.

Four bells had sounded. It was 6:00 AM, but the sun was not yet up that late in October. So Thache set a lantern on the side near the door.

"Where do you want these two, Captain?" Vane asked. Thache pointed to the long side opposite his lantern.

"The boys will take the ends, and you and Rackham sit by me," Thache said. "Does everyone know Jack Rackham?" he asked.

Besides Ody and me, everyone did.

"Calico Jack Rackham, First Mate of the Ranger, meet two lads who have been a great help to me at home, Ody and Drake Saunters."

Rackham took a seat. Edward closed the tent flap, losing the feeble pre-dawn light, so he moved his lantern to the middle of the table.

"So, we're ready?" Vane asked.

"Aye," Thache replied.

"What's going on here?" The Crow asked.

"'Tis a trial, gentlemen," Vane replied.

Israel Hands stood at his seat and slapped his fists to the table. "A trial?" he asked. "About what? And am I here as judge or jury?"

"You're here as a man accused, Hands," Thache replied.

"But I'm your first mate, Edward. You should trust me above all others."

"In the past, it has been so," Thache replied, "but it seems you are finagling your way to take my ship, Israel. You've been talking against me to the men to get their vote. I saw that in the islands and on the way home, too."

"But that's our way," Hands replied. "The men are entitled to choose a new captain if they want. So they voted, and you won fair and square, Edward."

"I did. But you kept playing the basilisk, Hands. You were plotting even when we were on the high seas and came upon the *Rose Emelye*. And from what I've seen in Bath, you are still at it, aren't you?"

"What do you mean?" Hands replied. "And why are these boys here?"

"They are witnesses, I believe," Vane replied. "Now sit down."

"You can't bring these boys as witnesses against me? What do they know about our business?" he asked.

But Vane pushed him to his chair. "Sit."

"We will start with The Crow. When I caught this man robbing my house, he said he was after a document signed by Tobias Knight and me. He wanted proof I was guilty of pirating and that Tobias Knight was in on it. He was after that paper because you asked him to get it, Hands."

"You can't believe that, and surely not on the word of this Crow. I signed that contract the same as you, Edward. Why would I turn that over to anyone else? If I prove you a pirate, I'm proven one, too. What good would it do me? My neck would stretch as tight as yours."

"Coleman. You gave me that answer in my house, and these boys heard you. Tell us how you answered that question."

"I … err," he stammered.

Vane laid a pistol on the table. "You what?" he asked.

When The Crow didn't reply, he set the other gun beside his first, tapping the fingers of both hands near the triggers.

"I … I said Hands wanted that document to turn over to Edward Moseley, so he could prove Thache guilty and shed doubt on the honesty of Tobias Knight and Governor Eden."

"Why would I do that?" Hands screamed, raging as he faced Adler.

The Crow stammered, "Because Moseley promised he'd help you get a ship and keep you out of trouble once he had control of the governor." Then he stood, reaching out to the captains. "He said that. He did."

Hands pounded the table. "Who's to say Adler didn't make all that up? He impersonated you, Edward. He and some farmer pirates robbed William Bell, hoping you'd be thought guilty of it. How can you trust an underhanded skunk like that against me? What other proof do you have?"

Edward turned to me and then Ody. "Boys, do you have proof of who is telling the truth here?" he asked.

"Well, we found your silver cup in Hands' things," I said. "Crow was looking for it, too. They wanted to set you up as a robber with that."

Ody nodded. "And when I patrolled the woods in Plum Point, Caesar and I heard The Crow and Hands plotting for Moseley's trackers to search on Plum Point for that contract. Hands passed silver to The Crow, and I reckon he used it to come here."

"Caesar heard this?" Thache asked.

Ody nodded, "Aye, he's a witness, and there's more. After you left to meet Vane, Caesar and I spotted the two trackers. Drake sounded the alarm, and Tobias Knight's men came to investigate. The last I heard, they had not caught the men, but they saw signs of them digging on Plum Point."

Thache stood, enraged. "Why didn't I know about this?" he asked. "You put my wife in danger! I should strangle you with my bare hands."

"That's not the worst of it, Captain," I said. "Ody saw them; they wore Tuscarora eyepatch paint."

"My poor wife," Thache screamed. "You'll not have my ship, nor my trust, not ever again. I'm done with you, Hands."

Vane nodded. "You're right, Edward. 'Tis time to get rid of the rats." Then he stood, took a gun in each hand, and turned to Jack Rackham, saying, "You know how I feel about mutiny, don't you, Jack?"

I thought he'd drop Jack Rackham with one gun and Hands with the other. So, I twisted toward Edward, saying, "Don't let this happen. It's not who you are, Captain Thache. What would your wife say if you killed someone in cold blood?"

He growled at me, and I leaned back, petrified.

"He's right, Edward," Vane said. "You don't have murder in you, but 'tis no bother for me. Besides, if you don't kill one of them every once in a while, they won't remember who you are."

Edward took a deep breath and raised his guns above the table. "Oh, I have murder in me—especially to anyone bringing harm to my wife," he said, scowling. "Sit down, Vane. This is my rat."

The Captain put his guns under the table and crossed his hands. Then, after glancing at Vane, he glowered at the two men across the table and blew out the lantern.

One gun fired, and the blood-curdling screams of Israel Hands drowned out the blast.

Ody, forgetting the other gun, jumped up and ran to Hands. "He's bleeding, but his leg is still there. Ody grabbed a blanket and tied it around Hands' knee."

"Argh," Thache spat. "We can't watch him bleed out. Go for Asjen Neuvo. He's bunking on *Adventure.*"

I started to run for help, but Thache stopped me. "Wait. You said you had more to tell me."

"Oh, yes, Sir. 'Twas about your wife."

I didn't want to tell him Mary was having trouble with the baby—not when I'd be the messenger in front of his loaded gun.

"Well. What is it, boy?"

Ody stepped between us. "She's fine, Sir. She was upset about the Indian rumor, but she's over that now. But she wants you home soon."

I stared at Ody with eyes like saucers as I prayed he was telling the truth.

He nodded, saying, "It's true, Sir."

Then he ran for Asjen Neuvo, and I alerted Olwyn to prepare to sail. Soon Asjen slowed the bleeding. And when Hands had a proper bandage, we loaded him and Asjen on Olwyn's boat to head for better medicine in Bath.

But Ody and I didn't wait for Olwyn to leave. Instead, my cousin pulled me into the trees and tapped Grandma's pendant. But before we commuted to Grandma, I asked, "Are we going to be in trouble for lying?"

"Oh, for Pete's sake, Drake, tell me one person in Bath who isn't lying?"

I nodded, and we vanished to Plum Point—me first, with Ody right behind me.

61 The Prodigals Return

Aurora Saunters

If willing a thing could make it happen, my grandsons would have been beside me on Plum Point Landing. But the pink glow on the creek had faded to blue, and I still sat at the summer house fiddling with Ody's hair pendant. Had it been an hour—or two—since I watched Ody commute to his cousin? I couldn't risk waiting any longer.

But then, just as I decided to go to Ocracoke after them, Drake and Ody appeared, nearly knocking me off the summer house railing.

"Oma! Have you been waiting out here since I left?" Ody asked.

I grabbed them both in my arms and held them tight. "Thank goodness. Now I don't have to choose between a pirate banyan or going home without you."

"Ah, you have more faith in us than that, don't you, Grandma?" Drake asked.

I pushed him back to be sure he was all right. *But what was the blood on Drake's shirt?* And Ody had spatters from *chest to thighs*.

"Are you hurt?"

I grabbed Ody's shoulders. "What have you been up to?" Then I spun Drake around, gasping as I asked, "Whose blood is that?"

"Oh," Ody said, looking at his clothes. "I forgot about the blood."

"And …?" I asked, impatient for a straight answer.

Drake looked up and down the creek before whispering, "Israel Hands. It's his blood."

"He's shot," Ody said. "But don't worry, he isn't dead."

My heart raced, and I put my hands to my head, asking, "Did you shoot him?"

Both scrambled to reply with a chorus of, "No, not us."

Ody answered my question before I asked it. "Captain Thache shot him."

Drake added, “But I don’t know how he’s still breathing. It was at point-blank range, and Ody loaded the gun.”

“What?” I gasped. “Were you that close to him?”

“He was breathing because I loaded his guns by the Captain’s instruction—one with a musket ball and one with no more than powder.”

Drake wagged a finger in the air. “Oh, that explains it. That’s why he crossed his hands before he blew out the lantern.”

Ody nodded. “He knew which gun was which, and Charles Vane was right about one thing, the Captain is no murderer.”

My head was spinning. “Charles Vane was there?” I asked.

“Aye,” Drake said. “Vane was going to kill Israel Hands, and I believe he wanted to kill Jack Rackham, too.”

“You were with Calico Jack Rackham? What in the world did you boys get up to?” I asked. “Ody said you’d finish your mission and come home. Was killing Israel Hands part of the plan?”

“Well, no,” Ody replied. “That was more Vane’s idea, but we saw what happened.”

“Shouldn’t you be proud of us, Grandma? We did what you wanted,” Drake said.

“In what universe was this what I wanted?” I asked, aghast at my grandson’s notion.

He smiled as if the answer were obvious. “We survived outside our time without anyone guessing our secret.” Then with a slap to Ody’s shoulder, he added, “And we did it together. We thought on our feet.”

I threw up my hands, “OK, fine … for now. But where is Israel Hands?”

“He’s coming on the boat with Olwyn. Asjen Nuevo is with him, too. But it will be hours before they get here.”

“What a mess,” I muttered.

“It’s not such a mess, Grandma. We can wash the blood out. Or you can. You’ve done it before.”

“I’m not talking about the blood or even Israel Hands getting shot in the knee.”

“How did you know it was his knee?” Ody asked.

“That’s not the problem nor the time for it. How will we explain your returning from Ocracoke before Olwyn’s boat arrives?”

I sat down with my chin on my fists, and the boys sat on either side of me as we solved that riddle.

“No one else here knows we left,” Ody said, raising his palms. “That should simplify things.”

“True,” I said. “And Asjen will take Hands to a place with more medicines and instruments—probably to Dr. Maul if he’s at his office in town.”

"That solves it, doesn't it?" Drake asked. "Except for Olwyn, it won't be obvious to those on the boat that Ody and I shouldn't be here yet."

"Hm. I'm not sure it *solves* the problem, but it might delay suspicion for a while," I said. "Give me those bloody clothes and …."

A new voice interrupted my instructions.

"What happened here? Are you hurt?" It was Marybeth. "Why are you at the landing at this hour? Is Edward coming?"

Ody and Drake stammered for an answer, but I was thinking on my feet this time. "No, no sign of Edward yet. These silly boys wanted to try frog gigging, and they brought more harm to each other than the frogs."

"Oh, my goodness. Well, go change your clothes, and I'll soak the blood out of these," Mary said. "Mother has breakfast ready, so be quick about it."

When they looked at me for permission, I shooed them on. "Do as the lady asks; I need to think." Then the boys followed the scent of sizzling bacon, and I sat in the summer house, fitting the loose ends of lies together.

Israel Hands would rant about Edward shooting him, but between the pain and whatever medicine Neuvo found to ease it, thoughts of my grandsons would fade into a dream. What would a couple of out-of-place boys matter to him, anyway?

Tobias Knight's men were looking for Moseley's trackers, and with Hands working for Moseley, Knight would keep a lid on any lies Hands tried to spread.

Crow warned his cronies he was leaving Bath, so no one would expect to see him. But we would have to watch Moseley; he might find a new hooligan to do his dirty work.

And how much had Asjen Neuvo learned about Drake and Ody? Would he bring time wrinkles to Plum Point? We didn't expect him to visit the farm until Edward returned, so I had days to worry about handling the mysterious doctor.

Marybeth was our biggest worry. She kept more of her food down lately, but she pined for Edward. And Mrs. Thache believed in her husband despite her confusion about his loyalty to the crew. Unfortunately, only Edward could ease Mary's mind, and based on historical records, she would face heartbreak soon enough. With our current problems settled to the best of my ability, I joined everyone at breakfast, hoping it would be the last day of our wait. But three mornings later, Edward had not yet returned.

Drake and Ody stood by Marybeth on the Bride's tower each night. Mary stared toward Ocracoke with the North Star charm clasped in her fist, wondering what Edward was doing.

The boys had a good idea of what was happening, and I knew how Edward's days ended, but we couldn't tell her. We could only watch as Marybeth endured the pain of waiting.

We were time travelers, and there was more than one downside to that so-called *superpower*. For one, we couldn't speak of it. Keeping secrets was stressful to the boys and to me, too.

62 November Ice

Marybeth Thache

Even by the fire, I huddled within my shawl; November had arrived wrapped in a chilly wind. But it had been days since my husband left to meet Charles Vane, and life without Edward affected me more than cool weather; it chilled me to the core.

The household was tired of me asking when he'd return, but my husband's absence hovered over Plum Point like an icy overhang.

Mother stood beside me shaking her head. "With the way you stand vigil in the tower, 'tis no doubt you'll be the first to spot Edward's boat, so you tell us when he gets here." Her knife grated as she scraped the trenchers into the slop bucket.

We were all edgy. But my husband was among murderers, and I had a child to protect and childbirth to fear. 'Twas I who walked on the point of that sharp blade.

Aurora Saunters sat at the washbasin, and Mother passed her the trenchers asking, "Aurora, why don't you answer the girl? You know the future; tell us when he's coming home."

Widow Saunters focused on scrubbing her dish as she replied, "Because I don't know the answer." Then she raised her face, weary of Mother's accusations. "Just because you imagine I'm a seer doesn't make it so."

Mother wiped her hands on her apron and patted Aurora's shoulder. "Forgive me, friend. 'Tis probably the change of seasons that puts us on edge."

Aurora agreed. "'Tis true. I spent a winter in the north once, and massive shelves of ice cracking at the end of winter made us all fidgety."

"What's so bad about winter ending? Flowers can bloom then, right?" Drake asked.

"Aye," Aurora said, "But ice cracking at the end of a frigid winter means falling ice shelves, icicle daggers, and melting, which can bring flooding or thinner ice over the lakes."

"She's right," Hetty said, "I love the falling leaves of autumn, but I always worry about the winter ahead. Do we have enough wood or food put by?"

"But this isn't a season change," Ody said. "It's early November, mid-fall at most. What season change is that? We're barely past Halloween."

"Then, this must be the season of ghosts and ghouls," I said.

"Like that ghostship Captain Thache told us about," Drake added.

Mother hung her towel to dry, and while the boys lifted the dish basin to empty, she asked, "So do you believe in ghosts instead of seers, Aurora Saunters?"

"The Captain sure believes in ghosts," Drake said as he and Ody lugged dishwater through the porch door. "He saw the ghost of Henry Morgan twice when he was a boy."

Mother shook her head. "That sounds more like an omen than a ghost," she said.

But I wanted Aurora to answer, so I prodded her, "Tell us, true, Mis'ress Saunters. You don't believe in ghosts, do you?"

She cocked her head before replying, "I've seen things beyond my understanding." Then with a shrug, "There is more to the world than I'm privy to."

"But ghosts?" I asked again.

"I do not believe I've ever seen one," she said. "But I sometimes feel the presence of those I loved dearly—my parents, my husband."

"Do they speak to you?" Ody asked.

"Not usually," she replied. "And if I hear words, they are in my head as if I thought them myself. But on special days, I sometimes see something beautiful or unexpected."

"Like a birthday gift?" Drake asked.

"Yes, like that. Or when I'm confused, I find a sudden clue to a path forward, and I feel my loved ones are with me through the struggle."

Engrossed in what Aurora said, Mother stopped working—something far from her habit. "Do you think these are ghosts speaking to you?" she asked.

Aurora shook her head. "I don't know all the workings of this world, so I can't say it's what folks think of as ghosts. Maybe my loved ones loved me so well that I conjured their memories to comfort me. And, maybe, they were such a part of me that I remember beyond what I heard them say or saw them do. But, on the other hand, perhaps I knew them so well that their lives were a testament to all they ever would do, and that's what sustains me in hard times."

The faces of Mother and the lads were transfixed, just as I had seen them during Edward's stories. Mrs. Saunters had lifted them from the creaking floorboards of our farmhouse to the realm of spirits. I was raised, too, but work brought us back to the ground.

Mother broke from the spell first. "All right, boys, off with you. It will take Caesar and the both of you to patrol Plum Point."

Ody sighed, "Come on, Drake; we have a lot of ground to cover."

While Drake found his hat, I reminded them, "Well, at least Tobias Knight said the trackers won't bother us again, and he's sure they were only white men disguised as Tuscarora."

"Yes," Mother agreed. "That nightmare isn't at our door yet."

"No, but we don't want Edward returning to a house unprepared," I said.

So, we worked another day, and late that afternoon, while I was on the Bride's tower, clouds of good fortune sailed over the creek. Finally, the sails of *Sam Bellamy* brought Edward home.

I called out the good news, and the boys were the first to the tower.

"Hurrah!" Drake shouted. "Maybe everyone will be less nervous when he's here."

Even beaming from ear to ear, I could still speak. "Yes, what a relief. It's like the ice finally cracked. The waiting is over. Things can return to normal, at last."

Ody shifted his gaze from the sails toward me. "But don't bad things happen after the ice cracks? The floods and such?"

"It doesn't have to be bad. Sometimes it just opens the rivers to water the farms," I said.

"Well, I wouldn't worry about it, either way," Drake said. "Edward makes us step lively when his temper blows, but he's a rock star at conquering nerves. He'll calm us all down."

"A rock star?" I asked. "What's that?"

"Oh, he meant a guiding star or maybe a solid rock," Ody said.

"Well, whatever he is, I'm glad he's back," I replied.

But Edward didn't come home immediately; he first stopped to see Tobias Knight.

It was over an hour until he reached the porch, sweeping me off my feet and into his arms. I beamed as he stood with both hands on my face, his soft eyes staring into mine. But then I noticed only a hint of a smile under his furrowed brow.

"We must talk, my love," he said. "Ill winds are blowin', and we have hard choices."

And there it was. It began as a long, low, nerve-wracking screech, and it grew worse, creaking and cracking as the shelf dangled, until finally, the ponderous, frozen boulder crashed to the ground.

That was the ice cracking. And it froze me solid.

63 Winds from Four Corners

Marybeth Thache

Someone gently shook my shoulders.

"Marybeth? Did you hear me?"

My husband's voice snapped me to consciousness. "Edward," I said.

He loosened his grip and held me at arm's length. "Yes," he replied. "Did you hear what I said?"

I nodded. "Decisions. Hard choices." Then I grabbed his forearms. "What has happened?"

He pointed me to the rockers by our bedroom window and closed the door before joining me, taking my hand in his.

"I'm a hunted man, Marybeth. The pirate hunters are on their way, and 'tis just a matter of time till they come here."

"But, how? Why?"

"The merchants of Charleston are after Charles Vane, and they already captured Stede Bonnet. Nassau's new governor has set Benjamin Hornigold after Vane, too. And they don't mean to stop till they find every pirate in the Atlantic."

"But, but you're not a pirate now, Edward. Surely, they won't come for you. And wasn't Benjamin Hornigold your friend?"

"Men make choices, Mary. And some old friends are pirate hunters now. Benjamin Hornigold is one of 'em."

"But they can't come for you when the King's Pardon protects you, can they, Edward? And Eden and Tobias Knight will vouch for you, won't they?"

The corners of his eyes dropped further. "They have enemies, too, my love. And their enemies are mine now."

My tummy tightened, "So is Benjamin Hornigold on the way? Will he come to our house?"

Edward sat back, his shoulders eased, and I relaxed a little as his grip softened. "He will not come to my house, but he may come to Ocracoke, and he may not be the first one."

"What do you mean?"

"Governor Keith of Pennsylvania put out a warrant blaming me for piracies along his shores. Witnesses saw me there, and given my history, 'tis enough."

"But that had to have been in July on your trading mission for Bath. You didn't take any prizes on that voyage, did you?"

"No, but I was there, as were other freebooters, and I reckon if any are takin' prizes, they figure I'm one of 'em."

"Well, if he doesn't charge you, does that matter?" I asked.

"He names me as one he believes took the King's Pardon and then fell back to pirating ways. And he claims that when the Pardon ended on the 6th day of September, anyone caught pirating in the province should be brought in for justice. He's offering a bounty of £200. That's on the head of any who help a pirate, too."

"*Rose Emelye*," I whispered.

The name was enough for Edward to cast his eyes to the floor, sadly bobbing his head.

"But the Admiralty Council absolved you of that. So that protects you, right?"

"Aye, it does. But the pardoning date is past, and Pennsylvania wants me."

"Does Keith know where you are? Can they come for you here?"

"Some of my old mates know I'm off the Carolinas, but men from other provinces can't come for me in Eden's domain. Still, I'll stay out of Pennsylvania, for sure."

"What of Hornigold?"

"He'll try to catch me on the open sea, and if he suspects me of doing wrong, he'll have grounds to chase me. But I reckon he'll not catch me. He's a shark's mate for sure, but he's no match for me."

"This will change things for us forever, won't it?" I asked.

"But Knight had a sliver of good news, too. England is in another war with Spain."

"How can war be good news?"

"Well, it ain't war that's good. Not exactly. But England isn't alone in this war. France and other nations are on the same side. And Knight believes the kings will need more ships to help in the fight, meaning more chances to sign up as a privateer, which brings a second chance at a pardon. We don't have a signed proclamation yet, but Knight is sure it will come soon."

"But does that mean you'd have to go to war again? Please say no."

"My darling, when have I not been in a war of one kind or another?"

I touched his shoulder. "Try to find another way. No one has found you yet, Edward. You're safe for now, aren't you?" Then I remembered. Someone *had* found him. So, I asked, "Can you trust Charles Vane?"

"I believe so. Vane sees us as on the same side. But he had ninety crewmen on his ship, and I welcomed him to take a few of my men who wanted to be sea rogues again."

"And those men? Can you trust them?"

"Not totally. Not all of 'em. Vane took The Crow with him. But Coleman has good reason to fear Captain Vane, which might keep him in line."

"So, we are safe here, aren't we? What choices must we make?"

"I'll speak to Tobias Knight again, but I should get you to the safest place possible. We need to think about where that may be."

"Edward, this is my home. I can't live on a ship. What about the baby? He shouldn't be born in the middle of a war."

"My love, I cannot control the choices made by kings and where they place their pawns." He stretched his arms wide as he said, "But here is the measure of what I am—what I can offer you."

"You are my husband, strong, loving, powerful."

"Aye, and what you want of that is yours. But I also have a ship, and I knew from the first time I stood on a deck that one who masters a ship has the world at his feet."

"I know nothing of sailing, Edward. And I only know the wide world from reading and stories the sailors tell. So, I wouldn't know where to choose, and if I picked a place, I wouldn't know how to live there."

"Look at your North Star, my darlin'," he said, tapping the charm at my neck. "It's a ship's compass showing the directions of the four winds and all the corners in between. I can sail to any of them. I can offer you the world, my dear wife."

"But I only know this corner," I said, fidgeting with my necklace. "How could I choose?"

He stroked my hair, smiling. "With sickness, drought, and war, this corner has been frightening enough; we can surely find one safer. So, here's what we'll do. In the next few days, I'll tell you what lies in each direction, and we will choose together."

I touched his face. "Anywhere will do as long as I can be with you and keep our child safe. But Mother should be with us, too. I could never feel safe while my mother is in danger."

"I'd take her anywhere that pleases you, but she must choose to go."

"Yes, of course."

"So, decide where you want to go and see if your mother will come."

"And what will you do while we decide?" I asked.

"I will fit the ship to be ready for us should we sail. And now that Israel Hands is off my crew, the rest of the men will be with me. I'll choose the best and the most trustworthy to sail with us."

"Yes, Israel Hands, your first mate—the man you shot on the island. What do you know about him now?"

"Asjen is with him, and the good doctor will do his best for Hands, and watch out for my interests, too. But I reckon now that Hands won't be makin' captain, he'll find other ways to live."

"Can he bring you harm?" I asked.

"As I said, Asjen will let me know what he's up to."

"And how can I help?" I asked.

"Keep yourself healthy and strong, so you'll be prepared for travel if needs be. You'll have the babe to consider. And just in case, settle your business here."

"The house belongs to my mother, Edward. We can help her, but 'tis her job to settle her affairs."

"You're right, my love. We'll have a crew meeting soon."

He meant our crew on Plum Point and agreed that I should tell Mother about our decision first. When we opened the bedroom door, we found Mother and Aurora on the settee, clasping hands as they waited. But Mother stood as soon as we set foot in the room.

"We do not know what you were saying, but we heard the strain of it. Tell me what upsets my daughter," she said.

"Trouble may be comin' our way, good Mother," Edward said. "Marybeth knows how the winds are blowin', and I reckon you need to know too."

I squeezed Edward's arm more tightly for courage, hoping to make Mother understand our desperate situation. "Men from all corners may be coming after Edward."

Her chest rose as she asked, "So, will you be leaving us again so soon, Captain?"

My husband put his arm around me as we stepped closer to her.

"'Tis my hope it won't come to that. We have friends and some protection here, and the enemies have no right to be here. But If they come, I'll be ready to meet them on the sea or Plum Point."

"So, will you bring a battle to our home?" she asked.

"'Tis my hope to avoid a battle, but if it comes to that, my first duty is to protect my wife and family, including you, Widow Bellieu."

"I reckon you won't be able to avoid it. Aurora won't tell me so, but I can see it in her eyes. That trouble will be here, and so will I."

I put my hand on hers. "Mother, in the worst case, Edward can take us away from the danger. He says we only need to choose where. Perhaps you'd like to see Bristol again or meet Father's people in France."

She huffed as she lifted her chin. "Your father knew what he was doing when he left the old country, and I will stand by the home he built us. Daughter, you may follow your husband, but I'll be here on the Point, no matter what."

Edward nodded, but he squeezed me tighter. "We have some time, Hetty. Perhaps you will change your mind when you know more of what may come." Then he grinned, "You'll want to see the little nipper when he arrives, even if he does favor me."

Mother's eyes glistened as she left for her room. But then she turned, and her tears dried as she glared at Edward, her lips drawn tight. Then she said, "You listen to me, Blackbeard. You take care of my daughter. And her baby should be born on dry ground, not a rocking ship. I saw babies born in the black hold of a ship when Bert and I crossed the sea, and it ain't pretty. My daughter's fit for better than that."

Edward nodded, "Understood, Ma'am. Dr. Neuvo might sail with us, but I'll remember what you say."

She grunted, saying, "You do what you must, Captain Thache, and so will I." Then she slammed the door to her room, and we heard nothing more from her that night.

But since the news was out, Edward turned toward Aurora. "We may as well tell the rest of the house," he said, and soon Ody and Drake joined their grandmother on the settee, and Edward pulled two chairs closer to tell them what we had learned.

"Boys, your grandmother has already heard there might be more trouble in Bath soon. You've been a great help to us here, but it might be time for us to get you home."

Drake's eyes widened, and both boys turned to their grandmother. She patted their hands as she replied to Edward.

"You needn't worry about us, Captain. We've made our plans, and we can contact relatives anytime."

"Oh, aye," Edward replied. "Well, we've had one squall after another, haven't we, Widow Saunters? It must have been a rough stay here for your family."

Aurora smiled as she replied, "Nonsense, we have enjoyed your hospitality, Captain, and since your family still has its share of upsets, we'll help you prepare for what's coming if we can."

The Captain scratched his chin, "Well, since you can get yourselves home without too much bother, perhaps you will stay till I get the lay of what's happenin' here in Bath—or at least until my mother-in-law is speakin' to us again."

I reached for Aurora's hand. "'Twould be a comfort to have you."

"How can we help, Captain?" Drake asked.

"First thing is to keep your eyes open for trouble. Then, I'll need to talk to Tobias Knight again, and we'll stock the ship for a voyage." Then he looked toward our three guests on the settee and asked, "Can you stay another day or two?"

Aurora squeezed my hand, "Of course, Captain. We can manage that."

Edward grinned ear to ear and slapped his thighs, saying, "Then I reckon we better see if there's any stew in the pot. I don't believe Hetty will be servin' supper tonight."

So, Aurora took charge, and together we brought food to the table. Then after we cleared supper, the Saunters family and I enjoyed the air on the porch until Edward, eyes bleary from studying his charts, joined us.

"Have you found a peaceful corner of the world yet, Edward?" I asked.

He pulled his lips so far left that they nearly hid in his beard as he replied, "It won't be France for sure. That would put us in the middle of the war, and England is in it, too, so we best stay out of their shipping lanes."

"Where then?" Drake asked.

"North of here, maybe," Ody suggested.

Edward tossed his head back and forth, "Possible, I reckon. If I give Pennsylvania a wide berth."

"I wouldn't worry about it too much, Captain," Ody said. "If you must go, you'll find a corner of the globe you like. And if fate agrees, perhaps you can stay right here."

"There's a happy thought. Let's go to sleep with that on our minds." I said. And we tried to do just that.

64 A Chorus of Whispers

Aurora Saunters

After we left the porch, I closed the bedroom door and braced myself against it, searching for the best path for my family. Edward needed a plan of action, and Marybeth and Hetty had decisions to make. But what should time travelers do? I needed facts.

So, as quietly as possible, I reached into the secret pocket attached to my waist and unfolded my page of notes about Blackbeard's life, looking for facts, specific times, dates, and names.

I had remembered correctly. Edward would not be traveling to Europe or Maine, or anywhere else.

Science fiction writers spun time travel stories with various possible outcomes and unintended consequences. But did any of those storytellers get it right? What could I trust?

Vincent Peregrino was the most well-versed time travel scholar I knew. According to him, new evidence could change our *perception* of the past, but nothing—not even a time traveler—could change a historical *truth* in any significant way.

He and those in his time-travel think tank contemplated the unanswered riddles of space-time physics. And to this circle, the no-change hypothesis was more than a respected guess; it was an immutable rule as solid as any proven law of physics. But that was their opinion; it takes testing to elevate a theory to law. There were precious few ways to test time, and outside of astronauts traveling in space, none were at the level of human experience. And unless my grandsons and I did the unthinkable and broke that law, Edward Thache would die in battle on November 22, less than three weeks away.

Marybeth was a different matter. We didn't know the date of her birth or marriage, and there was only unsubstantiated evidence of her name. We didn't even know where she was at any precise moment, but there *was* a record of where she was *not*.

There was no sign of her aboard *Adventure* when Edward fought Lt. Maynard. So, unless the ladies of Plum Point found a hiding place undetectable to the Royal Navy, she and Hetty did not sail with Edward.

So, what purpose did I have here? Should I collect the boys and leave right away? What difference could it possibly make?

Drake commuting to Ocracoke with Edward's hair proved our family descended from Captain Thache. At least, that was consistent with my understanding of our family's ability. Unlike Ody's bugle, Edward's hair was not an emotionally charged object taking us to the charging event. Instead, it worked like our hair pendants, and that was proof of common genes—ancestry.

But if Edward was our ancestor, how did his line reach the Saunters family in our century?

Edward had a daughter in Jamaica, but records showed she died childless, and there were other possibilities, such as unrecorded children. But what we had witnessed in Bath—and the fact that we commuted there—added to the overwhelming likelihood that we descended from Marybeth's child.

That put us smack dab in the middle of the biggest and best-known time-travel paradox, preventing your own birth while traveling to a time before you were born. Such an event fell somewhere between bad manners and a physical impossibility, but time-travel science was in its infancy at best, and respected theories weren't yet laws.

So, did we have a path out of this mess? What should we do to keep from wreaking havoc with time?

While short of a solution, I settled on two primary principles. We should keep Baby Thache, our ancestor, alive. And, since stress is a killer, we should do our best to relieve the anxiety descending on Marybeth and her mother. If a third point existed, I hadn't found it yet. So, I took those two tenets to bed and fell asleep wrestling with how the boys and I could work toward those goals. The best idea I came up with was to follow our routine and look for opportunities to support my two objectives. It wasn't much, but I was tired.

Dawn finally came, and I started breakfast. When Hetty joined me, she had little to say, and her tired eyes showed she had not slept much either. But as usual, she directed us toward our farm chores.

Then when Caesar rowed to Knight's plantation, Edward rowed with him. The boys joined Marybeth, collecting the final remnants from the apple crop to dry in the sun.

I convinced Hetty we should air the bedding. After all, my family would leave soon, and we might as well leave her with fresh sheets.

Once we shook and spot-cleaned the linen, we had time alone in the backyard as we pinned everything to the line. The task allowed me to apply my tenets, but Hetty had an agenda, too, and she made it clear as soon as she spoke.

"I'm not going to leave this house, Aurora," she said.

"Nor *should* you," I replied. "Not unless you choose it."

"Bert and I built it."

I nodded, "You're right to follow your heart, Hetty. This place is full of memories."

"Aye. 'Tis," she replied. Her gaze drifted to those long-gone times. And when the memories spilled over as tears, she wept into her apron, only raising her head to speak between her sobs.

"But my girl will leave. The Captain will take her to some country I don't know. What will I do then?"

"Things will work out as they should. You'll be fine."

She sniffled as she asked, "Do you *know* that? Is that what you *see*?"

I ignored her *seer* probe and replied, "It's how it looks to me, yes."

She dried her eyes and threw another quilt over the line.

After that, we discussed more mundane things like ripening pumpkins and the likelihood that the weather would hold long enough to dry apples.

Edward returned as we shook wrinkles from the last blanket, and the news he brought carried hope and despair in one stroke.

"Where's Mary?" he asked as we met on the back porch. "She isn't in the woods alone, is she?"

Hetty was in no mood to speak to him, so I replied. "She's gathering apples with the boys. They should be along soon."

"I should find her. Knight had news."

Hetty spun round. "What news?"

Edward paused to peg his hat on the porch wall while we wiped nervous hands on our aprons, waiting for his reply.

"Well, here 'tis," he said. "You might want to sit down."

Hetty fired her words at Thache. "Tell it."

Edward nodded, saying, "Tobias showed me correspondence from Virginia. There's talk of another Tuscarora uprising. The letter said there are signs of a war party gathering just north of here. He's worried."

Hetty's chest rose from a series of inhales with no exhale. Finally, she asked, "So, you'll stay then? And protect Plum Point as you always promised?"

"'Tis the riddle," he replied. "I'd never want to disappoint you, Mother Bellieu, and I'll use every bone in my body to keep Mary safe. But with a lean crew and enemies coming from every side, perhaps the best way is to take her away from here. That way, I have a battle on one less front, and I'm more practiced at watching the sea than the land."

"So, have you decided then?" Hetty asked.

"No. Not yet. But I should tell Marybeth how it is."

Hetty wrung the hem of her apron, fighting not to cry again, so I tried to ease the tension. "You know, Captain, since you are undecided, perhaps it would be good to prepare for either case."

"Prepare to stay and go, too? How can I do that?" he asked.

"If you go, you'll need provisions for the ship, and whether you go or stay, Hetty needs food for the winter. So you'll be stocking up on supplies no matter your path."

"True. And *there* is our plan," he said, smacking his fist to the table. "And 'twill be diverting work for Mary. 'Tis a good idea, Widow Saunters. Whether it be a month's voyage with a crew of twenty or winter supplies for up to ten farmers, we can do that."

"Well, don't count on taking food from my stores," Hetty said. "I don't have enough for twenty pirates."

Captain Thache ignored his mother-in-law's insolence and winked as he replied, "I reckon I'd better pitch in my share, then."

When Edward set off to the orchard, Hetty turned to me, nearly in tears again.

"She'll go with him now for sure. She survived an Indian attack once and can't endure it again."

"Edward will be gentle when he mentions it to her. Winding her up about it won't be good for the child."

She gasped at that thought, then moaned, "My poor girl." And she gave in to a few more tears.

I patted her back, "Things will …."

She wouldn't let me finish. Words mixed with sobs as she said, "Things will work out?"

"Aye," I replied.

She shook her head. "I can't see how this will end well."

I sighed and continued tidying the kitchen as she absorbed the truth from the Captain's news.

Over the following days, Edward set up a system for gathering supplies without alerting Bath that he may sail. Wallace started his Tuesday visits again, bringing items from Edward's list. And each time Olwyn Finch stopped at our landing, Edward heard what the whisperers had to say, and he gave Olwyn a list of provisions to look for as he sailed over his circuit.

Edward directed as Caesar, Drake, and Ody stacked barrels and crates to make room for even more kegs and barrels filled with supplies. Hetty had a few hot words for Edward over that, though.

"Don't ye be clutterin' my cellar so's I can't reach what I need, Edward Thache," she said. "And don't think ye'll take my food stores and leave me here to starve."

Edward's patience wore a bit, but he kept good humor. "Well, now, Good Mother, ye wouldn't want your daughter and grandchild to starve, would ye?" She scowled at him, so he added, "Don't ye fear, Hetty. My men know how to live off the sea. We won't need much from you besides fruit, beans, and grain."

"Well, grain isn't easy to come by," Hetty said. "I reckon I can spare some cornmeal, though."

Then I had an idea. "Oh, how about this? Can you trade some of your sugar, Edward? Send my grandsons or Wallace with sugar to swap for flour in Bath."

"Aye. 'Tis a splendid thought, Widow Saunters," the Captain replied. "Olwyn might find some for us around the sound, too."

I turned to Hetty. "You wouldn't mind a bit more wheat flour, would you?"

Wheat flour was a treat for Hetty, and the promise of it stopped her complaining.

But then, one day, we had more news from Bath. Wallace had discovered it, and Ody and Drake carried it to Plum Point. A pair of Virginia strangers had come to town to investigate Edward Thache. Sal and Wallace saw them with Edward Moseley, and the rumor was that they were there to find out where and how the Captain lived on land—his routines, the ways he communicated, where he stored valuables.

Edward immediately sent a message to Tobias Knight, and they met secretly a few times after. When Knight heard of Wallace's reports, he and Eden began to separate all records involving Edward's business dealings with them and store them in hidden places.

"You'd be wise to do likewise, Edward. These Virginians have no cause to stick their noses in our business, but it sounds like Moseley is still up to no good. Watch your back, my friend."

So, during the second week of November, Edward added to his tasks. On top of gathering provisions and watching for more spies, he went through his papers again to ensure there were no dangers for those remaining at Plum Point.

There were a few trips to Ocracoke as he ferried small portions of his provisions each time. Olwyn Finch helped with that, too, and it was Finch who brought news from his sources that stirred the whispering winds into a storm.

65 Vultures Circle

Marybeth Thache

Olwyn's boat reached Plum Point while there was just enough twilight left for the men to shift supplies from our cellar to the landing.

I watched from the porch as they loaded barrels, and Olwyn chatted with my husband. The boys followed Caesar to the backyard, and after Edward helped shove Olwyn's crew toward Ocracoke, he joined me. A letter fluttered in his hand as he climbed the porch steps, but he dug the fingers of his other fist into his palm, a sign he was trying to put a cork on his temper.

"What is it, Edward?" I asked as he plopped into the rocker beside me.

"'Tis a letter from Charles Vane," he replied, handing the message to me. "Read it."

I increased the lantern flame and turned the page toward the light to read.

> *My Dear Friend,*
>
> *I enjoyed hearing about your story of the Rose Emelye and how it came to be burned. Your ability to wrestle with a problem amazes me, as always. However, sources tell me that the Toison d'Or arrived in France, and Captain Bouyer has since given a deposition about how they lost Rose's cargo on 24 August.*
>
> *One such document has already reached Virginia, and others will follow. I have no idea if such reports interest you, but I felt it my duty as your friend to make you aware.*
>
> *Keep an eye on winds from the north.*
>
> *V.*

"*Rose Emelye* again," I said, returning the page to him. "Vane was careful about what he said."

"Aye," he replied, lifting the lantern chimney to set the page afire. "He was wary of enemy eyes."

"August 24th was the date, yes?"

He nodded. “Aye. ’Twas before the chance for the current pardon ended, but while I was under its protection, sworn to follow the agreement. When this news reaches Eden, he can annul my pardon if he wishes to. And since September 6th has passed, I’m prey for any pirate hunter.”

“And will he do that? Will Eden annul your pardon?”

“I cannot say. The Governor has devils at his heels, too.”

“Will you ask Tobias Knight’s advice?”

He nodded. “I will, but I must do that soon. Olwyn brought more news of trouble with him.”

I gripped the arms of the rocker and closed my eyes, bracing for the bad news.

“Olwyn makes many stops on the sound, and Swan’s Bay is the home of Moseley’s friends. They get news straight from their government friends in Virginia.”

I gasped. “Have your enemies already heard about the depositions from France?”

“Perhaps, but that isn’t all. The whisperers heard Virginia’s Governor Spotswood promises £100 for me, dead or alive. Besides having ships of the Royal Navy cooperating with him, he has engaged some shallow water vessels, and he means to fit them with guns.”

“Shallow water vessels? Why is that important? What does it mean?”

“It may mean nothing. But shoal boats can navigate Pamlico Sound, and the creeks, too. So, they may be preparing to come here.”

“Virginia gunships coming to the Carolina banks—is that legal?” I asked.

“Not without Governor Eden’s approval.”

“And the Governor would never agree to that, would he?” I asked.

“No. I don’t think so, but ’tis another matter for the attention of Tobias Knight.”

“Tell him quickly, then. Go now if you must.” I said.

“Not tonight, my love,” he said. “He’ll be abed, and it would do me well to sleep, too. I’ll speak to him tomorrow.”

Our conversation shifted as the household joined us on the porch. Aurora noticed the ashes at Edward’s feet, and Mother grabbed a broom to brush it away.

“Have we missed your stories, Captain?” Drake asked, propping against a porch post.

Edward struck a broad grin. “Nay, lads, they haven’t begun yet. Which would you like to hear?”

“You never told us about the second time you saw Henry Morgan’s ghost,” Ody replied. “Tell us that one.”

“I’ve heard that tale,” I said. “’Tis long, and we are all tired.”

"But 'tis a good tale, my love, and much better with the rattlin' chains and moaning winds."

"Another time, then," I said.

"Oh, very well. Then, ask me three questions, lads. I'll answer those tonight, and we'll save the scary parts for another evening."

Both boys grinned, but Drake spoke first. "I'll go. What did he look like?"

"Aye, there's a lad who knows the heart of a tale. So here it is. After my family moved to Jamaica, we settled on an old plantation. Ye see, the earthquake of 1692 ruined much of the island, and plantations failed. And many owners died or gave up, leaving the lands for others to farm. Since my father had commanded ships and sailors, he was a natural choice to run a plantation and be master to the enslaved folk who worked it. So, for a time, we lived in a house once occupied by Sir Henry Morgan himself."

Mother tapped her foot. "That wasn't the question. What did he look like?"

"Aye, yes. To the point, then. Well, that house had an attic like this one. I called it the guard house. But instead of a bell tower, they had a proper Widow's Walk where old Henry kept a watch on the nearby town in one direction and the port in the other. But as I told you, he had died by then.

"One stormy night, I heard shutters rattlin' around that boardwalk, so I climbed up and battened them all tight, but even with storm winds blowin', I heard steps following me. So, I hurried into the guard room and hid behind an old leather chair to watch who might enter.

"Soon, a shadow filled the doorway, and the silhouette brushed water from his sleeves, kicked his boots against the door frame, and dumped out his hat brim before he collapsed in the chair I hid behind.

"Then he called, 'Come out now.' When I crept from my hiding place, he grabbed my wrist with his cold, wet hand, pulling me before him. One eye squinted, and one flashed red when lightning streaked the sky. Then both eyes opened wide as he said, 'I've seen 'e before. Why are you following me, boy?'"

"Why was he there?" Ody asked.

"Well, fair enough; the second question goes to Ody. Here's what Sir Henry told me."

"After I denied I was following him, he said he heard wailing in the house and came to see who it was. I told him it was my mother. She suffered from sickness the whole time she lived in Jamaica.

"We talked a bit and finally agreed he was Sir Henry Morgan's ghost. So, I told him I knew something about his life and planned to be a sailor, too, as my father had been.

"And then he asked me my name. When I told him Edward Thache, Jr., he nodded, saying, 'I know why your mother wails. She moans over what will become of you and begs for God to spare you,' he said."

"And was he any help?" Drake asked. "What did he tell you?"

I nodded, "And that is the third question."

"Aye," Edward replied. "He told me what helped him through life, hoping it might provide a path to follow. But like any good sailor, he loved stories with riddles, so he answered in three parts."

"Oh, good. Three more parts," Ody said.

"Fast parts, I hope," Mother said.

Edward grimaced. "Oh, for pity's sake. Sorry, lads, the ladies are bossy tonight."

"First, know what you're good at and use that to do what you must."

"You used that one for sure," Ody said. "You know all about sailing, and you've made your livelihood at it."

Thache nodded as he continued.

"Second, know yourself and make clear people know who you are before they meet you. Let them know what's comin' when you're on your way. It saves time and trouble."

"Like when you make them fear you from the look of you?" Drake asked.

"Aye, and from his reputation, too, like keeping his word," Ody added.

"And moving on to step three," Hetty said.

"This one is my favorite," I said. "You can linger on this one a bit."

"Third—my good wife's favorite—anchor your heart. Morgan claimed that women are many things at once. Some men see them as playthings or servants, but deep down, men know 'tis the women who make the world worth fighting for because 'tis they who lure us home again."

"And this sailor has anchored his heart with me," I said, smiling as I reached for Edward's hand.

"'Tis three asked and answered. Now, shoo!" Mother said.

The others hurried to their rooms, but Edward held me on the porch a while longer. Then, he took my shoulders in his hands and stared at me with his soft eyes. "I know what I must do, my darling. I must use my skills, reputation, and love for you to choose the best way to end this."

"You're leaving then?" I asked.

"*We* are, I hope," he replied. "You are my anchor, and I can't start new anywhere without you in my world."

"So, you plan to raise the sails?"

"I think it's time, and if we move quickly, perhaps we can slip through their nets."

"When will you leave? Do I have days?" My voice faltered. "Or is it only hours?"

"I'll talk to Tobias Knight in the morning. After that, we must decide where to make a stand."

"What can Knight say that makes a difference?" I asked.

"He may have ideas I haven't considered."

"So, is Tobias Knight's imagination my best hope for keeping my home and family?" I asked, barely able to stand.

A nod was his only reply, but then he added, "Perhaps I'll dream up another way."

"I'll pray for that," I replied.

"Then let's dream together, my dear," he said.

And soon, fatigue drove us to our room, too. We closed our eyes, and I pretended to fall asleep as I examined each possibility, detesting them all.

Edward didn't sleep either, and if he dreamed, it was while he paced the room in his nightshirt, arguing with fate and the ghost of Henry Morgan. I roused to call him back to bed, but he had found a place to watch the world from our room. He stood with his head against the highest glass pane and fists clenched atop the sill. His nightshirt was as black as his hair, and his silhouette loomed against the moon. There he stood, still as a figurehead muttering against approaching unseen enemies.

The last words I could understand were, "They'd do well to remember who I am."

66 The Tempest

Aurora Saunters

Captain Thache popped his head into the house kitchen with a short "*Good Mornin'. Have ye seen Caesar?*"

When I shook my head *no*, he dashed to his den.

Next, Ody pushed through to the porch, and when he brought in more firewood, I asked, "What's the Captain up to this morning?"

He waited until his logs quieted from their rattling drop to the log bin, then replied, "I can't say. When I was in the stairwell, I heard him rolling his charts. Do you think he's decided to leave?"

I had no answer other than a shrug.

We filled our trenchers as usual, but as soon as Caesar knocked at the back door, Edward grabbed his coat and hat, and they were off to Knight's Landing.

Marybeth's head raised in alarm as her husband dashed away, and my grandsons looked to me for an explanation.

"Shh," I mouthed. "Easy does it."

But it was not meant to be an easy day.

I finished the kitchen chores and took up mending with Marybeth on our porch. The girl pretended to sew but couldn't keep her eyes from Knight's Landing. Soon Ody and Drake joined us to help watch for Edward to arrive with his answers from Tobias Knight.

When he returned around mid-morning, the boys ran to the landing to help tether the boat. Then they followed Captain Thache as he bounded up the boardwalk, leaped over the steps, and bounced into a chair beside his wife with a decision that would shake the foundations of Plum Point farmhouse.

"I talked it over with Knight. He agrees. We should leave."

Mary twisted the shirt she held as she asked, "So, he had no better ideas? What did he say about the Indians?"

"The Tuscarora situation still has him on edge, but there's been no change."

She dropped her needle and leaned toward Edward. "Then shouldn't we stay here where there's a fort, food, and medicine?" she asked.

"We'd be better off in a place with no hostile natives," Edward replied. Then he leaned till they were head-to-head and whispered, "He didn't like what Olwyn reported. That upset him even more than spies in Bath. He agrees. If the pirate hunters are coming, I should be gone when they arrive."

"I see," Marybeth said, her face draining white.

"He says St. Thomas is the place to get a letter of Marque. He believes my best bet is to sign on as a privateer. And it makes sense. This time, Spain has riled four nations, England, France, Austria, and the Netherlands. And none of those countries can come after me if I'm an agent of any in the Quadruple Alliance."

"But what about the pirate hunters? Aren't they swarming around the islands? What if they find you before you get your letter?"

"I'll dodge 'em," he said. "They won't see me till it's too late, but if we stay here, we're geese waiting for the guns. We must leave, and soon."

Mary rose to her feet. "How soon? And must I leave, too? I have no idea what St. Thomas is like. Will we have a roof over our heads?"

Hetty joined us on the porch, grabbing her daughter's arm. "He has no idea, either, girl." Then she pushed between Thache and his wife. "Is this true? Do you plan to carry your wife and unborn babe on a cruise dodging pirate hunters? Can your sloop repel cannon fire?"

Edward gently took her forearm. "Come with us, Hetty."

"So, do you want me to face the cannons, too?" she asked, jerking her arm from his grasp.

Edward raised his voice as he lifted his hands to the heavens, "Well, do you plan to face the Tuscarora alone? Will you and Marybeth keep them out of the house? I can hide from a few ships on a big sea, but you can't hide from a tribe in your yard. You're safer with me."

Hetty put fists to her hips. "I'll not leave my house. I don't care if the Tuscarora burn me out. I'm staying here," she said, stamping a foot as punctuation.

"So, you'll have Mary pierced with flaming arrows, but you won't let a seasoned Captain sail her over the waves, is that it? How many attacks have you warded off, Hetty? Do you know how many sea battles I've lost? None."

She whispered her reply, but it was still a growl. "It only takes one."

Edward's face turned red as his neck stiffened. "I'm not about to start losing with my most precious treasure aboard," he said.

Marybeth watched as little Hetty stood chin-to-chest with over six feet of Captain Edward Thache. The widow reached up and pulled his beard to bring the face closer. "Ye'll not put my daughter in your stinking ship."

Thache's neck muscles twitched as he bellowed, "Ye'll not tell me where I can take my wife!"

Shifting his gaze from the spectacle was hard, but Ody first noticed the young wife.

"Marybeth," he shouted as he pointed to Mary swooning back into her seat.

"She's fainted," I said. "Bring water."

Thache growled as he pushed Ody and Hetty out of the way to fetch the water glass by his bed.

He returned, offering water with one hand and squeezing Mary's shoulder with the other. He spoke, but his words were indecipherable from the tension in his neck.

"Let me see," I said, kneeling by Mary's chair. It took the look of daggers to get Edward to let go of her, but when he realized how tightly he held her, he released her arm and settled back in the chair.

When Mary roused, I turned to one combatant and then the other. "You both want what you want, and you both want Marybeth to be safe. Now let's work out what we can do about that."

"The captain wants to escape his enemies," Drake said. "He can't take them all on at once."

Ody added, "And Hetty wants to stay in her home and keep her daughter safe there, although it's unclear how she can do that if the Tuscarora attack."

I nodded. "And Marybeth wants her mother and her husband. But the question is, if we can't have everything we want, what is the most important thing?"

Marybeth gasped out a few words. "To keep us all safe. I don't care if it's in Plum Point or an island in the Caribbean. I want the ones I love to be safe—Mother, Edward, the baby, and me."

"Edward, how will you do that?" I asked. "How can you keep everyone safe?"

"Well, I can't do it here," he said. "But I can sail to St. Thomas, where I'll find a safe port with good people to watch after Marybeth. Hetty can be one of them. Dr. Neuvo will sail with us, and I'll get Caesar's papers back from Tobias Knight. He'll guard my family with his life. Finally, I'll get a letter of Marque, and that will be the end of the pirate hunters."

"How about you, Hetty? What's your plan?"

"My plan is as it was when Bert was here. My family will stay in Plum Point; we will go to the fort for protection if the farm becomes unsafe. There are doctors and friends here to help Mary with the baby. Edward can return when things are calmer."

"But Bert isn't here now, Hetty. And are you sure the garrisons will return?" Ody asked.

"I don't want Edward to leave," Mary moaned. "How can I rest when he's too far away for me to know his danger?"

"Edward can stay if he wants to," Hetty said.

"But they are spying on me here, and the pirate hunters can come here, too," Edward said.

"And it won't be a sea battle if the Tuscarora attack," Ody said.

"So, whose plan is best?" I asked. "Marybeth, what do you think?"

"I'm not sure," she said.

"Then, let me ask this question first. If Marybeth chooses, will the two of you agree to it? She loves you both. Hetty, you love this house, and Edward, you feel safer on the sea, but do you each love her enough to let her choose?"

After a few silent minutes, I asked, "Hetty, what will you do if Marybeth chooses to sail?"

She nodded. "I'll reinforce Plum Point and plan to face what comes with my friends and neighbors. Together, we'd pray for Marybeth and her baby every day. My heart would be broken, but I've survived heartbreak and bad times. I can do it again."

"My turn then," Edward said.

I nodded, "What will you do if Mary chooses to stay?"

"I'll sail to St. Thomas, get the pirate hunters off my backside, and return for my family. My dear wife is part of me. I'd be less of a man without her. But I'd live with that hole in my heart till I can return to claim her."

Marybeth rested a hand on his knee. "I'd be a shell of a woman without you, too."

Edward smiled. "The worst part would be not seeing my baby and not being here to protect the little boy or girl and tell them stories. They wouldn't know their old Da. That happened to me once. I can't abide it again."

"You've heard them speak, Marybeth. 'Tis your turn."

"I love you both so much," she said. Then she turned to her mother. "You once told me that when I married, I'd become part of a family with my husband, like you were with my father. You said that the two people would become one, and where one goes, the other follows. You heard Edward, and he said what I feel. Separating us would bring us both harm. I can't hurt him, and I can't bear it without him."

Edward studied her face, and his smile broke through the beard as he clasped his hands around hers. "You'd choose life on a ship with me?" he asked.

"I choose life with you no matter where," she replied.

Hetty nodded as she lay her hand on top of theirs. She didn't smile as she said, "So be it. I'll help you collect your things in the morning."

Marybeth swallowed as she realized what her decision meant. "Wh … when do we sail?" she asked.

"Sooner is better. Three days, tops," Edward replied.

***

We had no cheers or stories that night. There had been enough drama.

One by one, the others drifted off till only Ody, Drake, and I were on the porch. Then, when I walked off in a daze toward the summer house, the boys followed.

They sat on either side of me, silent. I should have said something wise or hopeful, but it wasn't in me.

Finally, Ody spoke. "Oma?" he asked. "What's up with you?"

"Yeah," Drake added. "What's up?"

I blurted out my answer. "We must stop this. Marybeth can't go with him."

"Why not?" Drake asked. "I thought you just led them to that very conclusion."

"Because in less than a week, Edward Thache will die, and Marybeth will either die with him or hang as his abettor."

"But shouldn't we let what happens happen?" Ody asked.

"That's the point," I replied. "That's not what happened."

"Can't you talk to them and persuade them differently?" Drake asked.

"I just talked to them. How can I undo that?" I asked.

"Then we have to stop this," Ody said. "But how? Thache thinks it's best to bring her aboard. Mary wants to go, and even Hetty has agreed to live with that. So, what else can we do?"

Drake nodded. "I have an idea."

Ody rolled his eyes. But since I had no hint of a solution, I shrugged. And when I leaned in to hear Drake's plan, Ody did too.

67 Ghost Conjurers

Drake Saunters

After Ody heard my plan, he leaned back, gripping the summer house bench. "Well, now it's official. You're bonkers."

"You only say that because it wasn't your idea. It makes perfect sense."

"Oma, does any of this make sense to you?" Ody asked.

She tilted her head, sighing. "Give us a few more details, Drake, dear."

"OK, it's like this. We all agreed to the arguments of Marybeth and Hetty, but now, we need someone who can convince Captain Thache to change his mind."

"Who does the Captain listen to more than himself?" Ody asked.

I shrugged. "Easy-peasy. His mother, Elizabeth Thache. He'll listen to her."

"But isn't she dead?" Ody asked.

"Yes, but lucky for us, the Captain believes in ghosts," I said, grinning. *Why were they so slow to catch on?*

Grandma shook her head. "Drake, we are time travelers, not ghost-hunters. We can't bring Elizabeth or her ghost here. So, how will this plan work?"

I leaned forward again, hands between my knees. "Do you remember the morning you found me on the tower with old Mrs. Thache's portrait? She looks like you."

"Well, yes, you said so, but I didn't see it."

"Asjen Nuevo agreed with me. Your face resembles that of Elizabeth Thache—inherited traits, I guess. And better than that, I saw her in the flesh, and it's true; you look like her."

"But Captain Thache has never said so; I could never fool him."

"Do you remember the picture? She wore her hair pinned up with two silver combs. She had a silky, flowing shawl in the painting, too."

"So? Do you think I can find similar combs and shawl?"

"No. But I can. I can bring the exact ones from Jamaica, and no one will ever know."

"How can you do that?" Ody asked. "If you take them, the first disaster is that they'll find you. And if you steal the combs, you've changed history. Who knows what will come of that?"

"But I can replace them before anyone knows they are gone. It will work."

"So, what then?" Ody asked. "What if someone else sees Grandma dressed like Edward's mother? They'll figure it out."

"We can iron out the details," I replied.

Oma still had questions, but she wasn't shaking her head anymore. "Suppose we do figure it out," she said. "Suppose I can look enough like Elizabeth Thache to fool Edward; what could I say to him that will change his mind?"

"You'll say what I heard her say to Edward as a boy, what he's said about his mother, and … oh … what Sir Henry Morgan and Caesar told him, too. We can do this?"

"Oma?" Ody asked. "Are you going to try this lame idea?"

Grandma shrugged. "Well, we must do something. And if Edward's accent is anywhere close to his mother's …."

"Right," I said. "You're great at accents, and Hetty's from Bristol."

Grandma nodded. "It might work … *if* we have time to prepare. We need to know when and how Thache will sail. Timing is everything."

"We'll find out. The Captain will make plans tomorrow, and then we'll know what we're working with."

"Fair enough," Oma said. "I'll look at that portrait again. Her hair was whiter than mine. I'll see if Hetty has wig powder somewhere."

Ody was doubtful, but he joined in the planning. "Drake, you must write down everything you remember from Mrs. Thache, Asjen Nuevo, and the Captain's story about Sir Henry Morgan. Then, Oma can put it together into an argument."

"Yep, nobody argues better than Grandma."

Oma chuckled. "What's your part in all this, Ody?" she asked.

Ody scratched his chin, "I reckon I'd better figure out a private place with dim lights … somewhere ghostly. I'll look around the farm."

"Then we all have our jobs to do," Grandma said. "But first, we need to know the Captain's plans for sailing."

"Right," I replied. "We can't move without that."

"We must try," Oma said. "We can't save the Captain—at least I don't know how we can—but we might be able to save Marybeth."

"And our baby grandpa—to keep the space-time continuum happy," I added.

Oma grinned, "Let's hope so."

Early the following day, Captain Thache rowed to Knight's Landing again, and he returned with permission to sail to St. Thomas with *Adventure*.

"So, when must we leave?" Marybeth asked.

"As soon as the ship and crew are ready," he replied. "But I'll need to leave for Ocracoke and transfer the rest of the provisions to *Adventure*."

"I cannot be ready today," Marybeth said. "I need things for the baby and me in case it comes before we settle. And Mother … I need time to be sure she has what she needs."

"We can't dawdle, my love. How's this? Have your mother list all she may need from Bath and have the boys row it to Wallace. He can bring what he finds for Plum Point and me, and then he can bring you and the rest of my supplies Sunday evening. Tell him I'll be at Little Porpoise Island near sunset. That's not far to row, and we'll get a good start Monday morning."

"I'll be ready," she said. "But must you leave now?"

"Very soon, my dear. But we won't be apart for long. 'Tis only a day or two, and then we'll be together always."

She helped him gather his charts and gear and made a new star ribbon for his beard.

"I won't need a ribbon on this trip, my love," Edward said. "You'll be with me, so I'll be at home." Then they shared a loving kiss and a hug that neither wanted to release.

Next, Ody, Caesar, and I helped the Captain shift supplies from our cellar to the *Bellamy*. Then with a few added crewmen, they started for Ocracoke.

Once the *Bellamy* raised its sails, Ody tapped me on the shoulder.

"What now?" he shrugged. "The Captain won't be at Plum Point."

I shook my head, pondering the same riddle. "We know where he'll be on Sunday night," I said. "But how can we get him back to meet Grandma?"

Ody shook his head. "I don't think we can."

"We need Plan B. What else can we do?" I asked.

Ody shrugged and paced until he had an idea. "We can take Oma to him."

"We can't do that. First, we don't know if the beard-ribbon would work for Grandma, and second, neither of us can commute directly to Edward this time. It's not like Ocracoke. We can't know when he'll be alone."

"You could go with Marybeth on Wallace's boat. Then Oma could commute to you to play her ghost scene."

"Yes, that would work," I replied. "But there's one big problem. We don't know what Porpoise Island looks like, and we need to know we can make a ghost work there."

Ody tapped a finger to his head, smiling. "But we know someone who's been there. Wallace knows. He said so when he met Olwyn on the dock. So, Olwyn must know too."

"And we're supposed to row to Wallace today," I said, catching the excitement. "We can ask him what to expect."

***

We figured out the rest of the plan while we rowed to Bath.

Ody asked, "How much time do you need before you can return with the ghost costume?"

I shrugged. "Fifteen to twenty minutes, I think. It takes that long before Mrs. Thache falls asleep. Then I can grab the hair ornaments and shawl."

"Do that tonight if you can. And write out what you heard Mrs. Thache say that will help Oma persuade Edward to leave Marybeth behind."

"And what will you do while I'm zipping through time and writing a paper?" I asked.

"I'll make props for you."

"Props for what?"

"Props for a ghostly appearance—*if* there is a spot to make one."

"And if that doesn't work?" I asked.

"Then we're left with plan C—convince Marybeth to stay."

Luckily for us, the night Wallace spent on Porpoise Island was dark and scary. Of course, we didn't tell him what we planned, but when he spoke of the little island, his story of making his last stand told us enough.

"After the pirates left me and my head stopped bleeding, I walked the island to find anything useful to save me. It's shaped like a man's left hand," he said, holding out his hand, palm down. "I'd gauge it as a few hundred yards long and maybe 100 wide. The main channel goes left by the little finger, and the island points toward Brant Island Shoals. There's a swift side current around the thumb between this island and a bigger one, and unless the water is low, 'tis too deep and wide to cross."

"How did you survive?" Ody asked.

"Without Olwyn, I might not have survived, but I explored to find what I could. There was nothing to eat and no fresh water. The only animals I saw were rats and a few foxes chasing them through the swampiest part," he said, pointing to his thumbnail. "Their yipping was unnerving, and I didn't like walking through the moss that dangled from the cypress trees. I never saw a snake, but I feared I might, so I only stayed among the pines and cypress long enough to find vines and driftwood. Once I collected makings for a raft, I built a fire on the beach, hoping for a rescue."

"Do you think Captain Thache will camp on that beach, then?" I asked.

"Likely so. The shoals are too shallow for *Adventure*, so he'll bring a tender to shore and camp near the ship. He and his men will stay out of the swamp, I reckon. They'll only need to go into the grove side, near the thumbnail, if they want more firewood."

"Well, here's the list of items Thache would like you to bring. The top part is for Plum Point, and the end is to bring to him at the Little Porpoise," Ody said.

"You'll be bringing Marybeth, too," I added.

"Did she choose to sail with the Captain?" he asked.

Ody nodded. "They decided it's the best way. The Captain will be at Little Porpoise around sunset Sunday night. Then he'll take on your supplies and add Marybeth as a passenger on *Adventure.*"

Wallace bent his head over his hands as we left him. He likely wanted a better solution for Mary, and so did we.

Once we reached home, we put the plan to work. Before supper, I wrote everything I could recall that might convince Edward that Grandma was his mother's ghost. Ody carved whistles and other noise makers to use for the spirit of Elizabeth Thache.

Then when everyone went to bed, I made a quick trip to Jamaica for the silver hair pins and a white silk shawl. When I returned to Grandma, I delivered her costume, and she began writing her scene.

The following day we reviewed the final instructions.

"I ride with Wallace and Marybeth and encourage her to stay on the boat while I help unload. Then I escape to see the stage and arrange a few special effects."

"That's right," Ody said, "And while you're gone, Oma and I will try out ghostly voices and mannerisms, and she can test her speech on me. Then, an hour past sunset, you go to a secure spot so Oma can commute to you. I'll be in her room, so she'll come straight to me if anything goes wrong."

I nodded. "Then, once Grandma gets the lay of the swamp and how to make it ghostly, I'll lure Captain Thache to the scene."

Ody summed it up. "Grandma does her ghost scene, and hopefully, the Captain will send Marybeth back home."

"But whether it works or not, once the ghost makes her plea and Grandma returns to you, we will have done the best we can do, and I'll come back with Wallace and reset my last visit to Jamaica."

"That's it," Ody said. "But we can count on Oma. She knows what's at stake."

Marybeth and Hetty spent the rest of the weekend together, packing, planning, and laughing over baby names. They said repeated farewells, each ending with the promise to meet again as soon as possible.

As planned, Wallace showed up on Sunday afternoon, and we shifted supplies to and from the *PlumMary*, and while Marybeth waved to Hetty from behind a wet hanky, we shoved off for Little Porpoise Island.

68 Another Ghost Story

Drake Saunters

Marybeth sucked in her breath as she turned from watching as Plum Point vanished behind us. Whether she reflected on what she left behind or contemplated her new future, she remained quiet for most of the trip. But when the sun began to sink, and our destination might lie around the next bend, she whispered, "What will I do on Porpoise Island?"

"Let Edward be your guide; it's his domain. He'll keep you safe. But till your husband comes for you, stay on this boat with Wallace," I replied.

"Will you stay with me?" she asked.

"Someone you trust will be on this boat if you need us."

It wasn't long till we saw *Adventure* bobbing in the channel near Little Porpoise. Captain Thache waved to us from the shore, where the crew had lit a fire and were busy roasting fish. Their sea songs proved they were happy to be on the front end of a new voyage. Several of them stopped to shout greetings as Wallace pushed *PlumMary* ashore.

Marybeth took her first up-close look at pirates making merry. She studied their loose-legged pants, earrings, tattoos, and wild dancing, then turned to me, breathless. "There must be two dozen of them," she said.

"Aye, but they'll listen to the Captain, especially with no Israel Hands around. Vane took The Crow and others of Hands' followers, so these men are loyal to Captain Thache."

She nodded. "Edward can manage them."

"I reckon I can," Edward said, grinning as he approached the *Plum*.

After a quick kiss to Marybeth, Thache clapped me on the back. "And I thank ye again," he chuckled. "Are you sure you won't come along? I always figured you would sign up to sail with me."

"Not this time, Sir," I said, grinning. "I must return home soon. My job was to escort Mrs. Thache."

"Aye," he said, watching his men as they laughed at the jigs of others. "I should see to the cargo, but I'll fetch Caesar to keep Marybeth company." Then he turned to Wallace. "Ye'll stay to get Drake home, aye?" he asked.

"Aye, Drake can sail with me."

"Well, stay long enough to eat and rest a bit before you start back."

"I'll stay as long as Marybeth needs me, Captain," he said.

As I jumped from the boat to help unload, I pulled out the keg of rum.

"This is a gift from Oma," I said.

"Aurora sent this?" Mary asked.

"Aye, she paid the Window Bellieu for it. Grandma figures Captain Thache can do a better job if his men are happy." But, of course, I didn't mention that she thought her ghost show would appear more realistic through tipsy eyes.

"Send her my thanks," the Captain said. Then he pointed to the channel. "'Twill take a few trips to load *Adventure*, so do a little fishing if you like. We can always put a few more fins over the fire."

"Aye, Sir, I'll make a quieter camp back in the grove."

I watched from the edge of the trees as Edward tapped the keg for his men. Then, he took his place in the boat beside Marybeth and Wallace, and the three of them conversed as they watched Thache's crew ferrying goods to Adventure or cavorting around the flames.

It was time to make the final touches to my stage at the edge of the cypress swamp. The sky was dim, and fog hovered over the water and through winding garlands of Spanish moss. And when I hung my handkerchief over a knot at the height of Oma's face, I could gauge the light and shadow where she would appear. She'd be visible but faintly lit. That seemed about right.

Ody had given me a wind chime of sticks that rattled like bones, and he had spent his Saturday whittling river cane whistles until he made one with a low, mournful sound. I hung the rattle where Grandma could reach it and placed the sad whistle in the brush near me.

At about an hour past sundown, I hid behind a stand of brush, so no one could find me if they came looking, and when Grandma commuted, we'd both be undercover. With the brush as a blind, she'd have a moment to return to Ody if our plan went awry.

Then she appeared inches from me, blinking till her eyes focused. Her costume was perfect, the picture of Elizabeth Thache.

"Are you ready?" I asked.

She nodded. "Ody had a few ideas for the ghost, where I should appear and how I should bob and weave."

"Then I'll sit by the other fire and see if you'll make a convincing picture for Edward."

Grandma examined our setting and saw how to become ghostly among the brush, saplings, and fallen logs. The bone rattle worked, and when she felt at ease on her stage, she added another effect.

"Bring some of your embers here and here," she said, pointing to spots left and right of her center stage. "Put a bit of tinder and dry leaves under each. Then, I can make them flame as needed," she whispered.

She hid behind the brush while I peeked at the pirate camp. Asjen Neuvo and Captain Thache chatted with Mary in the boat. Caesar, Wallace, and his crew ate fish by their fire. The time would never be better.

So I returned to the fire opposite the swamp and signaled Grandma that it was time to begin. I played the flute softly at first, then gradually increased the moaning sound till it sounded like a woman wailing.

I peeked through the trees to see if Thache heard, and when Mary noticed the sound, she gripped his arm. Then the Captain stood, motioning for her to stay with Asjen, and I tossed the whistle into the brush as he came to investigate.

"Did you hear that?" I asked, pretending to look for the origin of the sound.

"I did," he answered. "Maybe some bird," he said. "Why are you still back here? Come join the party?"

"I dropped my knife around this fire pit," I said.

He bent to help me look, and as we crept around, a white figure began to fade in and out as Grandma threaded her way among the saplings. I jerked my head up, and then the captain saw it. "What was that?" he asked.

"I don't know. Wait here. I'll go see."

But before I was three steps away, he pulled me back and drew his sword.

"*Ned ... deee,*" a soft voice whispered from the darkness. The voice was not like someone calling. Instead, it blended perfectly in tone, note, and volume with the natural sounds of the swamp as if the birdsongs carried it. And when it repeated the name, the voice came from a different direction.

"Who is that?" Thache asked. He glanced at the boat, but Marybeth was still with Asjen Nuevo.

Then a small fire by the swamp flared up as if someone had stirred the coals. Moaning started low and faded to a whisper as the form of a woman floated behind the fire.

Grandma's costume was her gray cloak and hood over a long nightshirt and the white shawl of Elizabeth Thache. She walked behind the fire and rotting logs, giving the illusion of a floating woman. Deep in the shadows of the swamp, the cloak was invisible, but it floated around her, causing the outline of the white shift and flowing shawl to waver in the mist.

"Is … is that a ghost?" I asked.

Edward gulped. "'Tis … 'tis my mother."

"*Ned-deeee*," she whispered, this time chirping insects muted the voice.

I grabbed the Captain's arm as he started toward the apparition.

"*Not yet, my son*," she spoke as softly as a pine breeze, holding her vowels long and letting the consonants trail.

"Why are you here?" I asked.

"I heard wailing. Someone we loooove may be lossst. I … may be lossst. Nooo one will remeeember me. Nooo … leeegacyyy."

"Who is lost, Mother?" Edward asked.

"Youuu … aaaarre," she replied. "And aaall we love may be lossst. Even…." The voice trailed.

"Even who?" I asked.

"Eeeven the smaaaallest Neeeddie."

"Does she mean your son?" I whispered.

"A son," Thache gasped.

"Is your heaart like miiine, Ned?" she asked. "Be myyy legacy. Your tiiime comes sooooon. You will come to me, won't you? I've waited sooo looong."

"I have a wife, Mother," he said. "And she carries a baby. Is he the smallest Neddie?"

The apparition moaned. "The sea wants Maaaary… Saaave heeer. Saaave the baaaby."

"I'm taking them with me to safety, Mother. They will be fine."

This time the apparition moaned more loudly, crying. "Nooooo. Not across the sea. I could not survive the seeaa, and neeeither shall theey."

"What should I do?" Edward asked. Then he turned to me. "What does she mean?"

"Maybe what Sir Henry Morgan told you. Those three things? Could that be it?"

"It's as you and Ody said. I lead men. I conquer the sea."

"Aye," I replied. "Those are your strengths. What you were meant for."

Then the apparition added, "Uuuuse your streeength … your faaather's duuuty. Saaaave the ones we loooove. *Then come hoooome.*"

He nodded. "Like Morgan said. Home to the woman who makes life worthwhile."

When he looked at the fire again, the apparition was gone, probably covered in Grandma's gray cloak from head to toe, and the bone rattle covered the sounds of her backing away from the fire.

But the voice whispered in the wind once more. "'Tis tiiime … you were hooome with meee, Ned. Saaaave theeeem. Save uuuss."

This time the voice trailed into the sound of waves lapping on the beach. The wind rushed from where the apparition had been as Oma commuted to Ody in Plum Point.

The ghost had vanished.

Thache sat on the log, and then, whether from seeing his mother's specter or the words of her dire prophecy, he wept.

"Captain?" I asked. "What did that mean?"

He didn't say. Instead, he drew his sword, and with a determined face, he rushed to the swamp to search behind every tree.

"There's no one here," he said.

Then he returned to our log by the fire to answer my question but was slow to speak.

"My days are numbered," he whispered, "And if they are … if I join my mother soon, I can't protect Marybeth."

"Are you sure?" I asked.

He nodded. "They've told me all my life, and now I see it. Mother asked me to be her legacy and spoke of leading her family home. Henry Morgan warned me twice not to follow him."

I sat silently beside him as we pondered the moment. Grandma explained why he needed to sail without Mary, that his end was near. But I didn't want that. Edward Thache should win.

"Well, here's the truth," he said, his rumbling voice disturbing the quiet of night. "A battle awaits; if Mary follows me and I fall, she won't survive." He gripped his sword and turned to the boat, saying, "And neither will my son."

Asjen Nuevo had helped Marybeth remain calm, but she sobbed again as Edward returned, pale and sorrowful.

Caesar reached us first, and he whispered to Edward. "Some of the men are worried about a woman coming aboard."

Edward nodded. "Perhaps it won't be an issue." Then he turned to Marybeth, squeezing her hand in both his.

"What's wrong, Edward?" she asked.

"My love." He closed his eyes, shaking his head, before he continued. Then he looked deeply into her eyes. "I've … I've had an omen. I may not be able to survive this voyage. And if I don't live, I can't protect you. So, you must stay behind."

She leaned toward him. "Of course, you will survive. And where you go, I will go. If you don't survive, I will not either. I will be with you."

"Is it possible for you to stay here, Edward?" Asjen asked.

He shook his head, "Trouble will come here, and it will swallow us both."

"Maybe not," Wallace said. "I have a note for you from Tobias Knight. Read it first before you decide."

Grandma had told me about the letter from Tobias Knight. He encouraged Edward to stay in Bath—that perhaps Eden's enemies would be reasonable, and they could reconcile. He had word that the Tuscarora were standing down. But would that ease Edward's mind enough to stay?

"Where did you get this?" Thache asked.

"A man named Gannet gave it to me to bring to you. He got it from Tobias Knight."

"Does it mean we can stay, Edward?" Marybeth asked.

"It means it may be safe for you, my love, but not for my men. Not till threats against us are resolved. I'll speak to them."

So, Captain Thache stood before his men. "Mates, news has come to me that we may stay in Bath. Tell me how that suits ye."

"I thought the Governor wouldn't have us, Captain," one man called out. "Has he had a change of heart?"

"No, not exactly. He'd expect you to behave and settle down. Can you do that? Can you disperse and lose yourselves among the fields and woods and people? Marry among them and survive? If you stay here with me, you will die with me, too."

A red-haired man spoke first. "Some stay on land, Captain, but not I. If you must stay here, give us the ship to sail away."

"I know ye, lads. And while you have heart and strength, you aren't ready to face the storms and battles ahead if you sail."

"Then come with us, Captain," said a man with a tattooed face. "Take us to St. Thomas as we planned."

"Can you choose another Captain?" he asked. "Is there one you would trust?"

The oldest sailor there spoke up. "I sailed with you before we had *Queen Anne's Revenge*, and you brought us home safe every time. I sail under no commander besides Edward Thache, and if you head for battle, I'll be at your back."

"And I," a man no older than Ody added. "You put me on my first crew, Captain, and you treated me better than my own father ever did. 'Twas Edward Thache who showed me the world and how to fight for my place in it. I know nothing but crewin' for 'e, Sir. If ye die, I'll die with 'e. I wouldn't know what else to do."

Then one of the black crewmen stood. "Ye found me in chains on a slave ship, Captain, and I'd heard stories of what awaited me here. 'Twas my best day when you pirated *La Concorde* and made me a free man of the sea. What would happen to me if I left you? If the hunters don't kill me, they'll catch and sell me again." Then he raised his sword high, saying, "I'd rather go down swinging my blade for Edward Thache."

Another called out, "Aye. If we be sea rogues or shark food, we are Captain Thache's men."

By this time, Marybeth had gathered courage enough to stand behind her husband, and Edward turned to her.

"I must go," he said. "These men are my sons, too."

"Then I will go, as well," she replied.

If Ody were there instead of me, he'd follow her and help keep her safe. *Should I take his place? Or had fate chosen me for this mission to keep my cousin from following? Was I destined to sail, then?* But another spoke before I decided.

Wallace hesitated before stepping forward to say, "If Marybeth dies on your ship, so shall I."

I nodded, ready to volunteer, too. But as I stepped forward, Marybeth rested a hand on Wallace's arm and turned to me.

"Don't say it," she said. "You can't sail with us. Your grandmother would be heartbroken. Don't you have a mother and father to return to?"

"They will survive, but you may not be so lucky if you sail. It will take all of us to protect you, so I'm signing on, Captain."

Thache scratched his beard, speechless.

Marybeth touched my shoulder. "This isn't your future, and you can't risk losing what you might become, *who* you might become. You have a destiny that belongs to you alone."

"Your legacy," Edward whispered. Then he touched my shoulder, saying, "I'm honored you want to sail with me, but my wife's right. The battle I head to is not your fight, and if you go with me, you won't be there to lead battles fate means for you. And when they come, you'll be fit to fight 'em. I'm sure of that. If fate allows, I may be by your side to give your enemies a whack." He clapped me on the back, but his eyes softened as he turned to Mary.

He gently patted her hands as he said, "My darlin', I saw my mother in the grove. 'Twas she who told me my time was at hand, and she reminded me to do my duty and save my family. She said I must be her legacy."

"I don't understand," Marybeth said.

"I see it clearly now," Thache replied. "My father had children by his second wife. My sister has no children, so I'm my mother's only hope. She wants me to pass on the goodness she had inside her. You have that goodness within you, Marybeth."

"But what of your daughter?" she asked.

"She never knew my mother, and she knows little of me," he replied.

"Then what about you, Edward? Your goodness is your mother's legacy."

"What good I have is tarnished by my choices, and my time for reckoning has come. If you stay with me, we are all lost. I must finish what I started with my men. Please don't let all of me die on the sea. Keep part of my mother and me alive. Let me survive, my love. Let me survive in you and the wee one."

"You don't know what you saw? Perhaps it was a dream or some demon wanting to trick you."

"Then if 'tis a trick, I'll defeat the sea. I'll get my men to a safe place and come home to you, and we will live together till the end of our days. Please, go back to Plum Point, my love. That way, I'll surely survive, and so shall you."

"Then let your men have the ship. Let them go, and you stay with me."

He shook his head. "I cannot do that. These are my sons too. One hundred men came with me to Bath, and these remain. You heard them; they will follow me, even if they must die. But they'll have a better chance of living with me. I'll see them to St. Thomas if we can get there. And if we meet the devil on the way, I'll fight him with these men."

She sobbed into his chest, holding tight. "Stay."

He pushed her back so he could look into her eyes. "You married me so Bath could survive … so *you* could survive. Now help *me* survive." He winked, grinning. "At least the little me inside you."

Then he turned to Asjen Nuevo. "Will you help her?"

When he nodded, Edward turned to Wallace.

"If I can't keep my promise to keep her safe, will you do it for me?" Edward asked.

Wallace nodded. "I will, as long as she will allow it."

Then Edward stepped to Wallace. "Here," he said, passing him the iron key to the potato hole. Then he emphasized each word that followed, "*This is the key*. You mustn't fail. Keep this safe for my wife, child, and the welfare of Bath Town. But, please, take care of my family."

Wallace nodded. "I will."

Edward held Marybeth tightly, kissing her passionately for as long as he could, but the time came to part. As Edward led her to the boat, she leaned against him, holding her stomach. But when she boarded *PlumMary*, one hand rested against Edward's arm, and the other reached for Wallace's outstretched fingers.

She sat beside Asjen, and Edward bent to kiss her softly, one hand on her tummy, the other pressing his signet ring into her palm.

Then she jerked and pressed his hand tighter. "Did you feel it? The baby moved."

He grinned. "Of course he did. He will be a wild little nipper and need taming."

"He will need a father," she said.

Blackbeard chuckled. "I'll do my best to take care of that."

After one final kiss, he stepped off the boat and turned to Wallace. "You know what a treasure you have," he said. "You'd better do your best, too."

"Aye, aye, Captain," he replied.

Thache pulled at Wallace's headscarf and rubbed his hand over the scarred skull. "I'm truly sorry for your trouble," he said.

Wallace smiled as he grabbed his scarf, and before he turned to make his boat ready, he said. "I'm sorry for yours, too, Sir. Follow your star."

Then he and Caesar shoved *PlumMary* into the channel, and as the boat slowly pulled away, the Captain turned to Caesar.

"Will you go with them to guard Marybeth?" he asked.

"She has protectors," he said. "I will stay to defend you, as you have me many times."

The Captain nodded. Then he put a hand on Caesar's shoulder. "Do you agree to stay, knowing we may not survive?" he asked.

"I stand with you, Ned Thache," he replied.

"Then, will you do me a great favor?"

"Of course, I will if I can."

"See to it that none of these men hang. Do you understand? None of them, nor you."

He nodded grimly. "I'll see to it, Ned."

Edward sighed, clapping Caesar on the back. "I know you'll do the best any man could."

Caesar grinned.

"Oh, and one last thing," Edward said, returning the grin. "I'm going to dig out that silver cup. Will you get the wedding cup back to my wife?"

He smiled as he waved toward the *PlumMary*, and I saluted him back.

As we rowed away, I heard Edward shouting to his crew. "Let's make the most of this night, lads. Kick up a night for the stars to remember."

69 The Escape

Ody Saunters

Not long after the clock chimed seven and Oma had finished her part in our ghost story, she appeared on the Bride's Tower beside me. I grabbed her, relieved she was safe at Plum Point again.

"Did it go well?" I asked.

"We'll see when the periauger returns."

There was no one else on Plum Point besides Hetty. And she had been bolted in her room weeping since Marybeth sailed to meet *Adventure*. But to be safe, Oma hurried to change from her Elizabeth Thache costume and become the mysterious Widow Saunters again.

Several hours later, the *PlumMary* docked at our landing, and we breathed a sigh of relief to see that Wallace, Marybeth and Drake were safe. We were surprised to see Asjen Neuvo among the party, too.

Hetty ran to greet them, squeezing Marybeth till she begged for mercy. It was well past supper time, but Oma found cold meat and bread, and the stewpot was never empty.

But no one was hungry, and none of the *Plum*'s passengers wanted to talk. Marybeth left first, and even though we suspected she didn't sleep, she closed her door, separating herself from the world on the other side.

Drake, Asjen, and Wallace told us snippets of what happened, but words dragged like feet through the mud.

"You're too weary to row to Bath," Hetty said. "We will make room. Sleep here, instead."

Asjen felt he should check on the health of Tobias Knight and report what happened with Thache. And Drake should undo his last actions in Jamaica. So, I offered my bed to Wallace and rowed the doctor across the creek before returning to a cot in the crew's shed.

Each of us slept as we were able, and in the morning, Hetty and Oma roused me as they rattled pots. Drake made a racket, too, as he fetched wood for the fire. But over the din of the morning, I heard sounds in the forest and rushed to the others.

"Someone's here," I whispered. "Men, dozens of them may be on Plum Point. They're coming through the back woods."

"Get the axe," Hetty said. "Aurora, wake Marybeth and find whatever you can for a weapon."

When I returned with the axe, Oma barred the back door behind me.

"I'll fetch Wallace," Drake called.

But when they met on the stairs, Wallace already had his pistol in hand, and Hetty had pulled Bert's gun from over the mantle. I passed them all on my way to Edward's den, where, through the east windows, I saw men prowling through the sheds and animal pens.

Wallace joined me. "They're men of the Royal Navy," he whispered.

Oma followed him, adding, "They've come for Edward."

"What shall we do?" I asked.

Wallace held up a finger to silence me, and he pushed Edward's desk chair away from the window light and motioned for us to gather around. Marybeth took Edward's chair, and Hetty stood behind her with Bert's gun propped at her side. Drake and I stood on either side of Wallace, where we could watch through the window.

"It's the Virginians," Wallace whispered to our huddle. "They've come to find Edward."

"Well, good thing he isn't here then," Hetty replied.

"And they shouldn't know who else they have here," Wallace said, his eyes rolling toward Marybeth.

"Well, 'tis my home, and I'll tell them to leave it," Hetty said.

"Very well. Someone must speak for the house, and it might as well be you, but I'll stand by you. Everyone else should stay out of sight. Let's let the Navy guess at the force we have here. Then maybe we can avoid violence."

"I'll show them violence," Hetty said, hoisting Bert's ammunition pouch over her shoulder as she headed for the tower.

"Wait for me, Hetty. Wait till I stand with you," Wallace said.

"Then hurry."

The rest of us turned to Wallace for our orders.

"We need a way off this point, and our choices are the jollyboat or the ferry."

"But they're coming over land, and some are on horses," I said.

Drake nodded, "If they are mounted, they came from the ferry. We can't go that way."

"Oma, take Marybeth to the cellar," Ody said. "Mary will show you the hiding place there. Go there and wait till we come."

"I know where it is," Mary said. "We can do that."

"But you might need help with the rock screen; I'll come with you," Drake said.

"Be quiet as you move. We don't know where the men are or who may be listening." Oma said.

"All right, Mr. McNeil. 'Tis you, me, and Ody now. What's our part?" Hetty asked.

"Come with me. We can't see enough through this window. Let's go to the tower to see how many there are. Keep low till I say."

I crept along the tower wall, staying close to the floor but within reaching range of the spyglass, lantern, and bell rope.

Wallace mouthed, *wait till they speak.*

It wasn't a long wait.

"Hail! Is someone up there? I'm Captain Ellis Brand of the Royal Navy, requesting to speak with Edward Thache." The voice came from the backyard, so Hetty popped up over the wall in that direction.

"I'm Henrietta Bellieu, and this is my house. This land is not in Virginia; we are not a crown colony. Why are you on my property?"

"But you are subject to the laws of the King of England, Madam, and we are commissioned to find the home of Edward Thache."

"Captain Thache is not here. He's at sea."

And for a moment, Hetty and Brand bandied words about who gave such a commission and why it had no meaning in North Carolina until I feared the volleys would become musket balls.

Finally, Wallace appeared at her side, his musket visible but upright. "Captain Brand. I am Wallace McNeil here to guard Widow Bellieu while her family is away."

"Very well, McNeil," Brand replied. "My orders are to search the grounds of this plantation for proof of piracy by Edward Thache, known as Blackbeard. Unless you want to take on men of the King's Navy, open your doors for us."

"We will not," Hetty replied.

Wallace moved in front of her. "Sir, the Royal Navy has no authority in North Carolina, and the Widow Bellieu has rejected your request. However, if you wish, you may speak to Governor Eden or his secretary, Tobias Knight, and we will gladly oblige if they approve."

"Sir, my men are here in force, and we demand entry, or we shall make one for ourselves."

"Should we ring the bell?" I whispered.

Wallace shook his head no. But I lowered the lantern from the railing and reached for the bell rope.

Then Hetty raised her gun, aiming at Brand, and one of the attackers fired back, hitting the bell. The rope jerked from my hand, and the bell sounded once, but I grabbed it before it chimed again.

"Then we shall bar all our doors, Sir. You may not come in." Hetty shouted.

Wallace pulled Hetty from the wall and directed her to the attic hatch. "Go to the cellar. Find Marybeth," he whispered. "Let's make them guess where we are." And he motioned for me to follow.

I mouthed I'd be right behind him, but instead, I let the bell rope dangle, and in Edward's den, I grabbed a few long fuses like the ones we used to burn *Rose Emelye*. This time they'd do us a different favor.

Brand's men pounded on the back door, but I stayed low as I tied fuses to lengthen the bell rope. Then I slowly pulled the bell until it was almost horizontal and maintained the tension as I crawled toward the hatch.

Eight rings of the bell signaled imminent danger. Tobias Knight's men would respond, but I needed to time it well and be safely out of musket range before I let go. It would take Knight's men twenty minutes to reach our dock once the alarm sounded. We'd be on our own till then.

I couldn't go far down the block ladder without losing my leverage on the bell. So, I kept my arms above the hatch and my body and head below and pulled hard, producing two loud clangs of the bell.

"They're in the tower," Brand yelled. And musket balls thudded against the tower.

Two more strong pulls. Four more clangs.

Fists pounded on the back door. So this time, I pulled the rope tight with both hands, yanked it hard, and then released it, counting on at least two more chimes.

Then amid the bell ringing and muskets blasting, I ran down the stairs and through the cellar entry, where I could safely slip through the passage in the crawl space and join the others in the hidden tunnel.

Brand called as I reached the crawlspace. "You men, go around front. Find the other door." He was in the backyard.

Marybeth dug her nails into Drake's arm as everyone listened for movement from Brand's men. Horse hooves clopped over the rocks of the drainage ditch near the potato hole as Brand's mounted force moved to the front yard.

"We have you surrounded, Mrs. Bellieu," Brand called. "You have five minutes to respond to us."

"We need Tobias Knight," Marybeth whispered.

"He heard the bell," Hetty said. "He's on the way."

"Good word," Drake whispered, but Wallace shushed us, and I continued quietly rebuilding the rock screen that hid the potato hole from the cellar.

"Only two weapons," Hetty whispered. "'Tis not enough."

"Two are more than enough if we don't have to fire them," Wallace said. "Were there other weapons in Thache's den?"

Drake shook his head. "He took all for his voyage."

"Wait," Marybeth said. "He left a pistol for me in our room. A safeguard when he was away. I'll get it." But she froze as fists pounded on the front porch.

"Mrs. Bellieu. Your time is nearly up."

Wallace peeked through the hinges of the little door. "They are front and back of us," he said. "No one is at the side of the house. Maybe we can sneak out this way."

"We need a diversion," Drake said.

And in that instant, a sailor called, "Rowers, ahoy. They're coming from Knight's landing."

"Run now," Wallace said. "They're watching Tobias Knight's men."

"But where should we run?" Marybeth asked.

I figured I could move as quickly as anyone there, so I volunteered. "I'll sneak down the gut and move the jollyboat downstream when possible."

"We need to get Marybeth out first," Hetty said, shoving Bert's gun toward her daughter. "Here, girl, go with Ody. Take your father's gun."

Wallace unlocked the door, and I peeked through the sassafras stand. Horses stood in the yard where men watched Knight's men on the creek or continued hammering the front door.

A few windows shattered. The house was breached.

"Look here," a sailor shouted. "I found his sea chest."

"They're in our room," Marybeth gasped.

I rechecked the yard, and when I stood, craning my neck, The boats were nearer to Knight's landing than ours.

"This side's clear," I said. "Let's move."

"Not without Edward's flask," Marybeth said. She shifted the rocks in the corner to find Edward's contract bottle, two leather sacks, and a letter pouch. She tucked the bottle under her apron, making her small baby bump a little more pronounced; then she passed the sacks to Hetty and Oma and the pouch to Drake. "Edward must have left these. Keep them with you. Guard them."

I took Mary's hand, and when the coast was clear, she balanced with the butt of the gun as we slipped down the ditch to the gut, hiding among the reeds as we made our way to the landing.

"Stay in the reeds," I said. And I sneaked to the summer house, crouching behind it. Knight's men had left the dock. And the cypress trees and horses screened me from the men assaulting Plum Point farmhouse. Knight's boat was halfway across the creek, and one of the boatmen spotted me, raising his musket, hopefully, to cover me as I waded and crouched till I could untether the jollyboat and walk her along the banks to the gut. Then I helped Marybeth aboard and rowed a short distance downstream.

Once the boat was secure, we walked through the woods till we could see the rocky ditch leading to our secret door. Luckily, I had one of the whistles I made for Drake, so I sounded it. My cousin recognized the soft, low tones despite the fists pounding at the doors. I saw his sleeve as he waved from the sassafras.

"Keep your gun ready," I said to Marybeth.

She nodded, taking a spot where she could see anyone approaching from either the gut or Old Towne Creek.

Drake and Oma came next. They had no weapon other than Oma's walking stick, but I watched for them, signaling when they should move or stay still. They came straight across the gut and then through the woods to me. I pointed them toward Marybeth.

"They're inside the house," Drake said as he picked up a stout branch. I don't know what they are doing, but it's noisy.

Oma swapped her walking stick for Marybeth's gun and stood in front of her with the musket at the ready.

Next came Hetty. She moved from the sassafras but slipped in the rocky ditch, and the noise brought one of Brand's men running. Wallace fired from the sassafras hedge—not at the sailor but over the head of the horses. They reared and ran, forcing Brand's men to chase them down while Wallace struggled with the man chasing Hetty and eventually knocked him down with the butt of his pistol.

Then, once we gathered in the woods, our party boarded the jollyboat and found another hiding spot further downstream.

Drake shinnied up a pine to watch what happened until Tobias Knight's men brought order to the chaos. Both sides held guns steady while Chamberlain and Brand spoke. Then, Brand left his mounted officers to search Plum Point farm while he and the rest of his men rowed with Knight to his landing.

Once Brand's party were inside Knight's house, and the horsemen ransacked Plum Point, Wallace and Drake rowed the others to meet me at the upper gut, and we sailed toward Bath.

"Are we going to the fort?" Oma asked.

"No. Captain Harding's lot will be safer," Wallace replied.

I turned to Wallace. “Has Captain Harding had a change of heart?” I asked. After all, Harding had kept Wallace safe from Blackbeard’s men.

“Over the past year or so, Thache stopped here many times for supplies and careening, and Harding respects him. He disapproved of how the pirate crew behaved toward me and protected me from them. But he doesn’t think those Virginians have a right to be here either; he’ll keep Edward’s family safe.”

“That’s good to know,” Marybeth said.

“Harding was a good friend to Bert, too,” Hetty said. “He’ll surely remember those days.”

He did.

“I saw the invaders when they marched through,” Captain Harding said as he hurried us into his house.

“You’re very kind, Thomas,” Hetty said. “’Tis a bad day for me and my girl, too.”

Harding nodded. “We have a room in the attic that will do for the ladies. I’ll set up cots in Wallace’s workshop for the lads.”

Mrs. Harding waved to us in the hall. “I’ll bring tea,” she said.

The room was large but sparsely furnished with two beds, a few chairs, a table, and a washbasin. I checked the windows against prying eyes, but the house sat deep in Harding’s lot where no one except those he trusted would pass. It was as safe a spot as we could hope for.

“Those dratted Virginians,” Mrs. Harding said, fussing as she set the tray down. “Why should they stick their noses in our business?”

“We are sorry to be a bother,” Oma said.

“Oh, ’tis no bother. Just look at ye. Foreigners invade your home and cast you out with only the clothes on your back. Mercy! I’ll see if I can find night shirts for ’e.”

It had been a grueling two days for all of us, and tea with a plate of pork pies was comforting. Marybeth was the last to sit, but she pulled the Captain’s flask from her pocket, rattling the paper scroll inside. “At least this is safe,” she said.

Drake nodded. “Let’s see what’s in this letter pouch.” He pulled out an oilskin-wrapped bundle, the documents Edward hid from potential invaders.

We spread the documents to be sure of what we had. They included papers signed by Edward’s pirate company and a few orders and receipts from traders in Bath and elsewhere along the Atlantic seaboard.

Captain Harding looked them over when he returned from the workshop. “Edward kept these hidden for a good reason. These papers are dangerous,” he said. “And I wouldn’t want Brand to find them in my house. So, we need to move them.”

"I'll take them to New Bern tomorrow," Wallace said. "My family will keep them safe, and I reckon Mrs. Thache would be safer out of Bath, as well."

Harding nodded. "At least till Brand's men leave."

"Well, I wonder what this is," Hetty said as her leather pouch thudded against the tabletop.

"Open it, and we'll see," Marybeth replied.

So, Hetty dumped out her pouch, and jewels scattered over the table.

"What? No gold or silver?" Drake asked.

"Gold and silver make a heavy load if there's much of it," Wallace replied. "Emeralds, pearls, and even sapphires and rubies are lighter, travel better, and are worth far more than silver. I guess he had the voyage to St. Thomas in mind."

"Are they ours?" Marybeth asked.

Wallace nodded. "Edward spoke of caring for his family when he passed me this key. So, I guess this is his cut of the goods he brought to Bath."

Captain Harding confirmed it. "Edward had to sell his cut of the sugar and cocoa, as did Governor Eden on behalf of the town. The mariners who own Thistleworth took care of that. Most of the prize brought silver or goods, but Edward wanted something more portable."

He handed his gem sample to Marybeth. "Mrs. Thache, you should be able to care well for your family with these. Edward will be pleased."

"So am I," Hetty said, grinning. "I reckon that pirate did well for us in more ways than one."

"Will you tell him, Captain Harding?" Marybeth asked. "We left him on Porpoise Island, and I want him to know we have his gift, and if he needs it, we will get it to him somehow."

"I or some of my crew sail past there frequently, Mrs. Thache. I'm sure your husband meant for you to find this. He has what he needs, but I'll check on him anyway while keeping your secret treasure safe."

Mrs. Harding added, "You must keep yourselves safe until Brand's men have gone. We'll keep watch. You stay tucked here, and I'll bring what you need. I'll go fetch supper now, and you can enjoy it together before the men retire." Then her smile faded to a scowl, "I hate to think what those ruffians have done to Plum Point."

"Just ask if you need anything else," Captain Harding said, then closed the door behind him.

Hetty shook her head. "I bet those Virginians made a right mess of my house. I can't believe we will be holed up in this room, though."

"You're not to worry, Widow Bellieu," Wallace said. "I'll keep an eye on it for you. And once we get a clear chance, Captain Harding will move you to New Bern if you like. Then, my family can take care of you until we get Plum Point ship shape again."

"I want to see every bit of it repaired properly," she said.

"I'll see to it, and you'll be there as soon as it's safe," he replied.

Wallace turned to Oma, "And what of you, Widow Saunters? Will you join us in Beaufort?"

"No. 'Tis finally time for my grandsons and me to depart. That will give Marybeth and Hetty more room, and we should be going anyway."

"Do you need passage?" Wallace asked.

"No, we have relatives who will care for our travels," she replied, smiling. "We will leave near dawn."

Marybeth had remained silent since Captain Harding left us. A loose tear occasionally dripped over her cheek, but we could not cheer her. Thankfully Wallace had an idea.

"Mrs. Thache, your husband asked me to make something special for him, and he meant it for Plum Point. Would you like to see it?" he asked.

"For Plum Point?" she asked.

"Aye. It was because he loved you so much and to make sure I knew that."

"What is it?" she asked, brightening a little.

"'Tis a carving of you watching the waves for his return. He treasures that thought."

She smiled. "Yes, please show me." And she followed Wallace to his shop.

But Hetty turned to Oma. "Tell me the truth, and don't quibble about being a seer. Will Edward Thache return to us? Don't evade me. Tell me so that I can help my daughter."

Oma sighed, and from the way her eyes crinkled, I thought she might cry.

"Edward will not return," she said. "And it grieves me to say that Marybeth has unhappy days ahead of her."

"Captain Thache told her as much," Drake said, "And he asked her to come back to Plum Point to protect the baby. He said that would allow him to live on."

Hetty shook her head. "My poor, Mary." Then she looked up, adding, "Thank you for telling me. Now I'm prepared to help my girl. Does Wallace know?"

"Not for certain," Drake replied. "But Captain Thache led us all to expect it."

Hetty shook her head. "He's a better man than I ever thought," she said. "I wish I had been kinder to him."

"Oh, I wouldn't worry about that," Ody replied. "The Captain enjoys a little fight."

Hetty turned to Oma again.

"And will you stay to help?" she asked.

Oma shook her head. "Not this time. We would only be distractions, and there is no remedy for sorrow as deep as the loss of a husband. She will endure it, and only those who love her most can ease the pain."

Hetty nodded. "You know that grief," she said, "and so do I. But Marybeth has a baby on the way; eventually, she will focus on that."

Oma patted Hetty's hand, smiling as he said, "Yes, she'll have happy days again."

And even though Drake and I knew Oma was not a fortune-teller, we were comforted to know she believed happiness could return to Plum Point.

70 Last Visit

Aurora Saunters

The boys and I left Bath the morning after Marybeth and Hetty were safe in Captain Harding's house, but I was surprised to find that my grandsons had brought a few unexpected souvenirs. Ody had his ghost whistle, and Drake had two mementos, the blue ribbon tied around Blackbeard's hair and the gold star that once belonged to Elizabeth Thache.

They knew better than to bring the trinkets, and of course, I scolded them, but I placed the artifacts on my top shelf for safekeeping, where I forgot about them for years.

Then one morning, while I dusted the shelf, I accidentally touched the hair ribbon.

It tingled.

Captain Thache was dead, and his hair ribbon was like my grandson's hair charms. So, if the ribbon took me anywhere, it should be to Edward. But where and when would that be? My father's charm took me to his grave since he died. So, would it take me to the bottom of the sea? Would I go to Blackbeard's grave? And would it matter that he had not lived in my century?

I had no idea, but I surely did not want my grandchildren to experiment with it before I did. I'd try it with my walking stick for the return.

So, I pinched the black hair, and the commuting storm began. But I did not land on Ocracoke, where some guessed his headless body was buried, and I did not travel anywhere where his tarred skull might lie.

I arrived near the gazebo at Plum Point and took a moment to enjoy the view of Knight's Landing. Unfortunately, Tobias Knight died just weeks after the trial that pronounced him not guilty of conspiracy with Blackbeard, and I did not know who owned that plantation after he passed.

Further up the creek, Thistleworth stood regally among the trees on the knoll. Governor Eden had not owned the plantation for long and died of yellow fever just years after Blackbeard was killed.

I turned toward the Plum Point farmhouse, wondering if Hetty still lived there. But before I could step toward the boardwalk, a child's voice stopped me.

"Who are you?" he said.

A young child, wet up to his knees, stood by the little creek with a wooden boat in his hands.

"Careful, matey," I said. "I wouldn't want to fetch you out of that water."

He shrugged. "Why not? The water's fun to play in."

Then he walked to me as he asked. "Are you one of my Grandma's friends?"

"Maybe," I replied. "Is her name Hetty?"

"No," he answered, shaking his head. "Her name is Grandma."

He was a healthy lad, just past toddling, with dark, sparkling eyes and a dimpled grin framed by curls the color of a brown mink coat.

"I'll take you to her," he said, grabbing my hand and pulling me along the boardwalk.

"What's your name, lad?" I asked.

"Neddie," he replied. "Captain Neddie McNeil."

"And where did you get such a fine boat?"

"My Papa made it. He can make anything from stone and wood."

"Oh, yes. I remember a carver. That must be your father."

"Come on," he said, pulling so fast I had to tuck my walking stick under my arm. "Grandma is in the kitchen but won't let me in there. If you're her friend, she'll let you in, though."

We found Hetty Bellieu putting sugared plums atop a cake in the eating kitchen, and she nearly fainted to see me there.

"Oh, my stars! Aurora Saunters. I thought we'd never see you again."

After a few hugs and laughs, she stepped back to show us her cake.

"This is for you, Neddie," she said. "'Tis your birthday."

"I know," Neddie replied, grinning as he held up his fingers to count the years.

"Go on up. We're having your cake on the tower," Hetty said.

"I'll show you," Neddie yelled, running ahead.

I was surprised to find wooden stairs where the block ladder had been. And once we reached the tower, Marybeth was equally surprised to see me. After a long, hard hug, she stepped back to show off her young son.

"What do you think of this one?" she asked. "Isn't he a treasure?"

I chuckled. "He is indeed. He has your hair."

She nodded, "The color, maybe, but the curls and dimples are from his father."

"And what's this?" I asked, pointing to a carving of a young woman standing at the tower rail.

"'Tis Wallace's work," she said as she adjusted the wooden statue to look toward the sea.

"He's a better carver than I thought," I said. "You can almost see the hair blowing in the breeze. It's lovely."

Wallace huffed as he set a bulky bundle to the floor, then dropped his jaw to find me there. "What a surprise! Did Hetty invite you to the party?"

"No," I replied with a grin. "'Tis a happy accident."

Once Hetty brought the cake, Wallace fetched cups and tea, and we all listened as Neddie sang his own birthday song and told us his plans for the days ahead. Then, when my dress was covered with sticky handprints, he began exploring the bundle Wallace had brought.

"Is that a boat? Is it for me?" he asked.

Wallace lifted Neddie into his arms. "It is not a boat, but it is for you."

"For my birfday?" Neddie asked.

"Aye. Something for a fortunate boy."

Neddie scrambled down. "May I open it?"

"Let Papa explain something first," Marybeth said. Neddie crawled onto his lap. "You are an extraordinary boy," he said. "And for your birthday, I shall tell you a secret. You have two Papas."

"Two?" he asked, looking around. "Where is the other one?"

"He went to heaven too soon, but we want you to know about him, so I made a carving for you."

The boy scrambled down again. "Let me see," he said, tearing at the paper until he revealed Captain Blackbeard's bust.

"He's pretty," Neddie said, touching the curly beard. "I have curls too, but I can't see if he has dimples."

"Yes, he gave you your curls and dimples, too," Marybeth said.

"He did?"

"Yes, he did," Wallace replied. "And they make you the bonnie lad we love."

"Why doesn't the other Papa come to see me?" he asked.

His parents had planned for this day, and they had answers prepared.

"Where is he now?" Neddie asked.

"He lives somewhere between the sea and the stars, and it's hard for him to come here from there," Marybeth said.

"Do you see him when you look at the sky?" Neddie asked.

"Sometimes," Marybeth said, her voice cracking a bit.

Wallace set the bust on a podium he had made, turning the carving till it faced the statue of Marybeth. "I made this so we could tell you stories about him, and you could know something of your other Papa, even though he can't come to see you now."

"But you will stay and be my Papa, right?" Neddie asked.

"I will always be your Papa," Wallace answered.

"Then what should I call this one?" he asked, pointing to the wooden man.

"His name was Captain Edward Thache, and his mother called him Neddie, like you. But some people called him Blackbeard."

"Then I'll call him that, too," Neddie said, grinning. "Papa Captain Blackbeard."

We chuckled at his choice, but Marybeth added. "That's fine. Call him as you like. He was far more than his name allows."

When Neddie ran to race boats with his Papa, I helped Hetty and Marybeth with the teacups. After that, I had a few questions I hoped they could answer.

"Marybeth, I'll understand if you don't wish to discuss my last days here, but do you know what became of Asjen Nuevo? Did he stay to help with the birth?"

She chuckled. "That doctor is as slippery as you are, Aurora. Tobias Knight begged him to hide until Brand's men left, so he found a midwife for me and gave her all the necessary instructions. Then one day, he was gone. Brand's men would have taken him to Virginia for trial, but Knight and Wallace found a way to spirit him out of Bath in time."

"I'm glad he missed that," I said. "And I was glad to hear Tobias Knight was found not guilty of the charges against him."

Hetty added, "At least those villains, Edward Moseley and Maurice Moore, were found guilty. I doubt they got more than a slap on the wrist, but their crimes kept them out of office for a few years anyway. Knight was found innocent, and no fault was found with Governor Eden, either."

"Justice won out, eh?" I asked.

Marybeth's face went dim. "At least Justice won for those two, but not everyone."

I reached to pat her hand. "Your Edward was an amazing man."

She smiled, nodding. "I believe that somewhere he still is."

"Oh, and one more thing. Did I see your wedding cup on the shelf in the den? How did that make it back home?"

"Caesar brought it. He was on *Adventure* with Edward. They would have taken him to trial, too, but since he wasn't with Edward when he took *Rose Emelye*, and his job was to blow up *Adventure*, not to battle the King's sailors, Caesar was not found guilty of piracy. It probably helped that Tobias Knight had his ownership papers—an arrangement Edward made with him to keep Caesar safe. But he was on the ship after Maynard scoured it for evidence. After Maynard logged that he had the cup, Caesar found a way to hide it and bring it back to me in Bath, as Edward requested."

"That must have brought you great comfort," I said.

"Aye," she said, turning toward the carving of her first husband. "I can almost see him wink and his curls moving in the breeze." She shook her head. "Just like his son."

"Young Neddie will be quite a man," I said. "He'll be master of the sea and the land as well."

"Aye, he will," Hetty replied. "But is that your guess or a prediction?"

We all chuckled at the old joke as I replied, "It's just what I see."

***

After a short visit, I said I'd walk to the ferry and return to Bath. But, of course, I came home instead. There I returned Blackbeard's ribbon to my shelf, but in a new place, under the dome that kept charms made of family hair.

I'd decide later whether to tell my grandsons about my last visit. At least, I thought it would be my last trip to Bath, but I had to admit I wondered what kind of adventurer Neddie McNeil would become.

History of The Bones and Related Topics

Please note that these notes are brief sketches of historical topics related to this novel. Please refer to the sources provided for a more thorough treatment of topics of interest.

Bone 1: The Charleston Blockade

In May 1718, Thache and his fleet stopped traffic in and out of Charleston Harbor for at least a week while Thache demanded medical assistance and a chest of medicine. During the blockade, Blackbeard stopped at least five ships attempting to pass through the port, robbing these ships and holding passengers and crew captive. He collected clothes, jewels, and other valuables from the ship robberies. But he requested no payment from Charleston besides the medical aid, promoting the speculation that one or more of his crew were ill.

When researchers found the wreck of the *QAR* in 1996, a urethral syringe was one of the ship's artifacts, promoting the theory that one or more crew members suffered from venereal disease.

Stede Bonnet was cruising with the fleet as a passenger on *QAR*, partly because he was known to have suffered a severe wound, prompting speculation that Bonnet was one aboard who needed medical care.

Bonnet was a rarity among pirates. Unhappy with his life in Barbados with his wife and children, he bought a ship, *Revenge*, and hired a crew to sail as his pirates. Bonnet encountered Blackbeard near Turneffe in late 1717, and the *Revenge* crewmen had voted for a captain to replace Bonnet, as they found him unfit to lead. They asked Blackbeard to take them into his fleet and choose another Captain for Bonnet's ship. A man named Richards took over the command of the *Revenge*; **Israel Hands** took command of another captured sloop, formerly commanded by **David Herriot.**

At the time of the Blockade, Thache's fleet consisted of 300-700 men.

[Moore, pp. 172-173]

Bone 2: The Grounding of Queen Anne's Revenge

The reports of this event, all written after the grounding, are inconsistent with the date, but they loosely agree on June 10 or thereabouts, soon after the Charleston Blockade. Thache had a fleet of four ships at this time. Unfortunately, *Queen Anne's Revenge* was stuck on a sandbar, and David Herriot's sloop, *Adventure*, then commanded by **Israel Hands,** was also lost in the attempt to save QAR.

Some later eyewitness testimonies, including **Ignatius Pell** and **David Herriot**, both deposed in the *Trials of Major Stede Bonnet*, claimed Edward Thache grounded QAR on purpose.

Nevertheless, the men had time to recover most of the cargo and transfer it to a third sloop, probably originally named *Dolphin*, later renamed *Adventure*. Thache had a crew of 300 before the *QAR* sank. After some of the crew dispersed and some left with **Stede Bonnet**, Thache kept a crew of 100, including 40 white men and 60 negroes. After losing *QAR*, Thache and his men used *Adventure* (previously *Dolphin*) as the flagship, reducing their gun power to 8-12 cannons.

Researchers discovered the wreck of *Queen Anne's Revenge* in Beaufort Inlet in 1996. Salvage is underway. Visitors may view the recovered artifacts at **The NC Mariner's Museum in Beaufort, NC.**

[Moore, pp. 173-178]

Blackbeard's Queen Anne's Revenge Project (qaronline.org)

Bone 3: Acquisition of Adventure and Parting with Stede Bonnet

The pirate, **Stede Bonnet**, was aboard *QAR* with Thache when the ship sank. Bonnet and Blackbeard considered if the time was right to take the King's Pardon. When Bonnet went to Bath to claim the Pardon, Thache took valuables from Bonnet's ship but left his sloop for Bonnet's use upon his return. Thache stranded some of Bonnet's men, but they were quickly rescued by Bonnet when he returned. Bonnet attempted to find Thache to exact revenge but could not locate Thache and his crew. Bonnet may have made a stab at legal trading, but he was soon back to pirating, calling himself Captain Thomas (or Richards), and his ship was renamed *Royal James*.

Thache approached Topsail Inlet with four ships. After *QAR* sank and they lost Herriot's *Adventure*, Blackbeard's crew removed anything his pirates may have taken from Bonnet's *Revenge* and stocked the remaining Spanish sloop, probably named *Dolphin,* to keep for their use. Once Thache asked for his Pardon, and the Admiralty Council permitted him to keep the ship, they renamed it *Adventure*.

[Moore, pp. 176-178]

[SC Court of Vice-Admiralty, p V]

Bone 4: The King's Pardon

On September 5, 1717, King George I issued a proclamation allowing any pirate to seek a pardon within a year of the declaration. The purpose was to curb piracy and bring these sea rogues back to a law-abiding life. In the first version of the King's Grace, pardons were offered until September 5, 1718, but if pirates did not accept the pardon by September 6, 1718, they would become wanted outlaws. Bounties of £20-200 pounds, depending on rank, would be offered to those bringing a pirate to justice.

The original proclamation promised to forgive acts of piracy occurring on or before Jan 5, 1718, but the date was extended to July 18. This date was after Blackbeard's piracy at the Charleston Blockade. However, it would not cover Blackbeard's later piracy of *Rose Emelye* on August 24, 1718.

[Note: An affidavit from one of the French ship captains lists the date as September 4, but the French used the new Gregorian calendar, whereas, in North

Carolina, the old Julian calendar was still in use. There was an 11-day difference at that time.]

An extension of the September 5 deadline was offered in December 1718, but Blackbeard died before that date. However, it saved the neck of the convicted pirate, Israel Hands.

Blackbeard accepted his pardon soon after he lost *QAR*, but no record of that event exists. Governor Charles Eden granted the pardon, but due to the political intrigue in Bath and the natural ravages of time, many documents related to Edward Thache no longer exist.

However, we do have this mention from the hearing of Tobias Knight in May 1719, which supports that Edward Thache did accept the King's Pardon.

"... Tobias Knight doth further say in his owne Justification that when the sd Thache and his Crew first came into this Government and Surrendered themselves pursuant to his Majestys Proclamation of indemnity…."

And at the same trial, there is this from Governor Eden:

"Whereas the Honble governor having laid before this Board a Narrative of his proceedings about the Surender of Thache and his Crew to him …."

[Brigham, pp. 176-177]

[Documenting the American South, pp. 341-349]

Bone 5: Blackbeard's Marriage in Bath

David Moore's study of "Primary Sources related to Edward Thache" identifies two letters from Royal Navy Captains Ellis Brand and George Gordon to Josiah Burchette, the Admiralty Secretary in London, mentioning Thache's marriage. The Brand letter places the union near when Thache accepted his pardon in Bath. These letters reside at The National Archives in London with specific references in Moore's article.

[Moore, p. 153]

Mary Ormond: There is a letter referenced in both Brooks' *Quest for Blackbeard* and the Baily genealogy study for Blackbeard, in which Mrs. White claims that her great-great-aunt, Mary Ormond, was once Blackbeard's wife.

Both these sources trace family trees without finding a successful candidate for Mary Ormond, as the Ormond family was not in Bath in 1718. However, the Bailey source does indicate that if the letter referred to Mary Ormond's Aunt instead of Aunt Mary Ormond, there are possibilities of finding our missing wife. Unfortunately, her name would not have been Mary Ormond in that case. For this reason, I chose Marybeth and the fictional Bellieu family for the bride and her relatives.

[Bailey, pp, 273-276]

Not only is the marriage deep in the memory of the residents of Bath and corroborated by the sources mentioned above, but there is one more indication that the wife existed.

One of the oldest and probably least reliable pirate histories, The ***General History of Pirates***, by Captain Charles Johnson, claims that on the night before Blackbeard's final battle, a crew member asked Blackbeard if his wife knew where his treasure was hidden. He replied that only he and the devil knew, and the longest liver could take it all.

The entire scenario is suspect, and it may go more to proving the ***General History of Pirates*** is unreliable than providing evidence that Blackbeard had a wife. But even so, no matter where the question came from, it suggests contemporaries of Blackbeard knew he had a wife.

Bone 6: The Voyage to Northern Shores

Did Thache voyage to the northern colonies in August? Did he commit piracy on that trip? The following shows a timeline and supporting evidence:

Around **June 10, 1718**: *QAR* was at the bottom of Topsail Inlet. Stede has sailed north in his ship under a new name. Edward Thache has married and has permission to use his ship *Adventure* to make a legal livelihood. Bath suffers from poor crops, sickness, and a lack of men. Ships bypass Bath for more lucrative ports in Virginia and South Carolina. The town of Bath needed Thache's services as a merchant.

July 29, 1718: Bonnet takes a sloop manned by Thomas Read.

July 30, 1718: Bonnet takes a sloop manned by Peter Manwaring

August 7, 1718: James Logan writes to NY Governor Robert Hunter that pirates have been active in the Delaware Capes. He reported two ships taken on their way to Bristol, several taken for provisions, and another taken en route from Philadelphia to Barbados. His dates suggest pirates may have been there as early as July 23. No names are presented.

August 11, 1718: William Keith, governor of Philadelphia, warns his council of pirates and reports that Thache "has been seen for several days in and about this town."

Note that Thache being *seen* is not the same as evidence that he was robbing ships. And he has no report that Thache stole anything. However, warrants were signed for Thache's arrest. Later evidence adds more wrinkles.

A source I do not like to quote is *The General History of Pirates*, *GHP*, by the penname of Captain Charles Johnson. In the section on Stede Bonnet, we find that on…

July 29, 1718, Captain Thomas [Bonnet's assumed name] *"...took a Sloop of 50 Tons, six or seven Leagues off Delaware Bay, bound from Philadelphia to Barbados, Thomas Read Master, loaden with Provisions, which they kept, and put four or five of their Hands on Board her...."*

July 31, 1718, The last Day of July, they [Bonnet's ship] *"... took another Sloop of 60 Tons, commanded by Peter Manwaring, bound from Antegoa to Philadelphia, which they likewise kept with all the Cargo, consisting chiefly of Rum, Molosses, Sugar, Cotton, Indigo, and about 25 Pound in Money, valued in all to 500 Pound...."*

Though I resist quoting *GHP*, transcripts in the *Trials of Stede Bonnet* verify these robberies.

September 1718: Bonnet is captured, and information in his trials states that Read and his ship, Francis, as well as Manwaring on his ship, Fortune, are part of Bonnet's fleet.

Evidence that Bonnet was involved in the robberies does not prove Thache innocent of any but these two. However, we have proof against Bonnet and no proof against Edward Thache.

Perhaps Blackbeard was seen in Philadelphia, but he had other reasons to be there. Bath needed supplies. Thache had the means to find them. After all, the Admiralty Council allowed him to keep Adventure for legal trading.
[Moore,176-178], [SC Trials of Stede Bonnet]

Bone 7: Pirating the Rose Emelye

Sometime before August 24 (Julian Calendar), Governor Eden has grown weary of pirates misbehaving in town and suggests Edward Thache take his crew to St. Thomas—anywhere out of Bath.

Thache returned to Bath, claiming he found the ship abandoned, but a later deposition from one of the ships' captains proved it was pirated.

The following passage from Knight's trial shows that the Governor asked Thache to take his men to St. Thomas and that they returned with the ship Rose Emely between August 24 and September 24.

From the trial of Tobias Knight:

> *" ... Whereas the Honble the governor haveing laid before this Board a Narative of his proceedings about the Surender of Thache and his Crew to him and of Some disorders committed by them while at Bath Town and By what means they were quieted together with the manner of his clearing out for the Island of St Thomas and his returne to Bath Towne the second time with his bringing into this Government as he pretended a Wreck laden with sugars with a full account of his behaviour."*
>
> *Knight further testifies that he didn't see Thache again until around September 24 (Julian) when he came to him with information about the Rose Emelye, and the Admiralty Council investigated it.*
>
> *"...he sd Tobias Knight doth aver for Truth that from the time the sd Thache tooke his departure from this Government bound to St Thomas's he did never See the sd Thache or any of his people until on or about the 24th of September last past when he came and reported to the Governor that he had brought a wreck into this Government...."*

Bone 8: Visit to Tobias Knight with Cargo from Rose Emelye

Here we enter murky waters, which are delved more in the section on the robbery of William Bell. Bell claims that Knight carried cargo to Tobias Knight's house on the night of September 13/14.

Knight claims he knew nothing of this cargo until around September 24, when Thache brought information about the ship.

[**Author inference and artistic license:** From the conflicting testimony above, someone is lying or badly mistaken. Tobias Knight was on trial for his reputation, that of Charles Eden, and the continuance of government in NC as designated by the Proprietors. So, he had the motivation to lie, but as he said in his testimony, he had been ill for months, rarely able to leave his house. He remembers Bell coming to report the robbery, but he and his houseman say he did not see Thache, and even Bell says the same in one of his subsequent interviews (April 25, 1719).

The entire body of evidence brought to Knight's trial, and that's all we have of William Bell's story, is riddled with inconsistency. I'm not sure Bell lied, but he seems easily persuaded to believe a lie is true—more on that in another Bone segment.

In The Heart of Blackbeard, I let my characters poke holes in the story. Still, I write the scene of Thache delivering cargo on September 14, even though the accuracy of that date is unclear.]

Bone 9: Political Intrigue

Records indicate that a group of individuals in North Carolina hoped to shift Governor Charles Eden from his office, replacing him with someone they favored. Edward Moseley, Maurice Moore, and Jeremiah Veil are the names associated with this treachery.

The actions of this group that relate to this story are attempts to associate Governor Eden with piracies committed by Edward Thache. This becomes most clear in two events and several legal actions.

Lt. Robert Maynard killed Edward Thache on November 22, 1718. Thache's severed head and the surviving crew were taken to Virginia even though Virginian officers' invasion of the North Carolina Proprietorship was illegal. Removing North Carolinians to face trial in Virginia was unlawful. And to add insult to injury, the hearing meant to dishonor North Carolina's governor and his associates was also held in Virginia.

Event 1: In the following December (1718), Edward Moseley and Maurice Moore invaded the home of John Lovich, who had been given charge of the legal documents of Governor Charles Eden. These two locked themselves in the house for twenty-four hours, ransacking it for evidence of Eden's collusion with Blackbeard. They found no such evidence.

Event 2: The robbery of William Bell brings curious testimony to prove Blackbeard stole a cup in the creeks of the inner banks in an attempt to prove Tobias Knight was colluding with Blackbeard.

The primary Trial of Tobias Knight was held in May 1719. In this trial, depositions of pirates from March 1719 were used as evidence, even though these men were black and thus not allowed to testify, and they had been hanged shortly after giving these depositions.

In this trial, Tobias Knight was found not guilty.

Edward Moseley and Maurice Moore were convicted of invading John Lovich's home and were sentenced to pay a fine and banned from public office for three years.

Tobias Knight defended himself in May 1719 and died in June 1719 from a long illness.

Governor Eden died from yellow fever in 1722.

Of course, **Edward Thache** was killed by Lt. Robert Maynard and the invading Virginia forces in November 1718.

Edward Moseley and **Maurice Moore** survived their political embarrassment and lived on to provide meaningful service to the North Carolina province.

Bone 10: The Robbery of William Bell

This story is told within the account of Tobias Knight's trial in May 1719. You may read the transcript at the link below. I will attempt to sort the pieces for you, pointing out contradictions and unanswered questions.

The story is told by 1) William Bell in his deposition, presented in May 1719, 2) the deposition of four pirates who were supposedly part of the theft, written in March 1719 just before they were hanged, 3) the deposition of Israel Hands, who was in jail at the time of Knight's trial, 4) Knight's response, at the trial 5) corroborating testimony of Knight's assistant Edmund Chamberlain.

From the Pirate Deposition:

Note: This testimony was given after these men saw several white colleagues hanged in January 1719. They were convicted of piracy and soon hanged as well. In 1719, black men were not allowed to testify in court against white men. Their captain, Edward Thache, was dead, and as Knight pointed out, they feared for their lives.

Claims of the Incarcerated Pirates

- They agreed with Bell's robbery date of September 14.
- They delivered cargo matching the loot from *Rose Emelye* to Tobias Knight, arriving at midnight or 1 AM.
- Knight was at home, and they carried in the cargo.
- Thache stayed with Knight until an hour before daybreak and then left.
- They departed to Chester's Landing, stating it was three miles away, and saw a periauger near shore.

[Note: Researchers are not in agreement about the location of Chester's Landing, but researchers Bailey and others fix it near North Dividing Creek, about 10 miles from Knight's Landing. At roughly 3-4 knots for a periauger near shore and in creeks, this trip would have taken more than one hour, perhaps three.]

- Thache demanded they row so he could go ashore at Chester's house.
- They rowed to the boat carrying a white man, a boy, and an Indian.
- Thache asked for a dram and immediately jumped into the boat, and after some dispute, plundered the boat and robbed it of money, a cask of pipes, a cask of Brandy, some linen, and other things.
- Then Thache demanded they row for Ocracoke.

[Note: Knight and Chamberlain said Thache did not visit that night. Knight claims he didn't see Thache until around September 24.]

Bell's Story

- While Bell was onboard his periauger at Chester's landing on September 14, he saw a periauger pass going upstream. Then a little before the break of day, the same periauger returned and rowed to board Bell's boat.

[Note: The pirates say they left Knight an hour before daybreak, and Bell says Thache was at Chester's Landing at the same time, even though these locations are from one to three hours apart via periauger.]

- The attacker was a white man who asked for a drink, and Bell said it was too dark to pour.

[Note: Either Bell or the pirates are wrong about the time. If they left Knight and rowed for an hour (or 3), it would be daylight by then. And if the trip took exactly 1 hour, which is doubtful, how could it still be too dark to pour?]

- The attacker then called for his crew to pass him his sword and demanded Bell put his hands behind him to be tied and demanded to know where his money was, or he would be killed.
- Bell **asked the man who he was**, and he replied with a threat, so Bell fought with his attacker, who could not defeat Bell alone and called for his crew.

[Note: Bell did not know who his attacker was. But whoever the white man was, he couldn't overpower Bell.]

- With his crew helping, the attacker overcame Bell, rowed his boat to the middle of the creek, and robbed it of his pistols, £66, 58 yards of crepe, a box of pipes, and several other goods. And apparently, Bell only recently remembered one thing in particular—a silver cup of remarkable fashion being made with a screw joining two cups, one like a tumbler, another a chalice, and remarkably, Bell has just learned that such a cup was found on Thache's ship after he was killed.

[Note: Bell wasn't told his attacker was Thache until recently, and he didn't remember he had such a fantastic cup aboard his boat until recently. Is anyone suspicious yet?]

- Bell says his attackers threw his sails and oars overboard and then sailed away, leaving him there. But in two hours, he sailed to Bath to report this to the Governor, who sent him to Tobias Knight.
- Bell described his robbery to Knight, including the fact that the four crewmen were **either black or disguised to be black**. And that after he told all to Knight, he did not admit a periauger had been to his house earlier, nor that he knew Thache was in the country.

*[**Note**: On the day of the deposition, Bell said that he had later learned his attacker was Edward Thache, but on the day of the robbery, Tobias Knight says he named Thomas Undey and Fiteing Dick as his suspects. Knight's assistant, Edmund Chamberlain, says Bell claimed the assailants to be John Undey or Richard Snelling, known as Fitery Dick. At a later interview on April 25, Bell believed the assailant to be William Smith. Bell also admitted at this April meeting that he did not believe Edward Thache was at Knight's house on the 14th. By the time of the trial, he has acquired a new opinion, stating that he "has now learned the attacker was Edward Thache."]*

*[**Note:** So, the pirates left Knight an hour before dawn, and miraculously they arrived at Chester's landing an hour before sunrise. Then, after a beating, a robbery, and rifling of his boat, Bell still can't tell if the crew were black or pretending to be. I wonder why he didn't mention a big black beard or that the man was tall.]*

  - One more piece from Bell says that in the struggle, the attacker broke nine inches off his sword, and at the deposition, he presents that nine-inch piece of the blade as evidence for the first time. He found it in his boat.

[Note: I can't say what Thache's pirate rules may have been, but in every example that has survived, it is necessary to keep weapons in good repair. It's the first thing you do after a battle. It is suspect that on the day of the trial, Bell noted three bits of evidence he had not mentioned before: Thache's name, the description of a silver cup, and a piece of the sword.]

[The Silver Cup: facts and a writer's interpretation**]**
The silver cup on Thache's boat was probably stolen, but not on September 14. Thache had a fancy silver cup since he pirated the *Great Alleyne* in early December 1717.

The Great Alleyne carried a rich haul of silver plate, among other things, but Captain Taylor did not want to give his cargo to the pirates, so he hid the silver and fought to keep it.

Having to fight displeased Edward Thache; he'd rather win his prizes from frightening the enemy. So, he burned *Great Alleyne* once the crew was safely ashore.

Soon after, Henry Bostock was taken on board *QAR* as a prisoner for eight hours while Thache's men boarded his ship. Bostock gives us our only description of Edward Thache from an eyewitness, **"a tall spare man with a very black beard which he wore very long."** But Bostock also tells us that he saw **a very fine silver cup**, a wager cup, that Blackbeard had kept as his share of the prize from the *Alleyne*.

A wager cup, sometimes used at weddings, other times for celebrations and games, fits the description given by Bell for a cup found on *Adventure* after Thache died, one he had had for nearly a year.
[Documenting the American South, pp. 341-349]
[Good examples of Acts of Piracy are provided in Wikipedia with corroborating references.
https://en.wikipedia.org/w/index.php?title=Pirate_code&oldid=1142820475]

Bone 11: The Admiralty Council's Decision Regarding Rose Emelye
The Admiralty Council met in September 1718 to investigate the ship, described as abandoned, that Edward Thache brought to Ocracoke. The Council believed Thache, and around September 24, 1718, the Admirals allowed Captain Thache to burn the vessel once the cargo had been removed. [The date is indicated by previously mentioned references from Tobias Knight's trial.]
[Documenting the American South, pp. 341-349]

Bone12: Meeting with Charles Vane
The reported dates of this meeting vary, but they agree on the season, Fall. I suspect October. I can find no evidence for this meeting, but there is a logical purpose for it, and the legend persists throughout every history of Blackbeard and his crew.

Apparently, at this end time of the Golden Age of Piracy, **Charles Vane** sought Edward Thache at Ocracoke. Vane had recently been removed from Nassau by the new English Governor, Woods Rogers, and **Stede Bonnet** had been captured by Charleston merchant searching for Charles Vane. The supposition is that Vane wanted to ally with Thache to recover Nassau, but Thache didn't accept the invitation.

The event is reported as quite rowdy if one believes *GHP*. But wild or not, it persists in memory and legend as the last encounter of these two pirate leaders. Charles Vane was known for his reputation for brutality and cruelty. But outside the malicious reports in *GHP*, Edward Thache, though quite fearsome, was not known for killing anyone before the last battle for his life.

Bone13: Israel Hands is Crippled

A story in *GHP* has Israel Hands repeating how Edward Thache shot him, crippling him for life. He offers no reason, implying Thache shot him on a whim.

Israel Hands *was* crippled for life, and it probably saved his life at least twice, and maybe three times.

First, A shot at close range with a full charge would have been so severe that Hands would have bled out and died. Even in Hands' version of the shooting in *GHP*, he claims Edward Thache fiddled with his guns and shot in the dark, switching hands first. Perhaps this was to shoot Hands with the less powerful weapon.

Second, he was convalescing from his wounds in Bath and did not face peril on *Adventure* when Thache was killed.

Third, he was taken to trial in Virginia where he was convicted of piracy and was sentenced to hang, but his part in the trial lingered, and he survived until December when the pirate pardon's new extension made it to Virginia, thus saving Israel Hands from the noose.

Bone14: Meeting and Letter from Tobias Knight

When Robert Maynard searched *Adventure* after Blackbeard was killed, he found a letter to Edward Thache written by Tobias Knight. This letter is transcribed in the *Tobias Knight Trial and is presented here with minor adjustments to spelling and punctuation.*

> *"Novr 17th 1718*
> *My friend*
> *If this finds you yet in harbour, I would have you make the best of your way up as soon as possible [as] your affairs will let you. I have something more to say to you than at present I can write. The bearer will tell you the end of our Indian War, and Ganet can tell you in part what I have to say to you, so refer you in some measure to him.*
> *I really think these three men are heartily sorry at their difference with you and will be very willing to ask your pardon if I may advise to be friends again. It's better than falling out among yourselves.*
> *I expect the Governor this night or tomorrow, who I believe would be likewise glad to see you before you go. I have not time to add, save my hearty respects to you, and am your real friend.*
> *And Servant*
> *T. KNIGHT"*

Note that this letter is dated November 17, when Edward Thache was stuck on Brant Island Shoals. It would have been delivered to him there or near Ocracoke before he was killed on November 22.

The letter implies that Knight and Thache had conversations about his leaving around this date and that they had discussed the possibility of an Indian uprising, which now seems to be resolved.

He mentions three men with whom Thache has had difficulty, hoping all parties, including Governor Eden, can resolve their differences. And he refers to Thache as a friend for whom he holds hearty respects.

The name "Ganet" is unidentified. Researcher Kevin Duffus believes it is the pirate named Garret Gibson, as these names would be very similar when written in script.

I can find no better explanation in my research, but I found one remote alternative. A man with a similar name was involved in better relationships between Europeans and Indians, perhaps in a missionary capacity. In 1711, Tobias Knight was a member of the party that asked the queen for support against the Indians who were terrorizing the colony then. However, I found no direct connection between this man and Bath or Tobias Knight.

Bone15: Adventure is Stuck on Brand Island Shoals

According to Robert Maynard and his crew, Thache was observed stuck on Brant Island Shoals on November 17.

[Duffus, p. 143]

[Note of artistic license: Brant Island is underwater in this century, but part of it was dry land in 1718. But we don't know why Blackbeard was near there to get stuck in the first place.

There are several guesses but no facts, so I made a guess that fits my story. My first intention was to have Thache there as a rendezvous point for Marybeth. Boats from Bath could reach Brant Island in far less time than it would take to reach Ocracoke.

But my history nerd side got the better of me. I had no idea how much of Brant Island was above water in 1718, and I had no clue what the terrain would be like, so I invented Little Porpoise Island, near Brant Island Shoals, with a landscape fitted to my needs. In the story, Blackbeard plans to take Marybeth onboard before he and his crew sail for St. Thomas to become privateers for the Netherlands in the Quadruple Alliance War. It took supernatural measures to change the plans of Blackbeard and his wife.

The following day, Adventure became stuck in the shoals near Brant Island. That part is documented]

Bone16: Final Battle

Thache was killed after a valiant six-minute engagement with Lt. Robert Maynard. His head was taken to Virginia as proof of the kill, and it was then used as a deterrent to pirates.

[Moore:179-184]

Along Bath Creek

Please note that these notes are brief sketches of historical topics related to this novel. Please refer to the sources provided for a more thorough treatment of topics of interest.

A Town of Firsts

Bath Towne, originally Old Towne, was a town of firsts in North Carolina.

The First **Town** was established in March 1705

The First **Library** (1701) was probably in place in one of Governor Eden's lots when Blackbeard arrived. It housed a collection of books for laymen and parochial use donated by Dr. Thomas Bray, founder of the Society for Propagation of the Gospel in Foreign Parts. Each book and pamphlet was stamped "Belonging to the Parish of St. Thomas in Pamlico." By 1714, there were complaints that the books may be missing or misused. So, in 1715, trustees were appointed, including Christopher Gale, Charles Eden, Tobias Knight, and Edward Moseley, among others.

By 1760, only one volume, Gilbert Towerson's *Application of the Church Catechism* (1685), could be found. In 1890, that one book was given to the Episcopal Diocese of East Carolina.

The first official **Port: Governor Eden** petitioned the Lord Proprietors to name Bath as North Carolina's first official port of entry, a site to handle required local and provincial inspections and duties. Bath was designated as such on August 1, 1716.

The first **Church: St. Thomas Episcopal Church** was built in 1734, even though Glebe land had been set aside for the parish as early as 1705.

The first de facto **capital** of North Carolina was in Bath when the Carolinas separated in 1712. However, when **Governor Eden** moved to the Town on Queen Anne's Creek, later named Edenton, that area became the center of government. Then New Bern was named the official capital in 1746.

Evidence of the earliest **shipyard** occurred in 1707 when Captain Thomas Harding was contracted to build a sloop for Governor Thomas Carey.

[Paschal, pp. 14-17]

A Town with its share of Trouble

The Cary Rebellion: (1711 and before) The Cary Rebellion was an armed power struggle between Anglicans and Quakers to determine leadership in North Carolina. A notable encounter between the forces of Edward Hyde and Thomas Cary occurred along Bath Creek on May 29, 1711.

Yellow Fever: Rampant fever and death in the summer of 1711 continued to plague the population, even claiming Charles Eden in 1722.

Drought: Summer of 1711.

Tuscarora War: The first coordinated attack on settlers occurred in September 1711. The war continued until a treaty was signed in February 1715.

Along Bath Creek

Plum Point: There is no record of Blackbeard residing at Plum Point; however, that is his home in the memory and legend of Bath, NC. This point lies near the east side of the mouth of Bath Creek, and even on maps of today, the southern gut bears the name Teach's Gut. A great cauldron called Teach's Kettle once existed on the land, and legend says Blackbeard and his crew boiled tar in that kettle.

In his book, Baylus Brooks reviews documented owners of the point, and of course, Edward Thache does not appear on any deed. But then, there are no records of any event Thache was to have engaged in while in Bath County, not his marriage, acceptance of the King's Pardon, or his hearings with the Admiralty Council. Tobias Knight and Governor Eden must have been very thorough in hiding any connections between them and Blackbeard.

Thistleworth: This land belonged to Thomas Cary and later Charles Eden, but according to Bath County Deeds, Eden transferred his land to John Lillington, who, on September 9, 1718, transferred it to mariners, Steven Elsey and James Robins.

According to the eyewitness report of Joseph Bonner, Thistleworth was once adorned with a gracious plantation house, and beneath the house was a tunnel, sixty yards long, reaching from the creek to the cellar.

Knight's Landing: This is the name I used for the plantation owned by Lt. Governor Daniel, then his common-law wife, who sold it to Tobias Knight. It is now marked on maps as Archbell Point. The plantation lies opposite Plum Point on the west side of Bath Creek. It is adjacent to Thistleworth.

John Lawson was a founder of Bath, who spent much of his time exploring the flora and fauna of the inner banks as well as the various tribes who lived there before the Europeans. His book provides much of what we know about the native customs and the landscape of lands new Pamlico Sound.

[Gurganus], [Bailey, pp. 255-256], [Brooks, pp. 481-486], [Duffus, 209], [Lawson, p. 235] [Paschal, pp.17-32]

A Ghostly Presence: From Blackbeard's death in 1718, people occasionally see a ball of light crossing Bath Creek. This phenomenon, called **Teach's Lights**, has been witnessed by many citizens of outstanding reputation. Dr. T. P. Bonner reported seeing the light during every violent storm. He described the light as bright enough to see during a storm and about the size of a man's head traveling in a straight line back and forth between Plum Point and Knight's plantation, regardless of 40 mph winds. The occurrence lasted throughout the night described in his report.

[Bonner, p. 39]

Other Places – Jamaica

Jamaica and Sir Henry Morgan: It is likely that young Edward Thache, Jr. moved to Jamaica a few years after the death of Sir Henry Morgan. During his last days, he lived on a Plantation called Lawrencefield, owned by one of his former comrades, Lawrence Prince. Curiously enough, Prince was the Captain of *Whydah* when it was taken as a prize by Blackbeard's friend, Black Sam Bellamy. *[Cruikshank, p.48w]*
[**Artistic License:** While Edward Thache, Sr. ran a plantation in Jamaica, and young Ned had the opportunity to visit Henry Morgan's last home, I have no proof that it was the same plantation where Sir Henry Morgan lived the year he died.]

Bibliography

Bailey, J. S., Oden, J. H., & Norris, A. (2002). "Legends of Blackbeard and his Ties to Bath Town." NC Genealogical Society Journal, 28(3), 245–351.

Bonner, Lottie (1939), *Colonial Bath and Pamlico Section*. Aurora, NC: Lottie Hale Bonner.

Brigham, C. S. (Ed.). (1911). *British Royal Proclamations Relating to America* (1603-1783). Stanhope Press. https://archive.org/details/royalproclamations12brigrich/page/174/

Brooks, B. C. (2015). "Born in Jamaica, of Very Creditable Parents" or "A Bristol Man Born: Excavating the Real Edward Thache, Blackbeard, the Pirate." *The North Carolina Historical Review*, *92*(3), 235–277. http://www.jstor.org/stable/44113270

Brooks, B. C. (2016) *The Quest for Blackbeard*. Greenville, NC: BaylusBrooks.com.

Cruikshank, E. A. (1935) *The Life of Sir Henry Morgan, 1st Edition*. Toronto: MacMillan Company of Canada. Available at the Gutenberg Project.org.

Documenting the American South (2004) *Colonial Records of North Carolina, V2*. Chapel Hill: UNC.

Duffus, K. P. (2011) *The Last Days of Blackbeard the Pirate, 4th Ed.* Raleigh: Looking Glass Press.

Gurganus, Janice. Contributor (No date) Beaufort County Deed Book 1 usgwarchives.net. Available at: www.usgwarchives.net/nc/beaufort/beaufortdeeds.htm

Johnson, Charles (1724) *A General History of the Robberies and Murders of the Most Notorious Pirates:* London.

Lawson, John (1709) A New Voyage to Carolina. London. Available at this link: https://docsouth.unc.edu/nc/lawson/menu.html

Leslie, C. (1740). *A New History of Jamaica*. J. Hodges.

Moore, D. D. (2018). "Captain Edward Thache: A Brief Analysis of the Primary Source Documents Concerning the Notorious Blackbeard." NC Historical Review, 95(2), 147–185.

Nash, J.D. (1986, January). Eden, Charles. NCPedia; UNC Press. https://www.ncpedia.org/biography/eden-charles

Paschal, H. R. (1955) *A History of Colonial Bath*. Raleigh: Edward & Broughton Co.

South Carolina Court of Vice Admiralty (1719) *The Tryals of Stede Bonnet and Other Pirates*. London: Printed for Benj. Cowse.

Reed, C.W. (1962) *Beaufort County: Two Centuries of its History*. North Carolina: C. Wingate Reed.

Other Books by Patricia Cooper Baker

Top Shelf Series: Available at Amazon.com in paperback, Kindle

***Ody Saunters, Out of Time*:** Aurora Saunters first time travel adventure with grandson Ody in Old Salem 1783. Paperback and Kindle versions.

***The Babysitters of Virginia Dare*.** Coming Soon:

Freedom Tavern Series: Available at Amazon.com, paperback

Virginia Rose and the Tory War. John Cooper's family, including their youngest daughter, Virginia Rose, endure the uncertain times of the Revolutionary War. But the Overmountain Men will soon stop in Burke County on their way to The Battle of King's Mountain.

1784: The Birth of Morgan Towne. In 1784, Morgan Towne is established as the seat of government in the Morgan District. There is a new school and new religious organizations, too. Quarterly court meetings bring traffic to the county, bringing new problems and opportunities. John Cooper, his wife, and his children struggle to find paths to their futures after the war.

The Ghosts of Snakeroot Cove. What happens when John Cooper and his children find a woman on death's door living in a remote cove in Burke County? Who has been helping her since the death of her husband? Are the people who helped her slaves? And if they are, what will become of them?

A Christmas Tale from Freedom Tavern: How does Freedom Tavern celebrate Christmas? And how can Little Joe and Virginia Rose survive being lost in the snow on Christmas Eve?

***The Courtship of Virginia Rose*:** Coming Soon

Martian Spring Series. Available at Amazon.com, paperback, Kindle

Spring Unbound: Spring Graviston has had a rough time on Earth, but will her opportunity on Mars turn out better? She's unsure she can handle her new job, but she also faces the challenges of living in a new environment where no one knows her. And there's another mystery on Mars, too. Is she up to handling secrets that Mars wants to keep hidden?

Spring Unbroken: When investigators come to WayPoint Station, Spring faces new challenges. Do they suspect her of wrongdoing? How will the probe into the deaths of her coworkers affect Spring's new status on Mars? And what will become of her relationship with Collin and the secret they've kept hidden from nearly everyone else on the planet? **Coming this year.**

Follow the Author
https://www.facebook.com/BurkeTales
Contact the Author
Email: Cooperspeak@yahoo.com Website: **Cooperspeak.com**